A LOVE AS STRONG

MARION DANTE

UNUSUALLY TALL STORIES LTD

First published in Great Britain by Marion Dante

Cover design by Andy Bowden

ISBN (Paperback): 978 1 9996471 2 4

ISBN (eBook): 978 1 9996471 3 1

❀ Created with Vellum

ALSO BY MARION DANTE

Non-fiction:

Dropping the Habit

Fiction:

Searching for Love

To my parents Frank & Patricia (nee Colivet) Dante & my brothers Tim and Des, RIP

Dante Alighieri:

Love and the gracious heart are a single thing... one can no more be without the other than the reasoning mind without its reason.

Amore e 'l cor gentil sono una cosa...e così esser l'un sanza l'altro osa com'alma razional sanza ragione.

Chapter XVI (tr. Mark Musa)
La Vita Nuova 1293

1

SECULAR LIFE: FIRST STEPS

Tomorrow was Frankie's first day at school. She was excited and nervous. She had been a nun for sixteen years addressed as 'Sister' Frances. At thirty-seven, she felt anxious about walking into the staffroom dressed in secular clothes. Although the staff knew that she was leaving the convent what would think when the saw her without her religious habit. How would the parents and children react?

What shall I wear? My choice is very limited. I want to look my best. I've cut my nails, applied Ponds face cream and purchased pink lipstick. I washed and conditioned my hair before putting in rollers. No habit, no veil, just me. Barely eight hours before I present myself as a new woman!

She sat on the edge of her bed looking at the multicoloured, elasticated skirt that had she bought in Oxfam, wondering if it would be suitable for her new life. She had hung it on the back of her door of her room, so that she could gauge how it might look. She clasped her hand together, interlocked her fingers, rested her chin on them, bent forward and tried to recall what other members of the staff usually wore. She hung the pink t-shirt next to the skirt. She walked back and looked from the skirt to the top to judge if the colours matched. They did. Perfect, she thought. She sighed. She tried them on again and walked round the room. She looked in the mirror. The mid-calf skirt hung well but the top was too figure-hugging. She decided that it would be better not to tuck the top into the waist-band of the skirt. She would cover herself with her long navy-blue cardigan. One of her plastic curlers fell on her shoulder. She removed the curlers from the back of her head, pulled her dressing-gown over her night dress and collapsed on her bed. She fell asleep on top of the bedclothes.

FRANKIE WONDERED what had woken her. The door to her room was being opened. The landlady's head peeped through. Frankie wished she had locked the door. Evelyn's petite figure was wrapped in soft pink dressing-gown and matching fluffy slippers. Her curly jet-black curls bobbed as she tip-toed nearer holding a small tray.

'Are you awake, Frankie? So sorry. You said you had run out of milk. I brought you a cup of hot chocolate. Your first day back at school tomorrow. I wanted to check if you have an alarm clock.'

'Yes, thank you for the drink, Evelyn. It's lovely to see your smiling face. How thoughtful. I must have fallen off to sleep. I'll need to leave by six-thirty tomorrow morning. What time is it?'

'The ten o'clock news is over. Must be nearing 11 now.'

'Oh!'

'Best you go back to sleep then, Frankie. The chocolate should help you. Goodnight.'

Thank God she woke me from my nightmare, thought Frankie. I dreamt that I was running round the convent trying to hide myself before anyone saw that I was naked.

Frankie tugged off her dressing-gown, slipped in between her sheets, took the mug of hot chocolate from the locker next to her bed and blew on it. She tried to imagine how the staff would react when they saw her in ordinary clothes. How glad she was that she told them last week that she had left the convent.

Frankie woke up at five am. She was used to waking up at that time in the convent. It felt strange not going to chapel to pray the

Divine Office. Having been a sacristan she remembered all the feast days.

Hmm. Third of September. Feast of St Gregory the Great. Pope and Doctor of the Church. He was a man of courage. Fearless and resolute. He will be my model today. One foot in front of the other, she told herself. *I'm free. I'm happy my new life begins today.*

She danced a little jig.

She pulled on her skirt and t-shirt. She removed the rest of her rollers from her hair. She noticed that it had become frizzy. She poured water into a mug and dipped her comb into the water. She carefully combed her hair until the frizz disappeared. Water had dripped onto her t-shirt. She hoped it would dry without leaving a water mark. She stood in front of her mirror.

I don't look too bad. In fact, with my hair in shape and the pink lipstick and new clothes my image has much improved. My mother. She used to show off the photo of me as a nun. I'll have to send her a photo of me now. Her letter said that she will be back from Kerry again at the end of this month.

With the whish of the wind as the tube, Frankie reached to keep her veil in place and realised that she no longer wore a veil. She tripped down the stairs to the tube, part of the real working world. Clatter of heels, buying of newspapers. Zigzagging between each other. When she stepped inside the tube she was amazed that it was crowded at seven a.m. No one spoke. No one looked at each other. No one stood up and offered her a seat.

If I was wearing my habit, they would have given up their seat for me, reflected Frankie. Now I don't need a seat. I don't need that deference. I am strong and able. She caught sight of her reflection in a shop window as she walked from the station to the school. The new Frankie full of life.

Frankie hoped that the caretaker would not be around when she reached the school. He was. As she rounded the corner she saw that he was lifting the milk crates onto a trolley from outside the front door of the school. He greeted her, 'Good morning, Sr Frances. Have the nuns gone into lay clothes?'

'No...'

'You look attractive. No one would know that you are a nun. Shouldn't you still wear a cross?'

'I'm no longer a nun, Mr James. I'm Miss Danivet now. Of course, you can call me Frankie.'

'Oh! You are not a nun anymore... why?'

'It would take too long to explain all the reasons, Ken. I know I'm going to be asked lots of questions. This is my first day back at school.'

'Sorry Sister... Miss... Frankie... Don't worry, I'll tell the parents.'

Just as well I was able to inform him before the parents arrive. I will tell the children. I'm sure they will be happy to accept me as plain Miss Danivet.

She had spent the preceding days positioning posters, labelling work trays for each pupil and checking her stock of folders and reading books.

The previous day Frankie bought a sheet with a variety of small sticky pictures of dinosaurs from a charity shop. She set about attaching them onto each of the children's writing books. She had finished putting these books and sharpened pencils into their individual trays. Then she picked up a stick of white chalk from the ledge under the blackboard and carefully began to write 'Monday 8th September 1987'. Suddenly, the classroom door opened.

Frankie spent the next hour putting final touches to her classroom for her new intake of thirty, seven-year-old pupils. When she discovered that nineteen of them were boys, she decided to deliver the curriculum using a dinosaur theme. She had divided the class into four groups: Diplodocus, T-Rex, Triceratops and Stegosaurus.

A blonde head appeared through the open door of her classroom.

'Good luck, Sis... Frankie,' welcomed Vicky, one of the teachers.

'I think I'll need it, Vicky. Mr James volunteered to tell all the parents that I have let the convent...'

'Oh no! Trust him! You do look chic, Frankie. That's a lovely shade of pink. It brings out the pink on the skirt.'

'Thanks, Vicky. The tan suits you. Did you go to Greece, after all?'

'Thanks! Yes... as you can see, I soaked up the sun.'

'I hear the buzzer. Better go to the staffroom.'

As Frankie neared the staffroom she buttoned up her cardigan, brushed off the chalk from the blackboard, straightened her skirt and licked her dry lips. She hoped the staff would like her new image.

As she pushed the door open, she overheard lively voices:

'I don't believe you.'

'You made that one up? '

'In all my years... I've never heard the like. You sure you're not imagining? Who else was with you?'

Frankie hesitated. *Such hilarity. I wonder who they are talking about. It might be better if I don't go in. I don't want to draw attention to myself. I feel underdressed without my habit. I'm ignorant of many things that go on outside the convent. Even though I have been teaching for some years now I didn't relax and mingle with the staff much.*

Frankie stopped. She heard a voice from behind her, 'Cakes today. I like it when it's someone's birthday, don't you, Sister... sorry... Frankie?'

'Vicky's twenty-five today. Can you believe it? I think it's that girlish hairdo. Yours looks good too.'

'Thanks, Anne.' The year five teacher.

She doubted that it did.

Anne was pushing her through the staffroom door.

She's put her hand into the small of my back. She is propelling me in. I'll try and stay in the corner and listen into the conversation.

'Start again please, Vicky. Please?' pleaded Anne. We were just doing last minute...'

'P-s-s! This happened way back before Easter. It's September now. You surely don't want to hear it all again?'

'Oh yes, we do,' chorused everyone.

'Okay. How much did you hear?' asked Vicky?

'When you went to the coach pick-up point, it was late. By the time it arrived, everybody going on the trip had become friendly.'

'Yes. then I got friendly with four couples. Well, I think they were couples… might have been partners, Vicky.'

What is she going to say next? worried Frankie. *Usually I walk out when they discuss sex. Now I suppose it is better that I stay and learn...*

'Were older folk there, too?' asked Year 1 teacher, Teresa.

'Yes, although the coach was taking us all to the Netherlands, there were two separate groups; those of us who had booked for the bulb fields and the others who had chosen a cycling holiday. I took one look at the oldies in the bulb field group and wished that I was joining with the younger lot,' answered Vicky.

'Tell us the rest later. It's nearly time to go out to collect our classes.'

Still more to discover, thought Frankie.

'I've still got to go to the loo. Speed it up will you?' chided Anne.

'Alright! Yes, basically they all ended up as swapping partners… lovers… whatever.' continued Vicky.

Frankie nearly dropped the mug that she was rinsing in the sink. 'Swapping lovers?'

How they do that? she wondered.

'Sexy. Frankie… careful with your mug… you'll drop it… no wonder… who ever heard of such shenanigans?' shrieked Anne.

'There's Sister Sheila. The Head's going outside with the bell. Hurry up, will you?' urged Teresa.

'Okay. Briefly, even though we had become friendly while we waited to board the coach, none of that group came near me. They must have known that I was on my own. They all grouped at the back of the coach,' said Vicky.

'There goes the bell. The kids will be lined up. Go on.' Teresa said.

'Sr Sheila's holding the door open for us to go out.'

'Okay. Next morning I made up my mind to go cycling with them. I bumped into one of the woman on the way to breakfast. I asked her if I could join them. That's when she dropped the clanger.'

'Her exact words?' demanded Anne.

'Sorry Love. No can do. We're a group. We swap about. You don't look the sexy type.'

As they closed the door, Frankie heard the Year 1 teacher remark, 'D'you know, now that I've heard the story again I wonder why folk behave like that.'

Frankie was glad that she could slip away.

As Frankie followed the other teachers into the playground, she tried to puzzle out what had been discussed. Five classes of approximately thirty junior-aged children stood in silence. Each class was lined facing their class teachers. Some of the girls were wearing their green and white-checked summer uniforms. A few boys were dressed in short grey trousers but the majority looked smart in what their new grey uniforms.

Frankie noticed two of the girls at the front of her class looking her up and down and frowning.

'Welcome back to school, children! I hope you enjoyed a good holiday,' said Sr Sheila.

She pointed to the ten year line of children. 'Top class, lead in first. Then other classes follow your teacher into your classrooms.'

As Frankie's class of seven year olds were the youngest children in the junior department they were the last to follow the others through the door and along the corridor.

Inside the classroom, Frankie pre-empted the children's curiosity.

'Very good, children. You have found your names. Please sit and listen. I want to tell you a little about myself before we say our morning prayers.'

Frankie felt thirty pairs of eyes scrutinising her. She wondered what the children who had brothers or sisters in her class were thinking. She smiled back at them.

'Please call me Miss Danivet. Can you say, Good morning, Miss Danivet?'

Frankie felt strange when they chorused her new title.

'Let me explain why I am Miss Danivet instead of Sr Frances...'

'My mum said you've left the nuns. Is that true, Sister?' asked a boy.

'Your mum's right, Sean. I am no longer a nun. I don't live at the convent. Store your questions up. I'll try to answer them later. We'd better get on with our work, hadn't we?'

'Miss, I like the pictures of dinosaurs. We went to the Natural History Museum during the holidays,' called out one of the boys.

Frankie was relieved to find that once the initial lesson on dinosaurs began, the children seemed to refer easily to her as Miss Danivet.

The buzzer sounded. 'Oh Miss, we've only started writing.'

'Don't worry, Michael. You can continue after playtime. Before you stand up make sure your desk is tidy. Then carefully lift your chair from underneath you. Stand quietly. The group that places their chair under their table quietly will be first out to play. Which dinosaur will win? Looks like the Triceratops! Off you go. Maria, you lead them out to the playground.'

As Frankie walked to the staffroom she felt Anne tug at her arm and asked apologetically, 'I hope the staffroom chat didn't embarrass you, Frankie?'

'I was a little confused. Did I understand correctly? Four men married to four women swapped partners and slept with a man or woman that was neither their husband nor wife?'

'You've got it! Don't think this is the norm, Frankie.'

'I've a lot to learn,' replied Frankie.

Frankie decided that having lunch with the staff might help her to adjust to life outside the convent. She would to go into the staffroom and listen. Richard, who was the only male member, might be there. The previous year, when his classroom was opposite hers, he always volunteered to represent the school at religious ceremonies. He looked good in his tweeds and well polished, good quality shoes. Tall, thin, shaven, deep sunken amber-coloured eyes and always good humoured, he seemed shy but approachable.

Handsome men like him were happily married with children.

Frankie considered how she would feel if Richard was present in the staffroom when the kind of conversation that went on that morning was mentioned. She felt herself blushing.

2

TENTATIVE STEPS

It was Wednesday of the first week that Frankie had returned to school. She was putting away the PE equipment when she heard someone call out, 'Want a lift home?'

'No, thank you, Paula. I have a rail card.'

'I'm going your way. You look tired. It's no trouble. I'll wait while you pack.'

'Okay. That's very kind. I'll be quick.'

As Frankie gathered her jacket and brief case, she recalled that on the day she announced to the staff that she was leaving the convent, Paula, the school secretary, had laid her hand on her arm and said, 'Sister, if there is anything you need, just ask.'

Frankie wondered why Paula seemed to be so caring towards her. She knew that as school secretary, Paula would be privy to the staff files. Paula probably knows about her background.

Frankie saw that Paula seemed to be reading as she waited for her.

'Thank you, Paula. I hope I'm not putting you out. Are you are really going my way?'

Frankie had barely had time to put on her seatbelt, when Paula placed her hand on her knee, leaned nearer and affectionately breathed, 'Frankie, you must feel very vulnerable. I'd like to help you as much as I can. I hope you will look on me as a friend.'

A friend? puzzled Frankie. Margaret was my friend. She committed suicide. The nuns prevented us from being friends. I've just left the convent. I don't want to belong to anyone. Besides Paula's too old to be my friend. She must be fifty.

Frankie managed to smile. 'I appreciate your concern, Paula. It's very kind of you...'

'I've witnessed so many changes over the years that I've spent in this school. Can you believe that I was a pupil here from the age of five. Then I came back as the school secretary for nearly twenty-three years.'

'Sr Sheila is lucky to have you to support her work. Head-mistresses need reliable secretaries. Sr Sheila must value your opinion and confide in you,' replied Frankie.

Maybe I do need someone experienced that I can trust, considered Frankie. None of my family have replied to the letters I wrote informing them that I have left the convent.

'Confidentiality is the key, Frankie. My lips are sealed. What I learn about the private lives of others, I never divulge.'

'You've read my CV. You know my address, Paula. You know lots about me.'

'I do know your background, Frankie. Let me be clear. I offer you my friendship. It is entirely up to you to let me know if you wish to accept my support...'

'Paula, I am very grateful. I admit that I need help... it's difficult to explain...'

'I'm assuming that I know a little about how you might be feeling. You see, Frankie, I knew another nun who left two years ago. At first, she thought she could go it alone. Then she had a breakdown. I can't tell you anymore about her... but... Let's pull in near this bus stop, shall we?'

Paula stopped the car. She reached to put her hand on Frankie's lap. Frankie moved swiftly away.

'Paula. I'm sorry. I don't like anyone touching me. I don't want to belong to anyone. I need to be free. I...'

'Oh... I'm sorry, Frankie. I've invaded your space.'

'I'm sorry, too, Paula. I've belonged to the nuns for too long. For 16 years I did as I was told. Perhaps Institutionalised. I want to reclaim myself. I am determined to start again.'

'Determination. Will power. I respect that, Frankie. If you allow me I will support you when and if you turn to me for anything. I promise that I will not interfere.'

'Thank you. I feel better for letting you know my anxieties, Paula. '

'That's good. Shall I drive on now?'

'Thank you Paula. The road that I live in, is just...'

'I'll drop you at the bus stop opposite Raglan Road. '

'Ah... of course you know where I live!'

As she stepped out of the car, Frankie said, 'Paula, I'm sorry. I do appreciate your friendship.'

'I'd much prefer it that way, Frankie. Strong-minded people tend to achieve. You know that I care and will support you on your terms. Have a good evening.'

I've proved that I can speak up for myself. I have to acknowledge that these were positive things that I gained from being in the convent. The nuns taught to us how to behave, with what they referred to as 'decorum'. Convent rules and regulations compelled us to live a disciplined life. I've escaped from all that. I need to relax, form relationships. Maybe, I am inhibited by the nun's constant fear of us forming 'particular friendships'. I long to be loved. Perhaps Paula is right?

Frankie turned the key in the house. She placed her feet firmly on each step of the stairs. Entering her room she put the homework that she had to correct and the file with her lesson plans on her desk. She boiled water and stirred a packet of asparagus soup in a mug. Relaxing in an armchair she assessed the last three days at school.

THE NEXT EVENING when Paula asked Frankie if she would like a lift home, Frankie accepted.

As Paula drove, Frankie asked, 'Paula, were you in the staffroom on Monday morning when the staff were discussing 'wife swapping'?'

'Yes, I was, Frankie. It was then that I decided to offer you my help.'

'Really? Why?

'I watched you. You looked embarrassed when all that banter and well... knowing what I know, I marvelled at your coping skills.'

'Was there something in particular that made you think I needed help?'

'Yes. I watched you wide-eyed that lunch time, assessing Richard's response when Vicky was telling him about the 'wife swapping' experience.'

Frankie remembered that she had begun her lunch when Richard and Vicky walked in. She felt embarrassed when Vicky retold the wife-swapping incident.

'Richard seems to be friendly.'

'Is that why you refused the lift that he offered you after school on Tuesday? You said something about having to rush home. Do you realise the way he looks at you?'

Frankie felt herself blush.

'No, Paula. I don't know how he looks at me.'

'He's been asking around... of course he knows that you are single.'

Frankie felt her hands perspiring.

'Has he, Paula? Is he single? He brought that lady into school last year.'

'Anna.'

Frankie immediately regretted showing so much interest in Richard.

I wanted to find someone to love but this is too sudden. I do like Richard, though.

Frankie rubbed her eyes.

'Wouldn't he prefer Anna?'

'Anna? No. Anna is not his type. He's more reserved.'

When Frankie was getting out of Paula's car, Paula remarked, 'Frankie, Richard is a good man. He gets embarrassed easily.'

Frankie thought, *Richard has a lovely smile. He pulled out a chair for me in the staffroom the other day. Is he really interested in me? I feel goose bumps shiver down my arm.*

When Frankie reached her room, she tugged off her jacket and tried to squeeze her eyes into focus. She felt so happy. *Fancy Richard asking about me. I like the way he asked me if I liked my new class. He seems genuinely kind and caring. Maybe I should ask him for advice about our Religious Education programme.*

The next day's lessons prepared, Frankie looked at the photo of her mother. She wondered where she was. She felt sad that she had not been in touch with her for months. She knew that she had moved to near where she used to live. She was waiting for her to send on her address.

Frankie emptied her purse and counted her money. She had kept back £100 from the £6000 that the nuns had given her when she left the convent. She tried to calculate how much money she would need. She made up her mind to find out about taking money out of the cash machine in the bank foyer. She had paid fifty pence for a small loaf of bread. Was this too much? She decided to compare prices in different stores. It could be fun. *I'll have to experiment and catch up. I need to buy myself a proper shopping bag, too. I saw a light, mesh one when I walked through Ely's. Whoopee... when I get my salary at the end of the month I can buy myself a winter coat.*

Maybe my mother's sister, Doreen, who lives in Wimbledon, knows where my mother is. She might know more about Joe. Is he my uncle or my mother's friend? Perhaps I could visit her tomorrow after school?

3

FRANKIE'S AUNTS

Frankie had often listened to her mother bragging about Aunt Doreen's des-res on Wimbledon Downs. 'She's very grand,' Mammy used to say. 'She thinks a lot of herself, does Doreen... as for Joan... she's got such airs and graces... I don't know where my parents... God rest their souls... I don't know where they got Joan...'

Now that she had left the convent and was embarking on a new life Frankie decided it was time for her to visit her Aunt Doreen. She pushed through the crowds at Wimbledon Station, walked out of the station, crossed the road and climbed up the hill. towards when she lived.

As she walked, Frankie recalled that the last time she visited her aunt was two weeks before she entered the convent. On that day when she had tapped on the bay window of Aunt Doreen's four bed-roomed house, she was shown into her aunt's elegantly furnished front room. While her aunt made her a cup of tea, she noticed *The Times* cryptic puzzle sprawled over her coffee table. She contrasted her aunt's comfortable home to her mother's untidy flat. How could two sisters be so dissimilar?

This time, when Frankie reached Aunt Doreen's house, she was surprised to find Aunt Joan's Volvo in the drive. She wondered if it was wise to knock at the door. She was aware that while both aunts criticised her mother. Aunt Joan was more disapproving.

Frankie remembered the time when her Mam had invited them to visit them in their flat. They had declined. She suspected that they did not approve of the run-down estate in Brixton where she lived.

Frankie was wondering if it might be better to return when Aunt Joan was not visiting Aunt Doreen. As she turned to go, she noticed a curtain being pulled back. Aunt Doreen looked out. Before Frankie had time to ring the door bell, she had opened the front door.

'Well, what brings you here, Frankie? Why did you leave the nuns? Come in and explain yourself to the two of us. You surely recognised Aunt Joan's Volvo parked in the drive? '

'I came to say hello, Aunt Doreen. Is it convenient?'

'You're here now. You might as well come in. We've a new carpet. You'll need to take your shoes off.'

Frankie removed her shoes and followed Aunt Doreen into the front room.

'Joan, didn't I tell you that Frankie would turn up one of these days?'

Aunt Joan adjusted her glasses and looked Frankie up and down. She was holding a wine glass in one hand and fingering a holiday brochure with the other. 'Well. What have you to say for yourself?'

Frankie thought it best not to reply. She smiled instead. No matter what explanation she gave for leaving the convent, they would not be satisfied. She pulled a chair near to theirs.

Aunt Joan said, 'We're in the middle of a conversation. I'm not in the mood to coax you to respond. You'll have to wait.'

Why do I allow my aunts to intimidate me like this? I'm tired after my first week of teaching. I've coped with all the hurdles. The staff, the children and parents have accepted me as 'Miss Danivet'. Only two of children quizzed me. I've walked up the hill to Aunt Doreen's house. I should be patting myself on the back. If they would let me tell them all that I have achieved, they might congratulate me. Maybe not. Should I be brave enough to leave? They are making me feel unwelcome.

'Now where was I?' Joan said clutching Doreen's arm. 'Oh yes. I was saying, I plan to be married by Christmas. Not this year but next Christmas. You mark my words, Doreen, I'll be happily married!'

Her husband died barely a year ago, Frankie thought.

'Hello!' said Aunt Doreen. 'That gives you... let me see... it's the beginning of September... so a year and three months. That's all, Joan. Have you anyone particular in mind... lined up, as it were?'

Frankie thought, *Aunt Joan hasn't changed. My Mam's posh sister's as bossy as ever. No wonder my Mam wasn't keen to visit them. She only visited here once. That was after their mother's funeral.*

Frankie noticed Aunt Joan's knuckles as she pummelled her sister Doreen's wrought iron table. 'Come what may, I will marry the man of my choosing! Mark my words, Doreen.'

Frankie wanted to laugh as she watched her ash blonde hair ping-ponging back and forth. She admired her determination.

'Ouch! That hurt!' she exclaimed.

Frankie was fascinated by the chiselled wrinkles on Aunt Joan's tanned face when she suddenly levered her elbows sternly on the table. She leaned forward as though she was intent on demanding complete attention. Giving equal force to each syllable, she announced, 'I have set myself a goal. I am determined to live my life as I choose. I know Tim is only a year dead this July, but he told me to find someone else. 'You need someone, Joan,' is what he said. 'You... You are not the sort to be happy on your own. We love each other and I..."

Frankie watched as steely Aunt Joan concertinaed herself back onto the cushion behind her. She seemed to be rummaging for a tissue in her bag.

Aunt Doreen pulled some from a box and handed them to Joan.

Frankie nearly jumped when Aunt Joan thumped the arm of her chair and shouted, 'We've only the one chance at life. I'm 59. I don't want to be at home dreaming my life away.'

Frankie's lips quivered as she tried to refrain from smiling at Aunt Joan's performance.

Aunt Joan wiped a tear from her eyes and flung the tissues into the bin. She uncrossed her long, slim legs. Elegantly, she rose to her five foot five height. Standing erect, she waved her fists in the air above her head. Flecks of silvery grey tremored like lightening through her lime, figure-hugging dress, as she sang, 'I'm *not* dreaming my life away…'

Frankie glanced at Aunt Doreen crossing her fingers over each other. She watched her tilt her head and blink. Then in pleading tones she observed, 'You've obviously thought this through, Joan. It's a big decision. It's your life. Tell us more.'

Aunt Joan smiled. Aunt Doreen stood and looked down at each of them and asked, 'Let me get some drinks first. Would you prefer wine or tea? And what about you, Frankie? Do you drink?'

They've remembered I'm here, thought Frankie. 'Well… well, I don't mind. Whatever you're having, Aunt Doreen.'

'The Bollinger, Doreen! I left it in the kitchen. Let's celebrate my future!' replied Aunt Joan. She threw her head back and lifting the hand holding a glass above her mouth, she made gurgling noises and pretended to pour a glass of champagne down her throat.

Aunt Joan said, 'I noticed a carton of orange juice in your fridge, Doreen. Give that to Frankie. I suspect the only wine she has drunk was altar wine.'

No wonder my Mam keeps away from Aunt Joan, thought Frankie. She loved the drink but not the drama.

As soon as Aunt Doreen went into the kitchen Aunt Joan reached for a copy of *Hello* from the coffee table. She began to flick through the pages.

Frankie sat in silence admiring a seascape of Galway Bay and a beautiful Belleek ceramic vase with yellow and red freesias placed on her window sill.

When Aunt Doreen returned and passed the drinks, Aunt Joan clicked glasses with Aunt Doreen. Then she said, 'Here's to the new man in my life!'

'Here you are, Frankie. Orange juice for you.'

Frankie thought, she's too dramatic. She also seems to have forgotten her late husband. I would have liked a sip of the champagne.

Frankie suddenly felt Aunt Joan's eyes glaring at her. She seemed to be looking at her quizzically.

Then she said, 'I suppose *you'll* be thinking of marrying too? Were you forced to leave the convent?'

Before Frankie had time to reply she added, 'Your mother should never have put you in there. Have you ever even dated?'

Once again, Frankie judged that whatever she replied would probably not be satisfactory. Silence. She glared back at Aunt Joan. She pulled a face at her when neither aunt was looking.

Aunt Joan spoke next, 'For God's sake, spare us the trauma your mother put on us, bringing two children into this world, one so soon after another and then you.'

Frankie felt hot blood surging through her body. She wanted to grab and aim the fly spray canister on the corner shelf and squirt Aunt Joan. Instead she kicked the leg of the table.

She wanted to shout out, don't speak about my mother like that. Three children is not a big family by Irish standards. What did she mean when she added, 'And then you?'

Instead Frankie replied, 'I love my mother. You only have one mother. She is mine.'

Aunt Doreen intervened, 'Ah now, Joan, whatever you may think of Patsy, Frankie is right. She is her mother. Besides, things were different back in Ireland in those days. It's not Christian to keep raking up her past.'

Aunt Doreen smiled at Frankie. She asked, 'D'you know, I've lost count. Is it 37 you are, Frankie?'

'I was 37 last May 13th… sorry… for my croaky voice,' replied Frankie.' She added,

'I'll finish off this drink and go.'

'No, Frankie. Your Mam had her problems… nonetheless… don't mind, Joan. Her bark's not…'

While Aunt Doreen opened a packet of biscuits and arranged them on a plate, Frankie noticed that Aunt Joan seemed to gaze into the distance.

Frankie relaxed into her chair. While neither spoke, she wondered what her aunts knew about her mother that she didn't know. She recalled that Aunt Joan's only son was a professor of English at Harvard University. She knew that Aunt Doreen's twin girls had settled and married in Canada. Her aunts' children had achieved such high standards because they had received a good education. Frankie contrasted that with the opportunities that she had had. She wondered why her sister Mary, and her brother, Dom didn't seem to visit her mother. What was the reason?

'More?' requested Aunt Doreen, as she held the Bollinger over Aunt Joan's glass. Aunt Joan nodded. Aunt Doreen poured.

'God provides, you know,' said Aunt Joan. 'I fell in love with Andy while he was caring for his lovely wife. She was struggling with her cancer at the same time as Tim was dying. We needed each other. Incredible, how God provides.'

Could it be that Aunt Joan is saying that she fell in love with a man called Andy even while the two of them watched their partners dying with cancer? Frankie was puzzled.

'You never told me that, Joan,' remarked Aunt Doreen.

'No need. Ann and Tim were aware of the support we were giving each other. Tim and I used to meet in the car park before we visited or partners. We met in the intervals between visits and chatted. We sometimes gave each other lifts to and from home to the hospital.'

Frankie pondered. *What's wrong with Aunt Joan? Fancy going off with her friend's husband while her own husband was wasting away from cancer! This is all so embarrassing. Should I be listening to this conversation? So immoral? What a way to behave.*

Frankie felt like a cipher as the two aunts continued their discussion. She felt disgusted. She combed her fingers threw her hair and enjoyed the pleasure of being able to do this.

'Have you seen each other since the funerals?' Doreen asked.

'Well, yes. You've been introduced.'

'Not that Andy? Tall, to die for, Andrew McGill; the *Sporting World* Editor? Him?'

'I'm so glad you like him, Doreen.' Joan was giggling a girlie giggle. She has emptied her large glass and was half way through a refill.

Frankie sat forward on her chair. She felt curious.

'I'm delighted and jealous all at the same time,' responded Doreen.

'Oh, you're lovely!' Joan pouted.

Frankie reflected. *They criticise my mother for behaving badly but they are just as bad. I must go home before they become too drunk.*

Then Frankie watched Aunt Joan collapse, catlike, into an armchair. The late afternoon sun seemed to draw out the heavy scent of Aunt Doreen's geraniums to do battle with Aunt Joan's perfume. Frankie thought that it smelt like the fragrance that she often squirted on herself as she walked through Army & Navy store. She remembered that it was called *Obsession.*

Aunt Joan asked, 'So, Doreen, how do you suggest I lure Tim?'

'Surely you've worked that out?' retorted Joan.

This conniving is simply awful, thought Frankie. *They're both as bad as each other.* Joan ran her hands through her highlighted hair as she raised her head. *She has a twinkle in her eyes. She's beginning to slightly slur her words,* 'Andy and I meet up often... I've been introduced to his sons and his father too.'

Aunt Joan paused. Then she announced, 'Andy's been in my bedroom.'

Oh no... what now? wondered Frankie.

'Oh!' exclaimed Aunt Doreen in a curious voice. Frankie watched as she cupped her face, leaned nearer to Joan, as though coaxing her to reveal more.

'I had to think of something. What better ruse than to get him to lay down the wiring in my bedroom? Why are you looking at me like that? I needed Broadband installed.'

Frankie adjusted her chair. She had never imagined that Aunty Joan would allow herself to get so giddy. *She's obviously drunk too much wine. Imagine her enticing Andy like that. Maybe my aunts have forgotten that I am here? Neither of them has questioned me again. I feel as though I am a spectator at an Alan Ayckbourn play. Mam always said Aunt Joan was single-minded and ambitious. 'How d'you think she's won all her golf trophies?' she'd often remarked.*

Frankie decided to cough and alert her aunts that she was still in the room. 'Hmm…'

Neither of them seemed to notice. Aunt Joan said, 'I've started to plan our honeymoon… the Caribbean… lovely out there… away from it all.'

Aunt Joan is a schemer, thought Frankie. *Why is she in a hurry to get married at her age? She surely can't be thinking of having sex? Or is she? She has blatantly admitted being in love, even with me listening.*

'He can afford that. Lucky you, Joan, You can get up to all sorts out there,' congratulated Doreen.

Frankie let out a sigh. Neither aunt seemed to hear. Frankie imagined herself with a baby in her arms. Then she thought, *Wouldn't it be wonderful to be happily married? Unlike Aunt Joan, I am still young enough to have a child.*

Aunt Doreen turned to look at Frankie. 'You must have lived such a sheltered life in the convent, Frankie. What must you be thinking about our conversation?'

'I have a lot to learn, Aunt Doreen,' Frankie replied. She stood. 'I think it is better that I go home now. I'll leave my glass in the kitchen. Thank you, Aunt Doreen."

'Maybe you could carry the biscuits out? Here, put the empty glasses on this tray. Leave them on the table out there. Thank you, Frankie. '

Frankie thought that her aunts must not have realised that she could hear their discussion from the kitchen. She was startled when she heard the following:

'How's Patsy getting on with Joe O'Connor now, Joan? Frankie's he's splitting image… she's his double… with those freckles and all.'

'That eejit mother of hers. She's the ruination of our family, Doreen.'

'Shush, will you? I hope Frankie can't hear you, Joan.'

Frankie felt as though she had become rooted to the kitchen floor. She gripped the table. She wondered why the aunts had remarked that she was like Joe O'Connor. She reflected that uncles and nieces often resemble each other. But what makes my aunts so angry with my mother? She questioned. Will I ever fathom the truth?

Frankie decided to pretend that she had not overheard her aunts' conversation. She put her head round the door and called out, 'Goodbye now. Thank you.'

Both aunts looked in her direction. Aunt Doreen waved her hand sideways in the air. She continued to talk to Aunt Joan.

As Frankie walked home she wondered if anyone in her family would ever understand what it felt like to live alone in a room in someone else's house after spending 16 years as part of a secure community. However, she felt glad that she was free to live as she pleased.

As she turned the key into the house she thought: *Aunt Joan is starting out on a new phase of her life aged 59. She is driven. She is acting with conviction and determination. If she can marry at her age, I will prove to myself and everyone else that I can turn my life around. I will plan what I want to achieve in my life. I'll set myself goals. I'm determined to make my dreams come true too. I can marry. I'm young enough to have a baby. My family is respectable. My mother struggles. I will be a credit to my family.*

4

AWKWARD QUESTIONS

Monday morning. Frankie intended to place her purse in her staffroom locker before going to her classroom. She became curious when she heard the staff conversation:

'Weekends! Weekends! Too short... so much to do...'

'And have fun! Live... relax...'

Vicky noticed her. 'Morning, Frankie! Lucky you... you can do whatever you like now.'

'Got my lessons plans ready to hand in...'

'Lesson plans! They took up the whole of yesterday evening.'

'People think we have a nine-to-four job and long holidays.' It was Anne

'They don't realise all the preparation we've to do.'

'I've been washing and ironing. The lawn had to be mowed. Lucky, Jim did that,' joined in Teresa.

Frankie was tempted to tell these teachers that she was glad to return to school. That she had not spoken to anyone during the weekend. Her landlady' family went to the seaside. She missed her community. She didn't think that they would understand. She didn't want to say that she felt strange at Sunday Mass. She didn't know anyone. After church she walked around the shops in Wimbledon. Each time she saw her reflection in a mirror, she realised that her multicoloured skirt and green t-shirt were not fashionable.

She recalled what her Aunt Joan was wearing.

There is a sale in Ely's Departmental Store. I'll try on some more up-to-date clothes tonight on my way home.

Franking was pondering this as she began to walk to her classroom.

'Miss Danivet, can you please come into the office.'

Frankie was about to walk past the headmistress office when she remembered that was her new name.

'Yes, of course, Sister Sheila.' She stepped into the office and stood in front of Sr Sheila's desk.

'Frances, I hope you won't be offended. Sr Catherine put together this little parcel for you.'

'Oh! Thank you, Sister.' Whatever it was, was contained in an extra-large brown envelope.

'You might have met Sister Catherine at the celebratory meal we had on the 14th September. She was there when we went to the hall after the Parish Mass to welcome the new curate, Father Philip. It was on the Feast of the Exaltation of the Holy Cross. Remember?'

'Yes, Sister. I do. She's tall and slim.'

Why would I be offended? wondered Frankie. 'Shall I open it now?'

'Open it and see, Frances. The clothes may not be your size. You might not like the colours. Sister Catherine's aunt is always sending her clothes. Sister noticed that you often wear that floral-patterned skirt.'

Frankie reflected that although she had worn the same religious habit for years she looked forward to being able to choosing her own clothes.

'Thank you very much, Sister Sheila. The cream skirt will go with anything. I don't have a warm jacket. Thanks for that, too. It's getting colder each day. They both seem to be the right size too. Please thank, Sister Catherine too. I'll try them on when I get home.'

Frankie was grateful that Sr Sheila was looking out for her.

Frankie was anxious to prepare her classroom ready for that day's lessons. As she walked out of the office, Sr Sheila leaned her elbows on her desk and looked concerned.

'Frances, your cheeks look a little flushed. I really hope I've not embarrassed you. Why don't you sit down for a minute. You don't have to pretend to be pleased. Tell me honestly. Are you able to get clothes easily? Have your community given you a clothing allowance?'

A clothing allowance, thought Frankie. *Maybe the order of nuns to which Sr Sheila belongs are given a clothing allowance? Surely Sister must have noticed that my religious Order wore a modified form of the peasant dress that was in fashion over a hundred years ago? Sr Sheila's nuns had exchanged their habits for up-to-date suits.*

'No, Sister. The nuns in the Order to which I belonged, do not give clothes allowances. The Sisters have agreed to pay the rent on my room for September. After that, I will have my teaching salary.'

'But you must have money to pay for food, Frances? Excuse me... I'm prying. I'm sure your Sisters have provided for you. Sorry. '

'Yes, Sister Sheila. Mother Provincial has arranged everything. Clothes are not a priority for me at present. I'm fine, really Sister.'

'I'm glad to hear that, Frances.'

Frankie wondered if the staff thought that she was not dressed appropriately. She had been looking at the prices of clothes in shops. They all seemed to be expensive. Besides, she was not sure what kind of clothes suited her. She preferred loose fitting clothes that did not reveal her angular body shape. She was more determined to try more on tonight.

'Well if that is the case, Frances, how would you feel if the Sisters allowed you to have first choice from the clothes that are handed in to our Sisters? We are expected to give them to the needy. Sometimes we receive good quality, fashionable clothes.'

'Thank you, Sister Sheila. I would be grateful to look for clothes from the ones you have handed in.'

'You're smiling, Frances. That's better. What's amusing you?'

Frankie was remembering an incident that occurred one morning in the convent.

'Yes, Sister, I smile every time I visualise what happened when one of our nun appeared at breakfast wearing a yellow blouse.'

'Your nuns didn't wear colours, did they, Frances?'

'You're correct, Sr Sheila. That's what our Sister Superior said, 'The Holy Rule stipulates that you should be wearing grey, black or white.'

'Yes, you belonged to an Italian Order. Italians are known for making rules that they try to make others obey.' Sr Sheila laughed.

'That's what makes me smile, Sr Sheila. After reprimanding the nun, she looked out of the window in our refectory. There was a lovely display of brightly coloured begonias in the centre of the lawn. She turned to the Sister sporting the yellow blouse and said, 'Sister, didn't God make such wonderful colours? Red and blue yellow and greens.'

Sister Sheila's phone rang.

'Frances, I'm sorry about that call. You are probably eager to go to your class. Don't worry. I asked Sr Dorothy to take the register. She'll lead the class into assembly.

'I heard the buzzer. I was becoming a little anxious. Thank you, Sister.'

'You seem to be settling in well, Frances. Hopefully it will be possible to promote you to a higher salary soon.'

'Oh! That sounds good, Sister. The rail fare has gone up. I have discovered that it would be cheaper to purchase an annual ticket.'

'Each member of staff will be requested to re-apply for their job this term. '

'I heard the staff discussing that.'

Frankie was going to ask what that entailed.

'Is there anything bothering you at the moment, Frances? I wanted to make sure that you are settling in alright.'

'Thank you, Sister, I appreciate your concern. I'm trying to adjust and to life outside the convent. That will take time.'

'Have any of the staff asked you awkward questions, Frances? I know some of them can be a little inquisitive. They don't mean any harm.'

'They are all very kind, Sister. I try to listen and learn... but...'

'I thought of you lately when I recalled what a cousin of mine confided to me. She, like you, had not long left the convent. She became very upset when two of the parents made it clear to her in no uncertain terms that they regarded her as a deserter. She told me that she wanted to shout out for everyone to hear 'Don't judge me.'

'That must have been very unsettling, Sister.'

I have been dreading probing questions like this, thought Frankie. *I hope Sister is not going to ask me why I asked to be dispensed from my vows. Although I am angry with my superiors, I do not want to betray the Order to which I belonged. I can't forgive them for not admitting that my friend, Margaret, committed suicide. However, many good sisters help numerous people. I will remember the good I have received.*

'The staff have been very friendly towards me. I have tried to fit in as well as I can. Sometimes though, I pretend that I have had an exhausting weekend when all I have done is pray the Mass, go window-shopping and prepare my school work. I can't expect them to understand, Sister.'

Frankie hoped that answer would stop Sr Sheila querying her any further. She didn't want to confess that many times when she was listening to the six years olds in her class reading, she longed to give them a cuddle. She had found it hard enough to admit these feelings to Mother Provincial. Neither did she wish Sister Sheila to know that when she was a nun she joined the Prayer Group because she wanted to be hugged by Fr Derek. She remembered how she felt. Her heart missed a beat every time he strummed his guitar. Frankie was determined that she would not tell Sr Sheila about Margaret's suicide.

'Good, Frances. I am aware that you are adjusting to a new life outside the convent. I'll ask Sr Catherine to let you know when more clothes arrive.

5

EARLY MORNING MEETING

Frankie paced the classroom floor. She had not slept well the previous night.

She was holding the letter stating that she was required to re-apply for her teaching post.

Richard put his head round the classroom door.

'I thought I heard someone coughing. You okay? I'm brewing my usual buck-me-up drink. Shall I bring you one?'

'Oh Richard! I'd appreciate a cuppa. Can I give you this herbal tea bag to throw in a mug?'

'Yep, of course. The kettle must have already boiled. I'll be back in a jiffy.'

Great, thought Frankie! She squeezed her hands together, pinching herself. *He seems really friendly. Maybe he likes me. This is my opportunity to chat to Richard.* She'd ask him to give her some hints about the job interview.

'Here we are,' said Richard as he placed the mug on her desk. 'I brought you a ginger biscuit as well. You look worried.'

Frankie noticed Richard's muscular, strong hands.

'Can't stop worrying, Richard.'

'You won't have a problem, Frankie. I've seen how well you get on with Sr Sheila, Frankie. You know the children love you. You're good with them. You've had lots of teaching experience. You get on well with everyone.'

He has fathomless, amber eyes. I love his musical laugh. Paula told me that he has been watching me and asking about me. Why is he interested in me?

'Thank you, Richard. I, I well... it's the interview... that's very kind of you..'

Frankie could feel herself blushing. She was overcome by his praise.

'Sorry, sorry... I can see I have embarrassed you. I'll be off.'

Richard nearly reached the door. 'No, Richard, don't go. I'm getting hot and bothered because... There are other things worrying me.'

'I'm guessing it might be adjusting to your new lifestyle?'

''Tis indeed! I'm an awful eejit.'

Richard pitched himself on top of the teacher's desk. He winked at her.

'Yes! Only Irish folk say that! 'Eejit'... I love that word.'

When he smiles like that he has dimples. She couldn't take her eyes from him.

'Sure I am Irish! Maybe though, I'd better watch my p's and q's at the interview. '

'I think they'll love you as you are.'

Frankie felt a shiver from top to toe. *He's teasing me! What kind of after-shave is he wearing? Maybe it's the ginger from my drink? No it's more aromatic and intriguing... a cocktail of refreshing, inviting, alluring scents. Her inner voice scolded her. Steady, Frankie, beware...*

'Yes, Richard. So much has changed. I am getting used to being on my own.'

'Good.'

'When you were interviewed for your post, how many were there on the panel, Richard?'

'Let me think. At least four. No, it was only four. The Head, of course, the Parish Priest, someone from the County and one other.'

'And the questions? Are they to do with the job or can they delve into your past experience?'

'Both, I'd imagine... but the Head already knows you. Besides, she'll be anxious to keep you. You're good at your job. You must know that we all love having you on the staff.'

Frankie could feel her neck and cheeks getting hot. She felt a smile ease itself across her lips.

'Thanks Richard.'

'You have no need to worry, Frankie. You have proved that you are a good teacher. Speaking as head of Religious Ed, I have no doubt that with your experience; you'll have no problem in preparing your class for their First Communion.'

I'd better not admit that I intend to employ a less traditional approach than the one I witnessed being used last year, reflected Frankie.

'That's very assuring, Richard, I get great satisfaction from teaching seven year olds.'

It's a lovely age group, isn't it? They're so enthusiastic.'

'Yes. It's a privilege to prepare them for the reception of the sacraments.'

Richard began to laugh. He moved nearer. Frankie suddenly felt the edge of his hand brush against hers.

In a voice similar to that of a judge he asked, 'Miss Danivet, tell me more about your criminal past before I have to uncover it all for myself.'

Frankie laughed. She wondered what she should reply. Was he probing or was he genuinely interested in befriending her? She loved his humour. Did he realise that his hand had touched hers? Is this how romance begins? Is it sinful to feel tingling darting through her body? Suddenly she was conscious of a tear rolling down her cheek. She didn't know why. Was it because Richard had been so kind to her.

'Tears... are you crying? I'm sorry... what have I done? I was joking.'

Frankie took one of the tissues from the box that Richard held out to her.

'No, Richard. It's me that should be apologising. I'm a big girl. That impersonation was funny. I suppose having been in the convent for sixteen years, I am extra-sensitive. Forgive me.'

'Believe it or not, Frankie, I feel the same. Your private, personal life is your own business. Hands off! Keep to what is relevant to the job. That's what I did when I was interviewed. I didn't feel that I had to explain my marital status. People can make all kind of assumptions. My reasons are nobody else's business. If tongues wag about me I don't care.'

Marital status? I feel the same? Maybe he's divorced, wondered Frankie. Not wearing a ring, she noticed.

Frankie saw Sister Sheila quietly levering the classroom handle. She crept in behind Richard. She was holding a piece of paper. Frankie recognised it as the note she had placed on Sister's desk earlier that morning.

Sister called out, 'Are you free to have a word now, Frankie, or shall we meet later?'

Richard jumped off the desk and backed out of the classroom. 'I'll speak to you again later, Frankie.'

Frankie responded, 'Thank you, Sister. If you have a minute to spare, I'd be grateful to speak to you now.'

As Frankie followed Sister to her office, she wondered how old Richard was, if he was married. *Imagine that he took the time to talk to me. He even made me a cup of tea. This is the first time that a man has ever made me a drink. I feel light headed, almost dizzy.*

'Frances, you asked about the nature of the interview questions. You have nothing to worry about. This type of re-assessment is mandatory. Appraisals are the norm. My opinion is valued. Let me assure you that your position is safe.'

'Thank you very much, Sister. I wondered if my private life would be mentioned. Do you think that the priest on the panel would have objections to an ex-nun being responsible for the First Communicants?'

'I don't see why that should hamper your re-appointment, Frances. You don't intend teaching the children any heresy, do you?' Sister Sheila laughed. 'Besides, Father's sister was a nun.'

'Was she? Gosh!'

Frankie waited in her classroom for her turn to be interviewed. She knew that those with responsibility for the core curriculum would be called first. Richard would be one of these. Her fear of the interview had gone since Richard's reassuring words.

The classroom door opened. Paula announced, 'You're next, Frankie.'

Frankie felt confident at the interview. Dressed in the cream jacket and skirt that Sr Sheila gave her, she was aware that she looked her best. She was delighted and relieved by the praise she received.

She decided to look for Richard. She wanted to tell him her ordeal was over. She knew he would be pleased. As she passed the secretary's office, she saw that he was with Paula.

She noticed that they were looking through school equipment catalogues.

Oh well, it's Saturday. I'd better shop for food. Maybe Richard calmed everyone before their interviews. I really like him.

6

MEN

Tucked snugly under her duvet, Frankie felt the sunlight playing on her eyelids. She opened her eyes. Another Sunday. Throughout the years in the convent, when she had to get up early, she longed to be able to ignore the rising bell.

She strained her ears for noises. She was about to turn over when she felt compelled to go to Mass.

A little voice reminded her that it was a mortal sin not to go. The church obliges her to attend on Sundays.

Going to Mass could be the high-light of my day. I might meet someone interesting. If I don't go to Mass, I might be lonely. Afterwards I could visit the British Museum and do research for my class project.

Not wanting to disturb the landlady's family, Frankie crept round the room as she washed and dressed in her new clothes. She carried her shoes downstairs. She was about to close the front door behind her when Evelyn's jet-black curly head emerged from the downstairs apartment. She waved, 'Waiting for the Sunday papers, Frankie.'

Frankie rarely saw Evelyn's husband, Sergio. When she bumped into their handsome, twenty-two year old son, Carlo, she avoided making eye contact. Frankie worried that she would be embarrassed if they or she were not fully dressed. She always checked that there was no one around before she crossed the landing to go to the bathroom in her dressing gown.

Autumn dew made Frankie feel glad that she had worn a jacket. As she stepped outside, a paper boy was propping his bike against the house fence. No one else was around. She walked up the hill towards the imposing Gothic style church with its twin turrets.

She heard children chatting to their parents. *How I wish I had a child to chat to me.*

'I want my rabbit *and* my teddy bear, Daddy.'

'Take them both, darling. Hold your sister's hand… watch out for the cars…'

'Good to see you, Muriel. You seem to be managing well with that stick…'

'Lovely autumnal weather… the cold is creeping in…'

'Congratulations… You're first wedding anniversary! Come here… you both deserve a huge hug… and a kiss…'

Frankie smiled. She was even more aware of being on her own as she overheard these conversations from parishioners making their way from the car park through oak doors to a porch where a stone parapet dominated the entrance. She admired the grandness of the large church in this prosperous South London area.

Frankie noticed that no one held the church door opened for her. They knew that would have done had she been wearing her habit. The woman handing her a Mass-sheet and hymn book, didn't say, 'Good morning, Sister.' Where was she to sit?

She could choose now. In the convent she had been given a place. As she stood trying to decide, a man brushed against her as he escorted a woman up the middle aisle. When they reached the place where the woman choose to sit, he stood back to allow her to go before him. *Someday a man will walk up the aisle with me,* she mused.

Frankie admired the sunlight shining through the massive, traceried window. She missed not reciting the beautiful psalms from the Divine Office with the nuns that morning

To you I lift up my eyes, you who dwell in the heavens... Psalm 122

The church bells began to peel. The bells reminded her of the

Angelus bells that rang out three times a day in Ireland. They remind everyone that the Angel Gabriel asked Mary if she would be the mother of God. Nostalgic feelings.

I am my own woman now. I can choose how I live. I will choose where I sit. I refuse to be submerged in self-pity. Life goes on. She recalled what her mother had told her about her Dad.

'He was a grand man, a grand man indeed. There he is, pictured in the Munster Rugby Team. Sure, the whole of Ireland is proud of that team.' She used to say, 'Frank, with his beguiling blue eyes, the colour of the Atlantic and tossed, curly brown hair, he cut a fine figure. He didn't even need to raise his voice. He was loved and respected. All he had to do was express a wish. It would be instantly granted. He's up there in Heaven looking down on us. God rest his soul.' Frankie wished that she could remember him. She had not inherited his blue eyes. Hers were the same shade of green as her mothers.

'Excuse me! Sorry. May I pass by you. Thank you.'

'Sorry… of course… sorry I didn't see you.'

The man was wheeling a woman in a wheelchair past her. Frankie decided to hold her head up, straighten her back and walk confidently down to find a seat.

She settled into a highly polished wooded bench midway down the church. A young couple with a little girl positioned themselves in the bench in front of her. The husband pulled a pram nearer to them. The baby was dressed in blue. The girl clothed in pink lacy clothes, cuddled into her mother's arms.

If only I was that woman, she sighed. They look so happy. A complete family. Will I ever find someone to love me. Someone who would be the father of my child.

Frankie joined her hands in prayer. 'Dear God, help me to make my wishes come true.

She lifted her head, sat back in the pew and read the Mass leaflet. The Mass was dedicated to praying for vocations to the priesthood and religious life. Would she want to pray that young people experienced the life that she had left?

As she pondered this, the folk group started singing 'Turn to Me'.

Frankie had played this hymn with the parish folk group when she was a postulant. She recalled that the beautiful words were based on words taken from Isaiah. She found herself singing. The young woman in front, hugging her daughter, turned and smiled at her. The baby began to cry. The father took the baby into his arms and rocked him gently.

How lovely. Snuggling up to his father. Secretly, she yearned to marry a man who would love children as much as this man did.

The missionary priest preached about the need for young men and women to leave their families and their comforts to go out into the world to bring the Good News to all peoples. He recounted incidents where the Kiltegan Missionaries were accomplishing great success in Nigeria. Frankie thought of Margaret and her years spent teaching in Africa.

Frankie clasped her hands together and prayed, 'Forgive me, Father in Heaven, if I have made the wrong decision in leaving the convent.'

At the Offertory of the Mass, Frankie was passed the plate for donations for the recruitment of vocations. She realised that she had not brought any money with her. No one collected money from nuns. She had forgotten that this would happen. She felt embarrassed as she passed the plate to the old woman sitting next to her, who placed a five pounds note on the plate. *Why should I feel embarrassed? I have given eighteen years of life to serving the church. Any money that I earned as a teacher went into the convent coffers. I am beginning to be aware of the cost of living. The church isn't helping me now.*

When the priest told everyone to share the sign of peace, the old lady shook Frankie's hand, 'You've a lovely voice. God bless you.'

The little girl turned to shake Frankie's hand. Frankie wanted to hug her.

Frankie continued to feel conflicting emotions as she followed the others to the altar to receive communion. The comfort blanket of memories, rubrics, singing, the beauty of the majestic church mingled with her anger and confusion of feeling that she had spent a good part of her life hopelessly searching for love in a convent. *Maybe I should have left years ago?*

Seated back in her bench when the folk group started singing *'Open your eyes to the wonder of this moment, the beginning of another day...'* Frankie felt her eyes moisten. The rousing, hymn *'Follow me, leave your family...'* brought back memories of herself as a teenager. Visions of her meeting Margaret at the Westminster Vocation Exhibition flashed into her mind. She wished that she could go to the pulpit and warn people. They could end up like Margaret.

Frankie sat in her bench struggling with these emotions until the majority of people had made their way out of the church. She wanted to tell the preacher that he should not be encouraging young people to train to become nuns. He should at least warn them that they could become indoctrinated. She smiled when she remembered that it would be difficult to argue with an intellectual and educated Jesuit priest. Though she loved the church, she hated aspects of it. She loved the way priests and nuns taught, nursed, cared for the vulnerable. She loved the way they encouraged wealthy people to support those who were in need. She hated the fact that the church was male-dominated and guilt-ridden.

... but the smells of candles, incense and flowers... the music and rituals... These are my comfort blanket. I'm like a divorced woman, who, in spite of myself, is drawn back to the happy memories and benefits of my past life.

Seated alone in the church Frankie felt a tap on her shoulder.

'Good morning, Frankie! We thought we had missed you coming out. We spotted you going up to receive communion. We waited outside scanning the crowd. '

Frankie turned round. It was Paula dressed in an autumn brown suit. Frankie stood.

'This is my husband, Paddy.'

'Paula, what a surprise.'

'God be with you, Frankie. How are things?'

His handshake was warm, friendly.

Paddy's Kerry brogue delighted Frankie. 'How are things?' is the way Irish people used to enquire. That way of speaking could be translated back into Gaelic, 'Dia duit, a Frankie. Ca bhuil tu?'

Paddy gripped Frankie's outstretched hand firmly. He smiled, inclined his head and winked. A big man with wavy hair and blue eyes not unlike the Muster rugby player in the photo her Mam had next to her bed.

'Grand. Delighted to meet you, Mr Foley.'

'Paddy to you, Frankie. Paula has been telling me about you. We thought we might find you here. Would you have any objection to coming back with us for Sunday dinner? That's, mind you, if you have nothing better planned.'

Frankie hesitated. *I like Paddy's Irishness. Maybe I would feel more at home in marrying an Irishman. I'd love to know what attracted Paula to Paddy.*

'I would be imposing on you. No, I'll head back to my flat.'

'Come on,' Paula coaxed. 'I have had a glut of fresh vegetables from our allotment. We wondered if you would like to help us to consume them. That sounds posh, doesn't it? Let me rephrase… please, would you join us for Sunday dinner? You would be more than welcome.'

'Thank you. I'd love to.'

Frankie was happy to have a proper cooked meal instead of the sausages she intended heating in her microwave.

'Grand Frankie. We live in Merton. It's only a stone-throw away. Jump in.'

Seated in the back of their Volvo, they sped off and soon arrived on the spacious driveway of a red brick, detached house.

'I'm amazed at how countrified is it here! So near to Wimbledon, yet quiet,' remarked Frankie.

'Two storey, three bed-roomed, solidly built detached, town house in a country,' said Paula.

'You sound like an estate agent,' laughed Paddy.

'Come here, will you? I'll take you into the back garden. You'll be able to imagine that you are back in Killorglin.'

'Fuchsia! They line the boreens of Kerry.'

'Now, what did I tell you, Frankie? You see, even though the lawn is no bigger than a Hurley pitch, with all those nooks and crannies and secret hide-aways, it gives the impression of being far grander.'

Frankie watched Paula's reaction to Paddy. He slid his arm round Paula's waist. 'Come on, love. Put your estate agent voice on again and point out the lovely plants that thrive in this garden to Frankie.'

How I wish a man would put his arm around my waist, thought Frankie. She smiled delighted to see such affection.

Paula placed her hands on her hips.

'May I draw your attention to the two ponds, one oval-shaped and an elongated river-like one? This latter has a miniature Monet Bridge spanning it. On first impressions it appears to be rambling and carefree but, as you move closer, note the variegated greens and autumn hues.'

They all collapsed in laughter. Paddy kissed Paula. Paddy reached out and pulled Frankie into the hug. He laughed and remarked, 'What Paula has forgotten to confess is that the variety of pink and red fuchsias have been uprooted from gorgeous boreens back in Kerry.'

'Now for the tour of the house. Follow me.' Paula pointed.

She led the way into an immaculately clean, green and cream tiled kitchen. Everything was in its place.

'The dining room's next.'

Frankie's eyes were drawn to a beautifully prepared table. Light brown coloured furniture, brocade curtains, beautiful landscape paintings. Frankie felt that she was being immersed in a maze of autumnal hues.

'What would you like to drink? Guinness?' enquired Paddy.

''Tis a long time since I drank alcohol, Paddy. Last time I got drunk!'

'A nun. Drunk?'

'It was after a prayer meeting. They served altar wine. I thought I'd be okay. I wasn't. Felt giddy. May I have orange juice or lemonade, please.'

'Make yourself comfortable Frankie. Dinner needs the finishing touches.'

'Thank you.'

'Maybe I'll show you round the rest of our home while Paula gets the dinner ready to be served.'

Is Paddy leaving Paula to do the cooking, wondered Frankie?

Paddy ushered Frankie in and out of the rooms. Each one seemed better than the next. She contrasted them to the furniture in her flat and wooden tables and chairs that she was used to in the convent. Even in the convent's visitor's parlour, the comfortable sofa had been given to the nuns after one of the relatives died.

Will I ever have a house like theirs? thought Frankie. *I could if I set my mind to saving.*

'Paula's a devotee of the Boat Race, you know. Once the tennis season arrives, she seems to forget anything else.'

'We're very near Wimbledon here.'

'Indeed we are.'

'She looks after our allotment, too. You'd think now, wouldn't you, what with our terrific garden she's have sufficient, but no, growing all those vegetables is in her blood.'

'Is that where Paula grows all these vegetables?'

'Sure, her mother and her Ma did the same. It all ties together with serving up the traditional Sunday roast and Yorkshire pudding. Now don't get me wrong. Sure, don't we Irish enjoy a Sunday roast too?'

'I love a roast. I love the company. I appreciate being treated.'

'There's no doubt about it, Frankie, Paula is as English as I am Irish. I love her for that. She's as proud as punch of her father's medal for serving Crown and Country. God forgive them for what they did to our country, though. But sure it's all in the past where it should be. We can't go on holding individuals responsible for what those bullies did way back then, sure we can't? Paula's thoroughly British. The only child of older parents.'

As Paddy rambled on, Frankie tried to understand what attracted Paula to him. Paddy seemed to be more Irish than the Irish.

'Dinner's served,' Paula called out.

'Sit yourself down there. I'll sit here. Paula needs to be this end so she can go in and out to the kitchen. Don't you, Alana?'

'Yes. That's fine, Paddy.'

Paula placed plates of salmon laid on basil and toast in front of Paddy and Frankie.

Paddy prayed, 'In the name of the Father and of the Son and of the Holy Ghost…'

Grace said, Paula picked at a much smaller starter. She gathered the plates. She carried in plates of Sunday roast with all the trimmings.

Paddy sat watching Paula do all the work. Frankie asked, 'Can I help you, Paula?'

'Sit and relax, will you? Paula enjoys looking after us. Sure you do, my treasure?'

Paddy tapped Paula on her wrist as she laid his plate in front of him. Paula slipped back to the kitchen and returned with a much smaller portion for herself.

'Now tell me again, Frankie… what was it that made you decide to leave the convent?'

Frankie was not sure what to say that would not offend this God-fearing, fully-committed, Catholic man. *I won't tell him that I resent the church being so male-dominated.*

'Many of my friends have left over recent years. Since the second Vatican Council, there have been so many changes. The nuns live a very different life now.'

'You deserted the nuns?'

'That sounds very selfish, doesn't it? Let's say that we agreed that I could do as much good as a lay person in the teaching profession.'

It seemed to Frankie that Paddy was presiding over the meal and questioning her like Father Superior might have done. She wondered why he was not helping Paula.

'Thank you so much, Paula.'

'Isn't this lovely? Apple pie and custard. The nutmeg smells so tantalising. I am so grateful.'

The more Paddy bragged about his grand connections in the kingdom of Kerry and the number of priests and nuns God had chosen from the Foley family, the less appealing he seemed to Frankie.

Paddy continued, 'I always get invited over to Maynooth on St

Patrick's Day. I enjoy taking part in the festivities. I'm an honoured guest on account of being related on my mother's side to Canon Joseph Keane, Professor of Theology to the seminarians and other students.'

'You must feel very proud of these connections, Paddy. You have so many successful and influential relatives…'

'Yes indeed. I have every reason to be proud.'

Paddy put his hand on Paula's arm. 'It's a shame you can't manage to go over for St Patrick's Day, too, Paula. I suppose that 17th March usually falls during term time.'

Paddy rolled his lips ready to kiss Paula's cheek. Paula leaned nearer to him.

'She doesn't mind, do you, my love? Sure I shower her with all sorts… Anything she may desire to compensate! She'll never go without, will you, my treasure?'

'I will go to Ireland one day, Paddy.'

Paddy stood up. He levered his trousers up from the waist and patted his bulging tummy. He grinned like a Cheshire cat. Stretched and rolled his lips. 'That was grand! I won't be needing another bite today.'

Frankie felt glad that she was single. She accepted Paula's invitation to drive her home hoping that Paddy would do the washing up.

'Paula, I'm very grateful for your invitation to your lovely home today. '

'I'm delighted we managed to convince you to come.'

'I loved it all. The meal was delicious. I must start looking up recipes. I will invite you to my home when I manage to have one.'

'You will. You have a positive outlook on life, Frankie. I will help you all I can.'

'Thank you, Paula. You did all the cooking today. You must be very tired. You look pale and exhausted.'

'I'm fine. Really I am. Paddy does his part too.'

'Of course. He showed me round your lovely home. He likes entertaining, doesn't he?'

Frankie resolved never to marry a domineering, vulgar man like

Paddy. Being Irish is not necessarily the only attribute that would attract her. To marry a man like Paddy would be worse than being single. She suspected that Paula wanted to befriend her in order to enjoy independence and female company.

Later that evening Frankie looked out into the garden below her flat. She tried to envisage the kind of man that she wanted to marry.

She listed the reasons that she felt attracted to Richard:

- Tall, thin, shaven, fathomless amber coloured eyes and well formed lips
- Conscientious, good humoured, shy but approachable.
- Interested in religious education
- Looks good in his tweeds and well polished, good quality shoes.
- Seems to care for me.
- Winks at me.
- Accepts me as I am
- Respectful
- Polite
- His slightly sallow skin makes me wonder if he has Italian blood.
- He is most likely happily married with children.

7

CONFIDANT

'I'm passing your flat, Frankie. I can drop you off.' It was Paula.' It's no bother, besides, I enjoy your company. Paddy keeps asking if there is anyway we can help you. We are only too willing. Of course, we don't want to intrude.'

'Yes please, Paula. I'd love a lift. I'm so excited! I've been invited to a wedding!'

'Really? Gosh! Lucky you!'

'I've never been to a wedding! Except my wedding to Jesus. I want to know all about weddings!'

'Is that the invitation?'

'Yes. Paula, my landlady has invited me to her son's wedding. Here. Look at the lovely envelope. The card is really special... it's embossed, all gold and cream...'

Mr. and Mrs. Sergio Renaldo

&

Mr. and Mrs. Emma Wakefield

invite Miss Frances Danivet to share in the joy of marriage uniting their children

Emily Wakefield
and
Carlo Renaldo
Saturday 28th October 1989 12 noon
at St Andrew's Church Wimbledon SW19

Reception in joining Church hall
RSVP
Mr. and Mrs. Sergio Renaldo

'THAT'S A PRIVILEGE. She must like you.'

'I'm going to go.'

'RSVP. *Repondez s'il vous plait.* Have you replied, Frankie?'

'I thought that was what that meant. Yes, I told Evelyn that I am grateful.'

'Then she knows you're going. It's polite to respond so as soon as is possible.

Only the nearest and dearest are usually invited. The cost of a wedding is so high.'

'Are you free next Saturday, Paula? I haven't a clue what clothes to wear.'

'Of course I'll help you get an outfit. Saturday shouldn't be a problem.'

'Grea...'

'I'll just have to clear it with Paddy, first. He'll be fine. I'll confirm everything tomorrow. Is that alright?'

Paula's hazel eyes flicked layered brown and green, like the fossil resin in the necklace that she was wearing. Frankie suddenly felt that she had always known Paula. She wondered if she was replacing her mother.

'Is nine too early? We can spend up to three o'clock together if that is alright with you. I'll have to be back to prepare Paddy's dinner. We eat at six. It's pork tomorrow.'

'Nine it is. Where?'

'Meet you outside Wimbledon Tube Station. Paddy usually needs the car.'

'That's perfect for me, Paula.'

Just as I surmised, thought Frankie. *Paddy makes the rules in Paula's home. I don't want to be timetabled again. Poor Paula, Paddy seems to be so possessive.*

'Twenty-two years since we married. Such excitement.'

'What will you have to drink, Frankie?'

'I never know what to choose, Paula. I'm still not used to having a choice.'

'They brew excellent coffee in this shop. Why don't you let me treat you to a latte?'

Frankie handed Paula two pounds as she pushed a tray along the counter in Foster's Department café.

'No, Frankie. This is my treat. Allow me. You find a quiet place for us to relax.'

'Thank you, Paula. There are seats near the window.'

'Paula, I knew you would insist on paying. That's why I've brought some Ginger Nuts with me. Can I offer you one?'

'Frankie, you can't... put them away before someone...'

'Why? I didn't steal them. I bought them in Sainsbury's.'

'It's not allowed... you can only eat food in the cafe that you have purchased here.'

'Sorry. I hope I've not embarrassed you. Is it okay if I finish this one?'

'You are funny... but I suppose...'

'I'll put the packet in my bag.'

'Mmm... this black coffee's delicious. So smooth and strong.'

'Only professed Sisters drank coffee in our convent. It was percolated in a special silver pot. The Italian Sisters used to say that it was ready when a blue light shone from it.'

'Do you buy coffee? Do you like shopping?'

'No I haven't bought coffee yet. Shopping is a novelty. Now I can choose what I like.'

'I suppose you shop in Sainsbury's. Do you get the bus to your flat?'

'If I have a school dinner, I don't need to eat much in the evening. I only buy a little, like eggs and cheese so I can easily carry them.'

'What do you do about perishables... milk, butter? Have you a fridge?'

'No fridge. I put my milk in a jug of cold water. I keep that under the bath. I'm fine, really.'

'You should have a fridge. Ask the landlady. You said she is kind. A fridge's essential.'

'Honestly, I cope, Paula. I buy half a pint on my way home once every three days.'

'What about the doctor? Have you registered with a GP? You'll need to do that.'

'Yes, someone else recommended that I do... not yet.'

'Have you got a washing machine in your flat?'

'No. I take my washing down to Worcester Park. There's a laundrette there. I've bought a big laundry bag and my own washing power. I make sure that I have the correct coins for the machine.'

'That must be awful, Frankie. You must have to wait and watch the washing.'

'It's fine. I bring a book with me. Sometimes I go to the phone box. I try to phone my sister. She isn't usually in. My mother hasn't got a phone. She uses...'

Frankie stopped herself before she revealed that her mother used the phone in the pub.

'Do you put your clothes through the drier?'

'Yes. I make sure that I am there to remove my clothes from the washing machine as soon as it finishes. Last week while I was in the phone box, a man emptied my washing and dumped it on a messy table.'

'Oh dear! I wouldn't like that. Your washing must be heavier and damp when you carry it back home. I imagine you carry it on the bus?'

'Yes. When I arrive home, I take it upstairs and put it on the radiators before my landlady finds out. I open the window to stop the condensation.'

'It's a wonder you don't catch a cold. Make sure you register with a doctor?'

Next she'll be asking how I get on with Richard.

While Paula plied Frankie with questions, Frankie noticed that she had lines under her eyes and her shoulders were slumped. She looked pale.

'You look tired, Paula. Did you go to bed late?'

'I'm very well. Paddy and I follow a very regular timetable. We're both fit and healthy, thank God.'

Paula doesn't seem to like me asking her personal questions. Maybe it's because she's twenty years older than I am.

'Now tell me about Richard...'

She turned around to see Paddy coming towards them.

'Oh Paddy... Why...'

'Don't want to interrupt while you are shopping. Just wanted to make sure all's well.'

Paddy patted Paula's wrist. She raised her eyebrows. He smiled and left as quickly as he arrived.

I was right, thought Frankie. Paddy is possessive and controlling.

'He's an angel, Frankie. He slipped me £50 to go towards your outfit.'

'Oh very generous..isn't he good? I don't intend spending that much money.'

'You have no idea, Frankie. Clothes are expensive. A wedding outfit could cost at least a hundred pounds.'

'I bet I could get a lovely outfit from one of the charity shops in that posh area on Wimbledon Hill. Would you mind toddling up there with me?'

'Well, if you change your mind, Paddy would only be delighted to drive us there.'

'Is not that far.'

'That's true. Let's go.'

'There are lovely boutiques there. We can see what my age group wears. '

'Of course.'

'I will choose what is discarded by the rich folk to cover my shape and match my pocket.'

'You wouldn't think that place is a charity shop, Paula, would you? Big windows either side of the door. Look at the lovely displays. Shall we go in?'

'Why not!'

'Where do I start?'

'First of all, what size are you, Frankie?'

'I really don't know. I saw size 12 written under the collar of this blouse that Sr Sheila gave me.'

'You look like you're a size 12. That's cheap looking clothes on that rack, Frankie. You need something smart for a wedding.'

'Now for the colour… with auburn hair and green eyes, you'll suit greens and browns. That cream jacket you're wearing looks good with your colouring.'

'Oh Paula… what do you think about this beige and brown dress?'

'Lovely. Looks silky. What size?'

'12. It's sixteen pounds.'

'Try it on. The cubicle's over there.'

'Get undressed in the shop? Do I need to?'

'Do you want me to come in with you?'

'Oh no! Thank you. I'll cope.'

Frankie did not like undressing in a shop. She didn't want anyone to see her in her underwear. She tugged the curtains carefully to the edge of the cubicle. She checked that there were no mirrors over head her. She took her top off first and slipped on the dress. She pulled her skirt off from under the dress. She hung her clothes on a hanger.

'You okay in there, Frankie? Let me see?'

Frankie came out of the cubicle to show Paula.

'Lovely. Turn round, Frankie. Now lift up your arms. That top's a perfect fit. Shows off your slim figure.'

'That's what I'm afraid of, Paula. I don't feel happy in anything that's so revealing. It's too low cut, don't you think?'

'That's not revealing! You're going to a wedding. You might meet someone special there. Come on, Frankie. You must look you're best.'

'What have you in your hand? Is that another dress you want me to try on?'

'Yes. It's a lovely shade of green. Your size too. Try it on.'

'Oh good. And it's got a collar. I'll try it on.'

'Want me to help you with the zip?'

'No thank you. I'll manage.'

'Here I come... what do you think?'

'You look gorgeous, Frankie. Hold on. Let me fetch a jacket that will go perfectly with that dress.'

'Good. I'll need to cover my arms.'

'Try that on, Frankie. Turn around. Lift your arms. Perfect. '

'I do love this pale green dress. It's got a collar. It's complete with the jacket. Green matches my eyes... but is it too tight, Paula?'

'What's wrong with you, Frankie? You've got a lovely figure and a fine pair of legs. You need to show them off. You're a good looking, attractive young women.'

'I find all this embarrassing, Paula. I'm used to covering myself. We were not even allowed mirrors in the convent.'

'That's the past. You said that you want to move on. How often have you reminded me that you are your own woman now?'

'You're right Paula. I like this dress. The delicate brown pattern on pale green. The quality of the beautiful silky feel material. It brings out my colours and makes me look attractive. Why not look my best? My gifts are God-given.'

'Please let me pay for these, Frankie. Only £30 for the complete outfit.'

'I have the £30, Paula. I've got my outfit now.'

'What about the accessories, Frankie?'

'Accessories?'

'Shoes? A handbag? Do you want a hat?'

'Oh! I've got shoes. I've never had a handbag. After having my hair covered with a veil I certainly don't want to cover it with a hat.'

'I've only seen you wear black shoes, Frankie. This outfit is calling out for brown ones. Every woman has a handbag.'

'You know best. There are no shoes here. Shall we go to the charity shop across the road?'

'I noticed that there is a sale in the shoe shop next door. I doubt it you will find a pair of shoes and a matching handbag in a charity shop. Will you come and see how much they cost next door?'

'I suppose you're right, Paula. As you paid for the outfit, I can afford to buy shoes and maybe a handbag.'

'What size shoes do you take, Frankie?'

'Seven. No harm in looking.'

'Seven. Can you see any brown?'

'Yes! Oh, but they've got a heel.'

'And a matching handbag above them.'

'Try them on.'

'They fit. Did you see the price?'

'Walk up and down. Look in the mirror over there.'

'I can look down to see them. Thirty pounds for them and twenty for the handbag. Shall we try a charity shop?'

'Why? They look perfect. You say they fit and you like them. I still have twenty pounds that Paddy gave me.'

'Yes, you're right, Paula. I'll get used to wearing heels. They're only little heels. I deserve good shoes. I should have a handbag even though I've not figured out yet what I will put in it. Yes, we'll buy them. Thank you.'

Frankie felt cradled by Paula's concern. Would it be safe to discuss her feelings for Richard with Paula? She was glad that Paddy interrupted her earlier when Paula had asked her about Richard. Thank goodness she didn't refer to him again. Maybe she sensed that she didn't want to discuss their friendship?

'Thank you, Paula. Please thank Paddy, too.'

'It was a pleasure. Remember anytime you need anything just ask. Paddy's waving to me over in the car park.'

'Thank you both. Bye.'

As Frankie wandered down the hill, carrying her big bags, she wondered what it must be like living with Paddy. He was very opinionated. He was dominant in their relationship. Paula had to bend to his whims. Did she want this sort of relationship? Could she be choosey at her age?

Paula seems to have everything she could want: A big beautifully appointed and furnished house, a car, only the best clothes, heaps of genuine silver jewellery and Paddy's affection. Yet, she seems to belong to Paddy. He seems to control her life. What kind of love do they have for each other? Would Richard be possessive like that? Would he demand her to love him?

8

RETURN TO THE NUNS

As Frankie passed by Sr Sheila's office, she called out to her. 'Frankie, how would you like to join our community to celebrate the Feast of Our Lady of Lourdes after school tonight? After Mass you're welcome to join us for an evening meal. One of our Sisters can drive you home later. You're welcome to stay the night if you wish.'

What can I say? She knows I have not long left one convent. Why would I want to join another community of nuns? I might hurt her feelings if I decline. What to do?

'How kind of you, Sister. Yes… yes, why not. Sure, I'd be delighted to join you. I won't stay the night.'

'Good. If you come to my office after school, we can walk there together.'

Thank goodness she didn't expect me to sleep the night in the convent. I have a recurring nightmare. I go around trying to unlock all the doors only to find that I can't turn the key or there is no key or the hole or the door grows bigger and stronger and more like a safe or a prison door.

Throughout the day Frankie kept wishing that she had not accepted Sr Sheila's invitation.

I must be strong. Nuns still seem to have a hold over me. I no longer have a vow of obedience. Why didn't I say no. I should have made an excuse.

During this reverie, the caretaker popped his head round Frankie's classroom door.

'Excuse me, Miss Danivet. Sister Sheila says she's ready to go home.'

Frankie realised that she had to pretend that she was pleased to be invited.

'Frankie, you must be wondering why I am inviting you down to our convent only six months after you have left your own?'

'Well yes…'

'I have another parcel of clothes for you.'

'That is kind! Thank you, Sister. I've been planning to buy more fashionable clothes. A local shop that usually sells stylish outfits had a fire. They've discounted fire-damaged clothes. I've even tried on some trousers. At first I was embarrassed when I saw myself in the mirror, but I think I'll buy a pair.'

'Before we reach the convent I want you to know that I'm on our Provincial Council. In this role I help nuns who leave our Order.'

'Like me, Sister.' Frankie wondered if that is why she was invited. 'Sr Sheila, I am getting used to being on my own. Besides if I am going to find a husband. I need to find places where this will be possible.'

Frankie followed Sister Sheila round the side of one of the two semi-detached houses and through a side door that lead into an elongated rectangular room.

Sister switched on the lights. She pulled the thin velvety beige curtains that captured the remaining warmth of the day. The scent coming from a pink potted hyacinth drew Frankie's attention to a round coffee table in front of a framed photo of their Foundress.

'I'm fortunate enough to have an en-suite room. I'll leave you here. If you like, you could try on the clothes in the bathroom. You can relax on that comfy armchair. Mass is at six. I will go to the chapel to pray the rosary. Would you like a drink?'

Sister straightened the peter-pan collar of the beige blouse that she was wearing under her navy blue suit. The little silver cross on the lapel of her jacket reflected the light.

'Oh, just a glass of tap water will do me fine, Sister, thank you.'

Frankie was surprised that her headmistress has taken her into the privacy of her bedroom. Her wide single bed was in the corner. Her washing was hung over a drying rack. Delicious smells of roast roused Frankie's appetite.

When Sister returned she pulled an armchair closer to Frankie.

'I am aware of how difficult it is for our Sisters who for one reason or another have decided that God is no longer calling them to serve Him in Religious life.'

'Are you?'

'I hope you won't mind me saying this, Frankie. I have been observing you. Sometimes you are wide-eyed and startled by staff conversations.'

'Am I?'

'Vicky was worried that she had gone into too much detail when she described her trip to the Netherlands. She sensed that you seem to be bowled over by what was being discussed. '

'Oh! I...'

'Nothing to worry about, Frankie. Perfectly natural. To be expected.'

'Thank you, Sister.'

Everyone seems to be watching me.

'Some of the nuns who have left our Order have found counselling or psychotherapy very helpful. Would you be interested, Frankie?'

Counselling? I thought I was coping. I've had too much soul-searching already.

'Wouldn't that be expensive, Sister? I did have some psychotherapy before I left our nuns.'

'Just as I thought. I can give you good news on the financial front. Have you heard of the Causeway Group?'

'No, Sister.'

'We haven't got much time left before Mass. Let's join the others. We can pray to God to guide you. We'll chat later.'

Frankie wondered if all this intrusion into her life was worth the free meal. *I left the convent precisely in order to escape this type of guidance? I have had enough analysing and probing to last me a life time. How am I going to avoid getting all screwed up again?*

When the guitars strummed the plaintive E minor chord, Frankie felt her voice soaring, gathering volume and clarity in time and in tune with the opening lilt of *Where Are You Bound, Mary, Mary.* Many memories of Margaret flooded her.

How I regret not trying harder to have kept in touch with Margaret. Maybe I could have prevented her suicide?

From one hymn to another, Frankie's moods modulated. As she sang the various melodies throughout the Mass. *The Magnificat, Now The Green Blade Rises, The Lourdes Hymn* and *Walk With Me, Oh My God...* Frankie realised how much she missed all the singing.

'We're delighted you can join us for our feastday meal, Frankie. Come and sit next to me,' invited Sr Joan, one the sisters in the community.

At the end of a meal of lasagne and salad and tiramisu, Frankie sipped the glass of wine that Sr Sheila handed her. She accepted an appointment card entitling her to a counselling session. Later she wondered if it was the unexpected wine that has lulled her into agreeing to accept counselling. The nuns only imbibed a little wine on special feast days.

9

THE WEDDING

'Welcome again to our house, Frankie.'

'Thank you, Paula. I'm glad that I didn't have to carry my wedding outfit with me on the bus.'

'You'd never have managed. I took your dress and jacket out of the bag. I ironed the dress skirt. They're hanging in our guest bedroom. The shoes and accessories are safe there, too.'

'You're so kind, Paula.'

'Paddy won't be home before midday. He's got a job to finish. Builders have work to on Saturdays. No men around.'

'It's so good of you to allow me to dress here, Paula. My landlady was glad that I was going to be out of my flat today.'

'As mother of the groom, she's bound to be busy with all the Italian relatives on her husband's side.'

'I'm so excited, Paula. I'll try and sit where I can see all that is going on.'

Frankie pulled on a dressing gown. She wanted to be fully covered if she had to cross the landing to go to the bathroom. Her training reminded to be modest.

'Frankie, if you like, I'll help you get dressed.'

'This is a totally new experience for me, Paula. The only wedding I've been to was the one when I married Jesus!'

'You told me. This will be different. You'll see.'

'That gold pendant you found in Oxfam really goes well with your dress.'

'Thank you. I've managed to buy gold lip gloss.'

'Perfect. I don't suppose you have any other make up, Frankie?'

'What kind of make up?'

'Ah... that's what I thought. I've got some moisturiser, foundation cream... Smooth it gently onto your cheeks. I have what's called an 'Angel Light' shade. Now, for your eyes. How about using an eyebrow pencil, mascara... highlight your hazel eyes.'

'Gosh! Why do I need all these cosmetics? My Mam only ever wore red lipstick and dabbed a little 'Evening of Paris' perfume on her neck and wrist for big occasions.'

'Perfume... I've got Estee Lauder. *White Linen* that is what I use... It's a wedding, Frankie. Everyone wears make-up. Everyone dresses elegantly.'

'Oh well... here goes. Make sure you cover my freckles.'

She held her face up to the mirror and, with her forefinger, smoothed on the cream.

'Look at your nails! They are broken. Just as well you came early. You need a manicure. I've a light nail varnish. Let me file your nails.'

'I won't recognise myself by the time you've finished!'

'You must look your best, Frankie.'

'What do I do first? Get dressed?'

'Yes. I'll leave you while you go to the bathroom and get dressed. Doesn't that silky green dress and jacket look lovely?'

'They do, Paula. I'll feel so different wearing them. I won't be long. I'll give you a shout when I'm dressed.'

'Use the toothpaste and toothbrush that I've left out for you. Anything else you need too, Frankie.'

'You're so thoughtful. Thank you, Paula.'

Left alone Frankie felt the silk brush against her skin and hug her body. *I do have a shapely bust.* She began to think of herself as a real woman. The skirt of the dress was short. The bodice revealed her figure. When she looked in the mirror she was delighted that the pale green reflected the colour of her eyes and the brown pattern matched her hair. *Maybe, some man will find me attractive today? Maybe there will be single men there? If I am to marry and have a child, this is my chance. Perhaps I shouldn't be thinking like this?*

'You ready?'

'Yes, Paula. Come in.'

'Oh Frankie, you look beautiful! You do polish up well. Turn round and let me see. Lovely. Sit down on that stool. We'll do the make-up. Here, put this towel over your shoulders. We don't want to spoil that dress.'

'I have never seen so much make-up! First for me.'

Frankie felt strange having someone touch her face and neck. Does feel lovely, though.

'Won't that cream clog the pores on my face?'

'No fear of that, Frankie. Your skin needs feeding with plenty of cream.'

'I suppose it does. When I was gardening or looking after the chickens, the parts of my skin that were not covered were exposed to all of the elements.'

'Look up so that I can put on the mascara, Frankie.'

'Oh no… I can't!'

'Stop blinking!'

'I can't!'

'Hee-hee…'

'You've got me giggling, now!'

'This is so funny…'

'Oh no! Come on, let's try again. We've got your hair and your nails to do still.'

'My hair… it's just straight and…'

'It looks girlish and neck-length suits you. You've got your own natural auburn highlights. Let me comb some water through and give it a blow dry. That will give it some volume.'

'Oh… that sounds good. Thank you.'

'Take a look in the mirror. I'm holding it up behind you. See the back of your hair now?'

'Good idea. I have never seen the back on my head! You're right; looks much thicker.'

'Now for the manicure. Pop your left hand into this bowl of water... of maybe you would like to straighten your nails first. Use these scissors. I'll give you this nail file.'

'That better?'

'Yes. While your hand is resting in that solution, choose what colour nail varnish you would like.'

'The lightest one you've got... that see-through one, Paula, please.'

'No! Don't put on that ring, Frankie. You need to rest both hands on this cushion otherwise you'll smudge the nail varnish.'

'Do you like the ring? I bought it in Oxfam.'

'Why do you want to wear a ring? I thought you are looking for a man... do you realise that you were putting that ring on your wedding finger!'

'Oh ... oh I mustn't do that...'

'Certainly not. Men check that you are not married. They'll look at your wedding finger.'

'Thank goodness you are looking after me, Paula. I can't imagine going through this beauty routine on my own even for big occasions.'

'But see how good you look, Frankie. Put on your jacket and shoes now and stand in front of that long mirror.'

'I'm wobbling! These heels... oh here I go again... oh...'

'You'll get the hang of them. Practise walking up and down.'

'Yes. I'm going over on my right ankle again. No, I'm fine now.'

'Here's your handbag. I've put some tissues in there. Pop your lipstick in there, too.'

'I look like a real woman now. What a transformation, Paula.'

'Won't it be strange having the wedding in a Protestant church?'

'Yes. My landlady, Evelyn's an Irish Catholic. Carlo's family are Catholic, too. But they have chosen the Church of England for their son's wedding.'

'Yes, I've often admired St Mary's as I've passed.'

'When I first came to England, my mother wouldn't let me join the Brownies because their meetings were held in a Protestant church hall.'

'Frankie, you ought to know that Paddy's not too keen about you going into St Mary's for the wedding even though it is High Anglican. The only thing that consoles him is that since it dates from before the Reformation, it was originally Catholic.'

'High Anglican is apparently as near as one can be to being Catholic. In fact, some say that their services are very similar to those conducted in the Catholic Church.'

'Except, of course, for the Real Presence of Jesus, Frankie.'

'Do you think that's true, Paula? When we were training to be nuns, the old priest who lectured us used to say…' Good as Church of England clergy are, Anglican clergy have not got the power to change bread and wine into the Body and Blood of Christ.' He would explain that because Henry VIII turned away from Rome, their bishops broke the line of succession back to St Peter, and therefore the link to Christ Himself.'

'Frankie, do you think that's true?'

'I wonder? The Anglicans I've met seem to be sincere.'

'I agree.'

Frankie leaned nearer to Paula. She noticed the gold cross that she was wearing on a chain round her neck. She remembered that Paddy wore one too. The brown strings of both their scapulars were also always visible. She felt for her miraculous medal and the scapular of St Frances hidden in the crochet pocket that she pinned onto her vest.

'Paula, I hope you will not be shocked when I say that I question what we are supposed to believe.'

Paula threw her head back and clapped her hands.

'Thank goodness you said that, Frankie. I often wondered whether you remain indoctrinated. Don't say anything to Paddy, though. You'll have probably gathered that he'd be horrified to know that I've even the slightest doubt.'

'Isn't it far healthier to question, debate and discuss? If we don't engage our minds, we're as good as automatons.'

'Faith, the gift of faith… That's what Paddy will remind you.'

'I am so relieved that I can talk freely with you, Paula.'

Maybe I'll be able to tell her about my longing to be loved? I want to tell her about the strong overpowering feelings that well up inside me when I imagine that I am in the arms of a man who loves me. I want to have a child of my own. Perhaps going to this wedding will help me to understand the love that the bride has for her new husband?

'I'll drive you to the church, Frankie.'

'Thank you, Paula.'

'Boarding a bus, all dressed up in your finery, would be daunting.'

'I have never worn high heels before.'

'Hello! I'm home!'

'That's Paddy back.'

'Frankie's ready to set off. I'll drive her there.'

'Come down, Frankie. Give us a twirl before you go.'

Why is Paddy whistling? Is my outfit too revealing? Maybe, I should have worn a coat?

'Come on, Frankie. Let's make sure that you are at the church in good time.'

'Tell me, Paula, what has drawn these two young people from such different backgrounds together?' Frankie asked.

'Emotions, hormones. Extra strong feelings, Frankie. Anyway, how different are they?'

'Evelyn told me that her son, Carlos is touchy, feely and emotional. He takes after his Italian father. His wife-to-be is apparently reserved and shy. Paula, why are these two presumably intelligent, well informed and otherwise mature adults being catapulted together by their feelings for each other?'

'If only we knew. If only I had known. It happens. Others look on helplessly, often unable to warn them. Here we are. This is the church. Enjoy. I'll pick you up later. Around quarter to two. I'll park across the street.'

A heady concoction of melting perfumed candles mingled with red carnations, roses and apple blossom laced with laurel and other greenery, delighted Frankie's nose as she slid in front of a massive grey column half-way back in the almost full church.

Sitting here I'll be able to observe all the others. The altar is within my view. I'll be able to watch the bride and groom. My landlady has seen me. She smiled and waved. That chap seated next to me looks like Richard. I'll watch for single men. My opportunity to attract and be attracted... oh, how do I do that? Stand up straight and look confident? Remember that I am looking my best today.

The Ave Verum is drowning out all the commotion coming from Carlo's side of the aisle. Carlos keeps turning round and looking to the back of the church. His searching eyes smile round the congregation. He's hopping from foot to foot and clasping his hands together. He pats the red carnation on his lapel and wipes his hankie over his lips. Now he's winking up at the organist.

'He's trying not to look nervous,' commented the woman next to me.

'Those Italians know how to dress... such vibrant colours...' someone else whispered.

'Oh... oh... isn't she lovely?... a lily-white bride...'

'Here comes the bride!' someone exclaimed. Gasps and smiles. Frankie wiped back tears as the bride made her way on the arm of her father to the side of Carlos at the foot of the altar.

If only this was me. How I would love to be welcomed so lovingly by the man of my dreams.

'I take this woman...'

'I take this man...'

The giving and taking of rings, all happened in a flash.

Two, twenty-two year olds were wed.

Frankie wiped her tears. I am so happy that they are happy.

Why am I crying? I should be smiling. Their joy is contagious. Some day I'll find the man of my dreams. How I long to glide down the aisle into the arms of some one like Richard, a loving and caring man who really wants me. When I vowed to Jesus that I would be His faithful Spouse forever, did I really know what I was saying? If only I had foreseen how lonely I would feel for all those years.

While the congregation were moving around her, Frankie sat. She saw herself back in the Noviciate, struggling to meditate at six o' clock in the morning.

There I was, half asleep, seated on a hard wooden bench, seated between two other nuns trying to conjure up a picture of my spouse, Jesus. The only warmth that I felt was generated by rushing around during the previous half hour, washing in tepid water, making my bed, pulling on my Novice's habit and making my way down stairs in silence, to the chapel. The central heating was only switched on from 6 to 7 in the morning and again in the evening during the coldest winter months. Why did I do it?

'Here she comes...'

'Isn't she beautiful...'

'He's gorgeous... has his father's dark looks. He's gazing at her. She's holding his hand.'

Frankie searched for tissues in her handbag. She dabbed her nose. *What's going on in my head? Am I feeling guilty for having broken my promises? I wore white. She's wearing white. I made promises on my profession day. She made promises. Am I longing for love or am I pondering the futility of commitments, perseverance and vows?*

No, I'm longing for love, she decided.

10

THE BEST EDITION OF MYSELF

Why had Sister Sheila decided to invite a colour therapist to speak at the Staff Inset Day?

Frankie was determined to appear relaxed. She sat further back on her chair in the circle of chairs in the staff-room. She saw Richard peeping into the staffroom. Was he checking who was there before he entered? He combed his hand through his dark brown curly hair. He was wearing his usual brown tweeds. His matching tie had tinges of turquoise running through it.

Mrs O'Sullivan, dressed in her usual clashing reds, oranges and purple noticed Richard. 'The very man! The only man! Richard, can you tell me why Sister has invited a colour therapist to address us today? As you can see I adorn myself with a multitude of colours.'

Richard put his hand over his mouth. Was he struggling to hide a smile? He looked at the other staff. 'At our last meeting at the Education department, this therapist was recommended. I suppose Sr Sheila thought that we can always…'

Sr Sheila came into the room followed by a tall, slim, well-toned middle-aged woman.

'We are very fortunate in having colour therapist, Marilyn, to address us today.'

When the therapist asked the staff to think of their favourite colour, Frankie pictured a calm seaside scene. She wrote the word 'turquoise' on a slip of paper.

'Time's up!' called the colour therapist.

'I'm going to ask each one of you, what colour you chose and why you chose that colour. Frankie, you first.'

'Oh! I imagined myself at the seaside. Sea, sun and green fields. I chose turquoise. If you mix blue, yellow and a tinsey- wincey dab of green... you'll end up with turquoise.'

'Well done! I'll come back to you later, Frankie.'

Why did the therapist choose me first? What does the slogan on the wall behind her mean?

We can see with our eyes but colour can see deeper and further.

Have I revealed too much about myself by selecting turquoise? Richard is looking over at me.

'Jane. What about you? What colour and why?'

'Gold. I've heard that it has something to do with wisdom. Isn't that right?'

'Good.'

'Who's next?'

'It's me. I'm Teresa. I have chosen black. I wear black a lot. Don't know what that says about me?'

The therapist continued.

Frankie removed her cardigan, drank the water and grabbed a tissue to rub her eyes.

The therapist clapped her hands.

'Those of you who have done this before will be aware that the colour you have chosen provides clues about you. As promised, I will my share my assumptions in private.'

Not more scrutiny, dreaded Frankie.

'Don't look so worried, Frankie.' It was Richard. 'Remember this is a therapeutic exercise. Everything will be discussed one-to-one in that room with the closed door.'

'Thank you, Richard. I'm fine, really.'

I hope that Richard does not think that I look too tense.

The therapist continued, 'Take the colour silver, for example. The silver personality can be summed up in the phrase, 'Still waters run deep.' There is a constant yearning in silver people for spiritual harmony. Silver is the thread of cosmic intelligence. Silver characters have quick, penetrating minds; are unbiased. Allow others to have their own opinions, without the need to try and change them…'

Frankie felt her left foot being kicked. Richard winked.

Why is Richard winking at me? Do I look scared?

The therapist switched on the over-head projector. Under a heading, *Positive Silver Keywords*: it listed various positive and negative qualities.

'Just as well I didn't go for silver then.' Richard whispered.

The next heading on the over-head projector was:

An emotional silver cord is said to attach us to the spirit realm…

Richards leaned nearer and whispered, 'I knew that yonks ago!'

There are no body parts specifically connected to silver. The feminine part of the self is represented by silver whether in a male or female body…

Sister Sheila clapped her hands. 'Shall we break? The urn is bubbling.'

'Just in time. Saved by good old Sister Sheila.' Richard whispered loud enough for those nearest to smile.

A woman seated on Frankie's left side, thrust her arms and punched above her head before yawning audibly. Everyone talked at once. Cacophony!

Sister Sheila banged a ladle on the urn, 'Save us all queuing… hands up those who want coffee? Tea? Someone open a few windows, please. Stuffy in here'

'I've chosen an apple, Frankie.'

'Me too. Fancy taking some fresh air? We've a twenty minute break.'

Just me and Richard? thought Frankie.

He grinned. 'Come on.'

Frankie blinked a 'Yes'.

'Lets go outside.'

We're walking out together.

'I have been itching to tell you that I was delighted when you chose turquoise, Frankie!'

Richard's squeezed Frankie's shoulder. It felt as though he was massaging it. Quivering feelings titillated her spine. *Is it sinful to feel like this?*

'Are you okay?'

'It's good to enjoy the fresh air.'

'Wait 'til I tell you, Frankie.'

His puppy eyes look so caring.

'Tell me what?'

'While I was in Sister Sheila's office this morning, she was called out to the playground. My eyes were drawn to the book on her table titled *The Entire Book of Colour Healing*. Out of sheer curiosity I flicked the pages. By chance it fell open at *Turquoise*.'

Frankie started to quiver. She wondered what her colour choice revealed.

'Oh?'

'I think you'll be pleased with what it said…'

'Will I?'

'The turquoise personality is calm and balanced. It has a fire burning under their cool exterior.'

'Oh…' she put her hands to her face. *Are my burning cheeks as the result of my burning desire? What's happening to me?*

'Hi there, Frankie! You're first to go for private consultation. I've been asked to bring you in. Sorry to interrupt,' called out Teresa from the door.

Frankie felt Richard pull at the tail of her cardigan as she was turning to go inside.

'Let me tell you the best bit of my discovery, Frankie.'

'What's that?'

He whispered. 'If you can manage to peep into the colour therapy book, flick to page 80. Read what it says about Turquoise and the unifying process. I chose yellow. That together with some shades of green produces turquoise. It's to do with relationships.'

Is he making a pass at me?

Richard smiled. Then he winked.

Was Richard flirting with her? She hoped so.

11

THIRD DEGREE

Frankie had arrived early at school. She was waiting outside the staff car park.

The caretaker was late. Paula rolled down her car window

'Where were you after school the day before yesterday, Frankie?'

'Sorry, Paula. I forgot to tell you that Sr Sheila invited me to her convent.'

'You went to her convent?'

'Yes.' *I appreciate Paula's support but I value my freedom.* 'Yes, I am an independent woman now.'

'I waited for you in the car park. I couldn't see if you were in your classroom. I had to go. Paddy had a dentist appointment. He would never admit it, but he desperately needed me to hold his hand. My poor soldier!'

Using you again, thought Frankie.

'Hobnobbing with the Head. That's where your friend, Frankie was, wasn't it, Miss Danivet? Walked off into the sunset together, didn't you? Watch her, Paula!' declared the caretaker in a mocking tone. He pointed a wagging finger in Frankie's direction.

As Frankie ripped off her scarf and undid her coat buttons, she replied, 'Don't mind him, Paula. Jealousy! That's what's eating him. He wishes the Head would invite him too.'

'Not to worry, Frankie. As long as you're alright.'

'Actually Paula, I wanted to ask you something. '

'I'm out at an OFSTED course this afternoon. Do you want to come to my office while the children are at assembly?'

'Good idea. I had forgotten that Sr Sheila wanted to take the assembly on her own this morning.'

Frankie drew a chair nearer to Paula's. 'Thank you again for helping me to prepare for my landlady's son's wedding. I really appreciated you helping me choose my outfit-helping me dress. You are kinder to me than my family.'

'It was a pleasure, Frankie.'

When Frankie got into Paula's car after school that afternoon, Paula looked very excited. She wore a huge smile. Her eyes were dancing. She was clapping her hands.

'Frankie, you'll never believe what I have discovered about Richard.'

'Tell me before you burst.'

'You know that Richard and I went to that OFSTED meeting today?'

'Of course.'

'He talked about you, Frankie.'

'Oh... Paula! That's so... well what did he say?'

'I think he should tell you himself. It's all so exciting, Frankie.'

'You're hinting... you're teasing... I'm so curious...'

'Perhaps it's alright to just say this much... he'll explain. He said that you and he have something in common...'

'Now you've got me really curious, Paula. What is it?'

As if on cue Paula's mobile phone pinged. She took it out and handed it to Frankie. Frankie read, 'Look across 2 my car + wave if u'l let me drive u home.'

'Perhaps it's alright to just say this much... he'll explain. You have something in common...'

12

RICHARD'S REVELATION

Frankie hurried to Richard's car. He flung open the door of his silver Toyota Yaris. He jumped out and came round to her side to hold the door for her.

'Thank you for coming, Frankie. I want to talk to you.'

'Oh, good. I.. Paula's driving off...'

They both waved goodbye to Paula.

Frankie felt strange.

I have never been in a car alone with a man. He has such alluring eyes. He looks gentlemanly in his tailored suit. He is polite. Look at the way he leapt round to hold the car door open for me. Besides, Paula encouraged me.

He closed the door after he helped her find the seatbelt.

'I'll drop you home, Frankie... where...?'

'What did you want to tell me? There will still be time to catch a train.'

'Are you sure?'

'Of course. There are trains to Wimbledon every twenty minutes.'

'Frankie... I... well... I felt that perhaps I ought to tell you more about myself.'

'Why is that, Richard?'

His eyes are smiling. He has long eyelashes. She settled into the front seat.

'Those green flashing eyes of yours!'

'I am curious, Richard.'

'We have something in common.'

'Really? What? Surely you're not Irish? Maybe you're of Irish descent? What else could it be?'

'A few years ago I left home to join the Carmelite Order.'

Frankie felt her mouth drop open. *He's waiting for me to say something.*

'Gosh!... really? I didn't suspect that.'

'I haven't told other members of staff. Of course, Sr Sheila and the governors are aware. I should have remembered that Paula knows too.'

'Thank you for telling me, Richard. I went to Aylesford Priory.'

'That's where I was.'

'Really? Our parish priest organised a prayer day there. It's an ancient religious house of the Order of Carmelites. '

Frankie felt herself sigh.. She had imagined that he was married to a beautiful wife. She even thought that he had children. Maybe he was not married? He wasn't wearing a ring. If he wasn't, surely this would draw them closer.

'I thought you might have been there. Most parishes organise pilgrimages to their friary.'

'Richard, the caretaker is dangling his keys. He's waiting to lock the gates.'

'I'd better drive off. Shall we stop at a café? There's Rizzi's near Barnes. Is that okay with you?'

'That would be great. I want you to tell me more.'

'Good. You could say that we have both served time inside!'

'Ohooo... that's so funny... True! I sometimes feel that I've been in a sort of prison.'

'Join the group. I was in prison for sixteen years.'

They were both laughing. *I feel safe with this man she thought. Like me, he may be a little naïve. I hope he hasn't had any serious relationships.*

'I left religious life four years ago, Frankie. When I heard that you were leaving the convent, I felt that you might be struggling to adjust. I know I did… in fact'

'You said religious life. Were you training to be a priest?'

'I was a Brother. I had not decided whether or not to go on for the priesthood at that stage. We're here now. This is a quiet café. We can chat.'

'This is so extra-ordinary, Richard. I would never have guessed.'

Frankie followed Richard to a corner of the cafe. The only other customers there were three older ladies who seemed to be deeply involved in their conversation.

'I am going to have a cappuccino. What would you like, Frankie?'

'A latte, please.'

'They serve lovely pastries here. Freshly baked apple tart is delicious. Can you smell it?'

'Yes… and cinnamon. I love apple tart.'

'What would you like, Sir?' It was the waiter.

'May we have two apple tarts too? A latte and a cappuccino. Could you heat them? Is that what you would like, Frankie? Some cream, too?'

'Yes, please.'

Richard smiled. Frankie noticed his straight white teeth. He removed his jacket and loosened his silky tie. Frankie got a whiff of fresh sea-smelling aftershave.

'Why did you enter, Richard?'

'I was a boarder at Battersea when, as they say 'I heard the call.' It was before I was due to launch out into this big world of ours. I was naive, young for my age.'

'You were a boarder? You must have gone to a good school.'

'My father thought it best. I never knew my mother. She died giving birth to me.'

'Oh no, Richard! That must have been hard…'

'My aunts… my dad's two sisters… they were great. They helped to raise me. We used to fly to them in the holidays. They live in Florence.'

'When did you enter the Carmelites?'

'We'd had one of these retreats run by a Vocations director. I fell in love with the Carmelites in Aylesford. Off I went. As easy as that. My family was delighted that I was safe and would continue with my studies. How about you?'

'My mother... ah well... my father died. I have vague memories...'

'Sorry, Frankie. We've both lost parents.'

'My mother sent me to a convent school in Tooting Broadway. I went to the Westminster Cathedral Vocations exhibition. I was persuaded by the propaganda dealt out by the nuns.

'Easily done. They can be convincing!'

'Yes. My friend and I were fired up. We wanted to save souls... save the world...'

'So did the Brothers... some people criticise their enthusiasm. I don't and I won't.'

'We had fun and many a laugh. I suspect you did too?

'We did. Simple things amused us. I wonder if people who have not been nuns or brothers would find some of them funny, though.'

'I'm sure they wouldn't.'

He looked at me, one of those shy quick glances.

'Would you like me to tell you a story, Richard?'

'Please, do.'

'At supper one evening we were all sitting in silence while one of the nuns was reading from the Scriptures. The door bell rang. Sister Mary Brown went out to answer it. A few minutes later she reappeared. She couldn't stop laughing. Sister Superior rang a bell and signalled to the Sister to stop reading.

'Well, Sister Mary, come on. You look as though you'll explode. Explain what has happened.'

'Sounds hilarious.'

'Mary was sliding her back up and down the wall and gasping for breath. We started to giggle. '

'Wait until I tell you why she was laughing so much...'

'Can't wait...'

She said, 'It was Sean again, Sister Superior, only it's the way he goes about… oh… oh! He started off by saying, 'Sister I've some lovely manure in this here wheelbarrow which I'm prepared to feed to your lovely roses here and over there and everywhere…'

'Up to his old tricks!'

Richard was staring at her. She hoped that she hadn't said too much.

'I'll give you this and not count the cost of the labour as it is for your good selves. How about a fiver for the lot? Now taken into account that I had to work hard to get the stuff and furthermore I had to push it all the way up the long bumpy road from Fuller's Farm, I'm not asking much, am I?'

'You said no?' asked Sister Maria.

'Well I tried but you should have seen the antics he got up too. Oh you know the way he contorts his face and that whining voice of his. Sure, he should have been on the stage.

No. He kept on and on with 'You'll miss a grand opportunity were I not to put this here fresh manure down tonight while it's still live and active. Will I go ahead now, Sister? What do you say?'

'You finally brought him to see sense, Sister Mary?'

'Well, that's it, Sisters. What came out of my mouth was… What I said was, 'Sorry, Sean, we don't need your manure because we make our own!'

'Oh no! The nuns must have howled.'

'They were in convulsions. I was too. I imagined Sean jumping up and down like a leprechaun.'

Richard was laughing aloud. The women seated at the end table turned round to look at us.

'So it wasn't all gloom and doom, was it?'

'Certainly not. But it's not for everyone. I struggled.'

'So did I. I'm glad I left but…'

'I know I made the right decision. All male… predominantly male environment… maybe suits some…'

Frankie was not sure if it would be good to probe further at this stage.

'But the after-care? What about that? They've no idea about how…

well, I can only speak for myself. Our nuns didn't really know how to settle me back into Civvie Street. But then, how would they?'

'Not a clue. I don't know how easy you found it to get released from your vows. I'm still not completely free.'

'And you've been out four years.'

'My problem was that I didn't have a CV. Not one that anyone would take seriously.'

'But you have your teaching qualifications……'

'And a degree… but I had only taught in monasteries…'

'Your CV would be too revealing?'

'I became a milkman.'

'Honestly? You really had a milk round?'

'What else could I do?'

'Your father? You come from a good home…'

'My father wanted me to stand on my own two feet. Well, I suppose he didn't know what to do. Being a milkman was not what he expected.'

'Oh Richard… that must have been so difficult. Your father… has… is… ?'

'You're so caring, Frankie. To be able to share is helpful. My father and I are the best of friends now. He loves me.'

As Frankie looked into Richard's eyes, she began to feel that she was being mesmerised. It was as though she was in a trance.

It's a bit like having heaven now, thought Frankie. *I want to be enfolded in those gesticulating arms that every now and then stretch out towards me. His smile became a chuckle as his dimples deepen, I'm quivering. I'm being lulled.*

'You seem to be dazed or…'

'Sorry, Richard I am… happy and…'

He's reaching over. His hands are on mine. Oh, what a wonderful feeling. I moved my hand. He felt my hand again. I feel on fire. My face must be red. My blood is racing round by body. It's so lovely to be touched by him. His hands are so soft and caressing. I feel ecstatic.

'Frankie, thank you. I'll drive you home.'

'How kind… I'd love you to but maybe not this time.'

What would her landlady think if she arrived in a man's car? What would Richard think about her room? Should she let him see her room? She hadn't bought any food. She didn't even have milk.

'You look worried, Frankie. Maybe that was not a good idea. We'll have to meet again… soon.'

'No, I am very happy. It's just the landlady… I'

'You're right. We'll make another date.'

She hoped that she had not spoilt this wonderful time with Richard. She discovered that she need not have been worried. Richard drove Frankie to the railway station. His kiss on her cheek was the first since John had kissed her all those years ago at the disco in Tooting Bec.

13

COUNSELLING

Frankie opened her eyes, stretched her body and pulled up her duvet.

What a dream! I feel so happy. I dreamt that I lay in Richard's arms all night. My life is changing. I can be my own person. Where is Richard today? What does he do on Saturdays? What am I going to do today? Half past nine. Light peeping through the curtains.

Frankie pulled off the duvet and looked under the door to see if the stairway light was on. Her landlady usually switched it on when she rose each morning. She saw a letter. She realised that she must have stepped over it on her way into her bedroom the night before. She slipped out of bed to pick up the envelope.

That's Sr Sheila's writing. Why is she writing to me? She saw me in school yesterday.

Frankie tore open the envelope.

FRANKIE AS PROMISED, please find enclosed an appointment card for a counselling session at the Causeway *Group in Nelson Mandela Community Centre at 11 o'clock on Saturday 11th November. I managed to get a slot for you with a good counsellor.*

You are in my prayers.
Sr Sheila.

NO! I don't need counselling. All my life I have had to confess my sins. When I was only seven I was sent to Confession every Saturday. I remember the examination of conscience set out in our prayer book:

Have I done anything wrong today? Did I say my prayers properly this morning? Have I been selfish?

In the convent we had to confess our failings to Mother Superior on Retreat Days. Counselling is yet another means of getting me to examine my conscience. When the nuns started giving us personality tests they wanted us to analyse ourselves, examine our conscience and feel guilty over and over again. I've struggled to dismiss feeling guilty. I want to fall in love. Taking advice from the nuns is a retrograde step. What do they know about love? I am in love with Richard. I'm walking on air... at least I was until I read this card.

As Frankie put the card on her bedside table she picked up her photo of Richard. She had managed to slip this photo from the pile left in the staffroom after the Christmas celebrations. She kissed him lovingly three times.

Darling Richard, what do you think I should do? Maybe you agree with Sr Sheila. Counselling is recommended in convents and seminaries. If only you were here. If only you were holding my hand.

Frankie pressed the scarf that Richard had loaned her to her nose. A lightning tingle sped down her spine as she inhaled his nutmeg and ginger scent. She closed her eyes and swooned into his enfolding arms. He kissed her softly. She hummed '*... all I have to do is dream.*'

Frankie combed her hands through her hair, scratched the back of her neck, waltzed towards the window and tugged open the curtains. The weeping willow tree at the bottom of the garden was quivering in the November wind.

I no longer have to obey the nuns' orders. How can Sr Sheila know what it feels like to be in love with a man? The nearest phone box is half way to the Community Centre. I might as well go there to cancel my appointment.

Frankie walked to the Nelson Mandela Community Centre situated at the other end of Wimbledon. She stopped inside the door. She wanted to assess what kind of place it was. She read the sign to 'Causeway Group' where she had been told that counselling took place. A young woman strolled past her carrying a yoga mat under her arm. A lad of about eight scooted by on rollers skates. The smell of soggy, worn rubber tennis balls pervaded what looked like a series of hickelty-pickelty pre-fabricated rooms united by a corridor.

Frankie followed an arrow pointing to an information desk. It led to a narrow passageway with walls painted in shades of green. She pushed through double doors to face a middle-aged woman with a broad smile seated behind a reception desk. She placed the appointment card that Sister Sheila sent her on the counter.

'My name is Frances Danivet.'

'Ah, Good. Sister Sheila phoned to say you'd be coming. Welcome to the Causeway Group. I'm Margaret. You'll be seeing Peter O'Kane. He's always punctual. Perhaps you would you like to take a seat until he phones.'

'I'm really sorry. I only received this card this morning. I want to cancel. I know it's late…'

'Oh… Peter is expecting… Appointments are precious… It's too late…'

'Well I… I…'

'Why don't you tell him what your plans are?'

'Alright. I'll do that.'

Frankie wondered if Peter O' Kane might be a priest. *Will he welcome an ex-nun? Do I really want to speak to the clergy? I haven't left the Church but I can't imagine a priest who probably encourages young people to follow Christ into religious life being pleased to see a deserter like me. Maybe I could enquire about him? Would Margaret tell me?*

Frankie noticed the receptionist glancing at her.

'Don't look so worried. Do you mind me calling you Frances?'

'Frankie. My name's Frankie.'

'Frankie, Peter's very helpful. He's just phoned for you.'

Frankie knocked firmly on the door of Peter's room.

'Come right in, Frances.'

'Good morning, Mr O'Kane…'

He held out his hand. 'Peter. Please call me Peter.'

'Sr Sheila made this appointment. I don't need…'

'Yes. Dear, kind Sr Sheila. She asked me to fit you in as soon as possible.'

'I want to explain…'

Tall, lanky, grey haired, Peter seems to have x-ray blue eyes. *Is that a good sign? Will he be able to read my mind? Will he detect my fear of being made to feel guilty for leaving the convent? Will he sense that I am in love with a man who has left the Carmelite Order?*

'Sit down and make yourself comfortable, Frankie. Draw that armchair nearer so that I can get to know you. That's better. I won't bite. We'll complete this form with your details?'

Frankie perched on the overstuffed chair and folded her arms into her lap.

He has a melodious, monk-chanting, sort of voice. Friendly and informal. What would Richard think? I suppose there's no harm in giving Peter my details. Dressed casually in navy corduroy trousers, a denim jacket over a blue shirt, he seems a decent chap.

'My name is Frances Danivet. I'm known as Frankie to my friends. I—'

'May I call you, Frankie?'

'Yes. That's fine Mr… Peter…'

'Oh I remember. Sr Sheila has given me your name and address.' He lifted up a printed sheet.

'How are you feeling, Frankie?'

Frankie felt her hands joining. Her index fingers raised themselves to her chin. She pointed them across her lips.

'I see you're not comfortable about disclosing your feelings? Let's stick to facts. You're nodding. How tall are you? My guess is around five foot six or seven. Am I correct?'

'When you weighed yourself, what did the scales say?'

'You're nodding again.'

'Five foot seven.'

'How about your weight, Frankie?'

I'm not going to reply to this question. This is too personal. I don't want to talk about my weight.

Frankie lowered her eyes. She felt her top lip roll over her bottom one.

'Okay. I am six feet six tall. I weighed twelve stone last time I stood on the scales. Maybe you're happier with metric rather than imperial measures?'

'Nine stone.'

'That wasn't too difficult, was it, Frankie? You have green eyes that go so well with your curly auburn hair. What lovely freckles.'

Peter moved closer. 'Frankie, my friends call me a greyhound! They're always teasing me. They accuse me of eating everything in sight but remaining scraggy! I think they're just jealous because I can eat well and don't put on weight.'

He's trying to make me laugh... oh!

'So you're a slim healthy, fit, thirty-seven year old, lady with your whole life before you. Is that correct, Frankie?'

'Yes.'

He is grinning. I can't make myself smile back.

'Are you able to say how you feel, Frankie?'

Those penetrating pleading eyes! How am I feeling? Frightened, unwilling or unable to cooperate. I'm confused? What's going on inside me? He wants an answer. I hate this silence. I detest being looked at. I can't keep still any longer. I look at him. Oh... we're looking at each other.

Frankie heard ticking. A long silence. She read the sign on the wall behind his desk listing his qualification: Peter O'Kane BA (Hons) MBACP (Accred) UKRCP Registered.

She was disappointed that he saw her examining his framed documents.

'Impressive letters after my name... eh?'

She nodded.

He pointed to the badge that he was wearing. 'See' he said. 'Mr Peter O'Kane Counsellor.'

His eyes seem to pierce holes through me like spiky arrows. Is the ticking coming from a clock or my watch? My heart is pounding. My vision is blurred. Water is trickling from the sides of my eyes. He's handing me a box of tissues.

'Sorry.' My shaky voice sounds pathetic.

'Try me. I might understand, Frankie?' Peter pushed the tissues nearer.

He's probing too much, too quickly. I don't know him. I am my own person. I am not sure that I can trust him. I daren't look at him. I can feel him looking at me. I look at the floor.

He has not said anything for a long time. Is that his tummy is rumbling?

Frankie blew her nose. She watched Peter take tissues out of the box, bend nearer and hands them to her.

I'm wasting his time.

Frankie coughed. 'I'd like to go now.'

She tried to stand. She pulled up the collar of her coat. Peter stood. She raised her head and looked at Peter.

She saw his hawkish eyes pierce hers.

He is disappointed in me.

Frankie opened the office door. 'Frankie, should you wish to join us, the Causeway Group celebrates Mass at midday.'

'Thank you. I won't… I'll think about it.'

'One more thing. These counselling sessions are free. They get booked up very quickly. On Monday could you let our secretary know if you wish to take of this appointment next Saturday.'

'Yes. Thank you.'

Frankie nearly bumped into a woman. She enquired, 'Where are the ladies' toilets?'

'Down the corridor, round the corner and on the right. I'm going that way.'

Frankie didn't want anyone to see her crying.

The woman chatted, 'Nearly time for Mass. I always try to get in here before the other courses finished.'

'What type of courses are run here?'

'Lots! You must be new here. Why don't you come to Mass. We'll tell you all about them?'

In spite of everything Frankie was curious to know more about this Causeway Group. *Maybe I'll go to Mass? I know all about Mass. Nothing drastic can happen there.*

Frankie followed a group of other people into a big hall. A starched white cloth has been draped over a table converting it into an altar. Chairs were arranged in a semicircle around the altar. The sound of chattering grew nearer. More people entered through the swinging doors.

They're coming over to me. They're smiling, realised Frankie.

'Hello! I'm Susie... I'm Debbie... I'm John... You're new to this place. Welcome!'

There are too many names and faces to remember. They all seem welcoming.

Hymns were suggested. Readers volunteered. Others opted to take part in the offertory procession. Most of the men disappeared and returned dressed in Mass vestments!

Are they priests? Do the children who have come to join us belong to them? Catholic priests are not allowed to marry.

Half an hour later when Mass was finished, the woman on Frankie's right, leaned across her teenage daughter. 'Frankie, is this your first time at a Causeway?'

I must have 'bewilderment' and 'confusion' written across my forehead. What is going on?

'Yes I...'

'So that accounts for your... Well, I hope you don't mind me remarking that you look wide-eyed and wondering. Has anyone told you that these men are married and still consider themselves to be priests?'

'Really? I was always taught *once a priest, always a priest.*'

'You've got it. Precisely.'

'This is our son. His father is the second priest that was standing on the left?'

'Correct.'

Unbelievable, she thought. The only married priests that she knew in the Catholic Church were the Anglican clergy who have been allowed to be ministers after they have converted to Catholicism.

A drab, podgy older woman came up to her. 'I'm Barbara. What's your name?'

'I'm Frankie.'

'How did you enjoy that? A real family celebration. Take a plate and help yourself to food, won't you?'

'Thank you. Have you got used to married priests, Barbara?'

'Why not? Jesus may well have been married.'

'I suppose. We don't really know.'

'Come on. Tuck into this crispy bacon. Rashers as we call them back in Ireland!'

'Thank you.'

'I had my doubts too, Frankie. Two years ago, when I first met this Causeway Group, I had not heard of married priests. You may have worked out that most of us women there were nuns at one time too?'

'Barbara! Really? Ex-nuns too?'

'We need each other, especially since the hierarchy are not helping us to adapt to life after leaving the priesthood and religious life.'

'How do you help each other?'

'We meet on the first Saturday of each month like we did today.'

'Do you go to counselling? Oh, forgive me, maybe this is a private matter, Barbara. Sorry.'

'There's nothing to be sorry about, Frankie.

'Barbara, it's such a relief to be able to talk to another ex-nun.?'

'I understand. We have to insert ourselves back into life outside the convent. However, when folk hear that we have been in a convent, they don't expect us to know certain things about marriage and sex. Especially anything to do with real relationships.'

'You're right, Barbara. When anyone starts telling jokes I get scared that they may be rude. I become anxious, hot and bothered. Embarrassed.'

'I expect many ex-religious people feel that way.'

'Do you mind me asking you, Barbara, what religious Order did you belong to?'

'Not at all, Frankie. I was a Sacred Heart Sister for thirty years. I used to sew and design priests' vestments.'

'Marvellous. You were a machinist and...'

'Seamstress. When I left the convent, I had no certificates to prove that I had sewing skills.'

'Of course. That was before NVQ qualifications had come in.'

'I had no CV. Aged 61. I could not find a job.'

'What did you do?'

'I have almost finished a year attending the Westminster Counselling course. I hope to become a counsellor.'

As Frankie walked back to her flat, she was relieved that she had met other ex-nuns who had married ex-priests. She wanted to ask Richard if he knew about this group of people. What would he think about counselling? Did she need that sort of help?

Frankie reflected: *I have met a wonderful man who has also been in religious life. We've met without help.*

14

IMAGININGS

Frankie woke with a start.

'Oh… ah… sorry… I'm…'

Someone was knocking… 'Come… oh, I…' It was the landlady.

'I saw your light on, Frankie. I wondered if you're unwell. You're usually up…'

'Sorry, Evelyn. I was so tired. Is it late?'

'Good. You must have needed a long sleep. It's only ten o'clock. Drink this coffee… or sleep on.'

'You're an angel. Thank you. I can take my time. It's Sunday. Oh, Mass?'

'You're tired. Enjoy your rest. There's an evening Mass.'

Frankie sipped some coffee then curled back under her duvet.

I dreamt of Richard again. Dear Richard. I wanted to be with Richard. I wanted to ask him what he thought about the Causeway Group. I wonder what he would think. I dreamt that I had fallen asleep in his arms. Evelyn broke my dream. I dreamt that I was feeding my baby. My cuddly baby. Our baby! He's the image of his father, Richard. Will I call him Frank after my Dad or... I wonder what Richard's father's name is? He never talks about his parents. Wonder why?

If only my dream could come true. I will keep imagining that I am in Richard's arms. I'll close my eyes and carry on dreaming:

RICHARD IS INSISTING in driving me back to my flat. He says, when I reach the front door he presses his firm lips on mine. He holds me tightly. I can feel his strength and firmness. He follows me too my room. We made love, passionately, fondly and for ages. I hope I will have our baby.

There's nothing wrong in thinking, willing, wishing to be together. God wouldn't have given us all these body parts if He didn't intend us to use them. Fit them together. I need to go through it all in my mind. I can't make a fool of myself the first time I make love with Richard. I feel so warm and cared for as I surrender to him. But can I surrender to him?

The nuns talked a lot about purity and chastity. Our bodies are sacred vessels. We are to live on earth like angels so that our reward will be great when we meet Jesus, our spouse, in Heaven. How comforting is that?

I need to talk to Paula. She brought me closer to Richard. I should tell how our relationship is developing. How can I tell her about the feelings of sinfulness, guilt, the fear of Hell that is imbedded in my psyche? After years of covering myself up in all-enveloping-clothes and ignoring my bodily parts, how can I change now? Mammy never used the word 'sex'. It was a bad word in our home. In the convent we were told that marriage was solely to fulfil the requirements of God's command to procreate. A sort of a necessary evil. What will Paula think? Did she want to have children?

Am I lost in my imagination? Does Richard really love me? He only kissed me once. But those big tiger-cub eyes looked playful. Maybe he kisses other women when he invites them out for drinks.

It would have been no use meeting Paula after 9.30 Sunday Mass. I could not confide in Paula if Paddy was there. He asks too many questions. He blurts out everything. I want to discuss delicate matters.

Oh! Didn't Paula tell me that Paddy is going up to Westminster Cathedral this Sunday? She said he is attending a meeting for a select group of men chosen to become a Knight of St Gregory. I remember Paula saying that she would be at the last Mass today at 12 noon. What time is it now? A quarter past 11. I can make it to church in time.

FRANKIE SAW Paula kneeling on the bench where she and Paddy usually sit in church. On the right hand side of middle aisle six rows from the front. She crept in beside her and whispered, 'So glad you're here, Paula.'

Paula turned and patted Frankie's arm. 'Good, Frankie. We can stop for coffee afterwards.'

When Mass was over, Frankie followed Paula into the church hall where drinks and biscuits were being served.

'What are you up to this weekend, Frankie? Was it a busy week?'

'Yes, it was. Paula. Would it be possible for me to have a chat with you?'

'Of course... where? How about in my car? Shall we? We could take our coffee in one of these plastic beakers.'

'I hope you don't mind Paula. I'd love some advice.'

'Come on then. Take a biscuit and follow me to my car. We can have a good chin-wag there. We'll be snug-as-bug.'

'You're fidgety, Frankie. Are you embarrassed about something?'

'A little. It's putting thoughts into words...'

'Is it about Richard? I'm delighted that you both seem to be getting on so well.'

'Yes, it is about Richard. I love him, Paula.'

Paula put her beaker into the car holder and clapped her hands. 'Splendid!'

'Yes, but does he love me? I do a lot of imagining, Paula.'

'I've noticed plenty of signs of a budding relationship, Frankie. Winks, nods...'

'That obvious? I don't know what is real. I dream. I wish and imagine... it's...'

'Don't lose this opportunity. Your biological clock's ticking.'

'Biological clock? I know so little about things like that.'

'Your biological clock is important if you want a baby. You're ability to conceive doesn't go on forever. But maybe...?'

'I'd love a child of my own... our baby, Paula.'

'You could foster or adopt.'

'I suppose.'

'How old are you, Frankie?'

'Thirty-eight.'

'So your biological clock is most likely still ticking. In most cases women can safely become pregnant up to the age forty-two. After that there is fertility treatment. IVF in-Vitro.'

'Fertility treatment! That reminds me of my granddad getting the bull into impregnate his cows!'

'Ha! You know more about fertility than you realise, Frankie!'

'Maybe. But I'm still ignorant and embarrassed. Convent life cut me off from even thinking about men and their bodies.'

'It's not just nuns and priests who feel shy and ignorant about what happens in the bedroom, Frankie. My parents didn't tell me anything about such matters. Emotions rear and most of us just follow our instincts.'

'Really? I get emotional and almost out of control. Then I feel guilty and sinful.'

'Sinful? I can understand that. Many Catholics are tired of priests telling them that marriage is primarily for reproduction. When Paddy discovered that he could not have children, he decided that we should no longer make love.'

'Oh, I'm sorry Paula. I didn't think.'

'That doesn't worry me any longer, Frankie. We have sorted these matters out.'

'I didn't mean to probe.'

'You haven't. What do you really know about Richard, Frankie? Have you met his parents?'

'No but I imagine that he comes from a good background.'

'What makes you think that?'

'He wears good quality clothes. He dresses well. Tweeds and leather shoes. He speaks well too. He told me that he attended a good grammar school. He was training to be a Carmelite brother. He was in their seminary.'

'Good. I've never heard him speak about his parents though. I don't think anyone at school has. However, I've come to a similar conclusion about his background. Maybe you should try to meet his parents.'

'Yes, I suppose I am fortunate that you introduced me to Richard, Paula.'

'I couldn't help myself! I saw two lovely, lonely people. I wanted to match them up. Don't forget that as school secretary, I am privy to the information about your backgrounds.'

'Oh Paula, I must tell you what one of our ex-nuns did to attract a man.'

'Go on! This sounds good.'

'She asked a friend for hints. They were both at a party in a hotel. Her friend told her that smiling and winking at someone she fancies could do the trick.'

'Oh, no!'

'Oh, yes! There were pillars in the hall. She saw a desirable man sitting alone. She stuck her head out from behind one of pillars, coughed to attract his attention. Winked and smiled.'

'What... what happened?'

'Stop laughing... you're doubled up over that wheel. The horn will go off if you 're not careful.'

'He smiled back, stood, walked away and disappeared.'

'I'm not surprised.'

'But, wait. Later that evening when she was about to go home she met this same man at the exit door, arm in arm with a woman. Presumably, his wife!'

'Well she tried. But tell me, Frankie, what else worries you?'

'I get all hot and bothered when I recall things I imagine.'

'Try me. Tell me what you imagine. No harm in imagining.'

'I wake up cuddling my baby. I'm singing lullabies and rebel songs that Mam told me that my dad used to sing to me. I dress the baby in power-blue, soft woolly clothes. I spend ages dressing and undressing and playing with him.'

'That's a natural motherly instinct, Frankie. You probably imagine yourself in bed with Richard too...'

Frankie felt her hand spring to her face and cover her mouth. She lowered her head. She felt flushed.

'Yes… yes… how…'

'That's normal… most women feel like that…'

'Oh, Paula! This is such a relief… I want Richard to be mine forever. He will love our baby. We won't let anything happen to him. We'll put him in a rocking cradle next to our bed.'

Shall I continue? Paula is smiling at me.

'You don't think that I'm crazy, Paula?'

'Far from it, Frankie. Treasure your dreams and hopefully they will become a reality.'

'Thank you, Paula.'

'But you brought a smile to my face when I noticed you wearing a green top almost the same shade as Richard's shirt last week…'

'I wanted to match… oh dear! Not a good idea?'

'Perhaps not. Do you ever read Woman' Magazine, Frankie? I've got a pile at home. There are the Sunday paper's supplements too where all these sort of things are discussed.'

'We weren't allowed to read newspapers in the convent. Perhaps that would be a good idea. I might find better ways to please Richard. If I knew when it is Richard's birthday, I could look up what sign he was born under. My Aunt Joan used to do that.'

'Maybe I could check that out. However, not all you read in these magazines is true.'

'One thing I must keep in mind is that my mother smoked and drank. I don't want to repeat her mistakes.'

15

REALITY CHRISTMAS

It was Saturday morning. Frankie was wrapped up well in a long dark brown coat that her landlady had given her one evening. Despite the warmth she walked home from the bus stop, shivering.

Yvonne waved her off. 'You off doing your good deed, Frankie? You've wrapped up warm. Those colours suit your complexion. Bring out the green in your eyes.'

'Thanks Yvonne. The staff admired the coat. Thank you for that. I'll need it today. It will be cold out there fund-raising to help cancer patients. Do you like my green woolly matching gloves, hat and scarf? Lovely soft wool.'

'It was the woollies that I was referring to. You showed them to me the other morning. They were a bargain in Aly's, weren't they? Do you want me to drive you up to Sainsbury's?'

'Thanks Yvonne. I can catch a bus from across the road. I need time to prepare myself before meeting my Aunt Joan. No doubt she'll be issuing orders once I arrive. I've already been instructed that I am to collect a luminous yellow jacket, a sash and a collecting tin from a container inside the door of the store as soon as I arrive.'

'Military style then?'

'Sure is, but it's for a good cause, Yvonne.'

As Frankie approached the store she saw Aunt Joan chatting to the manager. She pointed to the box with the jacket, sash and collecting box. When she saw that Frankie had put the jacket over her coat, she beckoned her inside.

'No-one's over by the back door. Catch the people coming out,' she instructed.

Almost as soon as Frankie stood in her designated position, a large man with an official badge on his jacket addressed her, 'I presume you have a permit. You're aware that you have to have permission for street collections? Who's in charge of this collection?'

'Yes. I'm certain my Aunt Joan will have made sure we have all the necessary permissions. She's just gone to have a cup of coffee.'

He held out his hand to her. 'I'm sorry. I'm Edward Shaw. We get such a lot of requests to collect in Sainsbury's car park. I'm member of Farnham County Council.'

'I understand. I'm Frankie Danivet. My aunt has recruited me to help. She has organised a group of volunteers to raise funds for the Oasis Cancer Centre. Her late husband received wonderful care there.'

'I'm sure everything is in order. Did she tell you that you are not supposed to rattle your collection box?'

'I'm so sorry. It's just that Sainsbury's customers seem to look everywhere but at me!'

'That's a pity because they're not seeing your lovely smile! Is that your aunt waving to you?'

'No… no she's warm and cosy, still sipping her coffee. She's the lady seated in the café. She's at the window. She's wearing a pink jacket. Forty minutes more to go before my hour will be up! I'll stamp my feet and squeeze my hands.'

'I'll speak to your aunt. I hope your efforts will be rewarded. Bye for now.'

Someone was reading the label on Frankie's collecting tin.

'Oasis Cancer Centre. Good cause. Well done.' He dropped three pounds into the box.

'Thank you. Very grateful. Did you know that patients and their relatives coping with cancer can be helped with complementary therapies?'

'Yes. They're very good at the Oasis. I lost my husband just before Christmas last year.'

'Sorry. Christmas must be difficult for you. Thank you.'

I feel so cold, thought Frankie. *Music? Thank God for the Pogues! A brash Irish band. I heard them. The bit about Galway Bay is ringing out from the store.*

'You're shaking that tin!'

'Oh sorry! I just love the Pogues! I'll be careful.'

'You must be Irish? Where do you hail from? I'm a Dub.'

'Kerry. What we refer to as the Kingdom! I don't know why I love the Pogues. Their sheer irreverence rouses something deep inside me.'

'Good on you! You've a twinkle in those beguiling eyes. Here, I can't refuse you.'

'£10! Gosh! That's generous. Thanks.'

Who would guess that I'm a former nun taking great delight in such raunchy singing? Am I just airing my rebelliousness? Even Sister Sheila jigged around to it in the staffroom before one of the staff looked shocked and proceeded to spoil her fun by presenting her with a copy of the words of this super *Fairy Tale of New York* carol.

When she saw the cursing and swearing, she forbade the staff from playing the disc in the classroom.

'Oh, there you are, Frankie. I've been told that you have been shaking your collection box. People in Farnham voluntarily support many charities. Ours may not be one of those that they have selected. We invite people. We don't pester them.'

'Sorry, Aunt Joan. Have you come to relieve me?'

Here we go again. Only a fortnight ago I helped at another fund-raising event. As I was just about to reach out for something to nibble, Aunt Joan called out for all to hear, 'Put that canapé down. The food is for the guests.'

Looking extra slim in her magenta jacket, pencil line velvety black skirt, black patent, high-heeled, sling back shoes with matching hand bag, and that flouncy hair-do, Aunt Joan doesn't intend to take her turn proffering a tin in this winter blast.

'Frankie dear, you must be cold. I want to reward you for your efforts by inviting you to join me in the café for coffee when someone else comes out to replace you.'

'Soon? I have been out here for more than an hour.'

'Yes. Thank God, that awful substitute for a carol has finished. Call that music? Such bawdiness! I'll mingle with the Oasis Supporters' Committee until you're ready. Catch my attention when you are replaced.'

Why does my Aunt Joan thinks so much of herself? How can she be my Mam's sister? My Mam loves the Pogues. When they mention Galway Bay in the Fairy Tale of New York carol, she gets to her feet and jigs about. I'm prepared to put up with the bitter cold and the condescending attitude of Aunt Joan to support this wonderful Oasis Cancer Centre. What a brilliant slogan, 'One for every hospital' Every hospital should have a therapeutic centre.

'Good, Frances. You're just in time. Take this ten pound note. Buy a black coffee and the biscuit they supply with it. You can have a pain du raison. The queue seems to have gone now.'

'Richard told me that 'lattes' are very good. A blend of milk and coffee...'

'Percolated coffee. Proper coffee. None of these pastiches that unfortunately I have to put up with here. Don't follow the trend, Frances. Black coffee is the nearest you'll get to proper coffee in here.'

'Richard knows a lot about coffee. I think he is of Italian descent.'

'Who is this Richard? '

'Richard is a friend... a boy... maybe I should say a man friend.'

'Huh! You must be joking, Frances. I hope you are not going to fling yourself in front of some poor man. Oh dear. I hope you're not planning on marrying. How naïve!'

'Eventually I do want to marry. I love Richard.'

'Love, Frances? I hope you are not going to be a replica of your mother.'

My mother is my mother. How dare Aunt Joan denigrate her!

'What do you mean, Aunt Joan?'

'Love! What can you know about love? All those years in the convent. Is this the first boy! Man? Is he the first male that you've laid your eyes on?'

'Richard teaches at my school. He is…'

'Enough said. Remember that it is important to move in the right social circles. Your mother… well… If you want to know about men, Frankie, come to me for advice.'

Frankie clenched her teeth. Her right foot began to hit the floor. She wanted to shout at Aunt Joan. She had thrown back her head and laughed at her. She hated her too for the way she had spoken about her mother. Then she smiled in her head recalling the way Aunt Joan ensnared the man she was planning to marry.

'You foot is going up and down. Are you that cold?'

I have to get away from you and take control of my feelings.

'I need to go to the loo. I need to take my woollies off, Aunt Joan.'

'You mean the *lavatory*? Frances, dear. I've got a lovely brochure to show you where Andy and I have booked to spend our Christmas this year. He's coming to collect me and take me home in ten minutes time.'

Maybe if I take my time I'll be spared the brochure?

She's waiting for me as I emerge from the lavatory. *She looks ready to thrust the brochure at me once I hand her the coffee.*

'Here we are, Frances. I see your cheeks are not so flushed. You have calmed down. Sit down beside me. Let me show you. See, here… pull your chair closer. Let me show you.'

Calmed down? I'll have to restrain myself from throwing the coffee over her. She's proceeding to read it to me, clearly enunciating every consonant and rounding her vowels. You'd think she is broadcasting to the nation. Where are the cameras?

'The Cotswold Lodge Hotel in Oxford offers comfortable, luxury accommodation in a relaxed and inviting setting. The hotel combines traditional charm with refined, modern amenities making it ideal... Frances, see the picture of the four poster bed.'

'Lovely.'

'Your cousin, my son Paul, pleaded with me to join him, his wife and their baby at their home in Canada, but I had to put my new life with Andy first, Frances. You'll probably understand one day, dear. Oh I nearly forgot to give you this card from Aunt Phil. She wants to do her duty by you, too.'

Dear Frances,

I have booked lunch for us at Giovanni Agozzino's Zero Quattro's Sicilian style restaurant in Wimbledon. I have fallen in love with the atmosphere and the authentic regional food served there. Consequently I have frequented this restaurant on numerous occasions since September when I returned from my holiday in Taormina. They have such a varied menu with dishes such as marinated swordfish in grain mustard served on iceberg lettuce and pomegranate and tagliatelle baked 'a cartoccio' and so many more delicacies...

I am sure you will find it all fascinating and a change from the traditional Christmas food you will have with your mother over Christmas.

I will meet you in the restaurant next Saturday 11th December at 12.30.

Happy Christmas

Aunt Phil.

How my life has changed! In the convent I accepted the food that was served. There was no choice. We had to eat what we were given. I did not know how much food cost.

Both my aunts have no idea of the life that I live. They don't realise the changes I need to make in order to adjust.

I have not heard from my mother for ages. How can I go home to her at Christmas? How is it possible to explain to any of my relatives how much the life that I have lived for the past eighteen years has changed me? Even if I could locate my Mam, I know that she and my sister and her family prefer to relax with a drink and cigarettes either at home or in the pub. They discuss topics of no interest to me with people who have nothing in common with me. I feel awkward and out of place. Do they care that I don't fit in? They don't know what to do to help me to fit in. I no longer want to fit in with them.

'You don't look overjoyed, Frankie. Have you something else planned?'

Aunt Joan would make fun of me again if she found out that that I was hoping that Richard would invite me to spend Christmas with him. He popped into my classroom a few times lately. He smiles, winks and laughs at my remarks but he seems to be too busy.

'No. Nothing definite planned yet. I am very grateful to Aunt Phil. The restaurant seems perfect. I'm delighted to accept Aunt Phil's kind invitation.'

'Remember my advice, Frankie. You have a lot to learn about men. I am always ready to point you in the right direction. I know more than most on this topic.'

'I'll bear that in mind, Aunt Joan.'

I'll never broach that topic again with you. You have trampled on my fragile wishes and dreams.

FRANKIE WAS DETERMINED to make the Christmas celebrations special for the children in her class at school. On the day of her school party, she arrived at school laden with nibbles and presents that she has bought the previous night. Sister Sheila followed her into her classroom. As she was unpacking, Sister threw her arms up in the air and exclaimed, '*Ta tu fluairseach*!'

'Thank you, Sister. I had forgotten that lovely expressive word, '*Generous to a fault... giving in plenty.*' Am I right?'

'Yes. Generous to a fault...'

'I want this to be the best Christmas ever for little Barry and big bold Nigerian Iffy. Sure, they lack so much at home. I bet Christmas will be a bleak time for them.'

'May God bless you, Frankie! Come down to the staffroom when you're ready.'

When Frankie entered the staffroom Richard was there with Sr Sheila.

Richard beamed a smile at Frankie as she closed the staffroom door behind her.

'Good morning, Frankie. You're bright and early, Frankie. Sister tells me that you have already been busy preparing for your class party.'

'Yes. I love watching the children enjoy themselves.'

Richard turned to Sister Sheila. 'Not long to go now, Sister. I expect you'll enjoy the true spirit of Christmas with your community.'

'Yes indeed we do, Richard. We've begun the Christmas novena. I love all the beautiful Advent hymns we sing, 'Veni, Veni Emanuel…'

Frankie returned Richard's wink.

I wonder if Sister noticed that Richard winked at me. She must know that we both know all about the ceremonies and rituals associated with this cheerful nine days preparation for Christmas.

'Shall we put the mince pies out before the staff arrive, Frankie?'

'Good idea.'

'I'll leave you two to do that. I'll get the box of chocolates that I have in my office.'

As soon as Sister left the room Frankie felt Richard's hand on her shoulder. He whispered, 'Tesoro. My treasure.'

Frankie turned. Their noses touched. He smiled and gently drew back.

'I love Advent, Frankie.'

'Me too.'

Frankie thought that he seemed to be struggling to keeping control of his feeling. Is he frightened?

'I like the rose-coloured vestments that the priest wears on the third Sunday of Advent.'

If I kiss him now someone could come through that door. Sr Sheila is coming back. He called me his treasure but does he really love me? He wanted to kiss me. Maybe he realises that we are not in a safe place?

Frankie responded: 'I love it all. Lighting the pink candle on the Advent wreath. The recitation of psalms from the Divine Office.'

'Did you sing, *Like the dawning of the morning…?*'

Frankie watched Richard put the plate of mince pies on the table. He put his hand on hers.

'Oh Richard... I love...'

'Shish... Sr Sheila will be back..'

'You must know that lovely advent song... *Like the Dawning of the morning?'*

Richard started singing, *'Like the dawning of the morning, on the mountains' golden heights...'*

Frankie smiled. The next lines fitted in well with her wishes for them to have a baby. She joined in. She and Richard continued together:

'Like a secret told by Angels,
Getting known upon the earth
Is the Mother's Expectation
Of Messiah's speedy birth...'

'That was lovely Richard. You must have been in the choir.'

'Happy memories. I love Advent. I love that song."

Especially the last words, *'Like a mother's expectation of Messiah's speedy birth'* thought Frankie.

'Did you have to clean the convent from top to bottom during Advent, Frankie?'

'That's the drudgery that I don't want to remember, Richard. All the sacrifices that we had to make. Hard work, no puddings or jam. Nothing sweet. All so that we would merit heavenly rewards when we die.'

'It was the same during the weeks leading up Easter? The four weeks of Advent penance and prayer was not as hard as the seven weeks of fasting in Lent.'

'All that mortification and asceticism and reliving the sufferings of Jesus that seemed to drag on in such an atmosphere of gloom and doom.'

'We're free of all that now, Frankie! Let's forget the gloom and enjoy our freedom!'

Frankie was about to give Richard the special Christmas card that she had hidden in her locker for him.

'I hear footsteps. That sounds like Vicky's high heels clip, clipping.'

'Lovely mince pies! Morning to you, Frankie and Richard. They're from Sr Sheila. It's a tradition on party day.'

'Morning, Vicky. Sr Sheila brought the pies. That red dress suits your fair complexion.'

'That shade of orange is lovely on you, Frankie. Richard you always look smart in your tweeds. Love the green shirt.'

'The children expect us to dress in our best. Just as well we don't try to compete with them though.'

'You're right Frankie. I was just thinking that Sr Sheila doesn't have to worry, though. She wears her habit every day.'

Frankie was glad that Sr Sheila interrupted this conversation. She did not want to remember the religious habit that she had to wear for so many years.

'Here we are! I'm sure we're all counting down to the big day. I have put the box for your Christmas cards up there. Enjoy the mince pies. Help yourselves to some chocolates, too. Mrs Kearns brought them for the staff again this year.'

'Thank you, Sr Sheila. Must thank her. Very generous.'

VICKY WAVED her hand in the air and looked longingly out of the window. 'I can't wait to jet off out of this cold, dark climate to sunny Johannesburg for the duration.'

'Well I hope you are luckier than we were in Spain last year. Just as cold as it was here, if not colder when we landed there. No, we're staying in good old Winchester. Mother invited Will and I and the two boys.'

'What about you, Richard? Are you flying off?'

Frankie waited for Richard to answer. Instead he stood, turned and opened his locker. Was he purposefully walking away? Frankie wanted to follow him. She wanted to give him the Christmas card she had written. She thought it might look too obvious if she went after him. She tried to listen to what the staff were discussing.

'Jean, would you ask Arnie from your class to light the candles on the Advent wreath at the assembly this morning? He is sensible and safe with a lighted taper.'

If only Richard had answered that question. *I want to know where he will be. I imagine him going somewhere lovely in the Lake District. I can visualise him in an Alpine type hotel nestled between snow-clad peaks. If only I could snuggle up to his log fire far away from staff with their happy families.*

As soon as Frankie had dismissed her class for lunch she carried her Christmas card to Richard's classroom. When she peered through the window in his door she saw that he seemed to be absorbed in what he was writing. She tapped and opened the door.

'Sorry to disturb, Richard. I wanted to give you your Christmas card.'

Frankie noticed that Richard was turning over the letter he had been writing.

'Thank you, Frankie! How thoughtful. I feel embarrassed. I haven't bought one for you. So thoughtless.'

'Don't worry, Richard. I don't expect one. You may not even like it.'

O Lord I hope he does not think that I have gone over the top. He has begun to slit it open.

'Big one too! Thank you.'

She watched Richard face go red. He rubbed his forehead.

Maybe I shouldn't have chosen a card with the words 'Happy Christmas to Someone Very Special?'

'Thank you, Frankie. That's very kind.'

He is holding out his hand to be shook. No kiss! I'll back out of the room.

'Have a lovely Christmas, Richard.'

'You too, Frankie.'

What have I done? I thought a big red card for someone special was just right. Richard responded with a hand shake. No kiss. I bet Aunt Joan would have laughed aloud and made fun of me if she had witnessed what had happened. She would have remarked on his turning over the letter that he was writing when I interrupted him. Perhaps he really does have a girlfriend. He is probably going to spend Christmas with her. I really am naïve.

16

MARRIED BLISS

Frankie caught sight of Paula, admiring some hydrangea, as she opened the door into Jasper's Garden Centre.

'Glad you found it, Frankie. You look cold. Come here 'til I warm you up with a hug.'

'Once I enquired, half the passengers on the bus knew Jasper's Garden Centre. They were all giving me directions.'

'Relax! You're cold and stiff! Don't you like me hugging you, Frankie?'

'Of course I do! I'm just not used to hugs. Can't remember my mother hugging me. Physical contact was not permitted in the convent.'

'Come on. Let's remedy that. I know where there's a lovely cosy nook. Follow me. My treat. You'd like a hot mug of coffee and a toasted tea cake, wouldn't you?'

'Just what the doctor ordered! Thanks.'

The Bing Crosby and David Bowie version of *The Little Drummer Boy* carol was being played as Paula and Frankie queued for coffee in restaurant. Paula was humming the tune.

'Isn't this cosy? The cushions on these wicker chairs make them comfy. Shall I hang up your coat?'

'I didn't notice the coat-stand. Thank you, Paula.'

'Tell me, Frankie, are you looking forward to Christmas?'

While Paula was rubbing her hands together, Frankie was pinching her fingers.

'The truth?'

When Paula nodded, Frankie replied, 'I hate Christmas.'

'Frankie, you're face is contorted. Your eyes are like darts ready to hit out at someone. You, of all people, hating Christmas? The celebration of the coming of Jesus. Love coming to this world.'

'I know. I know!'

Frankie crouched forward her hands covering her face.

'Your coffee will get cold. Take a sip. Tell me what is troubling you.'

Frankie warmed her hands round her mug. Paula's purple mohair polo neck jumper and matching jewellery reminded her of the liturgical colours worn by the clergy in Advent and Lent and other penitential periods.

Paula looked round to check that the middle-aged man, sitting alone at the nearby table was not listening to their conversation.

'Christmas is for children, Paula.'

'Neither of us have children. I love wrapping up presents and writing cards to everyone in Paddy's family.'

'Paula, I'm dreading my first Christmas outside the convent. My sister, Mary, sent a note telling me that mother has moved into her home in Streatham when she is not in Ireland.'

'There you are, Frankie. You could have a lovely Christmas with your mother.'

'That is the last thing I want, Paula!'

'I don't understand. Why?'

'It's difficult to explain. Why wouldn't I want to spend Christmas with my own mother? Because I am different now. We have grown apart. She enjoys drinking and smoking. Convent life changed me. I'm determined to find a husband and have a family of my own. I would love to have a baby. '

'What about your sister? Wouldn't it be lovely to get to know her better?'

'My sister, Mary, is eleven years older than me. She's fifty. She and her husband, Bob have two grown-up children. Her daughter, Ciara, has a baby boy. We have grown apart. From what I've heard, they live similar lives to my mother.'

'You have a brother, too?'

'My brother, Dom, is divorced from Trish. He lives in Australia. Paula, they have long established customs and lifestyles that do not include me.'

'Gosh, it was very different for me. I loved my adopted parents. Every year I used to enjoy making a fuss over them at Christmas. Even when my mother was in a nursing home, we brought her to our home to be with us at this special time of year. '

'I sound pathetic, Paula. My mother's two sisters aren't very empathic. One aunt had me collecting for cancer patients. The other is taking me out for a restaurant meal.'

'You see, they have made an effort to keep in contact, Frankie. What about the Christmas preparations at school? Didn't the children help you enter into the spirit of it all?'

'Celebrating Christmas with my class was my salvation. It's really a time for children, isn't it? I found that difficult too. If only I could have taken little Barry home with me I'd have given him the time of his life. I don't mean by that I'd have showered him with presents. His alcoholic mother doesn't know what time of day it is. There doesn't seem to be a father around. No, I would love him to bits. I do love him.'

'Frankie, you're still young enough to make your wishes come to true.'

'My loneliness hit me hard when I hear the staff going on about their Christmas plans for their families. I'm not resentful of them. I just wish I had some of their happiness. There is Richard… well I can't help wondering and imagining.'

'Come on. Out with it, Frankie! Tell me. Oh… you're blushing.'

'Shish, will you, Paula! I can't…'

'I've been watching you two. I caught you and Richard winking to each other. He was resting his hand on your shoulder as you leaned into your locker...'

'Oh Paula... I really like him. A lot! I wish... I'd love to spend Christmas with him...'

'I bet it was you who took his photo from the pile on the staffroom table? It was... you've gone all red again!'

'I carry it around in my bag. Here! Look! Am I crazy?'

'Not at all. He is handsome. Amber eyes. Tall. Slim. He's told me his single. He had a similar early life... in the seminary I mean.'

'If only we could be together over Christmas. I would love that.'

'From what I see, he would too. He is always secretive about his family life.'

'Is he? I wonder why?'

'Maybe the awful time he had from Anna...'

'Anna? Who's Anna? I overheard Vicky mention her name. Who...'

'I wouldn't worry about Anna, Frankie. She turns up... no... she's definitely not Richard's type. Believe me, they had a huge row.'

'I hoped that I was the only one that...'

'Unclasp those hands. Straighten up. Be your strong self again, Frankie. I suspect Richard is longing to be with you just as much as you want to be with him.'

'I hope you're right, Paula. On the last day of term I gave him the loveliest Christmas card I could find. He looked embarrassed. I don't know if he liked it. Maybe I was too bold.'

'Very few men remember to buy cards. He was probably embarrassed because he hadn't bought one for you.'

'When I walked into his room he turned over a letter that he was writing. Maybe that was to this Anna. She might be his girlfriend.'

'Stop the guessing, Frankie.'

'You're right.'

'That's settled. You're coming to Cornwall with Paddy and me this Christmas. We already planned to invite you.'

'Oh Paula, what a generous invitation. I am grateful but you want to enjoy each other. You don't want a third person hanging around you. It's only one day. I'll go to church...'

'Paddy suggested I invite you. I wanted to find out your plans before I invited you.'

'Oh Paula!'

'Think about this while I go to the Ladies. Mull it over, while I'm away. Won't be long.'

Frankie's mind was considering the few options she had.

How can I opt out of this? How can I intrude on a married couple loving each other when I long to be in Richard's arms but he hasn't offered any invitation. I will be very lonely. The landlady will want to take care of me. That would create an extra task for her. I don't want to be by myself. Wouldn't it be wonderful to accept Paula's invitation?

Alone, Frankie overheard Irish accents coming from the table behind her. She turned to see two young men chatting.

Before she fully realised what she was doing, she addressed them, 'Good to hear the accent. What part are ye from? I hail from Kerry.'

'The next county. We're both from Cork. We've been over here for a long time. How about you?'

'Me too. I came over when I was a teenager.' Frankie laughed. 'Not that long ago really!'

Paula arrived back. Frankie introduced her to the men.' This is my friend, Paula. I'm Frankie.'

'One of the men pointed to his friend and then to himself, 'Kieran. Donal.' They waved and smiled.

Paula sat down. She whispered, 'I can't leave you alone, Frankie! Be careful.'

'I was just saying, hello.'

'They could misinterpret that.'

'Really?'

'Oh, you're an innocent abroad! I'll have to keep my eye on you! Well, did you consider Paddy's offer... our proposal to spend Christmas with us?'

'Thank you, Paula. I'd love to come. But only if I can pay my way.'

'That's settled then, Frankie. Did you hear that?'

'Hear what, Paula?'

'That twittering. Coming from the beams. Look up. It's a robin.'

'Maybe he's cheering me on!'

'Showing me that I do have friends who are helping me to be independent.'

'Good. Paddy has already booked our hotel. He booked the room next to ours for you. He hoped you'd come. It's easier to cancel a room than to get an extra room as we near Christmas.'

'A hotel! I've never stayed in a hotel before.'

'A lovely hotel in Cornwall.'

'I heard one of the parents saying how beautiful it is there.'

'We know it well. We've spent two lovely Christmas's at Coral Beach Hotel. It has everything you would expect of good hotel: excellent facilities, great food, fantastic location and friendly staff. It's a delightful location in Austell'

'Sounds idyllic. I'll pay my way, of course.'

Frankie considered: *I hope it won't be too expensive. The money that I have saved will be well spent.*

'Paddy told me to tell you that you are not to worry about the cost. '

'I have money ready to pay for my room. Please assure Paddy.'

Frankie thought, *I'll bring proper presents and have money ready to pay whenever I can.*

Two days before Christmas was the date set for their departure. Frankie had packed the travel bag that Paula had lent her. She was ready at the front door of her flat when Paddy and Paula arrived to collect her.

'All aboard! Off we go!'

'Not so quick, Paddy! Mind that... she's about... Oh, Paddy... why do you have to drive so quickly? Have you clicked your seatbelt, Frankie?'

'Paula, I'm driving. It was you who planned to travel to Cornwall via North Devon. Then we will need to head towards Barnstable. Then through Bideford and down the A39 to Bude. Barnstable to Bideford is 7 miles; Bideford to Bude is 27 miles. Do you realise how long that will take us?'

'I know... I know, but...'

'From the Devon border to Land's End is approximately 75 miles. Bude to Torpoint is approximately 40 miles; Newquay to St. Austell is 15 miles…'

'Now you see what Paula's really like, Frankie.'

'Welcome to married life, Frankie.'

'Don't worry about me, both of you. I'm so delighted to be included in this adventure. I'm tired too. It's lovely and comfortable back here. I think I'll have a nap.'

A nap? I'm petrified. Paddy is driving at top speed. We're not out of London yet. What is his driving going to be like on narrower roads? thought Frankie.

'What Paula is not taking into account, Frankie,' said Paddy, 'is that the days are shorter in December. We want to get to the hotel in daylight.'

'Oh, I see.'

When Paula played Christmas carols, Frankie fell asleep. She awoke as the car pulled to a stop.

'I'm delighted that you were lulled to sleep, Frankie.'

'Are we here?'

'Paddy has gone to books in.'

'What an imposing hotel. The redbrick reminds of Westminster Cathedral.'

'It's a family-run hotel, Frankie. It has an imposing frontage. Big sweeping entrance and gardens but it only has twelve rooms.'

'This will be my first time staying in a hotel, Paula. I haven't got a clue what happens…'

'Don't worry. Once we're checked in we'll explain everything to you.'

'Our cases are being carried in for us, Paula.'

A porter came and lifted the suitcases on a trolly.

'Let's follow Paddy to the checking-in desk, Frankie.'

'Oh what a lovely fire, Paula! A warm welcome. And the Christmas tree… looks real… just a few gold Christmas bells on the tree and attached to the lights. I like that.'

'It's a homely hotel Frankie. The wood-panelling, the dimmed wall-lights and of course the big side window with a supreme view of the distant hills.'

'Good choice, Paula. I understand why you return here.'

'I'm Mr Patrick Foley…'

'Mr and Mrs Patrick Foley and Ms Frankie Danivet. Is that correct, Sir? A double and a single.'

Frankie whispered to Paula, '*Ms!* Everybody will know that I'm single. After being called 'Sister' for years, I prefer not to have any title.'

'I agree Frankie. If men are given the title Mr. it doesn't signify that they are married. Yet when my name is prefixed with Ms my married status is proclaimed.'

'Good journey, Sir? Ladies? Roads not too crowded?' enquired the sallow-looking, low sized, male receptionist. 'Room numbers 204 and 205. Here are your keys.'

'This is yours, Frankie.'

Frankie whispered to Paula, 'Big and heavy!'

The receptionist must have heard. He laughed. 'Next time you come, we will have an electronic card-key.'

'We hand in these keys at the reception desk each time we go out. The lift is on our right. Follow me, Frankie,' instructed Paddy.

'Sir, dinner tonight is in the restaurant at 6pm. You'll find the menu in your room.'

'Frankie, your case has been taken to your room. There's only an hour before dinner. We'll freshen up and meet you out here on the landing at 6pm.'

'Thank you, Paddy. Do you change into different clothes for dinner, Paula?'

'I'll probably have a shower. Don't worry about wearing anything special tonight. I intend wearing these trousers with a different top. We're all tired.'

'Okay. I'll do the same.'

I've packed two pairs of trousers, one dress, two skirts and two other tops. If I wash the tops I hope they will dry.

'May I see your room, Frankie? I'll be back in a minute, Paddy.'

'Wow! What a wonderfully big room, Paula! Three large windows, too. I love the cardinal-red carpet. Same colour throughout the hotel. Smaller gold bells decorations over the bed and on the desk. Subtle.'

'Shall we check that you have a bath as well as a shower?'

'Ensuite! Lucky me!'

'You're easy to please, Frankie. Yes the bathroom is the same as the one in our room. Lovely cream-coloured tiled.'

'Soap and shampoo… is this a shower cap? All free?'

'What isn't free, Frankie are what's in the fridge. Did you notice it in the cabinet under the television?'

'Oh… hidden away. Just as well I only drink on special occasions. What about the fruit?'

'Yes the fruit is for you. They treat us to nuts at Christmas. All yours.'

'It's lovely and warm…'

'The thermostat… if you need that adjusting Paddy will do that for you. I never touch them…'

'Thanks for explaining everything, Paula.'

'It's dusk. I hope we will still be able to see the garden, Frankie. Yes, there's an outside light. Come over and have a peep.'

'It's big and well kept…'

'It's landscaped. They employ experienced gardeners.'

'We were the gardeners in the convent. I don't remember it being referred to as 'landscaping'!'

'It's beautiful all year round. They plant annuals, perennials, various bulbs, roses, a great variety of colourful flowers, as well as trees and shrubs. It's a year-round gardening show. unlike London Cornwall enjoys a temperate climate.'

'Oh look, there's a thrush.'

'The couple who run this hotel told us that bird-watchers… twitchers, stay in this hotel. I remember them telling us that the cold temperatures bring seasonal migrations to a fever pitch.'

'I'll have plenty of room in this double bed. The pink rose-patterned duvet and arm-chair covers are lovely. The colour scheme is warm and feminine.'

'Glad you like it, Frankie. I must go and unpack. See you soon.'

This room must cost a lot of money. I hope I have brought enough with me.

'Let me push in your chair, madam. Here's this evening menu.'

Gosh! What happens now? wondered Frankie.

'What can I offer you to drink, madam?'

'Do you prefer white or red, Frankie?'

'Just water, please.'

'Would you like a soft drink too? You'll find the list at the bottom on this side of the menu.'

'No, water please.'

'Would madam prefer still or sparkling?'

'Oh... as it comes from the tap.'

'We'll have a bottle. We can share, Frankie.'

Paddy handed Frankie the menu. Nothing was priced. Frankie omitted the starter and chose a main dish. She declined the dessert and coffee.

'You're being very abstemious or are you not hungry?' enquired Paddy.

'I'm not that hungry tonight, thank you.' She lied.

As they sat and chatted, Frankie wondered how the bill would be split. She hoped that it would be itemised and that she would have the correct money. No bill came. They said goodnight to the waiter and stood to go to their rooms.

'Paddy, forgive my ignorance, but as this is my first time in a hotel I don't know how to pay for my meal. Do I go somewhere? Is there a bill... ?'

'Oh my... We should have said. We have a special deal. That includes the food... the lot. I'm sorry I... Come to think of it'. Paddy cupped his chin in his hand, 'Is that why you did not eat much? 'Tis I who feel embarrassed now.'

'No. I'm fine, Paddy.'

Frankie decided that no-one was to blame. This initial predicament was a lesson. *In future I will ask as each new experience presents itself.*

'Frankie, before we part. I usually get up at about 8. I like to go for a walk round the grounds before breakfast... if you...'

'Frankie, won't want to do that, Paula. She...'

'That sounds good, Paula. I'd love to see the grounds.'

'Fine. If you really want to join me I'll meet you at the bottom of these stairs at eight-thirty. Sleep well. Night, Frankie!'

Frankie opened her door. She reflected, *You two have each other to cuddle. If only Richard were here. I wonder where he is. Maybe he is with someone else?*

'Did you sleep, Frankie?'

'I read. I fell off to sleep with my book in my hands.'

'A good book?'

'An Enid Blyton story.'

'A children's book?'

'*The Land of Far-Beyond.* I found a copy in a charity shop. I remembered that we used to read it when we were training to be nuns.'

'It's for children! How old were the girls being trained? What was the age range?'

'Eleven to twenty-seven. It's supposed to be an adventure story based on John Bunyan's *'Pilgrims' Progress.'*

'Why would a twenty-seven year old... was she a teacher?'

'Yes.'

'Why would she want to listen to an Enid Blyton story?'

Here we go again. Paula is quizzing me on every aspect to my convent life. I want to move on and live in the present. She tells me very little of her married life. Paddy seems to watch TV. He appears to want Paula for himself. He holds her hand a lot. He squeezes hers. They look into each others eyes. I bet that if I was not here they would kiss. I wish Richard was here.

'Darling, I'm so thirsty. I long for a drinkie!'

Drinkie! Paddy reminds me of a boy who wants his mother to look after him. He sometimes speaks in a childish, whiney, pleading tone, with upturned palms and pleading eyes.

'Paddy, have you told Frankie about the lovely little church you've found for Midnight Mass?'

'Indeed I haven't. Don't go spoiling the surprise, Paula.'

Paddy put his finger over Paula's mouth. 'Hush, Darling. I was biding my time until we've seated ourselves somewhere comfortable for our tea. Very good of you to pay for us, Frankie, but there's no need. Here, what about in this little corner? How's about that?'

While Paddy was driving them around the country side Frankie was trying to think how she could repay them. She was glad that they had accepted her offer to treat them to afternoon tea.

'Well now, as Paula has already hinted, the church we have been told about was built before the Reformation. What's more, Midnight Mass is to be con-celebrated by a community of Dominican priests. Isn't that grand?'

'Interesting.'

'Will ye excuse me now? I'm going to request a little more bainne… milk.'

'Okay, love.'

'He's not forgotten his Gaelic, Paula.'

'You look tired, Frankie. Do you want to go to midnight Mass?'

Frankie reflected, *Part of me is being tugged to Midnight Mass, the other bit is pulling fiercely in the direction of a cosy night in my huge bed. I'd better not say that to Paddy. He's coming back.*

'Thank you for finding out about the church, Paddy. I expect there will be carols leading up to Mass?'

'You're right! If it's like back in Ireland or even in London, we'll have a job finding a pew after a quarter past eleven, isn't that right, Paudie?' Frankie smiled when she realised that this was Paddy's pet name for Paula. Such endearment.

'Correct. I suggest that when we have finished our tea, we wear our warmest clothes, ready to leave after we have had our dinner.'

'Always practical. What would I do without you, my love?'

He's leaning over to kiss her… he noticed me watching… he's holding her hand. I'll look at the Christmas tree. I'd love to be loved.

'Thank goodness we can warm ourselves in the car. You warm enough, Frankie?'

'Yes, thank you, Paula. Lovely clear, starry night.'

'Wait until the church comes into view… there we are. Isn't it like a Bethlehem scene?'

'Nestled at the bottom of the hill, silhouetted against a starlit cold still sky… the Madonna and child over the entrance.'

'Open your window, Paddy… I think I can hear the carols…'

'Paula… I'm trying to find a parking place as near to the entrance as… here… no… you eejit! Woman driver… oh here we are… crowded already…'

'I said I would drive. You know how het up you can get…'

'If you hadn't asked me to roll down my window just… well we could have glided into that first place… Sorry, Paula… I…'

'Frankie what must you think of us? Parking always brings out the worst…'

'So many cars already. You've found an excellent spot to park.'

I hate being in situations like this. One minute they are all lovey-dovey and the next they argue. When I marry I will make sure that we set out what each of us wants from the beginning.

'You noticed the statue of Our Lady with the bambino over the entrance, Frankie. This is a Dominican Church and…'

'The Dominican Order are the often referred to as the Preachers. They brought the Rosary to the people… isn't that right?'

'Of course, you know that, Frankie… sorry, I should have remembered that with your background…'

'No Paddy. This is my first time in this church. We gain an indulgence the first time we set foot in a different church too, don't we?'

'D'you know I had forgotten that! You're quite right about the rosary. When you enter you will be able to admire the beautiful stained glass windows depicting each of the fifteen mysteries of the rosary.'

'Tell Frankie about the cupola, Paddy.'

'Beautiful! Octagonal. Look up and around at the mosaic stations of the cross… the… is it Caen stone that the high altar is made of, Paula?'

'You're right, Paddy. Try and get close to their crib. Wait until you see that, Frankie. Count how many creatures are hidden in the foliage surrounding the nativity scene.'

'I can hear... That's from Handel's Messiah... *Tidings from Zion... Jerusalem... Behold your...'*

Frankie began quietly to sing.

As soon as Paddy pulled opened the wooden carved doors, Frankie saw an usher beckoning to him. As indicated he walked straight up the middle aisle and over to the right of the church. Paddy and Frankie followed.

When they were seated Paula exclaimed, 'Perfect! We couldn't have desired more. Right next to the crib and in front of the high altar.'

'Didn't I tell ye I'd get you a good place...?'

Frankie turned to see Paula's reaction. 'Well done, Paddy. You managed all that by yourself!' She smiled at Frankie.

'Isaiah... that's from Isaiah... they have a such a good choir and that organ... the scent from the candles on the altar... the stained glass windows... so much to enjoy...'

'All so prayerful. Sit back and take it all in, Frankie. Remember to count the creatures around and above the crib...'

When Frankie looked across the aisle, she noticed that there were two rows of Dominican nuns seated there.

They look so prayerful. Their habits make them look the same. They have lost their individuality. I love my red duffle coat. I pray too. I used to love praying the Divine Office. I love the psalms. I could still recite lauds and vespers. Richard might pray the psalms.

Paula whispered, 'Handsome young altar servers... the tall one with black curly hair. Bet he has all the girls running after him!'

'I noticed him, too. It's a well groomed congregation. They all look smartly dressed. The church is crowded. We were fortunate to be ushered to this bench.'

Paddy leaned over Paula to Frankie, who was on the outside of the bench, 'Shish... please pass the booklets along, Frankie. '

'Certainly Paddy. I've just noted that they have printed the music and the words of everything. It's a veritable treasure. I'll take that home with me.'

Frankie looked around. She was glad that Paddy had taken them to such a lovely stone church in the care of the Dominican Order of priests, nuns and lay members. She recalled so many other inspirational Christmas's in Ireland and in the convent.

'The nativity scene is poignant, don't you think, Frankie. The Christ Child, Mary, Joseph, ox and ass and shepherds are all carved out of such lovely wood. If I remember rightly, they are sculptured from Italian walnut wood by one of the friars. You can smell the wood. It's such a lovely aroma. Especially when it's mingled with the candle wax.'

'It's all so lovely Paula. Thanks to St. Francis of Assisi, we have this tradition of the nativity scene. I'm so glad you invited me.'

Frankie joined in singing 'Veni, Veni Emmanuel 'in full voice. She felt proud of being familiar with the Latin version. The Gregorian chant, together with the smell of the incense, the candle light, the ceremonies, the ritual, familiarity with the responses, lulled her into scenes down her memory lanes. Her 'comfort blanket' was wrapped tightly around her by the time she sang the Adeste Fidele with all the vigour she could muster.

'Top that now… you couldn't, could you? Every single part from the way those priests conducted celebrated the coming of Christ into this world and our re-living of it in the Mass. Where would you be without it? Wasn't it pure heavenly?'

'Paddy's so happy!'

'You sang beautifully, Frankie. You have a lovely voice.'

'Thank you, Paula. I sang my heart out. It was good.'

Frankie remembered singing the Introit to the Latin Mass in Gregorian Chant *Dixit meus.*

'Once we're back in the hotel, we want you to come to our room for a night-cap and to give you your Christmas present, Frankie.'

Frankie was glad that she bought a silk tie for Paddy and Swarovski crystal brooch for Paula. She had carefully wrapped each one in red tissue paper inside gold wrapping paper. She had written 'Happy Christmas' and 'Thank you' on tags delicately attached with gold thread.

'You didn't have to buy us any presents, Frankie.'

'After all you have both done for me, Paddy? Shall I give you yours first, Paula?'

'As Paddy said... no need... yes, I'd love you to go first.'

Paula used her manicure scissors to slit the sellotape from the wrapping.

'Oh what a lovely... gosh... you went to some expense... really, Frankie... Swarovski... brooches are so glittering... I love it... let me give you a huge hug.'

Looking over Paula's shoulder, she saw Paddy giving her the thumbs-up sign. Did his wide-eyed look show that he might have been feeling a little put out that she up-staged him with her present, she wondered. Was he confident that the present he had chosen would be superior to anyone that Frankie had chosen?

'Your turn. Open yours, Frankie.'

Frankie felt the edge of an oblong box.

'I wish I had given it to you before we went out in the cold tonight.'

'Such lovely wrapping, Paula. Delicate pink tissue paper... and twine... what you call string... but this is raffia... darker pink... goes well...'

'Keep going... never mind the wrapping. There. I hope you like it.'

'Oh lovely! Lovely and soft. Oh Paula. I was wishing I had a white scarf. My pink one clashes with my red coat. Oh, and its lamb's wool!'

'Now your turn, darling.'

'No. Frankie was about to give you her present.'

Frankie watched Paddy tear off the wrapping and tissue paper with which she had taken such care. He screwed the wrapping into a ball and threw it on the bed without reading the label.

'This is a perfect colour tie for me, Frankie! Green for Ireland. Silk too... good quality. Thank you.'

Frankie was glad that he didn't rush over to hug her. He threw her a kiss. Then he turned round on his chair. He bent down and produced a Sainsbury's shopping bag and took out an unwrapped jewellery box. He moved swiftly towards Pauline seated on the dressing table stool holding the box. He kissed her while squeezing her waist with one hand.

'Only the best for you, my love!'

Please God, make me disappear. This is so embarrassing.

Paula opened the unwrapped box.

'Paddy! Diamonds again! You're too good to me.'

She read the receipt... so many expensive presents. So much jewellery!

'I knew you would want the receipt just in case...'

'Thank you, my love.'

'Try them on, darling. Lean back and I'll undo that necklace. Here, let me help you.'

Did Paddy want her to see the receipt so that she would know how much he spent on her? He is going to kiss Paula again. If only I could slip out into my own room. I knew he would. He has.

'I'll put this beautiful necklace and matching earrings on when you open your present from me, Paddy. Go on...'

Frankie watched Paddy tear off the green and red Christmas paper wrapping and open a long box.

'Well chosen, Darling. When I wear this silk scarf and the gold cufflinks I can hold my head up high... I'll be the envy of all. Eh, Frankie? You surely agree?'

'Stunning, Paddy! Silver looks so aristocratic.'

'Well said!'

'Let's celebrate! What will you have, Frankie? Champagne? Sherry? Wine? The fridge is well-stocked.'

'No. Thank you just the same.'

I don't need to witness Paddy becoming even more amorous. Now's my chance to escape.

'May I wish you both a very happy Christmas and a huge thank you for everything. I'm off to bed now. See you...'

'Oh no... not before we have a big hug.'

Frankie closed their bedroom door and opened hers.

No matter how expensive my presents were they can never outdo the diamonds that Paddy constantly showers on his wife. Does he think that he can buy her affection or is he generous to a fault?

17

FIRST COMMUNICANTS

Frankie looked in the mirror. *I will make myself look as attractive as I can today. It's my first day back to school after Christmas. Richard said that orange suits my colouring. I'll wear orange lipstick and wear my green and orange woolly top. Hopefully, my shorter hairstyle will, as Paula says, enhance my appearance.*

As Frankie walked from the rail station to the school car park, she wondered why Richard had not sent her a Christmas card. Had he spent Christmas with his family? Did he meet Anna? When she turned into school, she was glad that his car was already parked.

Opening the staffroom door, Frankie was greeted by Sr Sheila and Paula, 'Happy New Year, Frankie!'

'I hear you enjoyed Christmas with Paula and Paddy.'

'Yes. I was very fortunate, Sister. Had a wonderful celebration. Should stand me in good stead for this New Year. Happy New Year to you both, too.'

'Richard was looking for you, Frankie.'

Frankie smiled in response to Paula's wink. Sr Sheila had her back to them. She was making cups of tea.

'Would you like tea or coffee, Frankie?'

'No, thank you, Sister. I want to put my things in the classroom.'

Frankie hoped that Richard would hear her footsteps as she passed his classroom door.

She was delighted when he tapped on her door. She wanted to sound cheerful and welcoming. 'Come in, Richard! Good to see you.'

That's a different aftershave scent. There seems to be a touch of lavender and amber? Was that a Christmas present? He's leaning over my desk. His face is almost touching mine.

'Frankie, I wanted to catch you before the bell rings. Back to the grind again.'

He looks serious.

'Did you have a good Christmas?'

'Yes... yes... Frankie, I wanted to talk to you before Sister Sheila makes her announcement. I need to apologise for not telling you about the meetings for the First Communicants. Especially as it's your class that is involved.'

He didn't really answer my question about Christmas. Why is he so secretive? Does he live alone? Did Anna buy his new aftershave? I love him even when his firm lips don't break into a smile. They still turn up at each end, in a beguiling way as though he is pretending to control his feelings.

'Don't worry, Richard. It's our class's turn to take the school assembly. I can only focus on that at the moment.'

'Fine. That's understandable. All will go well, I'm sure.'

When Frankie was guiding her year three class through to their assembly, she caught sight of Richard.

Is that a new tweed jacket? I didn't see it properly earlier when he was sitting behind his desk. He looks very smart.

She felt light-headed.

I have an urge to feel his stubble. I'm sure I could make him smile. I wonder if I should throw off my jacket. Make myself irresistible? Maybe the room temperature has risen? Richard looks serious, seated next to Sr Sheila in front of the stage. Now he is standing, mounting the stage and facing the Junior School classes.

'Good morning, everybody.'

'Good morning, Mr Canto.'

There's softness in his eyes. His voice sounds velvety. We have not met since our meeting in the café on the Friday that the school broke up for our Christmas holidays. I waited for a phone call from him all day Saturday and Sunday. Nothing. He knows that I live on my own. Did I imagine it all? I'm good at imagining, so good that I'm beginning to wonder if the attention he shows me was a dream.

'I have the pleasure of welcoming class three to guide us through assembly this morning. Thank you, Miss Danivet. '

The children sang a Palm Sunday hymn, *Here comes Jesus, riding on a donkey.* Then they waved their palms and re-enacted Jesus' procession into Jerusalem.

Frankie noticed that Richard was following her class back from assembly to their class room.

'Each one of you can give yourselves a pat on the back for offering us such a wonderful assembly class 3. Fra... em... Miss Danivet must be very proud of you.'

Richard's winking at me. His hair has been cut. His tie looks silky. I want to lean back nearer to him as he lowers his face closer to mine. He whispers, 'I'm really sorry that we have had to make changes... all my fault... I should have set things up sooner. Could we snatch some time at lunch to discuss the First Communion meetings, Frankie? As the seven year olds in Linda's class next door are involved, I will ask her to join us.'

He put his arm on my shoulder. I'm mesmerised. The children are talking. I must clap my hands to bring them to order. They seem very far away. I'm feeling happy. My classroom assistant is looking at me. What must she think? She seems to be such a happily married, cuddly older woman.

'What's come over me, Mrs Prince? Thank you for stopping them.'

'He looks like a bit-of-all-right. I think that is a new jacket that he's wearing. Smart. Wonder where he's off to after school. She must be back on again then, unless... you okay, Frankie?'

Who must be back on again? What is Mrs Prince implying? Bother. I'm on playground duty. I could have asked her during elevenses. Oh well, nothing for it but to keep guessing until lunch time.

Feeling curious, Frankie dismissed her class promptly. When Linda had returned from leading her class into the dining hall, she came into Frankie's room to wait for the meeting with Richard.

'What's this about having to change the First Communion arrangements, Frankie?'

'First I heard of it too, Linda.'

'Oh Richard, shall we sit around my desk?'

'Yes. Good.'

Richard carried a chair over for Linda and himself.

'I suppose you two have been wondering what's happening? I apologise once again. I should have organised a meeting after school this evening but I have to dash off tonight. So sorry. Let's get down to arranging meetings for the First Communion classes.'

Why is Richard rushing through the arrangements? Linda and I must look like a pair of zombies. He must know that delivering the curriculum to a bunch of 30 lively seven years old is demanding. Lately many of both staff and pupils have been afflicted with bouts of various contagious germs.

'Thirty children of class 3 and 18 children from 3B are old enough to be prepared for their First Communion…'

Richard seems distant. What is preoccupying him? Where is he dashing off to after school?

Frankie felt incapable of listening to what Richard was saying. When he accompanied Linda and herself back to the staff room, he walked briskly.

When Frankie entered the staffroom door, she saw Richard open his locker, take out his mobile phone, stamp his way to the door, wrench the door handle and slam it closed.

The staff began questioning Linda, 'Did he say where he's going after school, Linda?'

'I don't suppose he mentioned Anna?' enquired Vicky.

'I thought those two were no longer in contact especially after that almighty row,' remarked someone.

'Surely he's not forgiven her? I hope he remembers that he came out worst. He was devastated.'

'Well, you never know. There's always two sides to every argument. We only heard one.'

'Wasn't that to do with Opus Dei or something?'

'Heard those words before… Did Dan Brown mentioned them in *Angels & Demons.*'

'Something to do with the church. Forgotten.'

Frankie felt tears. She blinked them away.

Something is worrying Richard. I'll have to be careful. Opus Dei translates as works of God. I wonder what it has to do with his change of behaviour. What's the connection between Opus Dei and Anna? He barely mentioned Anna. Was she his girlfriend? Has he gone back to her? My heart is going to burst!

Frankie wanted to ask questions. She didn't have enough courage. She kept her back to the group, pretending to search for something in her locker.

Tears? I'm a fool to think Richard was ever really interested in me. I must have imagined it all. Paula must know about Anna. I need to talk to Paula.

18

CHANGE AND CONFLICT

Meeting First Communion teachers, 3.30 pm today. Make sure you have relevant information at hand.

Mr F Canto.

'LINDA, did you find a note on your desk like...'

'I did, Frankie... what on earth?'

'It's a command... I can't believe...'

'She must be back! That Anna...'

'Who...?'

'I'm just about to take my class to the hall for their lunch... Lead on, Joseph... speak to you at the meeting, Frankie...'

Anna seems to have such a huge influence over everyone. I don't like what I hear. Maybe I'll learn more at the meeting.

'Richard looks so serious, Linda.'

'He's not himself when she's around, Frankie.'

Frankie looked across the staffroom table at Richard. He must have heard her approaching. He didn't raise his head to greet her.

Maybe Richard's mother has had an accident or is seriously ill? This is so unlike him. He is loved and respected by everyone.

'You both ready? This meeting is to give you instructions on how to proceed with preparing our classes for their First Communion.' Richard cleared his throat.

'Is it different from the way we usually prepare the children?'

Richard did not answer Linda's question. Is he preoccupied with more important matters? He was friendly this morning.

'You will both be expected to organise appropriate liturgies for the 9:30 Mass at the Parish Church throughout Lent. The parents or guardians of the First Communicants will have to demonstrate their commitment by attending a minimum of four of the six Masses.'

'What about the likes of Mrs Quinn? She'll never manage with the twin babies. She can barely get Joseph to school every day,' interrupted Linda.

Did Richard hear what Linda said?

He continued, 'Our Parish priest, Father Cormack, will meet you both at this time in the Parish house throughout Lent. You already have text books at your disposal. Should you require others, you are free to avail yourselves of any set aside for this purpose in my classroom.'

Why is Richard acting so formally?

'May I...'

'Permit me to conclude the instructions before asking questions, Miss Danivet. As I was saying...'

He's using my surname? I can't take any more of Richard's formal attitude. He is acting so differently. All that closeness... maybe, I imagined his fondness for me? I have not known him long enough to be able to judge.

'Have I made myself quite clear to both of you?'

'Will we take turns at being present at the Masses or are we expected to attend all of them?' asked Linda.

'Attendance? We surely don't just *attend* Mass. Participation in the celebration of Mass, or re-enactment of the Last Supper. Let's be certain that we know what we are about, Mrs Long, before presuming that we are able to impart these sacred truths to our children,' reprimanded Richard.

Mrs Long! Mrs... *formal titles. He's using her surname again. Linda must be looking at me. I am scared to check. The fridge noise is revving up. Did I switch myself off earlier? I probably missed much of what Richard said.*

Frankie saw the staffroom door being pushed open. The caretaker put his head around the door, 'Sorry to interrupt. Will ye be much longer? I could pop across home and lock up later if—'

Richard pushed his chair into place, gathered his notes and before banging the door closed, shouted, 'Lock up now, Mr James. We've concluded.'

'I just can't believe... Richard's gone mad. Tell me I'm right, Frankie?'

'Something must have happened to him. I mean... you tell *me,* Linda. Should I go all official and address you as Mrs Long? I have not known Richard long, but it was as though...'

'He's so weird that he's really funny. No he's not! D'you know, I want to laugh and hit him at the same time, Frankie. Strange...'

'Why the surnames? Has he ever done that before? He often forgets and calls me Frankie in front of the kids...'

'Let's get out of here, Frankie.'

Frankie followed Linda out to her car.

'I want to slam my car door closed...'

'I'm going to stamp my way to the train.'

'Sorry, I'm not going your way, Frankie.'

'That's fine. I need to sort my head out.'

'I only hope we're not in for another bout of... We'll see. Sorry, must rush... Late already. But we'll cope. We've got each other, haven't we?'

Another bout of what? Frankie wondered.

19

SCHOOL JOURNEY

Paula opened the door to her car. 'You look how I feel, Frankie. Have you clicked on your seat belt? Once we hit the A3, we'll be home in no time.'

'Yes... another day over at school. Oh Paula! I'm tired but it's more than... I...'

'It's Richard, isn't it? I thought that after that row he had with Anna...'

'Yes, he keeps avoiding me. Who is Anna, Paula?'

'She's not worth talking about, Frankie. She's not a teacher. She thinks she...'

'Come on, Paula... I need to know.'

'Concentrate on your work. Teaching is demanding enough. I'm sure you find preparing your class for their First Communion, administrating the SATS, writing those reports and parent's evenings... all this will zap your energy....'

'Did Linda tell you how Richard treated us when he discussed...'

'I know...'

We've turned onto the A3. Paula is silent. What is she hiding from me? Whenever the staff talk about Anna, they mention a row.

'Why is Richard treating us so formally? He called Linda and me by our surnames...'

'Don't be so impatient. Wait. You'll see.'

What is Paula implying?

Silence. Five minutes have passed.

'Aren't the Quinlan twins lovely children? I heard them singing a little song to Sr Sheila today.'

Paula is changing the topic.

'Please Paula; I really need to talk to you about Richard. My biological clock is ticking loud and clear: *Hurry up if you want your own child!* '

'Is it Richard or a baby you want, Frankie?'

'Both! I love Richard. Whenever he comes near me I feel... oh... I want to hug him. I want to be hugged. I feel, tingly, womanly... I'd love a baby too...'

'There's a folk group playing at the pub just around the corner from where you live. I heard John inviting the staff yesterday.'

'Technical John? The thin fellow who fixes our computers?'

'Yes. He's quite attractive. He's a Beatle's fan. I think he plays bass guitar in that band.'

'Paula! It's Richard that I love. I don't know anything about this John. Richard and I have things in common. He trained to be a priest. I was a nun.'

'I know. Remember it was I who told him about your background. I was just thinking that you have not met any other men.'

'That's true...... but it is... I don't know how to explain.'

'Tell me, Frankie. What is it that attracts you to Richard?'

'Our shared background is important. He knows the kind of life that I have lived. I love his vulnerability... I bet you didn't see him winking at me that time when the staff were talking about pop songs? He realised that neither of us knew these songs. When we were novices we didn't listen to that kind of music.'

'We're here. I'll just pull over, Frankie. Have you told Richard how you feel? Ask him why he is being so formal.'

'I will. I make sure that I get into school early tomorrow morning. He usually arrives about the same time as I do. Thank you, Paula.'

THE NEXT MORNING when Frankie boarded the train from Wimbledon to Clapham Junction, she noticed the couple who held hands every morning.

That could be me... but it isn't. I hope I will be able to talk to Richard this morning.

At seven-thirty Frankie arrived at school. She opened the staffroom door. 'Oh, sorry, to interrupt.'

Richard and Paula were the only ones seated there. They seemed to be engrossed in some paper work.

I'll go to my classroom. I'll find him later.

'Frankie, Sister Sheila would like to speak to you.'

'Thanks, Paula. You two look busy.'

'Up to my eyes with the form-filling for the school journey. Such a lot of paper work.'

'Go now. Sister wants to see you ASAP. Speak later.'

Frankie tapped on Sr Sheila's door.

'Good morning, Sister Sheila.'

'Sit down for a moment, Frankie. We have had a little sad news this morning. I hope... we all hope that nothing serious will come of it. Linda's two year old son, Paul, was rushed to hospital last evening with suspected meningitis.'

'Oh the poor little love! She must be worried sick, Sister.'

'Let's hope and pray that all will turn out alright, Frankie. Mass was offered up for this intention in our chapel this morning.'

'She'll be pleased, Sister.'

'She will. I have asked Richard to replace Linda on the school journey to Hastings.'

'Richard, Sister?

Maybe I'll be able to find out why he has been behaving differently lately?

'I have arranged for a supply teacher to replace Richard and Linda. One will take over Richard's class while you are both are Hastings.

Linda will come into school when she can. She needs to be able to come and go to the hospital.'

'I hope all goes well for little Paul. We'll miss Linda.'

'Twenty-four children are going. We need four adults, two of whom must be teachers. Because these children are only in Years 2 and 3, I had agreed to send two female teachers. Strictly speaking, although we are within the recommended guidelines, the preferred staffing is for a male teacher to be there for the boys.'

Sister Sheila is looking straight at me. I have been thinking about Richard. I wonder if he wants to be on this school journey? I have not been listening to Sr Sheila's explanations.

'Yes... yes, Sister.'

'I noticed that you seem to have been avoiding Richard lately. That's a pity. You both seemed to be getting on so well. You need to resolve whatever prevents you from communicating with each other before you go on this school journey.'

Now is my chance to ask Sister about Richard.

'I'm sorry, Sister Sheila. I don't know what has happened. Maybe, I have done something to upset him. If I have, it was not intentional.'

'When did things change between you?'

'Richard started to address both Linda and I by our surnames. He began to act officially... seriously... it all happened very quickly.'

'Oh I see... You know about 'Opus Dei', Frankie?'

'That ultra traditional Catholic group, Sister? We suffered so much from them when they infiltrated the school where I taught previously.'

'Go easy on Richard. I am not at liberty to say much more.'

'Thank you for mentioning the Opus Dei group, Sister. That information throws a different light on Richard's behaviour.'

He must feel compelled to obey. Like me, he has lived an ordered, disciplined life for many years. Opus Dei lays down strict rules. Now I understand why he has been acting strangely. Sister is smiling.

'Congratulations on all the work your class has produced in preparation for the school journey. Well done. Lovely wall display on the Battle of Hastings. I've read nearly all the children's files. You certainly seem to have inspired them.'

'Thank you, Sister. I warned them that they had to work hard if they were to go on this school journey.'

'Sister, I presume that I won't need to change the plans that Linda and I made. We spent the last few weeks preparing a programme for this journey.'

'Although Richard has a senior post, you are in charge of this school journey. You have held posts of responsibility in your other school. What you decide has to be adhered to. Richard, Mrs Hughes and Mrs Prince will support you. You represent Holy Rosary School. Remember, we assure their parents that the children will be properly cared for.'

'You can rely on us, Sister Sheila. This will prove to be a productive and beneficial school journey. I am very sorry that Linda cannot join us. I hope that her little son Paul, will recover with no serious after-effects. I know meningitis is a serious illness.'

'I agree. Puts our grievances into perspective, Frankie.'

I wonder if Anna is a member of the Opus Dei. Is that what the rowing was about? But she could have been Richard's girlfriend too. Did I dream that we were in love? But then I recall that intimate evening that we enjoyed in the restaurant. Richard showed me so much attention. Those dreamy eyes... his strong arms. We kissed. He held me close. That was real. I'll have to find out about Anna. She won't be near us for a whole week.

When Frankie returned to her classroom she found a note on her desk. She recognised Richard's handwriting. She tore open the envelope. And read:

For the attention of Miss Danivet:

Sister Sheila has provided me with the plans for our school journey in Hasting. I have asked Mrs Prince to give me copies of any relevant notes. I assume that this meets with your approval.

Thank you

Mr Canto

Silly man! Is he angry because I have been put in charge? Children from mine and Linda's classes are going on this trip. We know the children we teach better than he does. I'd willing forgo this responsibility and hand everything over to him. I really must find out what is causing Richard to behave like this. He has never lauded his authority over me before. Neither of us have any need to compete.

'Miss Danivet, the coach for Hastings has pulled into the school parking area.' Alerted one of the staff.

'You must be excited, Frankie.'

'Yes I am, Paula. Thank you for coming out to wave us off.'

'It's not every Monday morning that the children are so keen to get to school early. All those mums over there hugging their precious offsprings!'

'What a racket! I'll have to calm them down before we board the coach.'

'Just to let you know, Frankie. Richard has been in the staffroom enthusiastically reminding us all that children gain greater knowledge of our history when they travel to place where an event takes place. He was quoting the Chinese philosopher, Confucius: *I hear and I forget. I see and I remember. I do and I understand.*'

'Good on him!'

'I told you to be patient, Frankie. Let me give you a hug. I've got to go back. Be thinking of you.'

'Should I begin tugging these darlings away from their mums, Frankie?'

'Rather you than me. I don't think they are ready yet, Sharon. I'm waiting for Richard to join us.'

'Is it true that *Sandrock House* is a convent, Frankie?'

'Yes Mrs... Sharon. You'll have to behave. The nuns will be watching you! Richard and you, Cathy, will be in a dormitory at one end with the boys. The girls will be with you and me at the other end of the sleeping quarters.'

These nuns don't know me. It will be a bonus to know what goes on in convents. But now that I am free from keeping the nuns' rules, surely I will feel liberated.

'Here comes Richard. The parents seem to be admiring his green and beige 'Berghaus' outfit. He's always kitted out for the job.'

'Oh good, Cathy. Sr Sheila has come to make sure all is okay. I'll ring the bell. I'll ask the mums to bring their children's cases over and give their little ones their goodbye hugs.'

Richard is helping to put the luggage into the hold. The parents are chatting to him. He's smiling and disentangling himself from the admiring children. Hopefully all will go well. We'll sort things out between us.

'Well done, children. Mrs Prince checked that all your luggage is in the hold. Thank you, Mr Canto.'

'Oh Michelle is still clinging to her mum, Mrs Prince. I'll help her on board. Here she is. Come on, darling. Let me wipe your tears. We'll take care of you. One more hug. Look, you're sitting in the front next to Sheena.'

'Nearly ready, driver. It's Tom, isn't it? I'll introduce you in a minute.'

'Yes. Everyone calls me Tom.'

'Mrs Hughes, would you and Mrs Prince sit half way down the coach? Thank you, Mr Canto. You're at the back. I'll sit at the front, next to the driver.'

'Of course, Miss Danivet. I dread these tearful goodbyes, don't you?'

'Mr Canto made sure that we've left nothing behind.'

'Thank you both.'

Finally the children were settled.

'Miss, can we sing *She'll be coming round the mountain*? It was a seven year old.

'Good idea, Chuka. We'll do the actions too. I'll stand to start you off.'

Frankie stood in the middle aisle. She had everyone's attention, including Richard's. She cleared her throat and began. Even the driver joined in.

'Can we have the song about an old woman that swallowed a fly, next, please, Miss?'

Frankie was delighted that they had arrived safely at the convent.

Only one child suffered from travel sickness on the journey. As soon as the coach drew up outside the convent, two nuns appeared at the door. Frankie looked at the honey-coloured stone house before her and the landscaped garden to her right.

When the driver opened the door, the nuns climbed on board the coach.

'Welcome! You're all very welcome. Plenty of room in our big house. You must be Miss Danivet.'

Frankie held out her hand.

'Yes, that me. Thank you, Sisters.'

Déjà vu! I wonder what it will feel like to be back in a convent? Familiar. I need to sleep well while I am here.

'This is Sister Una. I'm Sister Dolores. The children must be hungry. Why don't we lead them straight into the dining hall. With the driver's help, I'll get Jose to unload their cases. We could leave them in the hall until after our dinner.'

'Boys and girls, did you all hear what Sr Una and Sr Dolores said?'

'Yes, Miss Danivet. The microphone is on.'

'Food! Where do we eat, Miss Danivet?'

'I'm starving.'

'Refectory. That's where we eat. Follow Mrs Prince. In two's. Walk. Don't race.'

These corridors look the same as the ones in our convent. Wooden brown panels. Green painted walls. Notices. The Community Room. Silence. Not much hope of silence with these children. A huge crucifix hung on the wall facing the bottom of the stairs.

WHEN THEY WERE all seated in the refectory, Frankie's attention was drawn to one of the children. Barry was stretching his arms round all the food he could grasp on his table. He was lowering his head and making sure that the other three boys couldn't get hold of the bread rolls, jam, fruit or even the bottle of sauce.

'Look at Barry, Miss Danivet. Poor little soul. Looks as though he's frightened that someone will take this food away from him.' Mrs Prince whispered from behind her hand.

'I'm not surprised. When I visited his mother yesterday evening, she had been drinking. I don't suppose he gets a lot to eat. His mother had not started packing the clothes that the Social Services had provided for Barry's school journey.'

'I thought he was neglected. He has probably never had so much food.'

When the meal was over, Frankie rang a bell.

'What an excellent meal! Shall we clap our hands to thank the Sisters?'

'Would you like me to show the boys to their dormitory, Miss Danivet?'

'Thank you, Sr Una. That would be great. Mr Canto will…'

'Please Miss. What's a dormitory?'

'Sorry, John. It's like a long bedroom, sometimes with maybe twelve beds in it.'

'When the boys have taken their luggage from the front hall, shall I lead the girls to their dormitory, Miss Danivet?'

'Thank you very much, Sr Dolores. Mrs Prince will go with Mr Canto and the boys.'

At the entrance to the girl's dormitory there was an altar to Our Lady of Lourdes.

Frankie remembered her friend Sr Margaret who had committed suicide. She recalled the promises that they made. She prayed, 'Eternal rest grant to her O Lord. Mother Mary, please help me.'

'They're all so excited, Frankie. There'll be tears no doubt when we try to settle them.'

'The first night is always the worst, even for us, isn't it Mrs Hugh… Cathy?'

'I feel selfish having that lovely room to myself. I saw the cubicle that you're sleeping in. Sure you don't want to swap?'

'No. Thank you. I'll be fine, Cathy.'

This time I won't have take off a habit and veil and put on a night bonnet. I have a pink, floral matching night dress and dressing gown and matching slippers. When I walk up and down the dormitory I'll tuck in the girls. Make sure they are happy. If anyone cries, I'll be there to comfort them.

As breakfast was nearly over, Frankie rang a bell to gain the attention of the children and staff.

'We have a very exciting day planned. We're going to be driven to a museum where we will be able to see the Bayeux Tapestry. Who can remind us what the Bayeux Tapestry is?'

'Yes, Georgina'

'It tells the story of the Battle of Hastings. You're right.'

'Miss, it is like a huge strip cartoon showing us what happened at the Battle of Hastings.'

'Excellent, Michelle.'

'When you arrive at the museum, we will give each of you a questionnaire. On this tapestry we will see soldiers building a fort and others fighting with clubs.'

'Yes, Jack. We'll see Harold fighting William. Kings and castles, banquets and battles. So much to see and learn.'

Frankie saw Richard stand up and thrust his hands in the air as he called out, 'The sun is shining. Come on. Let's fill our lungs with sea air and run along the beach.'

FRANKIE FELT that she had to intervene.

Maybe Richard has forgotten that we need to say Grace? The children don't seem to know who to listen to. Richard is looking at me. I'll give instructions, 'Children, stand quietly. Let's pray our Grace after meals. Then we will walk to our rooms to collect our belonging. Make sure you have been to the toilet before you line up. At the front door, wait for the coach to arrive.'

'Who is going to volunteer to collect the sandwiches and drinks?' It was Richard.

Frankie was glad that he was co-operating with her.

When the children emerged from the coach, Frankie saw that Richard seemed to have difficulty restraining the boys. They pushed past the girls and dashed over the beach towards the sea. Barry began to throw pebbles at the seagulls.

'Mrs. Prince… Barry has a fistful of pebbles… stop him…'

Frankie looked up. She saw that Richard was forcing Barry's hands open. He was making him drop the pebbles.

I don't believe it! He is shouting. Poor Barry is howling. Richard must be unaware of Barry's background. I'll have to call him over.

'Come over to me, Barry. You must not throw stones. You could kill the gulls. What would happen if one of those hit someone? Don't you ever do that again. Promise me? Stay by my side now.'

'I can deal with Barry.'

'Perhaps it is better if Barry stays with me. I'll explain later.'

Richard is staring at me. I didn't mean to embarrass him. He looks as if he wants to reply. He is kicking the pebbles as he turns and makes his way back to the other boys. Oh dear! Was I too forceful?

20

CONFRONTATION

'This museum has such a big entrance hall, Frankie. Nearly all the children have come back from the toilet. They're getting noisy.'

'Give them space, Cathy. They think they're in the playground. It's time to quieten them now.' Frankie clapped her hands. 'Children! Children! Quiet please! That's better. Congratulations. You have been a credit to our school. You behaved very well in this museum. Well done!'

Cathy spoke up, 'Miss Danivet, what time are the Sisters expecting us back for lunch?'

'One o'clock. The coach should be here any minute to take us back to the convent. Tom said he would try to park as near to the entrance as possible.'

'Miss, the Bayeux tapestry is really long.'

'Who remembers how long it is?'

'Yes, Brian. How long?'

'Seventy metres, Miss'

'Well done!'

Richard was standing at the back of the foyer of the museum with his group of boys. He shouted out, 'Is not actually a tapestry. It is, in fact, embroidery. It is stitched, not woven, in woollen yarns on linen. The original tapestry is on display at Bayeux in Normandy, France.'

'Thank you, Mr. Canto. Today we saw the embroidered replica of the Bayeux tapestry telling the tale of William the Conqueror's invasion of England. We know that the real Bayeux Tapestry *is* housed in Bayeux, France. Hopefully one day you may travel there to see it. Today you learnt how the Normans dressed, what armour they used. Now you know more about their castles, their boat buildings. All that information will help you fill in the questionnaires we have given you.'

Frankie noticed the coach driver was standing in the entrance hall signalling that the coach was parked outside.

She heard Richard's voice, 'Boys! Are you ready? The coach is outside. We sit at the back. We're first on. Follow me.'

Frankie moved the girls and signalled to let the boys go onto the coach first. They marched behind Richard.

'Gosh, Frankie. He's disciplined those boys. Hope they keep up their good behaviour. Mr Canto must have reprimanded them.'

'I noticed, Cathy.'

Maybe there is a battle going on inside Richard? thought Frankie. He's looks stern and tight-lipped. There seems to be tears in his eyes. I don't want to antagonise him. I hope he doesn't think that I meant to embarrass him when he was strict with Barry.

No sooner had Frankie returned to her cubicle than there was a knock at the dormitory door. Richard's fists were still pummelling the panels as she opened the door.

'Richard. What is it?'

'Were you trying to undermine my authority?'

'Shish. The girls will hear you. Let's go to the room further along the corridor.'

What have I done? Richards face is raw-red and contorted in anger.

Frankie closed the door. Richard stood rigid.

'Frankie, it is my duty to ensure that discipline is maintained.'

'Of course. Why don't we sit?'

Frankie sat in an armchair. Richard looked round. He dragged a chair across the wooden floor. He continued, 'As a responsible adult, I am in no doubt that Barry Hartley's behaviour was unacceptable. I was in the process of dealing with him.'

Frankie wondered if she was wrong. She was about to consider apologising. Richard said, 'I demand... expect an apology for your totally unnecessary and undermining intervention.'

What is going on? His face is still taut. He has turned up the palms of his hands. Is he appealing to me? I'll tell him about Barry's background.

'Richard, I should have briefed you about Barry. I discovered more about his background the night before we departed. His father no longer lives with them. Barry's mother is an alcoholic. Social Services have provided him with all he needs for this school journey...'

'I read some of the notes that you provided me. Still my authority should not be undermined...'

'Barry is in my class. I know how he behaves in school. He responds better to kindness.'

Frankie stood. Richard Stood.

He's staring into my eyes. What now?

Richard turned abruptly. He stamped his way to the door and banged it closed.

He's breaking my heart. I feel like yelling and crying. But I'd better be careful. Something must be eating into him. Is Opus Dei responsible for that?

When Richard's group of boys arrived for the evening meal, Frankie noticed that he did not make eye contact with her.

'Frankie, we needn't have worried about the boys behaving themselves. Look at them; they're marching like little soldiers.'

'Mrs Hughes whispered: He's watching their every move.'

'He's pointing to Barry to sit next to him.'

Frankie noticed that Richard was looking after Barry. *He has taken on board the information that I gave given him. If only I had slept better last night. I dreamt that Richard crept into my cubicle and begged me to forgive him. He slipped into the bed and folded his body round mine. He turned me to face him. He kissed me on my forehead, then on my lips. He kept repeating, 'I'm sorry... please forgive me.'*

'What is the matter with you? The Richard I love doesn't get angry. Why... ?'

'I wish I knew... You know I love you, Frankie.'

'You seem to have changed. Tell me... what's the matter?'

'I have to do as I'm told... rules... responsibilities...'

'Rules? Opus...'

My dream was interrupted. Cathy was shaking me.

'Frankie, little Debbie is crying! Poor little thing. I tried to comfort her.'

After they wiped Debbie's tears and tucked her into bed, Frankie found it difficult to get back to sleep. She was trying to puzzle out how best to react to Richard.

'Good morning, Miss Danivet. I hope you're happy with our accommodation.'

'Thank you, Sister Una. Please call me Frankie when the children are not listening. We couldn't be happier with all you're doing for us, Sister. '

'Good! I hope the children will cope with the buffet breakfast, Frankie.'

'I'm sure they will be, Sister. Maybe I should remind them not to overload their plates.'

'Mr Canto is lovely with the boys, isn't he, Frankie? He asked me to choose a book from our library. I took it down to his dormitory last night.'

'What did you choose?'

'*Wind in the Willows*. That's my favourite. It turns out it is his too.'

'Excellent choice. I treasure happy memories of having that book read to me when I was at school.'

'Before I left Richard, the boys were resting their little heads propped against their pillows.'

'Comforting.'

'He was putting on voices for Ratty and Mole. The boys were a picture of peace and happiness.'

Thank God Sr Una sees the good in Richard. Frankie wondered if she was blinded by her need to prove that she was her own person.

I have to brief the children where we are going today. I will try to be confident without being assertive.

'Here come the boys, Frankie. I hope they slept well. Debbie is smiling now. It's hard for them being away from their parents.'

'Distract them. Keep them busy, Cathy. That will help them to forget their homes for a while. I'll tell them what we have planned for them today after they have eaten. First I need to tell them how the buffet works.'

'Mr Canto seems to be instructing the boys.'

Frankie stood. She clapped her hands. 'Mr Canto, would you please explain to us how best to collect our food?'

'I was telling the boys that it would be best if the children from each table go up in turn.'

'Children, I will come round and tell you when it is your table's turn. Line up behind each other. Take a tray. Take your turn. No need to pile your plate up. Take the amount of food that you know you will eat. When everybody's had their turn, those of you who are still hungry can go up for seconds. The Sisters have put out enough food for us all.'

'Most of these kids don't know how a buffet works. Richard explained that very well.'

'That's what I thought, Cathy. All four of us should share the responsibility. Even though there are more girls than boys perhaps Sharon should help Richard a little more with the boys.'

Frankie decided that she would prove to Richard that she was acting fairly.

Frankie stood and clapped her hands, 'Before we leave the refectory to go and get ready for the coach, I want to tell you about the exciting day we have planned for you. We are fortunate to be able to see the re-enactment of the Battle of Hastings.'

'Is that the real battle? Will there be soldiers with swords, Miss?'

'John, the men will be dressed in uniforms like those worn at the battle in 1066. We will watch the re-enactment on a video at the new Visitors' Centre.'

'Please Miss, we wrote about that in our project files.'

'Yes, you did. You'll learn more to-day. Twenty-two thousand people took part in re-enacting this battle. Listen and watch well. We'll be asking you questions tonight. I have a quiz prepared.'

Frankie's voice trembled but she smiled as she addressed the children. She was determined to put aside all animosity. *All seems to be going well. I can hear Richard checking with Mrs Prince, that the mid-day snacks have been put on the coach.*

'Frankie, after we have watched the video are we going to view the exhibits as one group?'

Frankie reflected, *If we split into two groups, Richard and I will not be at loggerheads. When I make a decision, I don't want to taunt him. I do not like to see him upset.*

'No. After we have seen the video we will split into two groups. Sharon will you let Richard know? Would you go with his group? We can reassemble to travel back on the coach. Thank you.'

It was Friday. Frankie was glad that she that she had not any further confrontation with Richard. When the children had assembled in the front hall of the convent, she had walked through the girls' dormitory to make sure that nothing was left behind. Richard did the same in the boys' quarters. She carried her heavy bag on her shoulders to the coach. She, Richard, Sharon and Cathy made sure that all the belongings were on the coach.

'Are you certain nobody has left anything behind, Frankie?'

'Yes Sister. You and Sr Dolores have looked after our luggage wonderfully. Thank you. Oh here is Sr Dolores. Good Sister. Would you mind coming into the coach to join Sr Una?'

FRANKIE CLAPPED HER HANDS, 'Boys and girls, I know you have something to say to Sr Una and Sr Dolores. Come up to the front of the coach, Debbie.'

'Thank you very much, Sisters, for welcoming us into your lovely convent. We hope you will like the present that we have bought you and all the Sisters.'

Debbie handed them the gift bag.

'God Bless each one of you. The best present is having you here. You're a credit to your school. Do you think that I should I peep inside this lovely bag?'

'Yes, Sister.'

'No need to stand children. When Sister has taken the present out, I'm sure she will hold it up for you all to see.'

'Oh! What a huge box of Quality Street chocolate! The Sisters love these. Thank you, children. Safe journey home. Come back another time. May the Lord go with you.'

As Frankie walked through the coach to chat to the children she was pleased to see that Richard was helping the children to finish off their questionnaires.

'It's been much better since we split into two groups, hasn't it Frankie?'

'Yes it has, Sharon.'

'Barry seems to be enjoying himself. Look at him smiling. He's asking Richard to help him fill in his answers, Frankie.'

'Thank you both. It looks as though this school journey has been beneficial for all the children. Perhaps Barry has been helped the most. You two have been wonderful. I'll make sure to tell Sr Sheila that her assistants are worth their weight in gold.'

Frankie felt as though she had been on two journeys.

Richard led me from rugged rocks to the sea edge. I've stumbled, been battered and sprayed. I hope we will walk side-by-side. If only we could hold hands again. Perhaps Anna will have disappeared by the time we return to school? Great, I knew Sister Sheila would be at the gate to welcome us back.

'Children, you're parents are here. You'll be with them in one minute. Wait. Sr Sheila wants to speak to you first.'

'Sister Sheila! Sister Sheila! We saw the Battle. Harold got shot in the eye... and...'

'Well, well! Is that right? Poor Harold! You all look as though you've had a great time, children. I have some very good news for you about Mrs Long's little son. He's improving. He is much, much better. Thank the Good Lord.'

Everyone clapped. Frankie could see that they were searching for their parents.

'There she is! There's my mum. She's brought Bono. I've missed our dog...'

Oh Lord! So that must be Anna. What's she doing here? She is holding her hands out to Richard. He has shaken her hands. Did she want to hug him? How inappropriate that would be in front of the children. Sister Sheila seems to have noticed. She is looking at me. I hope my facial expression did not betray my interest in how they behaved towards each other.

Sr Sheila smiled. 'Welcome back home! I hear you have all behaved well. Make sure you take everything off the coach, children. Your parents will help you now. Did you thank Miss Danivet, Mr Canto, Mrs Hughes and Mrs Prince for looking after you? Good. I knew you would.'

Frankie watched Anna accompanying Richard as he carried his luggage to her car.

Perhaps that is why is Anna is here. She's going to drive him home. Did Richard tell her about me?

'Frankie, I asked our cook to keep a hot meal for you in our oven. I didn't want you to go back to your flat without something to eat. You'll need a rest after the school journey.'

'How thoughtful, Sister. I'm very tired. I'll say goodbye and thank Sharon and... Oh... Richard is being driven off.'

'He's probably grateful for the lift. If you thank Sharon and Cathy, I'll thank the driver.'

Anna has whisked Richard away. Was he depending on Anna to drive him home?

'That's good, Sister. Tom has been an excellent driver. Sharon and Cathy are still smiling. They deserve praise.'

'Good. After you have eaten and rested, I have something that I want to tell you. I drove down from the convent. The car is over there. The coach man is about to drive off. All the children have been claimed.'

Frankie was glad that Sister Sheila enquired about the suitability of the accommodation and the conduct of the pupils as she drove Frankie back to the convent.

Is Sr Sheila being kind? What does she want to tell me? Has Richard said anything about my attitude towards him?

Lasagne and mixed salad was followed by apple strudel and custard.

'Come in and sit on this comfortably armchair, Frankie. You have taken a lot of responsibility. I was delighted to hear that all went very well.'

'Yes, thank you, Sister. I hope the children benefitted.'

'I'm sure they have learnt a good deal from that sort of trip. While it is fresh in my mind, I want to tell you how preparations for the children's First Communion are progressing.'

Is that why Anna came to meet Richard? wondered Frankie.

'Oh Sister! I will have to concentrate on preparing the children on Monday.'

'Good. I wanted to tell you that as the teacher with the responsible for religious education in our school, Richard, Mr Canto, has been instructed to accept the services of a music teacher appointed by the dioceses.'

'We have been working with the First Communion programme, Sister. We've already learnt the hymns that we selected. The children love doing the actions to these hymns.'

'Yes. I am aware of that. However, our parish priest, Fr McCormac has received instructions from the bishop. Until the music teacher arrives, I am not yet fully informed about them. That's all I am at liberty to say at the moment. I wanted to prepare you before you go into school on Monday.'

'But…'

'Sr Mary agreed to drive you home. You need to rest. Sister is waiting. Hopefully, you will be refreshed by Monday. Thank you for organising the school journey so well. Isn't it good news about Linda's son?'

Sister Sheila is unwilling or unable to tell me more about the music teacher. Paula had told me that Anna was a peripatetic music teacher. What are Richard and Anna planning? I hope they will not force us to change the hymns that we have already learnt.

Frankie's mind was churning but she tried not to show it.

'Thank you, Sr Sheila.'

Frankie pulled the door behind her.

21

UNWELCOME ANNOUNCEMENT

Monday morning. Frankie felt tired. She couldn't relax during the weekend. The news that Anna was going to help with the hymns for their First Communion Mass upset her. Linda and she had chosen hymns appropriate to their children's needs. Anna was not a teacher. She suspected that Opus Dei had something to do with that.

I wish I was not on the train on my way to school. If only I could get off, return home, climb back into bed and pull my duvet over my head.

She heard a lady say to a small boy, presumably her son, 'We're nearly at Putney High Street Station, darling. The doors are about to open. Ready?'

Frankie mused, *How I wish that I was accompanied by someone who loves me. I'm dreading being introduced to Anna.*

She entered the school grounds and pulled open the school door. The staffroom was quiet. Paula and Richard's cars were parked. *Here goes,* she thought, *I'll walk boldly into the staffroom.*

Inside Sister Sheila was standing at the head of the long table with a twig of cherry blossom. Paula was reading a catalogue. Sr Sheila was holding up the cherry blossom in her hand. 'Even an atheist, must praise the Almighty when the miracle of spring bursts out.'

'Beautiful, Sister. There's a cherry blossom tree in our garden too. Such a gentle pink. Magnolias also have that delicate hue.'

'Did you buy hyacinths bulbs this year, Paula?'

'We did, Sister. When I visit our nearest garden centre, I always buy a few potted bulbs. I love the scent. I can't resist them. Can you?'

'Welcome back, Frankie. Sister told me that the school journey went really well. I've not managed to speak to Richard yet. He seems to be pre-occupied this morning.'

Busy preparing? I wonder if he intends introducing the music teacher today, thought Frankie.

'Yes, Paula. The children were receptive. Well behaved. We'll soon learn how much they remembered. Our two assistants, Sharon and Cathy, were wonderful.'

Frankie heard the door open behind her.

'Thank you, Richard. You arrived just in time to hold the door open for me. I'll take these flowers into hall.'

Richard was holding a note. He came towards Frankie.

'Miss Danivet. Frankie. This is for you.'

'Thank you, Richard.

She looked into his eyes. He put the note in front of her on the table. He didn't hand it to her. He turned round and walked out of the room.

'Miss Danivet'. That sounds very formal. You'd better read it, Frankie.'

'Paula, things have changed between us. Listen to this:

'This is to inform you that Sister Sheila has asked Anna Fuller to take over the music for the First Communion Masses. Miss Fuller is a music specialist. We will have our first hymn practice at two-thirty this afternoon. Please ensure that your class arrives in good time.

'Sister said that she told you that Anna is returning. Apparently Bishop David instructed Fr McCormac to ensure that the music for the First Communion is within the guidelines.'

'Paula, Linda and I have already selected hymns appropriate to the age of the children. I will accompany them on the guitar. I may not have the best voice but between us we manage fine. Besides, you said that Anna... Miss Fuller is not a teacher.'

'Anna is a music specialist. She is a peripatetic teacher. She accompanied the children last year.'

'She doesn't know the children in my class or the group from Linda's class. Why is she being imposed on us?'

'My hands are tied, Frankie. When the Bishop instructs us to do something we have to obey. Fr McCormac passed to Sr Sheila instructions about the liturgy for the First Communion Mass. We have to comply. I'm afraid you will do as you are told.'

'I thought I had been freed from my vow of obedience when I left the convent. It seems that I still must obey. I'm going to see if Linda is in her classroom. See what she thinks.'

Linda arrived late. Mrs Hughes led her class from the playground to her classroom.

Linda was on playground duty at break-time. She had to rush home during the dinner hour. Frankie realised that she was not able to speak to her until it was time to follow the instructions that Richard had handed to her.

When Frankie lined up her class, she opened her classroom door. Linda's class were beginning to walk along the corridor leading to the hall. Frankie followed Linda's class.

Faith of our Fathers was being played. Anna was playing the piano accompaniment. It was a hymn usually sung by older children and adults. Two children from Linda's class were handing out old hymnals as they walked through the hall door.

'Linda, Richard handed me a note when I came back to school after lunch. Don't like the sound of it. Take a look at Anna. The woman in black...'.

'Year 3. Miss Danivet's class, sit here. Move along. Stop jigging about Steven.'

'Linda, Richard is not himself. He doesn't normally shout.'

Frankie signalled to the children to follow Richard's commands. She walked to the end of the first line of her class so that she could see

Anna. She was seated behind the piano. Linda drew up a chair beside Frankie.

'This Anna woman is about my age. Late thirties, is she?'

'Probably. With her black hair swept tightly back, those piercing eyes and a beaky nose, believe me, Frankie, she looks lots older than you do.'

While Anna was fingering through a hymnal resting on the piano stand, Frankie looked at her.

So this is Anna Fuller. She's layered in a black top, cardigan and long skirt. She is shorter than me. Probably five foot without those high-heeled, black leather pointed-toe boots.

'She's quite the attractive in a strange sort of way, isn't she, Linda? I like the diamond studded, crocodile style hair-clip drawing back her black curls. Not short of a penny…'

'You'll learn, Frankie. Look at her now… those dagger eyes are surveying and intimidating the pupils. Look. See how she stumps out the accompaniment with bony fingers!'

'Sheena, Stop! You too, Mavis! Stop whispering.'

Frankie warned the children, 'Mr Canto is holding the bell. He's looking in our direction, Mavis.'

'Before we begin, I ask each of you to pay your full attention. Anyone who whispers or even rustles the pages of your hymn book will be deprived of their play-time. They will sit inside in my classroom and write lines. Are you listening, Sheena and Mavis?'

'Yes, Mr Canto. Sorry, Mr Canto.'

'Everyone carefully, noiselessly, open your hymn books at number 938. Then listen to Mrs Fuller playing the hymn '*Soul of my Saviour*.'

Linda leaned nearer to Frankie. 'We're back in the dark ages! Such old fashioned words… *Oh Lord my God, when I in awesome wonder…* is much more appropriate.'

'Listen to the words. Listen carefully.'

'Richard is bellowing out the words…'

'And glaring each child into submission.'

'*Sanctify my breast…* What does that mean to a seven year-old? I know what Sean will be thinking.'

'Put that hymnal down now, Jason Matterson! Sit here! Face those of us who know how to behave. If you don't pay attention, you will not be prepared properly for the reception of these sacraments.'

Frankie fingered her hymn book. *I don't believe it! This can't be the same kind, caring, good-humoured Richard that encouraged me to apply for a full time post. Something drastic has happened to him since Anna has appeared on the scene. I'll have to find out as much as I can from Linda before she leaves to go home.*

'Linda, please can you spare time for a coffee in the café at the corner?'

'Oh, thank God, Frankie. That's what I was about to ask you. Grab your bag. Let's head there before anyone notices, especially Richard.'

'D'you know, Frankie, the sight of Anna takes me back to memories of screaming, shouting and banging coming from her room at last year's communions. She only left... can it be... maybe... most be over a year ago? Well not too long before we broke up for the summer hols.'

'That bad? Really?'

'Believe me. Whenever Anna used to go into Richard's classroom, a few of us would listen outside to the hullabaloo that went on between them. Then as sure as night follows day, he put up notices about the importance of the sacraments. He'd leave leaflets around inviting us to attend penitential services and days of retreat. Even Sister Sheila would raise her eyes to heaven as if begging the Almighty to come to our aid.'

This smacks of the same kind of domination by Opus Dei that I witnessed when I taught in Battersea, thought Frankie.

'Linda, have you heard of the Opus Dei Movement?'

'Yes... well, that's what Sister Sheila used to refer to when Anna was here before. What do they do, Frankie?'

'As far as I can remember, this movement was initiated by Jose Maria who lived somewhere in Spain about 1900.'

'Have you come across them before? They sound like a sect. Are they part of the Catholic Church?'

'Yes, sadly I suffered their infiltrating methods. They managed to convince the clergy that their aim is to promote genuine family relationships. Surreptitiously, they creep into positions of authority. Eventually they take over.'

'Frankie, I am all for family values, but this old fashioned approach is something else. I have nothing against saying the rosary, Benediction and the Latin Mass. My mother loves all these. When Anna was here, she took control of all the music.'

'What can we do, Linda? Do we have to let Anna take control again?'

'What can we do?'

'Richard has changed so drastically. I don't like what I'm witnessing?'

'Frankie, if Sister Sheila can't do anything about this Opus Dei regime, how can we halt their take-over?'

'We must try, Linda.'

'What did you think about the readings that Richard has chosen for Mass? I thought he would have selected simpler translations.'

'I have always paraphrased those more accessible readings taken from the 'Good News' version of the Bible.'

'The Bidding prayers are too difficult, too.'

'They're more suited to year 6 pupils than my seven year olds. He has taken these out of some prayer book.'

'Sorry I have to go, Frankie. Look. There's Paula drawing up outside.'

Paula opened her car window.

'Sister Sheila said she saw you two heading in this direction, Frankie. That was Linda driving off, wasn't it? Just caught her tail end as I rounded the corner. Pop in. Sister Sheila's worried about you both.'

'Is she worried about Richard and Anna, Paula?'

'There have been great goings on in my office these last few days. Anna…'

'I tried to talk to you about her but…'

'I know. I had hoped she might have… well…'

'I guessed it is to do with Opus Dei.'

'I knew you had dealings with them before. Anna's back with the Opus Dei group in the Parish. Father McCormac seems to have been unable to stop them.'

'Why?'

'Poor Father McCormac has his own problems…'

'He's an alcoholic…'

'Yes… that's apparently how Opus Dei managed to infiltrate yet again.'

'He needs help, Paula.'

'But Bishop David. Surely…'

'This particular Opus Dei group has been resurrected in London by a Monsignor Morrish.'

'I know. They adopt a fundamental approach to the liturgy.'

'I was hampered by them when I took the First Communion class in Battersea. They are so secretive. It's hard to pin them down.'

'I'll give you a lift home, Frankie!'

'Thanks.'

'Just a… Excuse me. Oh no! What's that driver doing? Did you see him cut out there? No indication. Just barge in. It's getting worse up this road. I used to go the other way. This is a quicker route but not if the likes of that lunatic are driving. Sorry Frankie. Opus Dei and Anna…'

'Yes, Paula. How did she behave last time she was in the school?'

'Last time round, she was advocating the recitation of the rosary after school. She wanted Fr McCormac to have Exposition of the Blessed Sacrament. Poor Sister Sheila, as a nun dedicated to God, how could she object?'

'Anna sounds as though she's some kind of control freak, Paula. A spiritual maniac. What was Richard's role in this?'

'Under some sort of obligation to comply, it would seem. After all, he has the post for Religious Education?'

'What did you do, Paula?'

'What could I do?'

'I don't know. Everyone seems to have to let the Opus Dei group rule the roost. Linda was bewildered too.'

'I'm sure she was. I heard your little ones singing *'Peace is flowing like a river'*, as I passed your door the other day.'

'You should have come in to see them doing the actions to that song. Waving their little arms imitating the flowing water. Why should they be forced to learn old-fashioned hymns for the more meaningful songs that are better suited to this young age group?'

'I agree, Frankie. Rest tonight. Tomorrow is another day.'

'Promise I will.'

'Do you mind if I drop you here tonight? There must have been an accident.'

'Of course. Thank you, Paula. I'll jump out here. Bye now.'

What interesting news to ponder. I thought Richard was a strong man. I suppose if Fr McCormac, Sr Sheila and even Bishop David are seemingly entrapped by the Opus Dei. Richard may have to obey orders. Have I misjudged him?

22

MIGHTY ROW

'Where is everyone this morning, Linda?'

'No one was in the staffroom when I came in. I crept past the Head's Office. I heard Fr McCormac speaking very loudly. Sounded as if he was laying down the law. May I come into your classroom for a few minutes, Frankie?'

'Come in, Linda! Something serious is happening. I noticed that Paula's coat was flung over a chair in the staffroom. That's not like her. She must have been summoned quickly into Sr Sheila's office. No sign of Richard. Bet he's with them.'

'When I told my husband that we are being forced to change the music and prayers for First Communion Mass, he was appalled. I've told him about the work we put into our preparation.'

'I kept going over it, Linda. Richard didn't look happy.'

'It's that Anna... She seems to have a hold over him. I sometimes wonder... Oh, there's the bell. We'll have to collect our classes. Speak later.'

'Look out the window, Linda!'

'They're all lined up beautifully. Some of them have no coats. They'll be cold at playtime.'

'No, Linda. Can you see the mothers near the fence? They're gathered round Sara's mother, Mrs Stalkey.'

'We'll have to go out and face the music. Come on, Frankie.'

Something's up, thought Frankie. She wondered why the mothers were glaring at her.

One of the children in her class handed her a letter. Franke glanced over to Linda's class. One of the boys in that class left his place in her line to give her an envelope. The children in both classes seemed to be watching every movement.

'Good morning Year 3. Codie and George, please lead your lines into class.'

'Trouble's brewing and no mistaking, Frankie, whispered Linda as she reached her classroom door. When both their classes of children were seated, they stood next to each other at their adjacent classroom doors. Linda tore open her envelope to show Frankie the letter from her one of her parents:

Dear Mrs Long,

I am one of a number of parents who are concerned about the way our children are being prepared for their First Communion. My daughter, Chloe, enjoyed the hymns that you and Miss Danivet taught them. Seemingly our children are now being taught other hymns with words that are difficult to comprehend.

Seven year olds children need to be helped to understand the Mass and all that is entailed in receiving her First Holy Communion. As you will no doubt appreciate, actions reinforce and explain the learning.

As a teacher myself, I am bewildered and confused at the substitution of more formal adult hymns for this age group. All the joy of participation seems to be lost in adopting this approach. I/we would be grateful, therefore, for some explanation and possibly a meeting to discuss these matters.

Sr Sheila has a copy of this letter.

I look forward to hearing from you

Mrs Erneston.

'OH LORD! Something will have to be done, Linda. The children are watching our reactions too. They obviously know there's something afoot. Tell you what, I'll call the register. Get my lot to keep their heads down while I skim through my post. Then I'll pop them into to you. Okay?'

Frankie closed her classroom door. After calling the register, she glanced through the letter that she had been handed:

FOR THE ATTENTION of Miss Danivet:

Last year my eldest son's First Communion Day was ruined by the interference of Miss Fuller, both in the choice of hymns and the order of service during the Mass on his special day. She has reappeared to lead the First Communion Day.

This time I am not prepared to sit back and let her take over again on the occasion of my daughter, Emily's, First Communion. I therefore wish to meet with you as soon as possible to discuss this matter.

I appreciate that you will probably not be free to contact me before the lunch break. My mobile number is: 0772737012070

Mrs O'Driscoll. (Mary)

AS FRANKIE FINISHED READING the letter, she heard the classroom door open.

'Good morning, Sister Sheila!'

Sister has arrived in her classroom.

Is she pretending to look relaxed with that switched on-and-off smile?

'Now children, I need to borrow your teacher, Miss Danivet, for a very short time. I know that I can trust this First Communion class to be on their best behaviour while Mrs Prince supervises the Literacy Hour. You know the routine well. There should be no problem with getting on with your work. Isn't that right, children?'

Sister Sheila beckoned Frankie to her room where Father McCormac and Linda were already awaiting their arrival.

They were barely seated when Father addressed them, 'I am aware that each of you has received a letter from a parent regarding the music and possibly the liturgy for the First Communion Mass. Let me make it quite clear from the outset that in this parish we work as a team under the direct jurisdiction of the Bishop and in keeping with guidance directly from the Pope. As both of you, Miss Danivet and Mrs Long are employed by the Governors of this school especially on matters relating to the Religious Education, you are obliged to comply with our guidelines on these matters. Do I make myself quite clear?'

Frankie and Linda nodded.

He continued, 'You will be aware that commercialism, encouraging extravagance and unnecessary expense, has unfortunately crept into the manner in which First Communions have begun to be celebrated. This has resulted in seven year old girls resembling brides in long flowing dresses and the boys being suited and booted like mini men. It's often resulted in the poor parents struggling so much to compete with each other that they are out of pocket for the essentials for months. Ridiculous! True?'

'Your nods tell me you agree. I'll go on to inform you about the music for the First Communion Mass.'

'The re-appearance of Miss Fuller, Father? Is that what you mean?' asked Sister Sheila.

'Yes Sister Sheila. Precisely. Anna Fuller has been chosen by the Diocese to make sure that the hymns are hymns and not happy clappy action songs with little or no doctrinal content. Surely you will each agree that sentimentality has no place to play when it comes to the reception of the Eucharist. May I remind each one of you that we are talking about the reception of one of the Seven Sacraments: Baptism, Penance, the Eucharist, and later on Confirmation, Holy Orders or Matrimony and The Sacrament of the Sick? Serious matters require quality hymns, not ones that come in and out of fashion and depend on out feelings. Any questions?'

Frankie felt her lips twitching: *A bully. A male domineering priest is what I am thinking. My anger is ready to erupt.*

Frankie looked over at Linda. She saw that her head was cast down over her chest. She scratched her head. She noticed that Sister Sheila was switching her lips from a smile to a pout. Father McCormac gathered his papers as if to go.

Frankie thought, *I can't keep silent. That would be cowering before these high and mighty know-all, rule-all, priests who for the most part regard women as amadans. Wasn't this the behaviour that led me to leaving the nuns?*

Father McCormac rose to leave them.

Frankie stood.

'Opus Dei, Father. Is there an Opus Dei group in this parish?'

There I've done it! She thought.

'Miss Danivet.'

Father Cormack looked as though he has been stabbed from behind. His face was rigid. His breath was snorting through his hairy nostrils.

'Miss Danivet, it is precisely the Opus Dei movement that we have to thank for coming to our rescue. Without... without this dedicated body of single-minded, self-sacrificing members of the church.' His hand was thumping Sister Sheila's desk. 'For whom the sanctification of their family duties is the most important part of their Christian life, we would end up diluting our doctrines and abandoning our moral obligations. Yes, thank God for Opus Dei.' His face twitched.

Frankie wanted to laugh aloud but managed to resist. She glanced at Sister Sheila. She looked as if she wanted to laugh too. She noticed a smile playing on her lips. Linda was wide-eyed and bewildered. She began to ring her hands.

A knock on the door. 'Sorry to interrupt. Would you like coffee now? Father? Sister?'

Paula had come to the rescue.

'Had we better return to our classes now, Sister?' enquired Linda.

'Yes, maybe. Just as well. You've finished, Father?' checked Sister Sheila.

Father McCormac looked directly at Frankie and Linda. 'I believe there were letters delivered by parents this morning. We have copies. Now that you both know how to prepare the children for the sacrament of the Eucharist, I will communicate with the parents in my parish.'

Once outside the door Linda patted Frankie's back. 'Congrats! You put your head on the block... but what now?'

'Well at least now we know where we stand. The responsibility is out of our hands and into theirs. We'll have to tell the parents to ask Father McCormac. Besides it's so close to the First Communion Day that I can't see how we can change anything for this year, can you, Linda?'

23

IN THE FRAY

Frankie was opening her locker in the staffroom. It was nearly seven-thirty.

'You've arrived at school before me this morning, Linda.'

'Couldn't sleep, Frankie. Had to get here to find out if anything else had happened about the First Communion Mass.'

'Any more letters?'

'Yes! This letter was slipped into my class register, I checked yours. You've got the same letter.'

'Let me see.'

PLEASE REFER any parent or guardian, who approaches you concerning the First Communion Mass, to either Father McCormac or Sister Sheila. We have answered all the correspondence we have received. Any further query should be put it in writing or' phone 01022370 for an appointment.

Signed: Rev Fr M McCormac

Sister Sheila McGleen

'THIS IS HOTTING UP, LINDA.'

'I wonder if more parents will waylay us today.'

'Peep through this window to see if any of them have arrived in the playground.'

'That's Mrs Starkey standing by the gate. Is the woman wearing the blue anorak, Mary O'Driscoll?'

'Yes. Seems they're the ringleaders.'

'They are not going to let this matter drop, Frankie.'

'Let's see if there are any more letters are given to us when we go out to collect our classes.'

The bell rang. On their way to the playground as Linda passed Frankie, Linda whispered, 'Look at the group clustered at the end of the playground.'

'I wonder if they have spoken to Sr Sheila.'

Frankie led her class into their classroom. They began their lessons. She felt glad that unlike the previous day, the first hour and half passed peacefully.

Break-time. She pulled on her coat, grabbed her umbrella.

April showers can be such a nuisance when I am on playground duty, Frankie thought. One minute the sun shines; the next I end up shepherding the children into the hall to prevent them from getting drenched. Thank God, we escaped that big blast from the heavens twenty minutes ago.

As soon as Frankie arrived in the playground, twins from her class ran up to clasp her by the hand.

'It will be our birthday soon, Miss Danivet.'

'Then you'll be seven, Andy and Amanda. What's it like when twins celebrate their birthday?'

'We're having a party. Mum says we can each bring six friends to our house.'

'We mostly play with each other. Who should we invite, Miss?'

'You're twins! You're lucky. You always have each other to play with. But I've watched you play with other children.'

'We do, Miss. Jamie makes me laugh.'

'My best friend is Fiona. She's bringing me a present.'

'Amanda gets girlie things... uck! Mine are much better... proper football. I'm going to play for Chelsea one day.'

'Sounds like you each will get what you like.'

'Miss, have you seen the DVD about the *Da Vinci Code*? My Mum and Dad were watching it again last night.'

'Why was that, Andy?'

'It was after Father McCormac phoned them about my First Communion. My dad said there is something in it about… He said it is to do with the *The Last Supper*. That was the first Mass, wasn't it, Miss?'

'There's a book too, isn't there?'

'Is there, Amanda?'

'Our Mum read it 'cause she's in a book club. She's says it's weird,' added Amanda.

'You'd know that DVD? Well, in it, one of the men hits himself. His back is bloody. I've seen it with my own eyes.'

'People might have done things like that long ago. Don't worry. It doesn't happen any more.'

I must speak to Sr Sheila about this, decided Frankie. The children should not be associating their First Holy Communion with the Opus Dei portrayal of flagellation that is printed in the Dan Brown's book *Da Vinci Code*.

Frankie noticed that Richard had come out into the playground and taken the bell from that stand where it was kept.

Why, I wonder is Richard ringing the bell to bring playtime to a close? That's the responsibility of the person on playground duty. Today it's my turn. I should be ringing the bell.

'Line up, children. Dermot and Laura, lead class 2 into your classroom,' ordered Richard.

It's misty. It's not actually raining. Break has been cut short by five minutes. Richard has not acknowledged my presence. Perhaps Sr Sheila has sent him out. His voice was hard and husky. His amber eyes look angry. His brown hair has a fiery red glint. He has changed his soft tweeds for dark, navy blue trousers. I hate to see him like this. He seems to be acting like a robot. I'll have to find an opportunity to talk to him.

24

FIRST COMMUNION DAY

On a cold Sunday morning in April, Frankie arrived early for the First Communion Mass. As she stepped from daylight into the darkness of the Norman-arched entrance to St Francis Church, Putney, she looked around for Sr Sheila. She noticed her in the Lady Chapel praying the Divine Office. Sister turned and beckoned Frankie over.

Frankie crossed between the benches.

'God Bless you, Frankie I'm glad you have come early.'

'I wanted to help, Sister.'

'I think it only fair to tell you that I'm not at all happy with today's arrangements that have been made for the celebration of this First Communion Mass. No doubt you'll have surmised that.'

'Sister, I suppose nothing can be done to change either the readings for scripture or the music at this stage.'

'No, dear. We can only do our best. Oh! Linda has arrived.'

When Frankie turned round, she saw Linda at the back of the church, near the holy water font, surrounded by a group of First Communicants and their relatives.

'I want you to know, Frankie, that I have done as much as I can to change the readings and bidding prayers to the ones that you prepared. I expect that you may contrast this service with the action-filled participation First Communion Mass that your nuns were in charge of last year. The sad thing is that Richard… Oh there's Siobhan O'Gorman arriving with her twins. I'll go to help her. Don't lose courage… you're doing a fine job.'

What does Sr Sheila expect will happen today?

Sister Sheila patted Frankie's wrist before moving swiftly across the aisle to adjust little Ciara's long white veil.

'Phew! Its twenty-five past nine, Frankie. So many people! It's like the League of Nations! Some of the children are dressed in such vibrant colours.'

'In past years the parents used to dress their children in white. Girls sometimes looked like brides. All dolled-up in long white dresses. I'm glad the African and Caribbean children are wearing their bright colours.'

'They're noisy, though. Such a lot of talking, hand-shaking and hugging.'

'Quite a commotion.'

'Not for long, Linda! Here comes Richard and Anna!'

'She's dressed in purple! Penitential colour.'

Frankie was standing at the back of the church. She turned to witness Anna and Richard walking down the aisle together.

'They've arrived when all the work is done, Frankie. Look! She's tottering on high-heeled boots.'

Frankie pondered. *Richard is not smiling. Why did he have to walk down the aisle with Anna? I dreamt that one day he would be waiting for me at the altar. In my dreams we're were smiling, we're happy. We spent such a lovely time together in that café in Battersea.*

While Anna arranged her music on the organ stand, Richard turned to face the congregation.

Four stern, military-looking African men, dressed in black soutanes and white starched cotters, took up their places, standing on either side of Richard. Silence.

These men presumably are from Opus Dei, thought Frankie.

Richard addressed the congregation, 'Good morning. It is nearly time for Mass to begin. Please take your positions. Miss Danivet will be seated half-way up the pulpit side of the church. Yes.' Richard pointed his finger at Frankie indicating the position that she was to take.

'Two rows further forward. Thank you.'

'Mrs Lyons, will sit opposite at the other side.' Richard pointed Linda to her place.

'Mr Yatumbi will sit at the right back and Mr Arabi on the other side.'

'What's happening, Frankie? We are being regimented? Richard is treating us like soldiers.'

'I can't believe that Richard is behaving in such a stern manner, Linda. Look. Sr Sheila is smiling back at us. I don't suppose that she agrees with this approach either. Obviously she trying to indicate that she is on our side.'

Frankie wanted to shout out, *I won't be bossed about!* She wanted to tell Richard to let everyone know that he does not really want to behave like this.

This is not the kind man I love. Surely he is obeying orders from Opus Dei members. Instead she looked up and welcomed the first rays of sunlight streaming through the rose window. She wished that this kaleidoscope of colours will suck Anna out and away into the sky to disappear forever.

'For the sake of the children, Linda...'

'Yes, let's pretend we're happy. Go through the motions. After all, it's the children's special day.'

'Our roles are diminished. Anna's playing the traddie hymns, Richard is conducting. Sr Sheila will lead the first row of children up to the altar to receive Holy Communion and the Opus Dei men will lead them back to their places.'

'We've prepared them, Frankie. They're in our classes. I'm cross.'

'Their parents are here. Let's see how they react to this, Linda.'

After Mass Sr Sheila spoke to Frankie and Linda, 'Thank you both, Frankie and Linda. Mr Yatumbi asked me to thank you too. He insisted that there is no need for you both to stay for the First

Communion breakfast. Maybe it's better that you leave it all to his committee.'

'Really, Sister?'

Sr Sheila, standing behind Richard, put her finger over her lips.

When Frankie noticed her compliance, she nudged Linda. They nodded and turned to leave the church.

'You look mesmerised, Frankie.'

'They want to make sure there won't be confrontation. Look over there, Linda? What's Mrs Stalkey saying to Father McCormac? She's waving her hands about. I heard her tell Eamonn to wait for her by her car.'

'Come on, Frankie. I'm driving you home. Let's get away from here.'

'Yes, Let's. Maybe the parents will have their say. I can't believe that I have witnessed Opus Dei being so dominant.'

The First Communion is over now, thought Frankie. *There is no need for Anna to return to our school. I hope she will go back to where she has come from. Disappear. Sr Sheila intimated that the Opus Dei group appear to have taken control of this First Communion Celebration.*

25

UNDERSTANDING

The coach arrived at the swimming baths with two classes.

'Shall I go with the boys today, Frankie? Mr Canto is leading them into the changing room.'

'Thank you, Cathy. Sharon went last time.'

'Come on, girls. The boys are always changed and lined up ready to start their lessons before you.'

'Bet they chuck their clothes into their lockers, Miss.'

'Maybe they do less talking, Maeve.'

When the children were handed over to the swimming instructor Frankie resolved to talk to Richard. She noticed that Richard was not watching the children. He was sitting on a bench near the pool. His elbows were resting on his thighs. He was gazing into the distance. He didn't notice Frankie approaching.

'Oh Fra... what is it?'

'Richard, we need to talk. You seem to have changed. Since the First Communion... I'm not... I don't know... What's happening to you?'

'About?'

'Can we talk about the First Communion Mass? The parents.'

Richard turned. He sat bolt upright. He was not looking at her. He cleared his throat. 'I hold the post for Religious Education in this school. It is my responsibility to ensure that the First Communicants were prepared—'

'You know that I have prepared children for this sacrament for years.'

Richard looked at her.

Frankie found herself stuttering. 'Do you remember… that night… you were so encouraging when I was going to be interviewed for my teaching job? You were so kind.'

'I… Father McCormac and the Bishop… I also have to obey…'

His voice seems shaky. Better not mention Anna, Frankie thought.

'Opus Dei? Richard, why did you follow their instructions for First Communion Mass?'

'Opus Dei. You should know, Frankie. Solid doctrinal values founded on tradition and years of sound Catholic teaching versus sentimental-driven notions based on vacuous trash that is an apology for Catholic teachings. The watering-down of Catholic doctrinal teaching.'

Richard's face flushed.

'Is that's what Fr McCormac and the bishop said?'

'Yes. Opus Dei. The bishop sent Anna to ensure we observed Opus Dei. I prefer tradition… I also…'

Frankie continued, 'Plainsong. Gregorian chant. The Latin Mass. Our superb Catholic heritage. I love these too.'

'Anna, Miss Fuller, regards guitar tinkling as moody sentimentality…'

'Do you, Richard?'

Richard's attention seemed to be attracted by someone behind me.

Oh no! It is Anna walking towards us. What was she doing here? She was not supposed to wear out-door shoes in the swimming pool area. She was almost skipping towards Richard. She must be oblivious to all the complaints that we have received from the parents.

'Sr Sheila said I'd catch up with you here, Ricci!'

She's ignoring me. Why did she have to turn up when I felt I could approach Richard again? I won't give her the satisfaction of acknowledging her presence.

'See you later, Richard. Maybe we could have coffee together. I'd better go to collect my class as they finish their swimming lesson.'

'GOOD PROGRESS, children. Iffey swam exceptionally. You all swam well.'

'Thank you, Mrs Hughes.'

'Climb out of the pool immediately, children. No pushing on the way to the showers.'

Sr Sheila has arrived. Why has Sister Sheila come?

'Shall I look after the boys, Miss Danivet? I see that Mr Canto is busy.'

'Yes. Thank you, Sister.'

'These children benefit so much from swimming, don't they Miss Danivet?'

'They do indeed, Sister. The exercise does them good. It is good for the ones who are more academically gifted to see that other children succeed in these sporting activities.'

'We all have our different talents, Frankie.'

'I hope you did not mind me taking the opportunity to speak to Mr Canto, Sister Sheila. I was not shirking my responsibility of looking for class. When Mrs Prince offered to accompany them to their swimming teacher, I wanted to discuss matters with Richard.'

'No. I'm sure you are both aware of your duties. I came here so that you and I could discuss some matters as we travel back to school.'

'Thank you, Sister.'

'Sorry… Excuse me, Miss Danivet but… Michael, your vest is back to front.'

'Yes, Frankie, we'll sit together on the coach as we journey back to school.'

Why is Sister Sheila winking?

'Sit next to me, Frankie. The children have lost and found all their belongings. We are counted and checked, ready to depart. Mr Canto is up with the coach driver and Mrs Prince is looking after those at the other end of the coach. We can chat in peace.'

'Sister, I'm wondering if...'

'I have good news... no need to look worried.'

Frankie and Sister Sheila clamoured into the first two seats.

'First, I want to tell you that I had the good fortune of being on retreat over Easter with some of the Sisters from your convent. All of the Sisters, without exception, were singing your praises. They said that they supposed you would be in your element again organising the First Communion classes.'

'Oh Sister, did they really? Was it Sister Dympna and Sister Colleen?'

'Yes.'

'I treasure fond memories of us helping the children to mime the readings and the hymns.'

'Children really come to understand the Gospel better through that process.'

'We were fortunate in working with a parish priest, Father Pat, who trusted us. He was as keen as we were to substitute appropriate liturgies for the each age group. He agreed with us that young children's attention span is very short. The parents were happy when they realised that their children learnt more by being fully engrossed in the movement and dancing.'

'Yes, Frankie, children also need to speak to God in their own words. They need to use familiar vocabulary in order to talk to God, Our heavenly Father, in words that they understand. That's prayer after all, isn't it?'

'But Sister, Father McCormac stated otherwise for our parish First Communion Mass.'

'Frankie, I'm not at liberty to reveal... My lips are still somewhat sealed. Try not to let anger rear up inside you. It is counter-productive... leads to disease... Disease. Besides, you'll see eventually. Have patience.'

'Sister, do you mind me guessing what really happened over the First Communion Mass?'

'Not at all. Tell me what you have surmised.'

'Neither you or Father McCormac really agreed with the interpretation of the liturgy that Bishop David enforced for our First Communion?'

'You're nodding, Sister. So it was an Opus Dei take-over?'

'Suffice it to say that eventually things had to be smoothed over and compromises, let's say agreements, were made. You will appreciate that due to confidentiality, I'm not able to disclose much more.'

'The parents, Sr Sheila?'

'The parents were placated. The good news is that on the feast of Corpus Christi we will celebrate another Communion Mass. This time it will be celebrated in the way we had planned to have it before the Opus Dei group took over.'

Frankie wanted to hug Sister Sheila. 'Oh Sister! That's wonderful. Does Richard know about this?'

'He will soon. I wanted you to know first, Frankie. You must have been wondering why Richard has been behaving differently. Linda, of course, will be told too.'

'Richard. Yes, he certainly has. Linda will be delighted. Sister, this is such good news.'

'There is much more to explain but I'm restricted… you understand. As for Richard and Anna, if I were you, I'd go easy on him. Things are not always as they seem.'

Frankie felt guilty about the way she had judged Richard. He had been kind to her before Anna arrived.

She reflected, *Surely he was not just being a supportive member of staff by showing kindness and consideration towards me as I settled in. Could I have misread the signs? After all, I know so little about relating to people? Oh no… I can feel hot tears trickling down my face.*

Frankie reached for her handkerchief.

'What's the matter, Frankie? Here, take one of these tissues. You're tired.'

'No, Sister, I have a confession to make. In the light of what you have said, I feel that I should tell you about what happened while Richard and I were on the school trip in Hastings…'

'I know all about that, Frankie. Richard, well… suffice to say that you and Linda had prepared this trip. I also noticed that Richard had begun addressing you by your surname. No need to mention it again, Frankie.'

Sister understands. How fortunate, thought Frankie.

Sister leant over and gently rested her hand on Frankie's.

Frankie realised that whatever Richard recounted must have helped Sr Sheila to look favourably on her reaction.

Sr Sheila cleared her voice. 'Frankie, have you ever noticed that when you are angry or upset, everybody you meet appears to be in the same mood? It works the other way round too. When I smile, I discover that I have so many happy friends.'

'So true, Sister.'

'You're still young. You'll learn. Get together with Linda to prepare the liturgy for our Mass on the feast of Corpus Christi. The good Lord takes care of each of us.'

Frankie thought, *I wonder how Richard will react to this news. Surely Anna will go away now?*

26

A BETTER APPROACH

'The school hall is transformed, Sr Sheila!'

'Aren't the roses a lovely shade of red? Mrs Starkey managed to persuade the florist to donate the ones in vases on the two stands behind the altar, to our school."

'Is that the florist on the corner of this road, Sister?'

'Yes. Sr Carmel begged for the beautiful pink roses at Covent Garden market. They gave her those Irish Fire-flame roses in front of the window. See, they're a shade of orange with crimson veining. The strong, fruity fragrance that's pervading the hall comes from them.'

'You've got so many flower displays, Sister! I love the tall red and white gladioli around the hall.'

'The parents will be delighted when they arrive for the celebration of Mass today. Warm sunshine is streaming in through those windows radiating light on the beautiful posters and Eucharistic banners. The children's art work looks attractive displayed on the walls.'

'Mrs Starkey is helping Linda to arrange the Arum lilies in front of the scarlet roses around the altar.'

'Oh! Arum lilies remind me of the ones my Granny gave me for my First Communion.'

'I carried a bunch of those lilies on my First Communion day, too, Frankie. That was the custom.'

'Mrs Starkey must be glad that her daughter, Sara, along with all the other First Communicants, will lead the singing and the prayers on this feast of Corpus Christi.'

'Oh you're here, Frankie.'

'Yes, Linda. Everything looks fine. Who put out all the chairs?'

'The parents. A whole gang of them. They were so grateful to you, Sr Sheila, for allowing the children to have this celebration of their First Communion.'

Frankie thought of her first Communion day. Her mind flashed back to the other time she had worn a white dress. That was on her profession day when she discovered that the white dress she was given to wear, had been worn by other novices and stored in the convent wardrobe for many years. Hopefully one day, she thought, I'll wear a beautiful white wedding dress.

'Here we are, Sister. Where do you want me to put these tea roses that Mrs O'Connor brought?'

'Ask her if she would like us to use them to be strewn on the floor when the Blessed Sacrament is carried in?'

'She heard you, Sister. She's nodding.'

'Sister, do you mind me asking. Is Fr McCormac saying Mass today?'

'Not at all. I thought I told everyone. A missionary priest, Fr Sean Foley, has been asked to replace Fr McCormac because he and Mr Canto are taking part in an ecumenical course run by the Inner London County Council.'

Frankie felt very grateful. This Mass hopefully will be such a contrast to the one organised my Opus Dei.

'I wondered when I listened to Sara practising the first reading for Mass. You changed the wording, didn't you, Miss Danivet?'

'Yes, Mrs Starkey…'

'Call me, Maureen. Maureen to you.'

'Of course, Maureen. Scripture makes much more sense to that age group when it is taken from the 'Good News' version of the Bible.'

'Frankie, here comes Mrs O'Driscoll', whispered Linda.

'So the two ringleaders are helpers now, Linda!'

'Welcome, Mrs... Mary.'

'Morning, Sister. Morning, everybody! I meant to come earlier but I had to make sure my two ate their breakfast. They're so excited to be dressing up for this celebration of their First Communion.'

'Is it alright if Linda and I go to sort out the music, Sister?'

'Certainly, Frankie. Maybe you should call the children in from the playground who are doing the readings and bidding prayers. Give them a last run-through? Makes them feel confident.'

'Come on, Linda. Great to know that neither Fr McCormac nor Richard will be here today. I don't know how Sr Sheila managed to arrange that! Was it coincidence or clever manipulation?'

'Oh good. The children love to sing hymns that they understand, Linda. I watched them when you were conducting them yesterday. They looked so happy... engaged... totally involved. That Peruvian Gloria has such a swing in it.'

'Aoifa, when she shakes the tambourine and Iffey, on the drums, could wake up the jungle!'

'Any guesses what this new priest will be like, Frankie? I hope he has a brilliant smile and is a good conversationalist.'

Frankie wondered, *Did Richard ask to be on a course or did Sister Sheila arrange that? I wish I could find out if he feels pressurised into obeying Opus Dei.*

'Look all the people are gathering in the playground. I think Sr Sheila is calling in those children dressed in their First Communion clothes. We'd better be quick. Mass will begin soon.'

Sr Sheila stood in front of the altar facing the congregation.

'Children, before the priest begins Mass, I want to make sure that each of you is fully aware of what is taking place in our assembly hall on this very special day. Who can remind us what *Corpus Christi* means?'

'Yes, David. You have your hand up. What do those Latin words mean?'

'The body of Christ, Sister.'

'Excellent, David. At the Last Supper, Jesus knew that he was going to die the following day. Good Friday. He gave his Apostles the power to change his body and blood into bread and wine. Those of you who will receive the bread and wine today will be welcoming Jesus into yourself.'

Sr Sheila nodded to Frankie to play the introduction to the hymn, *Rejoice in the Lord Always*. Frankie was standing facing the congregation of parents, pupils and staff and strumming the chords G and F on her guitar. When the hymn was finished, she heard an Irish voice intone the prayer that commences Mass. 'In the name of the Father…'

She turned round.

That priest is from Kerry! I'd know the lilt in that accent anywhere. I should have guessed when Sister said that his name is Sean Foley. He looks handsome. Lovely smile, twinkle in his ocean blue eyes. Not that tall. Slim. Looks fit.

Frankie found herself looking closely at Sean. He's Irish. Gorgeous. Maybe Richard isn't the only fish in the sea. He's a priest… but I was a nun.

'Wasn't that a lovely, lively opening song to a very special Mass, children? You sang with all your heart and souls. Great accompaniment on the guitar and the other instruments. Well done! Come on, parents. Your children deserve a clap.'

Linda leaned over to Frankie to say, 'He's good, Frankie! So different from Fr McCormac.'

'Linda, I am no longer worried. If the children forget what we have rehearsed, it won't matter. This priest seems to understand us.'

'We can relax and enjoy the Mass. Everyone seems to be happy. Look at Mrs Starkey leading the readers up to the lectern. She has such a bright smile.'

Frankie found her eyes veer towards Fr Sean.

I like this man. He is at ease with himself. He puts everyone else at ease too. I wonder what he will say when he gives his sermon.

Fr Sean stood in front of the altar. He smiled as he rubbed his hands together and rested his chin on them.

'When I was small I used to get bored when grown-ups told me what to do. I hated it when my Dad would wave his finger at me and say, 'When I was your age…' so I'm not going to tell you what to do. What do you think of that, children?'

'Is it because we know what to do, Father?' a small voice shouted out.

'You've got clever children in this school, Sr Sheila. Well done, lad. You've got a little voice inside you telling you how to behave. Your conscience.'

This is great. Fr Foley has moved nearer to the children. He's asking them questions, telling them jokes. The parents are answering too. Everyone is responding to his engaging approach.

'Oh Frankie… he's very engaging, isn't he?'

'This is the final hymn, Linda.'

'*Happiness, Happiness, the greatest gift I've received…* How appropriate! The children are all in place with their instruments. Father Sean is nodding and grinning.'

After Mass, Frankie put her guitar into its case. She hoped that she would get a chance to speak to Fr Sean. She was delighted when he came up behind her and tapped her on the shoulder. She turned.

'Sr Sheila tells me that your name is Frankie. You hail from the Kingdom of Kerry, too. Small world, eh!'

'Sure, what would they do without us, Father? Yes, I'm Frankie from Kerry. I'm over here a good few years now. Do you live here in England?'

'Only here temporarily. Passing through from Kenya.'

That's where Margaret was. I wonder if they met? Big place though. I won't tell him that I was a nun. Not now.

'It must be hard work on the Missions, Father.'

'It's a privilege to work with such lovely people. Every now and then I need to re-fuel. At present I'm helping out at The Causeway Therapeutic Centre.'

So many coincidences! I like him. I have not been back for therapy for over a month. Maybe, I should go for another session. I wonder if he is a psychotherapist?

27

CONFUSED

'Morning, Paula. Have you time to chat?'

Frankie had planned this carefully.

'Sorry, not now, Frankie. Can you wait until after school? I've come in early to complete the ordering of stock for next year. I'm up to my eyes. Look at all the catalogues cluttering up my desk.'

'After school. Of course. As soon as the others arrive, you'll have to deal with the registers and all the usual demands too. No, that's fine.'

'Maybe, I need to be more efficient.'

'You're doing a grand job. Thought I'd catch you early. I should have realised you'd be busy.'

'Did you sign Richard's birthday card?'

'That's what I want to talk to you about, Paula.'

'Thought you might. Let's have a coffee in Dolce Vita near Putney Bridge.'

'Great. Thanks, Paula.'

I spent hours after school yesterday searching for a suitable birthday card for Richard. I looked in all the card shops in Putney and Wimbledon trying to find for an appropriate one. In the end, I bought two cards. I hope Paula will help me tease out the message that I really want to convey to him.

'Whoops! That was a near miss.'

'Oh Richard! Should have been looking where I was going. Sorry.'

'No need. Enjoy your day, Frankie.'

Wow! We nearly embraced. Lovely to feel his arm touch mine, even if it was accidentally. Gorgeously happy smile, too. Maybe I should give him the romantic birthday card?

As Frankie was about to open her classroom door, Linda popped her head out of hers.

'Psst! Do you have a minute?'

'Of course.'

'You missed the discussion in the staffroom yesterday after school.'

'What was it about? Paula's Paddy had a doctors appointment. She was giving me a lift. We had to rush off.'

'Sr Sheila came in as a group of us were heading home. She wanted to know what we thought about getting cakes for Richard's birthday.'

'Isn't it the person whose birthday it is that is supposed to supply the cakes?'

'Remember last year? It was the same the year before? Richard isn't mean. But he never brings cakes on his birthday. Does he like cakes? Maybe he would prefer not to draw attention to himself. Perhaps he's not keen on growing older!'

'You're probably right. He's not shy but seems to shun the limelight.'

'Sr Sheila suggested that after all his dealings with Anna, he deserves a cake.'

'Good idea. Let bygones be bygones. Hope that Anna never puts a foot in this school again. Are we clubbing together? How much?'

'Yes. Three pounds each. I volunteered to get the cake. Frankie, does he like cake?'

'Yes! I know he likes apple tart. He always chooses apple tart and custard whenever it's on offer at school dinners.'

'Good. That's sorted.'

'I'll pay you now. Thanks, Linda.'

I'm longing to talk to Paula. I don't know how much to divulge to her about my feelings for Richard.

Paula was waiting for Frankie in her car at the end of the day.

'Jump in, Frankie. I need a strong coffee. I'm sure you do, too.'

'Thanks Paula. Did you finish the ordering?'

'Sr Sheila came to the rescue. It's all in the post, thank goodness.'

Paula managed to find a parking space in Dolce Vita's car park.

'We're in luck. Why don't you grab that table in the cosy nook over there?'

'You grab it, Paula. I'll order. This is my treat. No use looking like that. I insist.'

'You're very authoritative! Real school mam!'

'Good! Now do as you're told... before you do... is it a latte? Do you like tiramisu?'

'Love it!'

'Thank you, Frankie. Two shots of caffeine, please. The combination of Italian coffee and tiramisu is heavenly.'

'Signorine! You're welcome. Please sit. I'll come. What can I get you?'

'Grazie. Due caffe and tiramisu for two, per favore.'

'Very impressed with your Italian. I love this little nook. Thank you, Frankie.'

'You deserve this. You have worked so hard these last few days, Paula.'

'You wanted to talk about Richard? Tell me what's happening, Frankie. I saw him almost embrace you when you bumped into him this morning. You were both smiling at each other.'

'Felix culpa! Accidents can sometimes be good!'

'Here comes our order.'

'Ecco! Enjoy.'

'Paula, I know it might sound trivial but I want to give Richard a birthday card. I found it very difficult to choose one that says what I really want to say.'

'I'm not surprised. How many years have I been married to Paddy? I still spend a long time selecting one for him. Besides, typical cards for men show them in the garden or playing football or golf. Many about drinks or with cars in them. I usually end up choosing one with yet another car on it.'

'Yes I suppose…'

'But choosing a card for Richard is different. What did you want to say to him, Frankie? I saw him winking at you the other day.'

'If only I knew, Paula. That's the problem. Here. I'll show you the two cards that I bought. See this one is… well…'

'Brush strokes. Impressionistic. Twirls of yellow and dark grey. Elongated slim couple. Him and her, blending into each other on the beach. Looking out into the sunrise. So romantic. Captures the momentary and transient. I know that Richard will love that.'

'But is it too romantic… to explicitly romantic?'

'You love Richard, don't you Frankie? Why don't you want to tell him? What message do you want to give him? What's the other one like?'

'This one. Another impressionistic one. I love Claude Monet. *Le Pont Japonaise a Giverny*.'

'That's lovely, too. A beautiful sunset scene. Peaceful, flowing river and the bridge…… What made you choose this one?'

'I feel so embarrassed, Paula. I want to tell you… I will. When I saw this card I remembered a lovely evening when Richard and I really talked to each other. We told each other what we felt… longings for happiness, love… dreams… fulfilment..'

'You're blushing. Do you want to tell me more?'

'I think I'll ask for a glass of water. I'll signal to the waiter.'

'Do. There's no need to tell me more than you want to. I understand.'

'Thank you.'

'Richard and I have a lot in common. We both spent time in religious life. Anna came between us. She seemed to have had a hold on Richard. Now he seems back to his old self now. The bridge… I wanted the bridge to be symbolic. To show that we can meet each other half way…'

'Perfect.'

'I was wondering if I should write this poem by Henry Longfellow inside. It's the one entitled, *The Bridge... And far in the hazy distance... Of that lovely night in June...*'

'Delightful poem. Meaningful. The poem goes with that card. Did the green envelope come with it?'

'No. I had to ask the shop assistant if it was alright to swop that envelope. I know Richard loves the colour green. I wanted to shoot out of the shop when that assistant asked if I wanted any further help.'

'Why?'

'I don't know. I felt that I was revealing too much. I wanted to get a card that would match Richard's personality. As well as the picture being right, the paper quality and colour, the wording or lack of it, even down to the envelope... everything had to be right.'

'This card means a lot to you, Frankie, doesn't it? How do you see Richard's personality? You don't have to answer if you'd prefer not to.'

Frankie took another sip of water. 'Okay. Richard is a strong man. He is his own man. He's strong and determined, discreet, principled. A man of character. Tall, handsome, has a good dress sense and those amber eyes... That's what I admire about him.'

'He is not swayed by fashion or trends?'

'No. Tweeds and good leather shoes. No gaudy ties. He's not Irish but I like to think that my father wore tweed, tailored suits too. Not all the time, but when he dressed up.'

'You love Richard, Frankie. He's the man for you. You've come alive enumerating his qualities. I bet you enjoyed him brushing up against you this morning. Was it really an accident? There's colour in those cheeks of yours.'

'Oh Paula!'

'Are you going to give him a present?'

'You've guessed my other dilemma. Should I? Would that be too much?'

'Not for someone you love. What sort of present were you thinking about? A tie?'

'A really good pen, perhaps? I did think of purchasing a voucher for a meal for two. That was when I wanted to see if he would take me out or if he was still in contact with that dreaded Anna.'

'I doubt if he'll be in touch with her again. Has he ever given you a present? Did he give you one on your birthday? 24th May, isn't it?'

'On the staff card he wrote, 'May all your dreams come true, Frankie. Richard xx'

'Why do you doubt his intentions, Frankie? Those wishes are promising.'

'He's always paid the bill on the two occasions that we've eaten out but he's not given me a present as such. I'm not worried about the expense. I want to give him a present but I don't want to embarrass him.'

'Maybe something small but significant would be good.'

'That's why I thought I'd buy a really good quality pen. A Parker. When he holds it in his hand he might think of me. If he carries it round in his jacket, I could be close to his heart!'

'You're smiling. A pen it is and the card with the bridge it is then.'

'Thank you so much, Paula.'

'We've not finished yet. Have you decided what to write on the card that the staff are giving him?'

'I nearly forgot about that. Everybody will be able to read whatever I write. What sort of words do folk normally write?'

'Enjoy your special day. xx Lots of love and wishes .xx Have a wonderful day. Shame you had to come to school today. xx Some people will just sign their name. Sr Sheila is bound to mention prayers or something holy. I usually put Congratulations! Enjoy! And sign it.'

'I would like to put 'Love galore!' But that would really mean exposing my feelings. Some of the staff might think I'm presumptuous or naïve. Maybe that would be too bold.'

'Frankie, how much proof do you want? He's been opening doors for you. Mind you, he's polite to everyone. I saw him wave to you through your classroom door, window. But I do understand.'

'I think I'll put 'Wishes galore' from the Irish Gu leoir!'

'And two kisses? Almost everyone else put two kisses. You must have given birthday cards to each other in the convent.'

'Not when I was there. Maybe they do now? We did not celebrate out birthdays. We celebrated our patron saint's day instead. I loved mine. Everyone loves Francis of Assisi. We were given a holy picture on our feast day. Sr Superior would write something pious on it.'

'I can't imagine not keeping my birthday. Birthdays are so important.'

'I agree. You'll never believe what I did?'

'Come on. Tell me. You're laughing.'

'I found some old birthday cards in a box at school. I did a cut-and-paste-job on them. I made envelopes. I wrote birthday wishes from Mother General, the Pope and Sr Superior pretending that they sent them to me. I addressed the envelope to myself and posted them through the convent letter box. When the Sr Superior opened the letter box she found cards addressed to me! All our post was opened. She must have read them.'

'You're a rebel, Frankie.'

'Just a bit of fun. I displayed the cards on a table at the end of the refectory. The Sisters laughed and Sr Anne, the cook, made an apple tart and put it on the table to share at tea time. Everyone was delighted.'

'Unlike Richard, you crave the lime-light! Did you receive a card on the feast of St Francis?'

'Yes. I did. Saints were important in our lives. We celebrated the feasts every day at Mass. I was sacristan for a time. I learnt all about the various colours of the vestments to be worn on special feast days.'

'I suppose there is a Saint Richard?'

'How strange that you ask that. You must be psychic. I looked up St Richard. Very interesting.'

'I thought you might. Was he called, Richard the Lion Heart?'

'This Richard of Chichester was born in 1197, in the little town of Wyche, eight miles from Worcester.'

'Long ago.'

'He and his elder brother were left as orphans. Richard loved studying but he gave it up to help his brother farm his impoverished estate. His grateful brother wanted him to take over all his lands. He refused both the estate and the offer of a brilliant marriage to study for the priesthood at Oxford.'

'Like our Richard, he also studied for the priesthood.'

'But this Richard perservered. In 1235 he was appointed chancellor of that university. Later St. Edmund of Canterbury appointed him chancellor of his diocese.'

'Noble and generous like our Richard.'

'His age? Three years older than you.'

'Forty-three. He let that slip. We were both sixteen when we entered.'

'What about Richard's star sign? Did you find that out too?'

'Yes! We've both got the same star sign. We're both Gemini! Apparently, those born under the sign of the 'Twins' are thirsty for knowledge and new experiences and sometimes even mischievous.'

'That's you. I don't know about Richard.'

'I'd better drive you home, Frankie. Paddy will wonder where I am.'

As Frankie slipped into bed that night she reflected on what Paula had said about Richard's demonstrations of care for her.

I wish that I could give Richard the present of a meal-for-two. I would take him to the Bellevue Restaurant. Linda told the staff that her husband took her to that French restaurant to celebrate her birthday. She said that they had enjoyed 'Non-intrusive service, a calm atmosphere and the best food that they had eaten in some time.'

I could wear the lovely green dress that I wore to the wedding. I'd need to get my hair cut. If I ordered a taxi, Richard could drink the wine. We could make up for lost time and really enjoy ourselves. Oh wouldn't it be wonderful to get closer, hold hands, kiss and maybe dance afterwards. Who knows what might happen then...?

Frankie fell asleep imagining herself in Richard's arms.

AT SCHOOL the following morning Frankie heard a tap on her classroom door. Linda's head appeared through the door. 'Here you are, Frankie! We're trying to get everyone to sign Richard's birthday card before he arrives.'

Frankie wasn't going to tell Linda that she had her own special card.

'Am I the last one, Linda?'

'Nearly. Come on. We're all in the staffroom. He'll be there any minute.'

When Frankie reached the staffroom, she noticed that Sr Sheila had spread the customary oval shaped table cloth in the centre of the rectangular table.

'Oh good, Frankie. There's a seat here. That's the card and the pen.'

'Thanks, Anne.'

Frankie wondered if Richard would like the picture of a big bottle of champagne on the front of the brownish card. It had 'Happy Birthday' written inside. Frankie scanned over what the others had written. They were as Paula predicted. She wrote *'Wishes galore! Frankie*

Should I put kisses? Everyone else has.

'Quick! I can hear footsteps. That must be him.'

Frankie added xx. Anne grabbed the card.

Richard closed the staffroom door behind him.

The staff shouted out, 'Happy Birthday, Richard!' Sr Sheila handed him his card.

Richard gasped and put his hand over his chest.

'Oh my goodness! It's my birthday. I had forgotten. Big card! Lovely! Thank you. When did you write this?'

His amber eyes opened wide as he began to read the wishes.

Frankie watched him and thought, *He always looks so smart in his tweeds and polished shoes. His chestnut hair seems to have a fleck of gold. He must have had a haircut last night. The beige shirt suits his complexion.*

She wondered when he bought the gold and green tartan wool tie that he was wearing.

He's smiling as he reads each of the comments on his card.

Linda went out of the staffroom and returned carrying a long birthday cake created in the shape of a log with one sturdy lighted candle.

Everyone clapped. Sr Sheila began to sing, 'Happy Birthday to you' Everyone joined in.

Richard kept beating his chest as they sang.

'I'm so sorry. I should have supplied the cake. I forget it was my birthday.'

'That's what we thought! We'll forgive you this time. We're determined to celebrate. Actually we all agreed that you deserve this cake. We appreciate all you do for us and the children, Richard.'

'Thank you, Linda and each of you. I feel so embarrassed.'

'Frankie noticed that you seem to like apples so it's an apple strudel cake.'

'Thank you, Frankie. She's right, Linda. Anything with apples.'

In one breath he blew out the candle and cut the cake. Linda sliced and plated it and handed the plates round.

Frankie controlled her urge to hug Richard when he chose to sit down next to her. Linda handed the first plate to Richard.

'This is for the birthday boy.'

'Ladies first. This one is for Frankie... for remembering that I love apple cakes.'

As he handed Frankie the slice of cake he held onto her hand. He smiled, looked into her eyes, 'Thank you, Frankie.'

His touch is so tender and warming. His eyes are smiling. I don't want to let go of his hand. Frankie whispered to him, 'When you go back to class, look in the bottom left hand drawer of your desk. I've put a little surprise... .'

Frankie wanted to add, I love you, Richard.

'Oh, Frankie... you're too good to me. I...'

Sr Sheila clapped her hands. 'Sorry to halt the celebrations. We're already a little late. The classes have already lined up. Let's cover the cake over and we'll continue to celebrate at break time.'

Drat it! What was Richard about to say? I'm on playground and dinner duty!

Frankie did not manage see Richard until school was over. She was about to go out to Paula's car when Richard grabbed her.

'You deserve a big hug. You're so thoughtful, Frankie. That was a perfect present. A beautiful Parker pen. Here let me show you where I will keep it.'

Richard moved himself a little away from her and pulled open his jacket.

'I'll keep it here in my inside pocket, close to my heart.'

'I love to see that smile, Richard!'

'Come here, let me kiss you!'

Frankie heard the school-keeper rattle his keys. Richard did too. 'Oh… I'd better let you go out to Paula. See you tomorrow.'

Frankie kept eye contact with Richard as she reluctantly turned. She waved. 'Hope you'll carry on celebrating tonight.'

'Was that Richard?'

'Sorry Paula. I don't know what would have happened had the caretaker not arrived.'

'You're beaming. Obviously Richard was pleased with his present.'

'Oh Paula, that was so lovely! Richard is so… so wonderful.'

'You're meant for each other.'

'He loves me. I know he does. I love him…'

'You're not going to say, 'but?'

'Everything would be perfect if… I don't know. How did Anna get a hold on him? I'd love to know. What was it that she triggered off in him? It's weird.'

'What do you mean? Surely you should understand Richard better than anyone else. Anyway why worry about Anna? She's gone. She won't come back.'

'You're right, Paula. Opus Dei, traditional Catholic teaching, bishops and people like Anna can be very persuasive in insisting that we slavishly adhere to every iota of the doctrines.'

'Frankie, I can't believe you're worried about things like that. I don't understand Opus Dei. Fr McCormac and Sr Sheila are good people. You need to forget and forgive. Move on, Frankie.'

'I want to. That's what my counsellor advises.'

'Frankie, are you still going to the Nelson Mandela Centre for counselling?'

'Yes.'

'Talk to them. Surely they can help you.'

'Counselling helps, but I feel that I need to talk to you about some things that are worrying me. Do you mind, Paula?'

'Are you sure? Isn't counselling a private matter? I've never been for counselling, Frankie. If it helps to talk about it, go ahead.'

'In the convent we were engaged in so much analysis and examination of our conscience. When Sr Sheila suggested that I have counselling sessions with Peter O'Kane in the Nelson Mandela Centre, I was reluctant. I'd had enough.'

'Have they helped you to adjust to life outside the convent, Frankie?'

'Yes.'

'You don't sound certain.'

'When Peter began questioning me about my background I felt that he was intruding on memories that I wanted to forget.'

'What sort of questions did he ask?'

'He begun by enquiring about my family. My mother...'

'You've never really told me much about your family, Frankie. All I know you is that you are the middle of three children but...'

'Oh Paula, I thought I told you?'

'I don't think so.'

'Okay. I have a forty-five year old sister, Mary and a twenty-four year old brother, Dom. He has recently returned from Australia.'

'You have a sister and a brother? Are you in contact with them? What about your mother and father?'

'My father died when I was ten years old. My mother lives in Streatham with my sister, her husband, Bob, and their daughter, Ciara. I have a significant Uncle Joe, too. I know very little about him. Mammy seems to keep contact with him.'

'Frankie, you have a family out there. Do you meet them? Do they support you? Paddy and I thought that you were on your own.'

'That's exactly what Peter asked, Paula. That's what I had to face up to. One of his first questions was: Tell me, Frankie, how you relate to your mother?'

'What did you reply?'

'She has many problems of her own. She can just about cope with what life has thrown at her.'

'What about your sister, Mary?'

'I told Peter that Mary was totally taken up with her own family.

Besides she is too old to understand. She is also puzzled why I left the nuns.'

'Do you keep contact with your brother?'

'Each Christmas he used to send a card from Australia. I suppose that it was his wife that encouraged him. But now that he is divorced and back in England, I don't know where he lives.'

'Forgive me, Frankie, but I do not understand why you don't contact your family.'

'That's what Peter said, too. I told him that I need help to sort my life. They need help themselves. They can't help me. It's not just that. Also, for years we have lived very different life. We've grown apart. My mum smokes and enjoys a drink. I don't blame her or my sister. She needs to switch off. That's the style of life my mother lives and my sister does the same now. Going to smoky pubs is their habit. I guess it eased their worries about bringing up kids.'

'And your brother?'

'Dom. Dominic moved to Australia years ago but I didn't ever really know him because he was too young when I went away to the convent.'

'That's sad, Frankie. I suppose many families survive in similar circumstances.'

'It's not really surprising. This is how it is. I told Peter that I am very fortunate in having friends like you, Paula, and your husband, Paddy. Sister Sheila looks out for me, too.'

'You never give the impression that you're weak. Not many people have the courage to leave the convent and begin a new life.'

'I am strong. I am determined. I will cope.'

Paula stretched her hands across the table and caught hold of Frankie's.

'It will do you good to talk. I'm sorry I did not realise.'

'When I met Richard I was drawn to him, Paula. I yearn to be loved for my own sake. I had so many dreams. I have never been loved.'

'You want a child, don't you?'

'I long to have a baby. I wanted it to be our baby. I'll be thirty-nine next birthday. Richard will be forty-two.'

'Have you discussed your relationship with Peter? Oh sorry, maybe I shouldn't ask.'

'Of course I have spoken about Richard in all my recent counselling sessions. In fact, Peter has asked me to keep a diary.'

'That sounds excellent, Frankie. You will be able to tell him all about your struggle to choose the right birthday and present and of course what happened between you today.'

'You'll be late home, Paula. Thank you for taking the time to talk to me.'

'I didn't want to interrupt you. We were almost home. Are you okay?'

'Thank you so much, Paula.'

'I'll drive on and drop you off. So much has happened for you today.'

28

URGENT

My mobile phone? I must find it before it stops ringing? In my bag?

Frankie was walking back to her Wimbledon flat. She knew it was somewhere in her school bag. Hurriedly she moved to the side of the pavement. She rested her bag on the wall. Eventually she pulled the phone from the bottom of her bag. Fortunately, the caller had not rung off. Traffic was whirring past on the busy road. She had to speak loudly.

'Hello. Who?'

'Oh, it's Father Peter. Sorry. I'm so sorry... Okay. Fine. Don't worry I understand... Who? That's fine. Take care.'

She held the phone away from her. Sad that Father Peter has had to go to York. His mother was dying.

Then she thought: *Perhaps I should have said something about sending her my love and sympathy? I don't know her. Somehow I hadn't imagined Fr Peter as having a mother. He said someone was going to contact me? I started the diary that Father Peter asked me to keep. He wanted me to note down how I relate to people. Now he is not going to be there on Saturday.*

Two days later Frankie received a letter:

Dear Frances,

Father Peter has asked me to contact you to see if you would be interested in a few sessions of art therapy while he has been called home to be with his dying mother.

Other people attending the Causeway Group have shown interest in this approach I wondered if you would like to find out more about this healing process.

Barbara Dwyer has agreed to take part in this type of therapy. Maybe you would like to contact her on 077163654300. She has given me permission to pass on her number. Should you wish to contact me, my number is 075932852150

I look forward to hearing from you either way.

Sean Foley

Sean Foley. He was the priest from Kerry who celebrated the Mass at school on the feast of Corpus Christi. *I wanted to meet him again. God works in strange ways! My mobile phone is ringing. Just as well I have it in my hand.*

'Hello Frankie. We met some weeks ago at the Causeway Centre. You may remember me.

I gave you a lift home. I'm Barbara.'

'Oh. I was just about to text you. Father Sean gave me your number.'

'Excellent! He said he would. Was he asking you about art therapy?'

'Yes. I've met…'

'You've met Fr Sean? He's lovely, isn't he? Would you like to know how I heard about him?'

'Yes, please'.

'Margaret. You remember Margaret, the secretary at the Causeway?'

'The woman on the desk?'

'Yes.'

'This is what she said to me: Barbara, would you be interested in supporting a trainee Irish Art therapist?'

'Really? What did you say?'

Margaret didn't give Frankie time to reply. She continued, 'I immediately thought you might be willing to help when Peter told me that he had asked Father Sean to take on some of his clients while he has been called to his mother's bedside. Sean is a qualified artist who has completed art therapy training. This will be his first assignment. You have experience in launching therapist into their careers. What do you think?'

'You agreed?'

'Wait 'til I tell you what I replied to Margaret. Cheeky me, I said: Only if he's drop, down, gorgeous. Is he a priest? Did you say *Father* Sean?'

'He celebrated Mass at our school. He was friendly and good with the children. I was impressed.'

'I have had my first session. I can highly recommend him. I'm so glad that you like him too. All the paints are provided. All you have to do is to turn up. You are assured of his full attention because the sessions are one-to-one. After a week at school it will be relaxing to come here and paint on a Saturday afternoon.'

'Barbara, even if I had not met Sean, you have succeeded in enticing me to become a guinea pig for Father Sean. I'll phone Margaret straight away.'

As Frankie approached the Nelson Mandela Centre on Saturday afternoon, she looked forward to meeting Sean Foley. Margaret asked her to wait until Fr Sean had finished with another client. Suddenly a door opened further along the corridor. She heard a woman's voice, 'Thank you, Sean. I thoroughly enjoyed that session.'

''Tis good of you to say so. Hopefully, this type of therapy will be of help. Goodbye, Joan. God bless you.'

The portly young woman reached the door accompanied by Sean.

He is like a springy sprite with a Kerry accent. A leprechaun! mused Frankie.

After Sean waved the woman off, he walked to where Frankie was seated. Frankie stood. Sean held out his hand. 'Frankie. Lovely to meet you again.'

That's a warm hand shake, Frankie thought. There's devilment in his laughing eyes. I can imagine him leaping to the beat of the bodhran, dancing, weaving, twisting and turning with a smirk on his impish face.

'Thank you, Fr Sean. I'm wondering what art therapy will be like.'

'Ah now, sure you won't know until you have started. Come. Follow me and I'll explain.'

Frankie was delighted, *My heart is beating rapidly. Is it because he is Irish? Has he touched something inside me? He is a priest. I should be safe with Father Sean. Maybe he can lead me to finding the man of my dreams. Hopefully, that will still be Richard. I know so little about men. I still treasure memories of my father. He was a six foot rugby hunk with his tossed curls and Atlantic blue eyes. He, God rest his soul, was an independent thinker and a tolerant observer. I wish he was still around to guide me.*

After her experience at Colour Therapy, Frankie decided it was better not to reveal too much of herself.

Maybe, I can hold back on my choice of colours until I am ready. How am I going to restrain myself? Besides, every single thing I do will reveal something about me to a therapist. He will probably observe the colours I choose, the lines I draw, the way I sit. But I need to feel free. What's the point of going to the sessions if I restrict myself and become self-conscious? Isn't that what I got used to doing in the convent?

Fr Sean held the door open. 'Here we are now, Frankie. Sit yourself down there. Don't mind me. The idea is that you unleash yourself on the paper. Let the paint flow. Take it away.'

Frankie thought, I love Sean's lilting Kerry accent.

'Do I get any guidance? Is there a topic?'

'No. No rules or suggestions. It's all yours. There are no rights or wrongs. Do you have a recurring dream, Frankie? Some people do.

Why don't you just let the brush, the pencil, whatever, take you where it will. Choose whether to fill the paper or just draw a picture.

As long as you make some attempt, that's fine. There's glue there as well and bits of cloth. You must be used to collage if you teach seven year olds. Be seven again. Go ahead. Free as a bird, that's you. Off you go. Pretend I'm not here. Okay?'

'Such encouragement. I have no picture in my head. I'll do as you say.'

Frankie reflected, *I did not consciously select any particular colour. Green was the nearest.*

She painted hills. But ten minutes later a big black bull was raging out of her page leaving a trail of gored cows flattened behind him. She mixed glue with red paint for his eye, she felt Sean's knee brushing against her lower back. She turned to look at him. He looked at her. He winked. He smiled. He pursed his lips and tapped his chin.

She heard herself saying, 'Oh my Go… It's so obvious… males… men… sexuality… oh!'

'Is that what have here, Frankie? You realise that only you can interpret your painting?'

'I know that. When I am looking at the children paintings I always say 'Tell me about it.''

'Tell me about yours, Frankie? Tell me, has there been a roaring bull in your life recently? Were you one of the cows?'

What should I tell Sean? Is Richard the bull in my picture? Do I feel that I have been bullied? Surely not. Richard has been kind and loving. Is it men in general? What am I going to say? I don't know Sean yet. Father Peter is my counsellor. Tears! What a give away. If only I could squeeze them back into my eyes.

'Sorry, Sean. I don't know what…'

Frankie heard Sean drawn up a stool behind her. His arm pressed into her shoulder. His head bent close to hers. He pulled a hankie from his trouser pocket and handed it to her.

'Let your feelings come out.'

Frankie felt her whole body go into a kind of tremor. Her spine was tingling.

I feel weak. I want to be held. To be cuddled.

Frankie lent back into Sean's arms. He cradled her.

This feels so good.

There are footsteps in the corridor.

Sean pushed her back into sitting position.

'Tell me more about this painting, Frankie?'

Margaret called out through the opened door, 'Can you lock up when you go, Sean? I have to run. My husband is waiting in the car.'

Sean answered, 'Certainly, Margaret.'

'Frankie, perhaps you are not ready to reveal anymore today. Your painting is still wet. Would you like me to keep it safe for you?'

'Only if you can hide it away in a corner so that others cannot see it, Sean.'

'It will be safe with me. Don't worry about the paints. Let them dry.'

'I'll rinse the brushes.'

'Frankie, you have done enough for today.'

He opened his arms and hugged Frankie.

She felt that she could barely walk. The stubble, the closeness of his skin made her feel weak. When he stepped back from her, she searched his eyes. She smiled. He winked. She struggled to turn away and walk down the stairs and out of the centre.

What was happening to me? Is this what art therapists do? Was he playing games? I enjoyed being so close to him? I long to come back next week. He's a priest. I'll be safe with him. We both hail from Kerry. Celibacy is not right for every priest. But I love Richard.

29

TEMPTATION

'Good morning, Frankie! How long does it take to walk from your house to this centre?'

'About ten to fifteen minutes, Barbara. I'm amazed that I had not noticed this Nelson Mandela Centre before Sr Sheila made an appointment for me here.'

'Come over here. We can sit by the entrance and chat. When the sun shines through these windows, it's pleasantly warm, isn't it?'

'Nice and bright, too. Comfy chairs, as well.'

'How are you enjoying the art therapy? Isn't Sean lovely?'

'Wonderful! These last few weeks I have thoroughly enjoyed myself. I have been able to cry, laugh and relax.'

'I don't know about you, Frankie, but I find that Sean is keen to help me to interpret my most intimate feeling through my art work. He even hugs me.'

'I agree, Barbara, Sean's approach is very personal. He helps me to be myself.'

'He's so care-free. He encourages a spirit of abandonment. It's as though he wants us to regress into our childhood. Is that how you felt?'

'I hope that the children I teach get as much out of their art classes as I have from Sean's.'

'Do you provide glue and fabric as well as a good variety of paints?'

'Yes. We do collage, tie-and-dye and batique.'

'Batique?'

'They love batique. They use melted wax to prevent part of the fabric from being coloured when it is immersed in a dye. That how we made white clouds in a dark blue sky in our nativity scene. The children were delighted with the result.'

'That sounds very creative.'

'I enjoy watching the children enjoying themselves. In Sean's class I can be a child again.'

'When I was at school, our art classes were not like that, were they? I remember being given a picture to copy. Our work was criticised. Instead, everything I produce in Sean's classes seems to intrigue him.'

Franke questioned herself. *Why am I feeling jealous? Why am I bothered about Barbara liking Sean? Am I falling in love with Sean? But I love Richard. Should I try to put my love to the test by going to Ireland?*

'I'm tempted to sign up for the Landscape Painting course that he is running in Ireland.'

'Why not? Unfortunately, I haven't got the funds to cover the cost.'

'I think I will go on this course, Barbara. This school term has been very demanding. I need a break. The course coincides with half term. I'm off to Galway.'

Frankie felt that she needed to seek advice from Paula about the confusion she felt with her relationships. She had to wait until Paula offered her a lift home after school.

'You look tired, Frankie. Pop in. I'll have you home in no time. My car is parked behind Linda's.'

'Thanks Paula. You're very good to me.'

'I heard you telling Sr Sheila that you are going to Galway during half-term.'

'I made a quick decision, Paula. When I was talking to another ex-nun who is taking part in an art therapy class at the Nelson Mandela centre, I realised that I seem to know very little about love.'

'What do you mean? You love Richard, don't you? Maybe you have not been as close as you were before Anna appeared. You talk to each other now. Give it time. You'll soon resume your relationship.'

'Our art therapist has been very kind and loving towards me. He even hugged me.'

'Isn't he a priest? Frankie, I'm going to pull in here for a minute or two. There's just enough space beyond the bus stop.'

'He is a priest, Paula. But he may not be happy as a priest. I used to be a nun. Remember? I left the convent. He…'

'Frankie, he is probably being kind to you. Did he tell you that he loves you?'

'He… well, I'm not sure.'

'Why are you really going on this course? Is Barbara going too?'

'From what Barbara intimated he has been as personal with her as he has with me. I thought that Sean had singled me out. That he loves me. He put his hand on my shoulder. I am confused, Paula. That is why I wanted to talk to you.'

'Did he brush against you?'

'Perhaps. He kissed me when I was about to go home.'

'People kiss and hug when they are saying goodbye.'

'Yes. I suppose. We were instructed not to make physical contact when I was in the convent. I wondered if counsellors normally kissed their clients when they parted.'

'You've lived a sheltered life, Frankie. Perhaps you are reading more into Sean's dealings with you than he intended.'

'Sensitive? I felt aroused. Tingling. I decided to go on this landscape painting course so that I can find out if Sean loves me.'

'Did Sean encourage you?'

'No, Sean seemed surprised when I said I wanted to go on the course. I was the first to sign up.'

'It seems to me that Sean is not expecting you to go on this course. What is Richard doing during half term?'

'I overheard Richard telling Sr Sheila that he is going to Italy. He will not be around. That is another reason why I decided to take part in the course.'

'Frankie, you need to be careful. You may be infatuated by Fr Sean. Remember that he is a priest. I realise that you love Ireland. You probably feel that you will be at home there.'

'Oh Paula, you are right. What am I to do?'

'You have signed up. Go, but be aware of what we have discussed.'

When Frankie arrived in Roundstone, Clifden, Galway, she discovered that there were only five people on the landscape painting course. She had been booked into a bed and breakfast called *Tighe Misa*. She knew that Celtic name translated to 'my house'.

The white pebble-dashed bungalow was positioned away from the road. She knocked at the green door. The landlady opened the door to welcome her.

'Dia duit!'

'I'm so sorry. I've forgotten all my Irish.

'Bearla? English. Welcome, anyhow. I'm Nora. '

A middle aged, low-sized, smiling woman held out her hand to Frankie.

Frankie moved to shake her hand. 'Frankie. Frankie's my name, Nora. I'm delighted to be here in Galway. It was a long journey.'

'You flew into Galway?'

'Yes. I had to get a train to Victoria Station. Another from there to Heathrow. Then the plane to Galway and the bus here.'

'You must be exhausted. Leave your bags there, now. I've some apple tart and a cup of tea waiting for you. Would you like that, Frankie?'

Frankie learnt that Nora lived on her own. Frankie was her only guest. Fr Sean was staying with the parish priest. There were two Americans and an Italian man following the course. They were lodged in the house across the road from *Tighe Misa*.

'Frankie, I hope this room will suit you. It used to be my son, Donald's. I'll leave you to unpack. There is an extra blanket in the wardrobe.'

'Thank you, Nora.'

'There'll be a meal ready for you at six. Should you feel up to going for a walk along the boreen, go out of the house, turn left. That little lane will take you along by the field at the back of the house.'

'That's very kind, Nora. I think once I've unpacked I might nod off for awhile. I'll see.'

'Up to you now, Frankie. Feel at home. You'll find a key for the front door on the little table as you go out. I'll see you at six.'

Frankie reflected, *It is lovely to be home in Ireland. It doesn't seem to have changed much since I left it nearly thirty years ago. This bedroom does not look as though it has been painted or decorated for years. The floral wall paper is peeling off in the corners. There's a smell of moth balls in the old brown wardrobe. The electric plugs are still the round ones.*

AFTER HER EVENING meal and a walk down the boreen, Frankie went to bed wondering what the other people were like. The tolling of the Angelus bells in the parish church woke her up at six the next morning. She showered and fortified with an Irish breakfast, she walked a hundred yards to the parish hall. As she approached she heard Sean's voice.

'There is only one more person to come. Frankie Danivet.'

The door is open. I can see Sean waving me to come in.

'The top of the morning to you, Frankie. Come in and complete the group. Here. Let me introduce you: Gerry and Angie hail from America. Enrico is Italian. That leaves Maeve who lives a hundred yards down the road from here.'

'Hello! As Sean said, I'm Frankie. Lovely to meet you all.'

'Make yourself comfortable here, Frankie. As you can see, I've placed you in a row facing up to the street above. Fortunately we have good weather. Through this big glass window you can see the row of houses facing down this way. Can you all see them clearly?'

'I can see them, Sean. You want us to draw them?'

'Yes, Gerry. That's your first task. Pencil and paper and paint.'

Frankie began to look around. They were in an old stone bungalow that had been converted into education centre. She wondered if the original front window had been replaced by a much larger one to let more light into an oblong front room.

Frankie looked at Sean. *I guess he is not that long out of the seminary. He has been on the missions in Kenya. Maybe he is still in his thirties. The two Americans are old. About sixty? Enrico is probably in his forties. Maeve looks like a mother with a family. Could she be fiftyish?*

'Are you okay, Frankie? Are you warm enough? Was Nora good to you? She is a lovely woman. So caring. I thought you'd like *Tighe Misa*.'

'Thank you, Sean. I slept well. Nora made me feel welcome. I'm rubbing my hands together to warm them up, ready to start.'

Frankie found a seat next to Angie. She peeped over to see how she was getting on. She reflected on what she saw.

If that's her best effort, there's some hope for me. This woman's depiction of the lovely row of two up, two down terraced houses resembles what I can see before me. The pink, blue and yellow rectangles are like something a five year old child would produce.

'Sticking to your guns? Good for you, Gerry. You've a style all of your own. You know how to express yourself.'

Sean knows this woman. Surely what she has produced is an immature portrayal of the scene? The beautiful, historic houses of Roundstone deserve better treatment than that. He can't be serious.

As Sean moved nearer to her, Frankie was tempted to grab a sheet of paper to cover over her drawing. She had tried to apply the rules of perspective and proportion even though he had encouraged her not to allow herself to make such restrictions.

'Ah now, Frankie. While this is a landscaping course, we also want it to be a therapeutic experience.'

He squeezed her shoulder. She felt tingling down her spine.

'Oh yes. I have been trying to portray what I see. You want me to let my feelings guide me. Sorry.'

Sean traced his finger down the sketching of the pathway that she had drawn from the road to the bungalow.

'Ah well now, you'll appreciate the approach that we're adopting here.'

Frankie looked into his blue eyes. He held her look. He placed his hand over her hand.

His small, tanned hand felt warm. His bluey-green eyes were mesmerising. Frankie thought, I want to hug him.

'Keep trying, Frankie. Allow yourself to feel free.'

Sean licked his lips and winked.

I love his slender quivering lips. The left side goes down. Then he pouts like a mischievous three-year old.

'Okay folk. Time for a break. I guarantee you'll be surprised by what you see in that end café.'

Sean pointed to the cafe.

Frankie felt embarrassed, unsure what to think of Sean's behaviour towards her.

Observe how he acts with the others in the class, she told herself.

Frankie covered her art work and followed Sean's instructions to the café. Sean and Frankie arrived simultaneously. As she opened the cafe door, she saw him in the big wall mirror that reflected sketches of the scenes from outside. It was as though they were surrounded, enclosed, immersed in the local landscape.

'I'm captured. These are amazing drawings. They all link up. It's like an outline of the area. Clever! Look there's the slip-way and the hills. It's as though we're outside in. Did you do them, Sean?'

'I guessed you'd like it, Frankie.'

Frankie heard chatter. The others were approaching. She pulled out the chair at the table where Sean had seated himself in the corner of the room. He moved the sugar bowl and flicked a few grains.

'Frankie, there are six of us on our course. It is a landscaping course. I consider art to be therapeutic. Each person should feel relaxed. However, we need to remember that there are six of us.'

'You know me quite well, Sean. I am frightened to relax and reveal too much. I don't want to become too vulnerable. I'm struggling with such strong emotions.'

'That is why I am warning you to be careful.'

Gerry and Angie and another American arrived in the café. They began to marvel as they surveyed the mirror reflection of the art scene.

'Oh my Gad!'

'Well I never! Wonderful. Who's the artist?'

'It's himself. Sean!' declared Frankie.

'You like it? Come and join us.' Sean invited Gerry and Angie to Frankie's table.

'Really? Marvellous!'

'Here, let me do the honours.'

Sean leaped up like a greyhound.

Angie and Gerry asked Sean and Frankie. 'You two know each other?'

'Yes, Sean was my tutor on another art class. I wanted to continue on this course.'

Frankie dreaded all the questioning that could ensue.

'Oh, I wondered if you are Irish.'

'I am Irish but I live in England. How about you two? Both from the same part of the States?'

'Miles apart! One side of America from the other. Angie's from California and me well... I'm a New Yorker! How about that?'

Frankie wanted to ward them off asking her too many questions. She asked, 'Do your families come from around these parts? Is that what draws you here?'

'We're actually related through marriage. Yes, our family traces its roots to Galway. *If you ever go across the sea to Ireland, then maybe at the breaking of the day...*'

'What a lovely singing voice you have, Angie, praised Sean. 'We'll have a Ceili at the end of the course. Maybe you should sing that lovely song? Wouldn't that be grand?'

30

TEASING

It was just after nine that warm morning. Frankie had slept well. She was temped to wear her alluring lemon gingham dress with its fitted bodice, cup sleeves and flattering, flared skirt. Then she remembered that Sean had given instruction to dress appropriately for painting on the bog, 'You'll need to cover your skin. Mosquitoes are blood-suckers.'

When everyone arrived Sean gave his instructions and invited them to position themselves wherever they wished.

'Who'd like a dab of my Citronella? Frankie, did you say you've already been bitten? Here, take the jar and rub it on your skin,' offered Angie.

'Thank you, Angie. I always get bitten.'

My arms and legs have been covered for so many years I must not have built up enough immunity to ward off the insects.

Frankie observed Sean. He seemed to be in his element in the bogs. He did a quick demonstration at his easel. Whatever way he stretched his body he looked athletic, sturdy and supple.

While Sean issued his instructions, Frankie remembered that Maeve had invited her to go swimming tonight. *Maybe I could manage to entice Sean to join us? He's looking in my direction. I'd better listen.*

Sean was pointing to a rock. 'This rock is prominent in the middle of your picture. That's if you view it from here. I want you to use artistic licence. Move yourself around or move the rock. You understand I don't literally want you to attempt to haul the mass. This is the exercise today. Each of you will see this boggy landscape differently. The heather, the ruggedness will feature. It's your unique perception of the reality I'm looking for. Okay?'

When the instructions were over, Frankie was wondering which of the participants Sean would approach to help. With the memory of how close he came near her the previous day, she longed to experience the shiver that tingled down her spine when he came near her again.

Frankie called out to Sean as he was about to pass by her.

'Sean, would you look at my initial sketch? Once I get your approval, I'll be fine.'

Frankie had positioned herself at the end of the row in the hope that he would start at her end. She saw that Gerry was signalling to him too. He went to her. Frankie watched Sean. Soon Gerry and Sean were laughing and giggling. When Sean seemed to be moving away from Gerry, Frankie called out again.

'How about from this angle, Sean?'

Frankie thought that Sean had looked over in her direction before leaning over Angie's work.

He looks so amusing with her pencil between his teeth while he's rubbing out. He's pretending not to hear me. He's teasing me. I can play that game.

Frankie stood behind Enrico and patted him on the shoulder:

'Brava! Questa e veramente, buono.'

'Da'verro? You like?' Enrico pecked her on her cheek

Is he flirting with me?

Frankie asked, 'What do you think of my composition?'

'Well done, Frankie! I like but how about you make your rock little smaller? I show you?'

Enrico's cheek smoothed against Frankie's as he reached across her. He attempted to show her how to decrease the size of the rock in her picture.

The tobacco in Enrico's pipe smells of heather, bracken and autumn leaves. He's aware that he's helping me to tease Sean.

Enrico stretched out his sallow arm.

Sean shouted over, 'Frankie, it has to be *your* work. Enrico, she'll never master perspective if you sketch it in. Let me see.'

Enrico replied, 'You are so right, Sean. It is much better she struggle on her own than I rescue her, Maestro!'

Enrico moved back at the same time as Sean grabbed Frankie's easel. He began to erase most of her rock. He positioned a stool he carried around with him, nearer to hers.

'It is all about composition today. That is the object of the exercise. Decide on what you want included in your picture. Visualise the whole scene and sketch in the outline. Work on your perspective. That rock must blend in, not dominate the view. Consider where the light is coming from. Were it to come from behind that enormous rock, it would cast a long dark shadow.'

Sean spoke quickly in a clipped staccato high-pitched voice. His jaws and teeth moved as if they were struggling to get a grip, like slicing slippery ham. His eyes darted from the picture to the scene but they never met Frankie's. His sketching arm levered up and down and in and out in, machine fashion.

Frankie leaned nearer to him and whispered, 'Are you cross with me?'

Sean didn't answer. He scratched his nose and rolled one lip over the other.

31

SWIMMING

'Frankie, let's meet on the beach.' It was Maeve. 'You've brought the good weather with you, Frankie.'

'Sean says he's joining us today, Maeve. Is that okay?'

'Sure, isn't the sea big enough for the lot of us? Maybe we should invite them all?'

Oh no, thought Frankie. *I want Sean to myself. I'd prefer if you weren't here either.*

'Yes, that could be fun. I don't think the Yanks would brave the Atlantic waters, do you?'

'I'm hungry. I'd love to nibble the biscuit I have in my bag but you know what they say about not eating for at least an hour before a swim? I'm off! Hey... hey... here we go!'

Maeve had instructed Frankie to wear her swimming costume under her trousers and top. She brought her underwear and the key to the cottage rolled up in a towel to leave by the beach wall. Maeve pushed the keys to Maeve's car into a hole in the wall as Maeve had told her to do.

'Wait for me!'

As Frankie chased Maeve down the strandline, she was conscious of her pasty white skin puckered with goose pimples. However, memories from her youth of being totally acclimatised two seconds after a breath-taking cold plunge convinced her, that it's all worth the initial pain. It would be a rush to freedom.

Frankie was delighted, *Oh to be carried, careless and carefree, in salty water. Next stop America! Terrific! What could be more exhilarating? Maybe I was a mermaid in my previous life? Time is suspended in this state of effortless movement!*

She plunged again into the waves. She walked out as far as a big wave and let it carry her back to the shore.

Then she decided to do the breast stroke beyond the crashing waves.

Every now and again Frankie caught glimpses of Maeve far out in the deep. Her hands reached up and then she was immersed.

When Frankie looked up again she saw that Maeve was back on the strand. She followed her in.

'You're so quick.' Frankie chattered as she grabbed her towel. 'That was so cold.'

'Sure, amn't I in the sea nearly all year round? Even in the snow, I'm tempted.'

With the towel round her shoulders, Frankie marvelled as fully clothed Maeve ruffled her hair, squeezed her togs and pushed her wet swim suit into her plastic bag.

'I'll never be as quick as you, Maeve. My towel invariably falls from between my teeth. Without my glasses, I can't locate my underwear. When I find the specs, they steam up!'

Maeve looked up the beach.

'Wouldn't you know. Sean has arrived as we're ready to go? That your landlady's granddaughter that's following him, Frankie'

Frankie looked aghast as a young girl in a bikini ran past her and Maeve. Sean seemed to be wearing a Lycra swimsuit. As they both careered past, Sean shouted in Frankie's direction, 'See you here around six.'

'They're having great fun, Frankie. Look at them jumping over the waves.'

'They're squealing so much! Did you hear Sean say he'd meet me at six?'

'Yes, that is what he said, Frankie.'

Why does Sean want to meet me at six? Is he teasing me again? Maybe he wants to explain something to me. Perhaps he is annoyed by what happened at the art session yesterday. He is a priest. Priests have always been freer to do what they choose. Wouldn't if be lovely if he loves me?

'That Sean's got a wild streak in him, that's for sure. Hello! Are you here, Frankie? Your distant perusal of the horizon won't get us back to breakfast.'

'Sorry, Maeve. I was watching Sean.'

'You went to his classes in England. You know him better than the rest of us.'

Frankie wondered how much of herself she should reveal to Maeve. She began to feel hot blood surging up into her cheeks. She took off her glasses and wiped them on her woolly top and replaced them before responding.

'I took part in an art therapy course run by Sean. I felt I needed some support and was advised that this approach might help.'

'I've often thought of perusing that side of art myself. When my husband became ill, I wondered if it might help him.'

Frankie did not want to turn away from watching Sean. His cheeky grin earlier had intrigued her. Then she realised that Maeve wished to discuss her feelings with her as she led her back to her car.

'Sorry. Maeve. I am so distracted. Is your husband getting better?'

'He has testicular cancer. I'm very worried about his prognosis.'

Frankie put her arm around Maeve.

'Oh Maeve, that must be very hard for you both. Has he had chemotherapy?'

'Yes he has. We had to travel City of Dublin Skin and Cancer Hospital every week for six weeks. He's trying to regain his strength. T'is a heavy cross to bear but we keep praying. Thanks for your concern, Frankie.'

32

THE DATE

Frankie wondered if Sean really intended to meet her at six o'clock. Maybe she had misheard what he said that morning when he ran past her on his way down to swim in the sea. She was seated on the sea wall when church bells suddenly began to peal from the church behind her.

It was six o'clock. The Angelus bells were ringing. After years of reciting this prayer, she automatically began, *The Angel of the Lord declared onto Mary...*

God sent an angel to warn Mary that she was to become the mother of a baby that was to be born without Mary being married. That was a miracle. Is something miraculous going to happen to me?

Frankie wondered why Sean wanted to meet her.

I'm meeting a priest probably with the purpose of discussing an art course, so why have I taken such care with my hair and dress? Will Sean come from behind and enfold me in a massive hug?

A warm feeling surged up her spine. She threw back her arms from her turquoise pashmina and let it fall over her shoulders. She tossed her auburn hair casually back.

The tide was in, lapping against the wall, occasionally peeping over the wall anxious to witness what was about to happen. Frankie stood to rearrange the layers of her gypsy style dress. She sat resting her arms on her lap. She glimpsed the golden-tinged sun hovering on the horizon. She felt its rays on her eyelids before she gently relaxed and began to dream.

She leaned back. Sean's arms dangled over her. He tickled her. She kicked off her shoes. She was cherished in his arms. She protested, 'Let me down!' Unashamedly he plied her with kisses on both cheeks, her forehead and—

'?Come es il pronostico del tiempo?'

Oh-o-oo I must have fallen asleep. Must be the sea air.

A Spanish couple brought Frankie back to reality. When she opened her eyes, the hugging couple were blocking the view of the disappearing sun. The sea was pounding against the sea wall. She wrapped her woolly pashmina around her.

No sign of Sean? No hope now of my dream coming true.

She hoped that he would suddenly appear and invite her to walk along the strandline. Utterly disappointed, she stood to go. A blue Vauxhall drew to a halt. Sean emerged. He walked round to open the door at her side. He kissed her cheek. He waited until she was seated before gently closing the car door.

'Sorry, I am late, Frankie. You'll just love this gorgeous restaurant hidden in a little cove not far from the coast. Such a variety of fish just out of the sea.'

'Oh I…'

Still breathless, Frankie was being driven off. Sean was patting her leg. 'At last we can have time together. You look lovely. Turquoise is your colour. You are so co-ordinated too. Your necklace and your watch strap match. Sure you're a credit to yourself, Frankie.'

Turquoise. Richard loved turquoise. In spite of these memories Frankie responded, 'We're matching! Your blue shirt and pants tone in with mine. Did you consult my Colour Therapist by any chance?'

Sean leaned over the steering wheel and laughed a throaty laugh. He glanced at her and winked.

'What wonderful sunsets we get out here. No wonder it's christened an artist's delight. I just love it all, Sean. It has been a grand few days. Thank you.'

'The best has yet to come. We'll enjoy tonight. Wait 'til you see the view round this bend.'

Frankie questioned herself. *Is this for real? I'm five seven inches tall. He's barely five foot three. He's sparrow-eyed with a beak-like nose. Gauging from his feathery streaked hair, he's in his late thirties. He's a member of an order of missionary priests. He probably has not much money. I wonder if he eats out often. He has a vow of celibacy. Why am I imagining that he loves me?*

'Here we are, Frankie. This is where I bring my friends. Isn't it in a lovely setting nestled into the rock?'

'Sean, this is wonderful. The restaurant looks as though it has been carved into the shape of a cavern. Shells and fishing nets... so lovely.'

'Wait until you see the seahorses and even bigger shells. The walls are adorned with all the creatures of the sea. When we were swimming, this morning I thought you'd love it here.'

'Gorgeous. Thank you Sean.'

'Ah Fr Sean! You've returned to us. How are ye? You're looking fine, thank God.'

You're looking well yourself, Tom. This is my friend, Frankie. She's taking part in the art class.'

'You're very welcome, Frankie. An artist. Good for you.'

'Sean's the artist. I'm learning.'

Tom shook Frankie's hand and pointed to a table in the big bay window facing the sea.

'Ah sure, we're all learning all the time, Frankie. Isn't that true?'

'This is all new to me.'

'The first thing I want to tell you is that this is my treat.'

'Thank you, Sean.'

'I want you to know that because of what happened to me some time ago. One of my friends invited me to enjoy a restaurant meal. At the time I didn't have much money. So I thought I'd better play safe and only order the main meal. It was only at the when he insisted in paying the bill that I realised that is what he intended.'

'Did he eat a big meal?'

'Starters, main meal and dessert. The lot. I pretended that I was not hungry. So Frankie, I want you to rest assured that I'm picking up the bill.'

'Thanks, Sean. What do you recommend?'

'My favourite is the calamari with rocket and lemon mayonnaise followed by grilled scallops wrapped in pancetta on a roasted mushroom with salad and roasted cherry tomatoes.'

'That sounds very appetising. I'd love to taste that.' Frankie's taste buds began to quiver.

I feel that I am living the dream. Is this a date? I've never been taken out by a man. Sean is cheerful. He's Irish but he is a priest.

'Your art has revealed so much about yourself, Frankie, but tell me more. You intrigue me the way you're... well, you're like an open book.'

'Where do I begin?'

'I could swim and dive about in your enormous sea eyes. Your mouth says, 'ask me'. You aquiline nose is aristocratic and intelligent. You're a girlish, young thing, eager to explore.'

'Oh, my God! I wish it were all true. Tell me about you. All I know is that you are an Irish missionary who hails from the Kingdom. Do you come from a big Irish family?'

'Fair dues. Like you, I'm from Baile an Fheirtearaigh, Tra Li, or as the English say, Ballyferriter, Tralee. Any further out in the Dingle peninsula and you'd fall into the Atlantic. I'm the youngest of seven. I have three brothers and sisters, only two at home, the rest scattered world-wide. My Mam's hitting sixty next month but unfortunately my Da's long left us, God have Mercy on his soul. How's about that for background?'

'I'm curious, Sean. You're too young to have returned from the Missions. Did you say you were in Kenya? I hope you weren't forced back with ill health? malaria or worse?'

'Spot on. Two years in Kenya and malaria; but I'm dealing with it. Hence my retraining as a counsellor and art therapist. Hopefully, that'll be useful wherever I'm sent. It'll be helpful with other missionaries convalescing in our house in Maynooth.'

'Malaria!'

'You look worried, Frankie. Am I a disappointment to you? I'm not damaged or sick. I'm just retraining. I'm vital. Like a hare waiting for the cage door to spring open. Come on!'

Sean leaned over, grasped both Frankie's hands in his. Richard had done the same.

He's just a little boy to be rescued and cuddled back into warmth. I'd love to cradle him.

Breathing deeply, she managed to utter, 'If only I could tell you how I feel.'

'Ah come on now, you have me curious. Shall we walk outside? It's a grand evening. Shall we?'

Is this really happening? I'm more muddled than ever. Sean is giving me mixed messages. All through the meal he winked and joked. The waiter quietly served and removed dishes. They seemed familiar with Sean's behaviour. He must frequent this restaurant often.

Sean wrapped Frankie into her pashmina, took her hand and led her out to the strandline. The tide had gone out.

'Let's fling off our shoes and walk along the strandline lit by a rising moon. What do you think, Frankie?'

'Why not, Sean!'

As the walked along the beach together, Frankie became intoxicated with the magic of that moment. She grabbed Sean's arm. 'Race you to the waves!'

She lifted her skirt and raced. Sean was behind her as she splashed into the waves. She felt his arms grab her round the waist.

'No! No! Let me down! We'll get soaked.'

'I knew you were a mermaid. I'm going to fling you back into the sea.'

He's tickling me all over. My emotions are racing around my body. He is folding me back into his arms and kissing me. I am warm, muddled, fondled, subtle and willing. It's as if neither of us has a care in the world.

'Thank you, Sean. That was lovely.'

'You enjoyed that?'

'I did, Sean. Thank you.'

'I couldn't resist. Do you think it was not right for a priest…'

'Oh Sean, I don't know what to think. Love is so complicated. How can it be wrong to have fun?'

'Good. So you don't feel that I'm leading you astray?'

'I thoroughly enjoyed myself. I chose to respond to you.'

'Good girl. I'll drive you back to *Tighe Misa*. You'd better get the sand off those toes of yours. I've a towel in the car. Come on. I'll help you up over the pebbles.'

Sean's hands felt warm as he guided her to his car.

This is a night I will not forget. I feel loved and protected. Why have I missed out in experiencing such pleasurable feelings? He's more loving, natural than I imagine that other therapist Peter could be.

'The smell of the sea is something else! I love it.'

'Let's roll the windows down and fill the air with music, Frankie.'

'Let's!'

Sean began to sing, *'I'll Take You Home Again Kathleen, across the ocean wild and wide…'*

Frankie joined in.

As Frankie placed her feet on the tarmac, she felt she didn't want the night to end. Sean put his arm under her elbow and manoeuvred her to the door of her B&B. He whispered, 'That was a grand evening!' as he kissed her. 'Goodnight'.

Once inside, Frankie leaned against the stairs. *Have I been so caught up in my dream world that I'm unable to distinguish it from reality? Was it the wine? I'm not used to wine. Oh well when I get into my nightie, I'll be harming no one by letting my imagination run riot.*

33

CEILIDH NIGHT

What time is it? Where's my watch? Gone ten. I'll have to get out of bed. It's strange that I didn't hear the Angelus bells ring at six o'clock this morning. I shouldn't have drunk that second glass of wine last night. There are no classes on the last day.

This is the final day of the art course in Galway. Early sunlight streaming through the window of *Tighe Misa*, woke Frankie.

'Am I too late for breakfast, Nora?'

'Now, that's a silly question, Frankie. You should feel at home here by now. Sit yourself down and tell me about what you are going to do at the Ceilidh tonight.'

'I'm not much of a singer, Nora, but Sean won't take no for an answer. I'm going to attempt to sing one of Ronan Keating's songs, *When you say nothing at all...* Do you know it?'

'You sing? That's lovely. As it happens I do know that song. Himself, Rory O'Connor, in the grocers down the road, hums it all the time. It's a fine tune, isn't it?'

As there were no classes, Frankie walked down the boreen and across the fields practising her song. That evening she decided to wear another gypsy style dress to the Ceilidh. That dress was a combination of green and rust. She knew those colours enhanced her auburn hair and green eyes.

There was only a small mirror over the sink in the bedroom. After she had meticulously finished applying powder to cover over her freckles and touching her eyes lids with green eye-shadow she put on maple-brown lipstick. She combed back her auburn neck-length hair. She was pleased that the cotton-mix material in her dress made her feel free and lady-like. When she slid her feet into mottled patterned, flat dancing shoes and draped a green pashmina over her shoulders, she skipped from step to step down the stairs. Nora had informed her that she would be at evening Mass. She took the front door key with her before pulling the door closed.

Frankie could hear the song, *Oh, For One of Those Kerry Dances* blaring out from the parish church hall as she approached the entrance.

'You look gorgeous, Frankie. Those colours suit you.'

'Thank you. I like your shirt, Maeve. You must be one of the Irish dancing troupe.'

'I am, indeed. Come on, let's dance our way in. That's a fine tune, Frankie. Hold onto my arm. Come on.'

'Well! If it isn't yourselves! Aren't you both looking wonderful!'

'Thank you, Sean. You look as though you intend to do a fair bit of dancing too. Was it you who chose the *Kerry Dances* record? Your dancing shoes give the game away.'

Slim, fit Sean, with that lovely smile, hazel-brown, tousled hair and a twinkle in his ocean-blue eyes, looked gorgeous dressed in an olive-green shirt and matching trousers.

I determined to dance with him tonight, thought Frankie.

'What will you drink, Frankie? Guinness?'

'I think I'll keep off the alcohol at this stage of the evening, Maeve. Lime and soda, please. I love the song the band has started up. *I've been a wild rover…*'

'The Swift Band. They're local lads. Father and two sons. Play traditional and modern. They're really good.'

'Good combination. Suits young and old. Shall we join the others in our art group? They're seated at the table over in the corner.'

'Is this hall very old, Maeve?'

'Yes indeed. It's seen generations of ceilidhs, parties, and celebrations. I think my father had a hand in building it. The wooden floor in front of the stage was probably the first part of the building. Then the dancers wanted a cemented floor. See over there where they've pulled back the long trestle tables. That's the bit I mean.'

'Now when I look up into the rafters I can see years of cobwebs. You can smell generations of foot wear too.'

Frankie felt a tap on her shoulder as she carried her drink over to the table to sit with the others. It was Sean.

'Frankie, I want to make sure that I accompany you in the right key. Would you mind coming outside with me for a minute?'

'You play the guitar, too, Sean? I had no idea! I'll put my drink on the table and follow you out.'

This is my chance to enjoy Sean's company again, thought Frankie.

'We know so little about each other, Frankie. I didn't know that you can sing solo.'

'Sing? Wait until you hear me, Sean. I only agreed because you said everyone had to do a turn.'

Frankie watched as Sean rested his foot on a tree stump. He hummed as he plucked each string of his guitar and turned the screws to adjust them.

Frankie wished that she had her camera to capture the way he rolled his lips and his fingers moved as he tugged at each string. Every now and then he flicked his fringe back. He reminded her of a cowboy immersed in music. *He's turning me on,* she thought.

'Okay. I'm tuned. Now let's hope this pitch is right for you, Frankie. Can you sing the first few lines for me?'

Although Frankie wanted to be alone with Sean again, standing near him and experiencing his full attention, seemed to paralyse her.

She coughed, rubbed her nose, licked her lips and looked him in the eye. 'I don't think I can do this, Sean. I've dried up. I'm not really as singer. I'm sorry.'

'No need to get stage-fright, Frankie. You're out here with me. I'll sing a bit and you can join in. Don't worry. Let your inhibitions flow away.'

Sean strummed the tune and began to sing… *If tomorrow…*

Sean smiled and Frankie found her voice. Sean stopped singing and Frankie continued. Sean accompanied her until she finished the song. Still holding his guitar, Sean put one arm round her waist and pecked her on the cheek.

'You're terrific, Frankie. You've a gentle voice. All that hymn singing has done you good. They're all going to love you. Come on in. Let's rejoin the others.'

My emotions are rearing up. I feel as though there's a volcano erupting in my inner being that's thrusting out of control. Frankie tried to control herself.

When Sean and Frankie re-entered the room one of the band called over, 'Sean, does Frankie want to sing straight away?'

Sean turned to Frankie. 'Why not, Frankie? We're tuned and you're ready?'

'Might as well get it over with, Sean. Okay.'

Sean strummed introductory chords and nodded to Frankie to begin.

Frankie turned towards Sean. Her eyes met his. He smiled and winked. When Frankie sang everyone joined in.

When they had finished clapping, Frankie wondered if she really could sing or if folk were cheering because they felt she had tried. Sean slapped Frankie's back.

'Well done, Frankie. You've a lovely clear tone to your voice.'

Maeve opened her arms to embrace Frankie. 'Congratulations, Frankie!'

'Well done, Francesa!' Enrico hugged her. Gerry and Angie stood clapping and grinning to her.

'More! More! Everyone shouted. The hall had filled up. About sixty people had crowded into the room. Frankie moved away from Sean. He slowly and gently started plucking Sting's 'Fields of Gold',

Frankie watched Sean making his guitar sing. He plucked,

strummed and flicked.

It's as though the instrument had become part of his body. He walked up and down and backwards and forwards, sometimes lifting his head to one side and sometimes to the other, appearing to be carried away.

Frankie felt that when he modulated his tenor tones, he sent a tremor through her body.

I close my eyes and dream that I am in his arms.

Suddenly, Sean started singing rousing and rebel songs. Everybody joined in, *Only our rivers run free, Four green fields,* finishing up with *The Fields of Athenry*.

'Our American friends are loving this, Frankie,' whispered Maeve. 'Look at their eyes glazing over. They've got that comaglia, nostalgic look.'

'I can't wait to see them become nostalgic at the end of the night when we sing our national anthem, *Sinne Finna Fail.*'

When the band resumed, the dancing began.

Frankie wanted to move nearer to Sean.

I want to hold his hand. How can I do that without drawing attention to myself? I can't stop my eyes from following him everywhere. From time to time he glances over as though to acknowledge my attention. He springs up and down and weaves his way up on his toes with a bounce and a wiggle like a sprite little leprechaun. He smiles and passes witty remarks to all with whom he touches or holds hands. I can't hold his attention. So frustrating! I want him for myself.

The band stopped playing. Sean clapped his hands. He joined his hands. He addressed everyone:

'A huge thank you to each and every one of you for coming here tonight. We've enjoyed a grand night.'

Sean pointed to the band. Let's give them a big round of applause. 'The Swift Band will go far. Thanks, lads.'

'As midnight approaches, let us thank Almighty God for the friendship we shared, the beauty we enjoyed and the talent each one of us has shown tonight and during the art course that a few of us have taken part in.'

Frankie felt sad that both the course and the week were drawing to a close. After they sang the national anthem, Sean hugged each of the persons next to him. He began to go round the circle formed around him giving everyone a goodbye hug.

Frankie wondered if Sean held on to Maeve longer than he held her.

Am I imagining that? Why am I feeling jealous?

'You can't help loving him. He's a dote, isn't he?'

Frankie smiled at Maeve and thought, *That's all he is to you, Maeve; just a little dote. You can go home to your husband I'll be among the ones going home on my own tonight, wishing, dreaming and longing to stay with him.*

The crowd dispersed. They bid each other goodnight. Frankie waited to see if she could get near Sean before going home. She watched a group of people surround him as he turned in the direction of the church.

Desolated, Frankie put her head down and began to walk home alone. Suddenly she heard Sean's voice call her name. She turned. Sean beckoned her to come to him. He held out his arms. Embracing her, he drew her onto a bench. Frankie clung to Sean. His arms drew her closer. She longed for the warmth of his embrace to last forever. Her body throbbed, her heart beat faster.

'You're special, Frankie.'

Sean kissed her forehead.

'I love you, Sean.'

'I've teased you.'

'You're a flirt!' Frankie thumped Sean's chest.

'You're a teaser and a flirt!' Sean held Frankie at arms length.

'I'm a priest. I'm a therapist.'

'You're a man. I'm a woman. You've aroused me. My body longs for you. I love you, Sean.'

'I know. I am on fire, too. A priest is a man first. I can't switch off my God-given feelings.' Sean took Frankie's hand in hers. He looked into her pleading eyes.

'At this moment, Sean, I want us to strip off and...'

'Hey, Frankie, you know I can't do that. I have a vow of chastity.'

'I made a vow of chastity too. But I broke my vow. You can too.'

Sean dropped Frankie's hand. He moved a little away from her. 'Ah now, Frankie, you've got me wrong. I can't deny my feelings but that does not mean that I want to give way to my feelings.'

'I don't understand, Sean. I feel angry. You aroused my feelings. You told me that I am special. You hug and kiss me. You took me out on a date...'

'Oh! Hold on, Frankie. You came on a therapeutic art course. You already have a chap that you love. Richard, isn't it? I've helped you to explore your feeling.'

'Are you telling me that this was all a therapeutic experiment? I'm confused. I'm angry.'

'Why are you angry? You're able to acknowledge that you have wonderfully natural, womanly feelings. You're safe with me. Nothing will come of our love for each other.'

Frankie put her head in her hands. She wanted to cry but she couldn't. She pursed her lips. They began to tremble. Tears began to flow. Sean reached out to pull her towards him. She pushed him away. 'I wish that I had never...'

Sean continued, 'fallen in love with me. I hope you don't continue to feel that way. Frankie, I'm a therapist. I helped you to explore your feelings. I was aware that you had spent many years in the convent suppressing those feelings. I hope I have succeeded in convincing you that you are a real woman. Hopefully, you will deepen your love for Richard, marry and have the child that you long for.'

'I suppose... but how can a priest justify... well, falling in love? We're you in love with me?'

'First and foremost I am a man, Frankie. I do love you. I am a priest. I am a therapist. I have chosen not to fulfil my manly inclinations. Instead, I help others to recognise theirs. In the process I do not consider that I should be denied pleasure.'

Frankie thumped the bench. 'How many other women have you led on? How many have you used? You admit that you love me? How do you think I feel when you tell me that our love for each other has to stop now?'

'Frankie, you have Richard. Enjoy some of the things that we shared with him. You're aware that you're capable of being aroused. You're a real woman. Talk to Richard. If you like, tell him what has happened between us. Examine your love for him. I'm not available. I was a safe person to be attracted to. Perhaps deep down you knew that?'

Frankie combed her hands to her hair. She looked into Sean's eyes. Sean stood.

'I'll walk you home. You're broken-hearted. Rightly so. Remember that I love you. When you marry, maybe you'll appreciate the love that we have shared.'

Sean reached out and took Frankie's hand. They walked the short distance to her lodgings. Sean drew her to him in a gentle hug.

'Sean, I'm still muddled.'

'Goodnight.'

'Goodnight.'

She put the key in the door. He turned. She looked after him. She opened the door. She crept upstairs, undressed and fell into bed. She spent a restless night pondering on what Sean had said to her.

THE FOLLOWING MORNING Frankie was grateful that Nora had arranged for one of the parishioners to drive her to the airport.

'Go raibh maith agat, Nora!'

'Well done, Frankie! You have learnt how to say thank you! No need. I enjoyed your company. Come back again. Safe journey over.'

'I will never forget this holiday, Nora.'

'Treasure the good that has come your way, Frankie.'

Frankie looked towards the house where Sean was staying as the car faced the direction of the airport.

Frankie kept asking herself, *Was Sean right to expose my vulnerability? When I return to England, Father Peter will probably be back. Will I be able to discuss these matters with him? Should I?*

34

WEDDING PREPARATIONS

'Good morning Frankie! I heard you creeping up the stairs late last night. Did you have a good time in Ireland?'

As I opened my bedroom door, my landlady, Evelyn, was tip-toeing across the landing. After another restless night. I was hoping to escape from the house without having to chat.

'Thoroughly enjoyed myself, Evelyn. I hope I didn't make too much noise coming in late last night. Oh, and thanks for milk you left for me. You're so thoughtful.'

'It must have been lovely to be back in the country of your birth. My home too.'

If only she knew. I can't get Sean out of my head. I put Richard's photo on the locker near my bed. I kissed it before I fell off to sleep. Each time I tried to imagine that I was in Richard's arms, I remembered Sean.

'Yes, it was lovely to be back home in Ireland.'

'Nothing quite like it, is there.'

Evelyn smiled and brushed a black curl from her forehead. She was still in her dressing gown.

'Back to school on Monday.'

'Yes. Off to do a bit of food shopping this morning.'

FRANKIE WANTED to clear her head. She hoped she might bump into Paula in Marks & Spencer. She felt that she was a bundle of emotions. Hopefully, Paula would help her.

She wanted to discuss falling in love with Sean. Was it real or an infatuation? Would Paula be able to understand what had happened to her? She was in a daze as she walked into the shop.

Frankie was suddenly grabbed by the wrist and pulled aside at the door as she entered the store.

'Aunt Joan!'

'Glad I caught I you, Frankie. Need to have a word. Come with me to the café. We can have a latte together.'

'Oh! I didn't expect… yes.'

'It'll be my treat.'

Will it have strings attached? She wondered.

'Will you share a sandwich?'

'Watercress and salmon or egg and rocket?'

'I really don't mind. You choose.'

'We'll have watercress and salmon.'

As Frankie accompanied Aunt Joan to the restaurant she quickly looked to see if Paula was already there. She pushed their tray along, collected the serviettes and cutlery and carried it to the table while Joan paid. Aunt Joan had no sooner seated herself opposite Frankie, than she rested her hand over Frankie's.

'Now Frankie, I wonder if you can be of assistance.'

Oh! Oh! I knew there must be a catch. No such thing as a free meal.

'Because of your excellent training in liturgy, would you be able to help me choose the music for our wedding? The Friars at Shilford are very kind but they presume that I being the… well I don't go, but I am nominally a Catholic…'

'The Franciscan Friary at Shilford. Is that where you're getting married? I only arrived back from holiday late last night. I saw your letter was on the top of a pile. I'm so sorry, Aunt Joan. I had to buy food before I opened my post.'

'Yes. I sent you an invitation card. Yes, I'm marrying at the Franciscan Friary at Shilford. I discovered that a lovely clientele or should

I say, congregation, frequent that imposing church. Our kind of professional people. Well-connected and able to engage in meaningful conversations.'

She continued breathlessly, 'The Norman church in such beautiful pastoral grounds. The winding, tree-canopied approach. The sturdy beige, with a touch of yellow stone, looks as though is could have been quarried in Bath. That Assisi, Italian appearance. It's just perfect for us. Those little friars seem so appreciative of having us.'

Frankie observed, *Aunt Joan has not opened the sandwich. I hope my latte will not get cold before she shares the food. The elderly couple seated behind our table are watching Joan fling her arms up in the air as she gesticulates. No doubt her loud tones must be entertaining. Maybe she is unaware that she is attracting such attention?*

'I have been to the Friary on a few occasions, Aunt Joan. Shall I glance through their hymnal? Make a few suggestions?'

'You are a darling,' She tapped Frankie's wrist. 'That would be wonderful.' She beamed and leaned nearer. She whispered, 'No need to mention us though. The Friars assume that I am competent at this, which of course I am. I am just availing... well, just making sure that you feel you are part of it all. You know me. I want everyone to be appreciated.'

'It's no problem, Joan. I'll go along next Sunday. Then shall I call over to your home with...'

'No, no that won't be... what I mean is, there is no need to disturb Andy with these matters. No. You know the tennis club, don't you? Meet me there next Saturday morning at eleven. We can have coffee. Okay?'

WHEN FRANKIE ARRIVED at the Friary she felt overwhelmed by a sense of déjà vu.

So many memories. Poor Margaret RIP. I'll pray for her before I read the hymnal.

As she walked up the narrow path to the church the towering oaks in their rich autumn shades of brown, orange and crimson, shedding copious leaves, she reflected that they provided all who tread beneath them with rustling carpets. The Norman-shaped church with its spire thrusting heavenwards through clear blue skies, clamoured for admiration. She spontaneously joined Saints Francis and Clare in praising Mother Nature and God, our Creator.

Frankie joined the Sunday worshippers after they locked their big cars. They picked their way across the damp lawn to the entrance of the church. She noticed wooden crosses with the names of the departed members of the community in a garden at the side of the path.

Frankie recalled that her namesake, St Francis, instructed his followers that Sister Death reminds all that our lives here on earth are only a preparation for our wonderful existence in paradise.

Frankie's brown leather high-heeled boots clipped and slid on the cold tiled floor. She was glad that her long brown shirt and woollen beige jacket kept her warm.

She smiled to herself, *My clothes and amber jewellery help me to blend in with these distinguished people.*

She flicked her highlighted hair and slung her straw bag over her shoulder in an effort to shake off the memory of the years that she had struggled in the convent.

Eventually whispering, gurgling, crying and coughing was drowned out by the organ playing the *Crown him with many crowns.* Three older priests in red and gold Mass vestments, processed up the aisle to the altar.

During the sermon Frankie began to flick through the hymnal to search for suitable music for cousin Joan and Andy's wedding. After Mass she was thumbing through another hymn book when the organist tapped her on her shoulder. 'Are you searching for hymns for a particular occasion, dear?'

In spite of having been warned, Frankie replied, 'I'm searching for hymns for my aunt's wedding.'

'Come with me. I'll show you a selection of hymns and music that other wedding couples have chosen.'

Frankie left the church with seven leaflets with details of music recently chosen for such occasions loaned to her by an Anglican vicar, who had converted to Catholicism and was now in charge of liturgy.

When the trio stood in front of the tabernacle, with the red sanctuary lamp to their right, Frankie saw that the chief celebrant was the same podgy, five foot, sixty plus, greying friar that she had encountered. As his penetrating eyes surveyed the congregation she noticed that he looked intimidating and self-assured. She began to struggle with her anger. What would poor St Francis say?

She noticed a friar in his brown habit, bare-footed in leather sandals slipping though a doorway and a table laden with Fair-Trade purchases. Further, at the entrance, a medium sized, tweedy woman was handing out hymnals and leaflets. She switched on her smile as she said, 'Welcome.'

Frankie sat at the back left hand side of ten benches on the left of the aisle, with green leather kneelers that accommodated four adults. Her attention was immediately drawn to a carved wooden altar. The cross was decorated with a red background with gold patterns. Above, as far as she could decipher from the, Latin, 'Behold the wood of the cross on which died the Saviour of the world.' Either side of the cross and in proportion to it were the traditional images of Mary and Saint John. There was adequate room though, to allow people to peep through to what supposedly must have been the original white imitation marble altar at the back of the church. In the niches at the left side of the church were altars below statues of Saints Anthony, The Sacred Heart and St Francis. High arch-shaped, clear-glassed windows let rays of warm sunshine stream onto the polished parquet floor which also highlighted the gold and reds on the Station of the Cross with pictures depicting the journey of Christ to Calvary on the left walls. Above, on the vaulted wooden ceiling were several golden sun-rayed circles, a reminder of Saint Francis's Canticle of the Sun.

35

AUNT JOAN'S WEDDING

After Mass on Sunday, Paula invited Frankie to have a cup of coffee in the church café. 'I'm dying to know how you got on in Galway, Frankie.'

'I have so much to tell you, Paula. Shall we grab that table for two near the window?'

'Lovely. The students are serving today. I'll just signal to that girl delivering the drinks to show her where we're seated. I asked for a latte for you. Is that okay?'

'Perfect, Paula. I've been invited to my Aunt Joan's wedding. Here. This is the invitation:

Joan Attridge and Andrew McGill
invite Frances Danivet to the Franciscan Friary, Shilford
Saturday, the Fourth of October, 1991
to share in their joy as they exchange their marriage vows.
Reception at Chilworth House Hotel

RSVP

'HOW LOVELY. Is she on your mother's side? Your mother's sister?'

'Yes. Do you remember that I told you about my Aunt Joan? A very determined, successful woman.'

'Yes. Yes. I do remember you telling me that she planned to marry the husband of the woman that she met while her husband was dying.'

'That's her. My Aunt Doreen described her husband to-be as the 'to die for' Andy, the *Sporting World* Editor.'

'Good for her. How old is she?'

'Sixty-one. She's marrying for the second time. I'm thirty-nine and not married yet.'

'Frankie, I know that you're longing to marry and have a child. I wanted to ask you about Sean. The fellow who ran the Landscaping Art course. I want to know before we search for an outfit for this wedding? You know that I'll be glad to help you.'

'No need to worry, Paula. I'm delighted to say that I still have the outfit that I wore to the wedding of my landlady's son.'

'You looked very attractive in that pale green dress with the brown pattern. The colours are just right for your auburn hair and lovely green eyes.'

'Paula, I have the jacket, shoes and accessories too.'

'Aunt Joan must like you, Frankie.'

'More like she's using me, Paula. She even asked me to help her choose the hymns and reading. She wanted the Friars to think that she is a devout Catholic.'

'Never mind. Perhaps you wish you had married before she did. Come on. Tell me how you got on with Sean?'

'I honestly don't know, Paula. I'm as confused as ever.'

'What do you mean? How can you not know? Has Sean contacted you since you returned from Galway?'

'No. I was attracted to Sean, but I don't think I will hear from him again.'

'Oh, Frankie! Tell me. What happened? You followed him over to Ireland.'

'I know. I still have feelings for him. He's thoroughly Irish. He's funny, artistic, musical...'

'He's a priest.'

'He reminded me.'

'He's unattainable. Happy in his vocation. A counsellor. Richard is single. He shares your background.'

'I know, Paula. I have been taught a painful lesson. Infatuation. Love. You pointed these out to me before, Paula.'

'Good. You recognise that the love you have for Sean is infatuation?'

'No, Paula. I really fell in love with Sean. Let me try to explain what happened between us.'

When Frankie related what had occurred between Sean and her, Paula said, 'You poor soul, Frankie. What an experience. Sounds as though Sean led you up the garden path. Celibacy. That's what is wrong. Most priests most likely fall in love. Taking a vow won't stop their urges. It's human nature. God-given human nature. Those that feel like that should marry.'

'I agree, Paula. I wonder how many priests there are who legitimate their actions the way Sean does?'

'You'll have time to ponder this while you are at your Aunt Joan's wedding tomorrow, Frankie?'

Frankie recalled Paula's advice when she arrived at the Franciscan Friary for the wedding.

I'll sit near the back of the church and try to reflect on all that is happening. Aunt Joan won't notice. She'll be too concerned with impressing the relatives. Of course she has not invited my Mam. Most likely she has considered that she would not come up to her social standing.

'Such extravagance in juxtaposition with mendicant poverty!' It was a woman seated at a centre aisle side of a bench, third from the back of the church.

'Yes. Sandle-footed. Friars ushering in bridesmaids in plush crimson velvet gowns. Such a contrast. Are you a friend of the bride?'

'I nursed Joan's late husband. A lovely man. I'm Liz.'

They shook hands.

'I'm Frankie. Joan's a distant aunt. That's why I'm seated back here.'

'Lovely to meet you. I'm on my own.'

'The groom looks so handsome, doesn't he?'

'Very distinguished appearance in his jacket and blue and green kilt. Fine sturdy legs. He has an athletic stature too.'

Frankie admired Andy when he occasionally swivelled round in the direction of the laurel-strewn archway, awaiting his bride.

Frankie reflected, *Richard would look even more handsome in a finely hand woven Harris Tweed. My uncle wore a Barley or Hamish bracken tweed three piece suit. Richard seems to love tweed.*

Liz interrupted her thoughts, 'Joan is so fortunate. The groom is like Michelangelo's David. When he glanced to the back of the church, have you noticed how his ruby-rose button hole contrasts with his silver grey curls?'

Richard still has an abundance of chestnut brown hair, Frankie thought.

Frankie agreed that Andy was handsome. Although she was pleased to be able to chat to the nurse, she wanted to observe what was happening. She was aware of perfume from the bees wax candles and the incense mingling with a multiple sprays of greenery, roses and carnations.

Everybody seemed to be eyeing each other. Cameras flashing and mobiles clicking. Older people peeping over spectacles. Folk seem to be carrying out head-to-toe examinations of what others are wearing.

'Whoops! I knew it. A mobile phone was bound to go off.'

'You're right, Liz. Joan seems to be late. Maybe someone was trying to contact her!'

Frankie became aware of familiar sounds of the swishing of friars' habits and the dull clanking of their wooden rosary beads. Then the organ quietly began to play Marc-Antoine Charpentier's *Prelude to the Te Deum*.

'She's here! That's the Sinfonia from Solomon George Frederic Handel.' Nudged Liz.

Frankie turned around to watch Aunt Joan's entrance. She was dressed in a cream and scarlet red, full-length oval-necked gown. Her blonde streaked hair was enhanced with a delicate bejewelled coronet. Her gold and red rose bouquet matched high heel shoes peeping from beneath her dress.

Liz continued to commentate, 'Beautiful. Just like the Queen of Sheba, she advancing up the aisle.'

'Those bridesmaids are teetering down the aisle in matching patent leather high heels bestrewn with red berried holly. Aren't they lovely? All four of them.'

Frankie contemplated, *Aunt Joan is sure-footed and determined. She has adopted a sense of conquest. One day I will be a bride, mused Frankie. Richard and I don't need to have all this pomp and ceremony. I have no wish to impress folk. Love. Love is important. 'For richer or for poorer...'*

Liz continued, 'Dowdy Friar Stephen seemed to have smartened himself for this classy wedding. He usually looks as though he could do with a bigger habit. He seems to have lost weight. Found a barber. Someone has mended his torn cowl for the occasion too.'

'You're very observant, Liz. I agree the friars look very smart in their brown habits.'

Celebrant, 'Will you take this woman...'

If only this was being addressed to Richard, Frankie thought.

La Rejouissance from the Royal Fireworks by George Frederic Handel awoke Frankie from her day-dreaming. After she witnessed Joan and Andy gliding past, smiling graciously at each and everyone, Liz poked her.

'If you are on your own, perhaps we could stay together, Frankie?'

Anxiously Frankie thought: *How am I going to explain that I want to go home now? Memories of being lonely at the wedding party of my landlady's son's wedding added to my determination to opt out of these wedding celebrations. I don't want to feel lonely jigging to music that I do not know. When waltzes begin, inevitably the wives ask their husbands to be kind enough to give poor Frankie a whirl. There is nothing to be gained by remaining here. Most of Aunt Joan's friends are much older than me.*

'I'm so sorry, Liz. Thank you for your kind offer but I have another appointment. Unfortunately, I will not be able to stay for the rest of the celebrations.'

The concoction of wedding happiness and loveliness made Frankie feel sick.

I want to have Richard with me. I remembered Jane Austen stating that 'a single man in possession of a good fortune must be in want of a wife'? Where is my prince?

36

IMAGE

'What are you doing here, Paula?' Frankie was in the shopping centre.

'Paddy's just gone to park the car. He has to buy a new suit. It's a long story. He was determined to be in Earl House Department Store early this Saturday morning. He wants to avoid the crowds.'

'Are you okay, Paula? You look a bit pale.'

'No, I'm fine really. I'll just take a puff on my inhaler. All this rushing around makes me breathless.'

'Take your time. Have a puff. I hope Paddy finds what he wants. I've popped in for some cosmetics. Haven't a clue what I want, really. '

'Oh, you're back, Paddy. Look who I've just bumped into.'

'Lovely to see you, Frankie. Why don't you two ladies enjoy a cup of coffee while I visit the men's department?'

'Nothing quite like a cup of coffee and a tea cake to begin the day, Paula.'

'Look .The queue is building up in the café.'

'Why don't you find a seat while I queue? Black coffee and a slice of toast. I don't want you to get out of breath again.'

'Okay. There's a table over there on the right. I'll settle with you later.'

'Here we are. At your service!'

'You're an angel. Thank you. How did you got on at Aunt Joan's wedding, Frankie.'

'You know my Aunt Joan. Pomp and circumstance! No, she is very fortunate. She's married the man she planned to marry.'

'You're not jealous by any chance, Frankie?'

'A little bit. Do you blame me? No, she looked lovely.'

'Well, you'll have to hurry up, Frankie.'

'That's what I've been thinking about. I want a simple wedding... I'm confused. I need to work out what I really want. I love... I'm not sure. Maybe, I should take a break and give myself time to think.'

'About what? If you want a baby, remember the years fly by.'

'I know. I have been thinking about trying to mix with more people. Maybe I should join a club. I never wear make-up. I thought I'd get a few samples in this store today. When I left the convent I wanted to cover my body. I still wear clothes that I find in charity shops. I need to change.'

'Be careful. Image isn't everything, Frankie. You're still young. Oh, Paddy's waving to me. You mind if...'

'No. Of course not. See you Monday, Paula.'

Frankie was disappointed that she could not have spoken to Paula for longer. She had to walk through the leisure wear department to reach the cosmetic department.

She thought: *I love that image. Short skirts or shorts, or even leggings and neat fitting tops. How would I look in that outfit? One of the staff plays badminton. Perhaps I should get fit.*

'Well I never! Lovely to see you, Frankie. You live around here?'

It's Sister Marion, one of the nuns from the convent in which we were both members. She left over three years ago.

'Yes, Sis... Marion.'

'Just, Marion. How lovely to see you. I'm just going up for a cuppa! Why don't we... what is it you young ones say? Is it 'chill out? Want to chill out over a coffee? My treat. Need to get my act together before I tackle the shopping.'

Frankie was being ushered into the Costa Coffee by a sixty year old ex-nun.

'How are you finding life outside the convent, Frankie? Are you married yet? '

'No. I'm still adjusting.'

'Frankie, I'm sure you would prefer to be around someone younger… not an old fogy like me. I saw you looking at the sports outfits. My niece, Amy, plays badminton. Maybe you'd like to play. If you like I could let her fix you up with a skirt. Would you like that? She has a spare racket.'

'Thank you Sis… Marion. You were always so understanding. Sorry, I can't stop the tears. Someone's up there's looking after me.'

'Here. Take this tissue. You're coffee will get cold.'

'Thank you.'

'I'm not surprised that you get upset from time to time, Frankie. Sure it's not that long since I left. Granted, I was in the convent for 32 years. It's different for you. But should you need someone to talk to. Someone who won't let the cat out of the bag, I'm willing to help.'

Frankie was not sure that she wanted to talk to an older ex-nun.

'Thank you. I have made some friends.'

'Sure that's grand. I was just going to say that I could introduce you to my niece who's probably younger than you. If you like I could introduce you to Amy.'

Frankie reflected: *Perhaps I would be able to meet a mixed group if I were to take up badminton?*

'I like that idea, Sis… Marion. Would she mind?'

'Why don't you ask her? I give you her mobile number?'

'Thank you.'

'She's very friendly. I'm minding her 18 month old until she arrives home after six tonight. Give me time to fill her in. I promise not to tell her your background. You can do so should you wish. I'm presuming that's how you would want things to be?'

'Thanks.'

'Allow her time to feed the baby. I might as well tell you there's no hubby. So things being as they are; I lend a hand with a bit of cooking. Like me she's fiercely independent. She gets on with all the palaver that goes with putting Grainne to bed. Text her after nine.'

37

KITTED OUT

'Good morning, Frankie!'

'Hello, Paula. I thought I'd come to school early this morning. So much has happened during this holiday. I need to get back into the swing of things.'

'Can catch up with each other when I give you a lift home after school tonight? That okay? There's always so much to do on the first day back.'

'You're an angel, Paula. Thank you.'

Frankie pondered, *Should I tell Paula about my meeting with Sister Marion? Will she approve of the suggestions that she made to me? I need friends to help me to decide on the next stages of my life.*

By the time Paula was ready to drive Frankie home, she decided that she didn't need to tell Paula everything.

'You survived the day, Frankie. If we start straight away we might be able to avoid the Wimbledon crowds. It's the beginning of the tennis tournament today.'

Frankie decided that it might be better to tell Paula about Sr Marion and her niece Amy, after she met Amy in a café near Wimbledon Station.

'I am grateful for a lift, Paula, but I don't want you to be caught up in the Wimbledon crowds. I can catch the train tonight. That way you can by-pass Wimbledon.'

'You sure, Frankie?'

'Yes.'

'Maybe you're right.'

Amy texted: Frankie: Meet 4:30 café left outside station. Wearing pink top, black leggings. Blonde!

Frankie opened the café door. She looked round. She could not see anybody meeting the description Amy had given. She glanced at her watch and saw that she had arrived ten minutes too early. She ordered coffee and sat in a corner seat. At half past four she put her lesson plans away, hoping that Amy would arrive. A quarter of an hour later, Frankie texted Amy: Sitting corner café. Blue dress, brown hair. You on way?

Suddenly the café door was thrown open. A tall, slim, happy young blonde rushed in. Before Frankie had time to wave to her, Amy extended her hand.

'You must be, Frankie. Just as my aunt described you. Sorry, I'm late. Amy.'

Amy ordered a Classic Ice Mango drink. She sat opposite Frankie.

'Aunt Marion told me a lot about you, Frankie.'

'All good, I hope. She told you why I wanted to meet you, Amy?'

'You want to mingle more. You'd like to settle down. You're much younger than my aunt.'

'I don't know about being young. I wanted to have a family. I…'

'Do you mind me asking what exactly you're aiming for? Aunt Marion told me that you're interested in finding a man. Is that right, Frankie?'

'Yes. I'll be blunt. I'm nearly forty. I would like to marry and have a child.'

'You need to get onto internet dating ASAP if you are serious about having a child before your clock runs out. That's without IV treatment. Presumably you know what kind of guy you would like to meet.'

'Do you do that sort of thing, Amy? Is it safe?'

'No I didn't need to. I grew up around guys. I had lots of tasters. You'll have to catch up.'

I feel scared. Perhaps Amy's ideas are too risky for me.

'Thanks, Amy. I want to meet some men. I don't know about internet dating. Is it safe?'

'It's safe enough. Aunt Marion wouldn't do that but you're still young. We could begin by browsing. If you're serious, you'll need to strike while the iron's hot'.

'Browsing sounds fine. I'm willing to try that.'

Frankie felt that she was in a whirlwind, meeting Sister Marion's niece.

She's 26. She told me that she has a gorgeous baby and a partnership with a young man who is not the father. She seems to be perceptive beyond her years. She is kind. She has taken me back to her home.

'Here you are: What kind of dater are you? Once we know that, we will be able to focus on you.'

'What do you mean, Amy?'

'Are you an Insta-mate, The Overlapper, The 'Life in a box of chocolate' charmer, The Prince/Princess, The Peter-Pan Fan……'

'Gosh, Amy! I don't understand that!'

'I'm joking. This is the kind of jargon that this site uses. Have a go. Google it and have fun!'

What am I doing? I'm being encouraged to Find a date on Match.com. Amy is rocking her baby daughter, Grainnie, to sleep before putting her into her pram.

'How you doing? I'll pop a pizza in the micro.'

The title *Singles events* came up on the screen.

Frankie read: *match.com singles nights and events give members the opportunity to get together at venues near them and share a drink, enjoy an activity and get to know each other.*

She thought, *This feels so clinical. Should I tell Amy? Will she understand?*

'What do you think of that site, Frankie?'

Amy is looking over my shoulder. She's handing me a mug.

'Here, down that quick before she wakes up. You take sugar in your coffee?'

Frankie pretended that she was searching. She thought, *Everything seems so chaotic in Amy's home. She steps over toys. She had to clear a space on a coffee table for my drink. She removed piles of magazines and baby clothes before plonking a pizza in front of us. Now she's flicking Satellite news at six to see what films will be on later.*

'Oh! Grainne has woken up.'

Amy dropped her plate and handed the baby to Frankie.

'Hungry, darling? I'll just heat her feed. Won't be a sec...'

Frankie watched Amy manage to consume half a pizza, empty her coffee and change Grainnie's nappy while she felt immobilised, looking on.

'Now you said about a badminton skirt?'

'I was just wondering what kind of gear... I should wear?'

'Well, that's it, you see. The likes of Aunt Marion's age tend to wear skirts but if you... well it's up to you. Our lot wear leggings and strappy tops. Don't have to but well none of us would turn up otherwise.'

'These fit you? Take them home and try. Grabbed them in the sale without checking the size.'

Frankie looked. *They're black and skin tight. I hate black. I wore that colour for too many years. They look so tight and revealing. I need a large 'cover me up' tee shirt to hide my bits.*

'You sure? Thanks, Amy. I owe you.'

'No worries. Aunt Marion will see me right. Here's the racket she left for you. Fancy a run round the park to get Grainne off to sleep?'

We're out the door taking turns at pushing the pram. Amy is on her mobile, getting me an invitation to a Chinese restaurant 'do' the following Saturday. She probably wants to help me to meet and mingle there.

'Amy, I'll have to go home and recover for an early start tomorrow. I'm happily exhausted. I'm not used to this pace. Thanks so much for the gear and those trendy trousers. I'll see you soon and thank Marion for me too. Ciao!'

Frankie prayed: *Dear Jesus, what have I got myself into? Order, routine, timetables, a place for everything... please take me home to my little room where's there's just me to look after.*

38

SHOCKER

Frankie took a corner seat on the train to school on Monday morning. She heard her mobile phone ping. She pulled it from her school bag and read: *Piking nr station 8 Sat. Gang celeb 30 birthdy. Guys 2. Bkd so turn up. Probs? Text. C u Amy x*

This is a quick arrangement. Amy means business. I want to go. I am scared. What shall I do? She has booked me into the restaurant. If I don't want to go I will have to decide. If only I could discuss this with Marion. I can't back out. Amy's friends will probably be much younger than me. Guysx2? Does that mean that there will be two men in the group or that she has invited two unattached men?

Frankie's mobile phone sounded again. Another text!

Cum 2 me Fri nite chek gear u like? 8ok?

Amy is trying to help me. Marion has probably encouraged her. What harm can there be in going to a Chinese meal? I can make an excuse and leave them if I find that I cannot cope.

Frankie responds: *Yes! Thanks. CU Fri Frankie x*

All week Frankie managed to avoid telling Paula that she was going out to a meal with Amy's young friends. She felt that she ought to widen her social circle and discover what men other than Richard and Sean were like.

'Phone call, Frankie! Phone!'

'Evelyn. I'm coming.'

Who can this be? Whoever it is I will have to speak to them on the phone on the table leading up the stairs to my room.

Frankie watched Evelyn's petite figure close the door into her private part of the house after she handed the receiver to her.

'Hello. Is that you, Frankie? It's Marion.'

'Marion. Good. I was hoping you'd phone....'

'I...'

'Amy's address...'

'I know. I've been to her home. Fourteen Byron House, Wellington Estate. Lawn Road. Turn left out of Wimbledon tube station and walk a hundred yards, turn right and you'll be facing a four storey block of flats on your right. Amy lives in the third home on the second floor. Green door.'

'Oh... I forgotten... She did say something...'

'Thanks Sis... Marion.'

'Amy said to be there around six.'

'Six. That's fine. I'll be there. I mind her gorgeous little daughter, Grainnie.'

ON FRIDAY EVENING Frankie left her flat in time to walk to Amy's home. She questioned herself, *Why am I feeling so tired? Is it because I am frightened? Amy is only twenty-five. She has a baby. She works in the leisure centre three days a week. If she can cope, I should be able to cope too.*

Frankie knocked at house number fourteen.

'Come in, Frankie. You must be tired at the end of the school week. You're welcome.'

'I'm tired, Marion. But I'm fine, really.'

'Hi Amy!'

'Hi Frankie! Good timing. Aunt Marion is just about to put Grainnie to bed.'

'Oh, she's lovely. Her little eyes are closing. A bundle of pink.'

'Want to kiss her goodnight? Here, hold her a minute while I load the washing machine.'

A baby. A beautiful baby girl. If only she were mine. I've never held a baby before. This is a lovely feeling.

'She likes you. She's peacefully opening and closing her eyes as you cuddle her.'

'I'm ready, Frankie. Follow me into the other room. I'll fix you up before I get myself ready.'

'Thanks, Amy.'

Amy seated Frankie on a wobbly pink-topped stool before a mirror in Amy's bathroom discussing funky hairstyles! She waved scissors very near to her unruly red mop and talked about spikes, gel and VO5. Even highlights.

'Remember I have to show up in school on Monday, Amy!'

'I know! But these things wash out. I hold down a job too. Go on, be a devil! If you're going to hang out with our lot, you want to blend in.'

'Okay, spike me up. You're sure it'll wash out?'

'Of course. Okay if I give you a few blonde highlights? With a few snips and gel you'll have an amazing new look. I got a sample of L'Oreal Paris Luminiser for you too.'

'It will all wash out, Amy?'

'Ye, yea! Chill out, Frankie!'

'I'll certainly look different. Nobody will recognise me, Amy.'

'While the colour is taking, why don't try on a little black number that I found in the Oxfam shop on my way home. No worries. Aunt Marion forked out for it for you.'

FRANKIE WALKED home with shades of blonde highlights on a gelled irregular shaped hair-do and a slightly skimpy black dress. The next morning she managed to slip out early without the landlady seeing her. Amy had encouraged her to buy something to wear from New Look. She came home with a wide, bright green, shiny belt and a matching mini wrap, dangling green earrings and necklace and a pair of throw-away high heels.

As arranged, Frankie tottered on her heels to Wimbledon Tube Station to meet the others.

Amy waved to her. Before she joined her, a group of six lively lads and four girls emerged through the station doors.

They all look so young. I don't know how to behave. They're saying 'Hi!' and slapping hands. They're kissing each other. What am I to do? I want to run home now!

'Okay, you lot! You all know each other. Frankie's, the friend I said I'd bring along.'

'Hi Frankie!'

'Hi!'

'I'll tell you their names when we are in the restaurant, Frankie. It's only round the corner.'

Amy grabbed Frankie's arm and walked on. When they were shown to their table Amy announced, 'I suggest we muddle up and go guy, girl and so on. Okay? Agreed?'

Frankie found herself seated between curly haired Tim and loud Mark. Neither of them spoke for a while.

What do I say to these lads? 'Where do you work?' seems inappropriate on a Friday night when they most likely want to forget work. I'll try, 'Have you been to this restaurant before, Tim?'

'Yes.' Was his response. Then he bent over towards the girl next to him and snuggled into her arms.

Frankie was about to ask Mark seated on the other side of her the same question when he addressed everyone at the table. 'How about we all chip in with the drinks? Okay?'

'That okay with you, Frankie?'

'Yes. Yes that's fine, Amy.'

Amy was looking concerned but what could she say? worried Frankie. *I have never drunk much alcohol. One glass of wine was all I intended to drink all evening.*

Chinese music began to blare. Drinks were ordered to be shared. Everyone helped themselves to various dishes being spun round on a

Lazy-Susan revolving tray. The music was very loud. Nobody spoke to each other. Every now and then two girls stood holding their hand bags and left the table. Mark turned to wave to the girls at the other tables.

Bewildered Frankie wanted, wondered, *Is he meant to partner me? I'll never know since I can't make myself heard above the loud rock music.*

Amy came round to where Frankie was seated. She asked, 'You okay, Frankie? You keep smiling but… ?'

'Fine, Amy. You enjoy yourself.'

What I want to scream is 'I want to go home NOW!'

The music grew even louder. The waiters began to bring more drink round to every table.

I can't endure anymore. I'll tell Amy that I feel unwell and go home.

Suddenly the momentum built up. Everybody stood. The chairs were kicked back and everybody began putting their hands round each others waists and prancing round behind each other.

What is happening? Everyone is pulling at each others clothes. Everything seems out of control. A waiter is jumping up on the table. He is encouraging a girl to pull at his trousers. She's pulling them down. He is naked in front of me! Why do I feel excited and sick all at once.

Surely the waiters will take control now? But no. The chief waiter has come over with a balloon to put in front of the naked waiter's private parts. Another waiter is jumping on the next table with only a balloon covering him.

Most folk begin to leer, clap, cheer and giggle. The music blares. A girl takes a lighted candle off the table and chases the naked waiter round the table. Another girl aims a fork at his balloon.

It develops into a nightmare. Frankie threw a ten pound note for drinks on the table.

Frankie walked out. No one stopped her.

39

AFTER CHINESE SHOCKER

'Visitor! Visitor! You okay for a visitor, Frankie?'

The morning after the Chinese meal Frankie was woken by someone banging on her bedroom door.

Who's rattling the door handles? What's going on? The door is opening. Marion is standing behind my landlady, Evelyn.

'I'm so sorry, Frankie, but I wanted to see you,' stuttered Marion.

Frankie realises, *She'd heard about the goings on last night.*

'It's alright, Evelyn. Come in, Marion.'

What must I look like? Pyjama bottoms and a long T-shirt. It is Sunday. Frankie pulled up her duvet and pointed to the chair.

'Sorry S...Marion. I took a sleeping pill. Last night I couldn't sleep.'

'It's about last night that I've come. Sorry to arrive unannounced. Perhaps I should have texted you but I forget to charge the thing.'

'Amy told you.'

'When Amy told me about the hilarity at the Chinese do last night I had to come to see you. She said that you disappeared at some point. I wondered if you got home alright.'

'It was awful, Marion.'

'I am so sorry, Frankie.'

'I don't know what to think. Did Amy tell you about... did she tell you about the men stripping off?'

'Only after I quizzed her. It seems that it's no big deal for her. I tried to imagine what it might be like for you, Frankie.'

Frankie recalled an incident with Sister Marion and a priest some years ago. The older nuns used to try and hush up the matter. Although they still talked about Sister Marion fondly, they were instructed, that should she turn up at the convent, she was to be put her in the parlour as opposed to welcoming her into our refectory.

'Marion. Sorry, I still find it hard to address you without the 'Sister'. What I want to say is that I've had a restless night trying to figure out what was happening. Did Amy tell you that two men had their clothes ripped off? One of them was right in front of me?'

'Yes, Amy told me, Frankie.'

'I was shocked, I suppose because I had never seen... it was a revelation for me. But was he in the wrong? I was so embarrassed. But somehow... I can't explain.'

Why is Marion smiling? wondered Frankie.

'You're a fully functioning woman with all your instincts in good order. You were sexually aroused, Frankie. Plain and simple. You were embarrassed and rightly so. That is natural. Whether these men should be prancing around naked is another matter altogether.'

'Oh Marion, that's such a relief! That's precisely how I felt and still do. Embarrassed and excited all at the same time... and a bit curious too.'

'I don't know what you have heard about what happened to me long ago? I don't want to bore you but it might help to you understand.'

'I recall that some of the nuns used to hint. Something about a priest fondling you inappropriately. No one would say exactly what, except that you made allegations. When you were asked to prove them, you couldn't.'

'Not, I couldn't. I didn't want to get the Order into trouble. I didn't want outsiders to know that abuse had taken place.'

'What's the connection with what I experienced last night, Marion?'

'You said that you were embarrassed and excited. An inappropriate happening excited you. On the occasion when I was abused, I felt angry and excited. This puzzled me.'

'Why?'

'Yes. Why?'

'It's the human bit that comes into play. Our body parts are God-given. They were given for a purpose. They fit together and we are meant to use them primarily for procreation. That's what the Catholic Church keeps stressing. Procreation, I mean.'

'I was angry and confused last night.'

'I would have shown my disapproval by walking out. I dare say had you known what was going to happen, you probably wouldn't have gone. But have you gained from it?'

'I presume you mean that I know for sure that I am normal and can be aroused?'

'And you can choose, Frankie. You see, that's where things are different, where priests are concerned. The Church has tied these men into celibacy without taking into consideration their God-given human nature. *'Bees do it, birds do it etc…'*

'Okay. But if you don't mind me going back to what happened to you, why were the nuns so annoyed with you, Marion?'

'I don't know. Maybe it was because they were frightened to look at the celibacy issue. The priests told me to go to a solicitor if I wanted to bring this issue up again?'

'But would you have taken the Order to Court?'

'They knew that I would never have taken the Order to court. Wasn't I a member of that Order for 32 years? Of course I am angry at the priest who took advantage of me and I want him reprimanded. What I wanted was for them to talk about the difficulties priests encounter in keeping their promise of celibacy.'

Frankie was reminded of the love she had for Sean and his explanation.

'So why didn't you say that?'

'I did. However, once the word 'sex' is mentioned, they go into a tizzy. You know that the Mission of the Order we belonged to is all about preventing sin. Unfortunately, sex is so often linked with sin.'

'Sin. That's it. I feel so guilty because part of me was excited by what happened at the Chinese 'do'. Is that because sex is for producing babies? I was not thinking of that.'

'Now don't tell me, Frankie, that you have reached your age without realising that unless there is pleasure evolved, women might not so easily be enticed into child-birth. The pleasure, the attraction is the most natural part of our human nature. It's God-given. If you don't believe in God, it's still a big part of what makes us human. You agree? All that nodding of your head shows you do?'

'I do. I know so little. No one has ever told me what in detail… I've guessed but…'

'Okay. Women. We feel pleasure in being touched. When a man combs his hands through a woman's hair, strokes her face, neck, her breasts, her body reacts…'

'I know… my body is…'

'Frankie, that is meant to happen. Your body curves, tenses, tingles and enjoys this pleasure. The man's body reacts too. His penis tightens. He wants the woman to respond by opening up to him.'

Frankie had felt this when Sean held her close.

'Talking about this… I feel…'

'If a man was folding into your body. Penetrating you. You would want to abandon yourself to the pleasure you feel. If woman didn't enjoy this pleasure maybe, they would not be enticed into child-bearing.'

'Thank you, Marion. Deep down I knew this but I equated it with sin. I remember my mother telling me that she had to be churched. Women were required to kneel before a priest in church to be cleansed after they had given birth.'

'Thank goodness we have moved away from such practices. Nowadays, we are trying to understand same-sex relationships.'

'Am I to take it, Marion, that you think priests should get married?'

'Frankie, there's no 'should' but in my opinion I think they would be better off with the option or at least an 'opt out' clause should they find it too hard to restrain themselves. At the moment it is totally unfair, in my opinion that married Church of England clergy are welcomed into the Catholic Church to work alongside priests who are bound by celibacy.'

'We were always reminded that we should sublimate our feelings, Marion. I mean we should love Jesus and the priests should love Mary, Our Lady, and to wait to satisfy our deeper longings in Heaven. All those lovely hymns and prayers we sang helped to do that.'

'Frankie, did that really help? For a bit, maybe. Speaking for myself, the urges and raging hormones that welled up inside me were often uncontrollable. I think that's why there has been so much abuse in the Church. Men, out of control, struggling with very strong urges denied them by celibacy. It's unrealistic.'

'Why do you think the Church, even our present Pope Francis is so adamant about keeping the celibacy, Marion?'

'Frankie, financial considerations play a big part. Church of England clergy and parishes have a family to sustain. Nowadays a vicar could even belong to a trade union and claim a salary. Were the Catholic Church to follow suit, it would have to fork out so much money. Seeing that the Catholic Church won't even pay back the pension of those of us who have left the convent or priesthood, they will hardly agree to do that.'

'What about denial, Marion? I often think some of the hierarchy live in a world of their own where they close their eyes to what is going on with regard to sexuality.'

'I agree, Frankie. That is why youngsters are no longer joining. They are better educated and are not afraid of the threat of hell. They can think for themselves and are not going to be dictated to by the Pope, bishops and other clergy who won't even listen to them.'

'I suppose too they have so many different professions to choose from.'

'That's so true, Frankie. When I left home if you wanted to succeed in life, you aimed at being a teacher or a nurse or to work in a bank. There was the high calling of being a nun or a priest. It was considered a blessing to have someone in the family who heard God calling them to serve Him in the Church.'

'Marion, I am going to insist that you have that cup of coffee. You deserve that. One of my chocolate biscuits, too.'

When Marion suggested that it may be better not to meet up again with her niece. Frankie decided that perhaps it might be better if she would threw herself into her school work.

40

CLOSENESS

Frankie dreaded the end term. Tests, reports, Open Days, Parent Evenings and Sports Day. She was glad that Paula was not at school. She felt embarrassed after what had happened in the Chinese Restaurant. She also decided to resume a more natural relationship with Richard. She consulted him on ordering next year's stock for religious education lessons and assemblies.

'Are you staying to finish you're ordering again tonight, Linda?'

'I'm determined to hand the completed forms to Margaret before I go home, Frankie.'

'Margaret? Who's Margaret?'

'Frankie! She's our replacement secretary.'

'I knew Paula had fallen. Her husband has been driving her. I didn't realise that someone is taking her place, Linda.'

'For goodness sake, Frankie. Come in. Let me fill you in.'

'What's happened?'

'Where have you been that you haven't heard all the-goings-on? Margaret is not just replacing Paula. She is our new secretary, Frankie.'

'Oh my G... Why didn't I noticed what's going on, Linda?'

'Paula is your friend, Frankie?'

'She is. She… I feel awful, Linda. Tell me. What has happened?'

Frankie thought, *I must have become too pre-occupied with what's been going on in my own life. I've blinded myself to what happening to my friend and confidant, Paula.*

'Pull over a chair. Where do I begin? Surely you were aware that Paula fell over a loose tile in the corridor?'

'I had heard that she fell. Paddy came and drove her home from school.'

'No, Frankie. He drove her to St Stephen's Hospital. There she was told that she had broken her arm.'

'Oh no! I feel awful. I…'

Frankie watched Linda push the stock-ordering books away from her on her desk.

'Frankie, that was bad enough but Paula's husband, Paddy, has succeeded in making life very difficult for her. He demanded that Paula sue the school because she broke her arm on a loose tile in the school corridor.'

'Why did he do that?'

'In a way he was right because that is why we have insurance policies. Even Sr Sheila explained that the compensation wouldn't come out of the school finances.'

'What did Paula think about that?'

'She was embarrassed. She tried to persuade him not to claim. She will not return to school, Frankie. She has handed in her resignation.'

'Paddy is a good man. He respects the nuns. He tends to seek justice. He is a business man. If this accident happened at his work he would have claimed on his insurance. He also must have suffered seeing Paula in pain.'

Frankie reflected, *I have to talk to Paula. It might be best to wait until the morning. It's late. My landlady will be out shopping on Saturday morning. When I use the phone on the landing there will be no one around to listen.*

When Frankie was sure her landlady had left the house the next morning, she dialled Paula's number.

Fortunately, Paula answered, 'I'm glad you phoned, Frankie.'

'I feel so awful Paula. I didn't realise...'

'Could you come over this morning, say around eleven while Paddy is out?'

'Of course.'

'We can chat. Maybe you could join me down on my allotment. You know where my plot is, don't you?'

Frankie decided, *I need to catch the 10.45 bus or start walking immediately. Luckily I am washed, dressed and breakfasted. Paula has made it clear that she doesn't want Paddy to be there when we meet.*

Frankie rubbed her eyes. She felt that her legs were as heavy as lead as she walked towards the door of her room. She wondered what kind of relationship Paula had with Paddy.

As she opened the gate into the allotment, she saw that Paula was struggling. She was trying to cut some flaming red gladioli with her left hand in a sling.

'They look lovely. What are those flowers over there, Paula?'

'Oh they are Zinnias. Look, here is the seed packet.'

'Paula! Let me have those cutters.'

Frankie noticed how Paula was determined to cut the gladioli with one arm.

She's not wearing any make-up. That's very unusual for her. The rims of her eyes are red and her greying hair is uncombed. A thin smile is hovering on her quivering lips.

'What have they been saying in school?'

'It was Linda who told me, Paula.'

'I'm so sorry, Frankie. I should have told you myself but it escalated so quickly and now I'm reduced to this and Paddy... well.'

Frankie gently put her arm round Paula.

'I see you have come prepared with a flask. Shall we have a cuppa?'

'Playtime! I have two Jaffa cakes. Shall we sit on those little stools, Frankie?'

'You make yourself comfortable. Use this board as a tray. I'll be Mum.'

Frankie thought, *Paula face resembles a crumpled dish cloth. The one time yellowish-brown amber colour in her eyes seems to have surfaced its dregs. She has aged and looked grey. She seems older than my mother.*

In the midst of a riot of fading autumn flowers in the middle of an allotment, Paula explained how Paddy insisted that she sue the school for her breakage.

'He is good in his own way, Frankie, but very controlling. He has a good heart.'

'He likes to be in control?'

'He doesn't want others to take advantage of me. It's just that I wish he had… never mind. Tell me what you have been up to lately. I love a bit of gossip. How are you getting on with Richard?'

'Back to normal. You know what it's like at the end of term. Richard likes the new religious education scheme. He helped me chose the relevant books. He's very efficient.'

'I suppose you're both too busy as the term draws to a close to having time to go out together. Once you're on holiday, you'll be free to resume a proper relationship. I hope you'll both be happy.'

'I could hug you, Paula, if it wasn't for that arm!'

As Frankie poured coffee into the mugs, Paula continued, 'I'm glad that you have forgotten that priest that you met in Ireland. Richard loves you.'

'Would you like one of your Jaffa cakes, Paula?'

'Yes, Frankie. Paddy won't be back until late for his meal tonight.'

Frankie felt tempted to tell Paula about what happened at the Chinese night. However, she thought that she looked too fragile.

Silence. Frankie bit into the cake. She watched a robin on a branch. Paula coughed. The robin flew onto a branch close above them and warbled.

'No, Paula, I need to… I want to talk… to tell you.'

Frankie stood. Then she sat down.

'You've something to tell me, Frankie?'

'Not now, Paula. You're not well.'

'Let's go through that gate and settle ourselves down on the bench in the rose garden. We can chat there.'

'Let me help you up. It's difficult with that sling. I'll take the flowers. You lead the way.'

'Are you sure that you want to hear about my recent exploits, Paula?'

'Everything!'

Frankie felt embarrassed recounting what happened at the Chinese restaurant.

'I think that you've been very brave, Frankie. Marion seems to have been very kind. Her niece, Amy, helped you to experience a life that you didn't know existed. You've experimented.'

'Thank you for being so understanding, Paula. I have come to realise that Richard is the man for me.'

'Good.'

'How are you really feeling, Paula?'

Paula blew her nose. 'When I broke my arm I looked on it as an accident but Paddy was determined to get justice. That's what he said. God forgive me, Frankie, but I have my suspicions. I think that he really wanted me to give up work. Maybe he would be happier if I were at home with him. Oh, I shouldn't have said that!'

'Well, maybe you're right, Paula.'

'Frankie, sometimes you can be loved too much. Every time I blink, he watches me. Believe me, you can long to… no, I'm lucky, that every breath I take, Paddy loves me more. I suppose what I'm trying to say to you is don't be bowled over by love.'

'Loved too much?'

'You're eyes are wide open, Frankie! Don't worry. Paddy adores me. I only have to hint at what I'd like and it's mine. Look at these rings. They're the real thing. Cost a small fortune. I shouldn't have said what I said earlier. I only told you that to warn you about checking out why you feel loved before you commit yourself.'

Once Paula and Frankie parted, muddled thoughts thumped through Frankie's head, *Would I ever know what relationships and love are, really?*

As she walked home she prayed, *Dear Jesus, why is love so compli-*

cated? Richard has been kind to me. Was his concern just kindness? Why did he treat me so abruptly? What am I to read into Sean's attention? But what about poor Paula? What kind of love does Paddy have for Paula?

41

SPACE

'Frankie. Have you got time to chat?' It was Richard's head popping through her classroom door.

'Come in, Richard. I was just about to go home.'

'Good. Can I give you a lift?'

'Oh, could you? I'm exhausted.'

'Maybe we could stop for a drink?'

'Brilliant idea! A cold drink on a hot day. Perfect. The last day of term. Removing the names from all these lockers. It's a killer. You must be tired too.'

'I'll wait for you in the car. Take your time. No hurry.'

'Give me five minutes.'

Frankie thought, *Look at the sight of me... sagging tights, no lipstick. Hair all tossed. Better smarten up.*

Frankie headed for the ladies cloakroom. She hoped she'd brought some of those perfume samples she collected. *Thank goodness I have fresh tights in my locker, she thought. Don't want to look like Nora Batty.*

Five minutes later, arms filled with books and bags filled with presents from the children, Frankie pushed open the side entrance. Richard was there.

'What a load! Library books to return? I've got some too. Put them in my boot. Make yourself comfortable. I'll switch on the air-conditioning.'

'Thanks, Richard.'

'How about stopping at the Angel Inn? Lovely garden at the rear.'

'Great.'

'I love that old seat in the garden. Let's see if it's free.'

They walked round the side of the pub into the wild meadow.

'Look! They've done the garden up... oh... ohoo... the arbour... red roses... beautiful!'

'So romantic! That garden seat is the other side of the rose arbour... Let's tip-toe through, shall we?'

'The scent from the roses... gorgeous...'

Frankie felt Richard's hand grasp hers. 'A rose for your hair, Frankie. Smell this one?'

'Thank you, Richard... you're such a romantic.'

'Look at the names carved in the arm of this garden seat. Shall we carve ours?'

'The waiter might be a past pupil... better not, eh?'

'Here comes the waiter.'

'What can I get you?'

'You order first, Richard. I never know what to choose.'

'Would you like to try an Aperol Spritz? It's low alcohol, aromatic? I'm going to order one.'

'Sounds good. Yes, please.'

'Spritz. Two please.' The old waiter hustled into the pub.

'Peals of laughter from that table. This is the place for happy couples! They must be celebrating. Maybe they're just engaged.'

'I'm tired but it's a happy tiredness.' Frankie lent back on the bench. Richard loosened his tie.

'I'm exhausted, Frankie. But look at you... fresh... relaxed... lovely.'

'End of term, Richard. Yes but you have you have extra responsibilities.'

'That's true. Done that for the last few years. Frankie, you'll laugh. I think I'm losing my marbles!'

'What? Why?'

'Yesterday I found myself going back to double-check that I had locked the confidential staff file. Must be old age is creeping on...'

'Don't be daft! We all forget things. Besides, I can give you a hand. I'm good at doing dance drama with the kids. I can even make cups of tea when you have parents' meetings.'

'Would you really? It's natural to be tired at the end of term. Frankie, your help will be great.'

'Here come the drinks. Cheers! Now for the hols!'

'Cheers, Frankie! We've survived another year!' He reached over to click her glass.

'You've chosen a lovely garden, Richard.'

'I'm glad you've come here with me. I've been longing for us to be together like this. It also gives me a chance to apologise for the way I behaved towards you especially when Anna was around. I wish it had never happened.'

'Well, I suppose the way I acted didn't help.'

'No, Frankie. I've thought about this a lot. Should have been more sensitive. More respectful. I forced my opinion on you.'

Frankie noticed Richard's eyes moistening. She reached out to place her hand on his.

'Everyone has their bad moments.'

'Whenever I meet the nuns, they sing your praises.'

'Did you feel compelled to obey Opus Dei, Richard?'

'Opus Dei? Rules? It's strange. I find myself abiding by them, yet rebelling against them.'

'So many rules to be obeyed in the convent...'

'Yes. That's it. Same for me in the seminary.'

'And Anna? I thought you might have a soft spot for Anna.'

'Anna? No. I have never loved Anna. She's part of Opus Dei. On reflection it was stupid to allow her to have any say in the First Communion celebrations.'

'That's a relief! Your attitude towards me seemed to change so quickly... I... I was baffled.'

Frankie watched Richard's hand cover the bottom half of his face. He gradually moved his hands so that his elbows rested on his chest.

Then he reached out and grasped her hand. 'Frankie, I'm so very sorry. I've acted so badly. Please, will you forgive me?'

'How could I not forgive you, Richard? I understand now. Of course I forgive you. You silly man.'

Frankie felt herself blushing.

'Frankie, you're one in a million. Always willing to help, always cheerful. How could I be such an oaf. I value you, really I do. Do you understand?'

Frankie felt a smile cross her lips. 'Of course I understand. Years spent in religious life. No touching. No physical contact… not even at the sign of peace during Mass. I had to obey the same rules.'

'That's what I admire about you, Frankie. You understand. We share so much. We both struggled to break free of those restrictions. It takes time to adjust to life outside religious life.'

Richard moved nearer to Frankie. She felt his arm gently encircle her shoulders and draw her closer. She enjoyed the warmth of his embrace.

'Oh, that feels wonderful.'

'Frankie, would you come out to dinner before I fly to Italy?'

'Oh Richard, I'd love to.'

'My Dad has asked me to look after my aunt. My father's sister. She lives outside Florence. She's broken her wrist. Can't drive. She shops for herself and my other aunt.'

'Poor lady. That is painful. Is she in plaster?'

'Yes. For six weeks. She's a dear old soul. So independent.'

'You'll be doing the chauffeuring? Is she close to you?'

'My mother died in childbirth. Aunt Margherita looked after me for my first seven years.'

'What caused your mother's death, Richard?'

'I've asked my father that question so many times. A blood disease, I think? He's never told me. Must be difficult for him. He loved her dearly. Keeps her photo beside his bed. There's a big one in the front room, too.'

'Lucky you, staying in Florence. Surrounded by galleries… Museums. You'll be a great help to your aunts. I bet they adore you.'

'I wanted you to know why I'll be away most of the summer. Six weeks. But I'll phone you.'

'Richard, we've both learnt to put duty first. I'm planning on a trip to the Lake District. Yvonne, my landlady, has invited me to join a group of women walkers. Always wanted to go there.'

The sun was setting through the trees, casting a golden across the garden. Lights were twinkling on the bushes. A cold wind was picking up.

'Brrrr... let's go. Getting chilly.'

'Let me help you with your cardigan. Here... have my jacket.'

Richard hugged her as he placed his jacket over her shoulders. 'We'll soon warm up in the car.'

'That's better. Thank you, Richard.'

'I'll drop you off at your flat.'

'You sure? Traffic's busy now. I can catch the train.'

Richard smiled. 'I insist on taking you home, Frankie.'

He opened the car door and offered her the seat belt. 'Let's have some music, shall we? How about 'My Fair Lady?'

'Great! That's Eliza Doolittle... I'll put on my Cockney accent... *All I want...*'

Richard joined in...

'I love singing...'

'It's fun to laugh... life is short... enjoy... that's what I say, Frankie.'

Richard whistled. Frankie clapped and tapped on the dashboard.

When they reached Frankie's flat Richard walked her to the door. 'Thanks for coming out with me. Have you got your key?' As he turned to leave, he bent forward and kissed her on the cheek. 'Goodnight, Frankie. Have a great summer. I'll text you.'

She slid inside, dropped her school bags inside the door of her room and lay on her bed.

He kissed me. Why didn't I kiss him? You've got a lot to learn, Frankie. I'm so glad that Opus Dei hasn't got hold on him.

Frankie didn't hear the knocking.

'Frankie, are you there? Are you alright? Phone call!' It was the landlady.

'Oh! Evelyn. I'm coming.'

'It's your friend's husband. He sounds troubled.'

'Thanks, Evelyn' She picked up the phone. 'Hello, Frankie speaking. Something wrong?'

'Hello, Frankie. I tried phoning you earlier. Paula would like to invite you to our house for coffee tomorrow morning. Would eleven suit you?'

'Is she okay? Has the plaster been removed from her wrist, Paddy?'

'The plaster is off. Can we expect you at eleven? I'll have some nibbles ready.'

'Eleven o'clock. I'll be there. Thank you.'

Frankie decided, *I'll have an early night. Wait until I tell Paula that Richard is going to Italy over the summer holidays. What bad luck.*

Minutes before eleven, Frankie rang Paula and Paddy's doorbell.

'Welcome, Frankie! Paula's in the dining room. She'll be delighted to see you.'

'Yoo-hoo! Frankie. In here! Paddy has prepared a feast. He insisted on going to the baker's. Hope you're hungry.'

'Lovely to see you, Paula.' She bent over to kiss her. 'How's the arm? Weak, I expect.'

'I'm following the exercise regime that the physiotherapist gave me.'

'Paddy has prepared fruit and coffee cake, chocolate biscuits, a variety of nuts, bowls of strawberries and blueberries... trying to make me healthy.'

Paddy was at the door wearing his man-apron. 'What will you drink? Hot or cold? Coffee? How about a drop of wine, Frankie?'

'Coffee would be lovely, Paddy. Is it your birthday?'

'No. Knew you'd be tired at the end of term.'

'Are you exhausted, Frankie? It always takes me a few days to recover after we break up. How was school these last few weeks?'

'Everybody has missed you, Paula. Margaret tried her best but she is inexperienced. She'll never really replace you. She must have been fed-up hearing us saying.' Paula used to...'

'Can't imagine I was missed so much. How's Richard? I expect you'll be seeing more of him during the holidays.'

Frankie heard footsteps. Paula seemed to be looking over her shoulder. It was Paddy.

'At your service, ladies. Coffee for two. The milk and sugar are on the table. Help yourself to the cakes. Coffee. Cakes, this side.'

'Thank you, Paddy. They look so tempting. Marzipan. Delicious! You must have made them yourself.'

'Now you're teasing me, Frankie.'

Paula chose a slice of carrot cake. She covered her lips with her hand. Frankie sensed there was something wrong.

Paddy was hovering. 'Let me help...'

'Frankie, it's not good medical news, I'm afraid. Paula wanted you to know.'

'Know what?'

'Paula has been diagnosed with cancer in her left lung.'

'Oh no, Paula. I'm so very sorry... There have been so many advances in treating cancer. I'm sure the doctors will do their best to help you, Paula.'

'Yes. Paddy has been doing his research. Definite progress.'

'Doctors say a positive attitude helps.'

'We wanted to tell you ourselves. Sr Sheila has all the nuns in the convent storming heaven for me.'

'I'll pray, too. I'll light lots of candles in church. I don't know what to say.'

Frankie moved up the sofa near Paula and put her around her shoulder.

'My poor, dear friend. I will help you cope with this. We will all help you.'

42

SUMMER HOLIDAYS

Frankie arranged to meet Sr Sheila in a café in Battersea Park.

'You sounded upset when you phoned, Frankie. I am only too happy to help, Frankie. What's troubling you?'

'Thank you, Sister. It's not me. It's Paula. I visited her every week during the holidays.'

'How do you find her?'

'She's very unwell, Sister. She knows that she will not live long. She is frail, lost so much weight. She has been told that the cancer has spread to the other lung.'

'That is terrible news. You know I offered to visit her. Paddy said no. She is grateful for the prayers. She felt too weak to have visitors. I'm glad that she welcomes you, Frankie.'

'I try to do what's best for her, Sister Sheila. I like to speak to Paula alone. Each time I visit, we go through a similar routine. Paddy provides enticing food. Sometimes it's cake, biscuits and coffee. On two occasions he even prepared a roast dinner.'

'He is very kind. I don't suppose Paula is able to eat much?'

'No, Sister. She eats and drinks very little. She uses a straw to drink. Can barely suck 'Fortified Food', supplied on prescription.

Paddy is attentive. Sometimes even amusing. I watch Paula's face. I don't know what she really thinks.'

'Amusing?'

'Yes, Sister. He tells jokes. He puts on silly voices and prances about pretending that he is Eeyore or Paddington Bear and other characters. At other times he lights a candle, places a statue of Our Lady or a crucifix on the coffee table and recites prayers.'

'He's trying to take Paula's mind off her illness. Poor chap. It seems that he does not know what to do for the best. It must be so hard for him.'

'You're right, Sister. Paula said that Paddy loves her too much. How can that be, Sister? He must think that he is being kind.'

'What did Paula say, Frankie?'

'Paddy watches me all the time. He watches my every breath. If I blink, he knows. As soon as I gasp for breath, he puts my inhaler to my mouth. When the doctor comes or I go to the hospital, he speaks for me.'

'Poor man. He's very anxious. He is trying so hard to care for her. Can't face losing her. He knows he wouldn't have anyone else...'

'She told me that she is on private health care. Said it is BUPA. Paddy has demanded to see the specialists. He researches what they diagnose. He argues... discusses...'

'That could be awkward, I suppose.'

'Paula said that she wished that he would use a more conciliatory approach.'

'Maybe he needs counselling. Sounds as though he could do with some medical support.'

'I was wondering about that, Sister. He will certainly need help as the illness progresses.'

'I agree. Would it be good for you to have some time together while Paddy is not around? I know that Paula loves river trips. A parishioner gave me a ticket for two on the River Thames starting at Windsor.'

'That would be wonderful, Sister Sheila! Give us time to chat... but surely Paddy will want to go with Paula?'

'Maybe he will. Leave it to me, Frankie. I will come up with a plan.'

Several days later Frankie travelled by train to Windsor. She walked to the River Thames and waited in a tow path where people boarded the boats down to the lock and back. When Frankie saw Paddy's car approach, she rushed nearer to help Paula.

'Hello, Paula, Paddy.'

'Aren't we lucky with the weather. I'll walk you over to the French Brothers' Ticket Office. This part of the river is lovely and quiet. Only the Queen's swans squawking and splashing.'

'It's always peaceful early morning. Even when parents arrive with their children, this is a quieter area.'

'You two ladies, wait there. I'll sort out your boarding passes.'

'Thanks Paddy. Sorry you're not coming with us.'

Paddy handed them their tickets. They walked slowly across the wide plank onto the boat. 'Let's sit at the front of the boat.'

Frankie observed: An elderly couple were sitting at the other end.

A ruddy-faced older man dressed in a woolly polo-necked jumper helped them on board. When they were seated, he grasped the microphone and in a gruff voice began, 'Ahem. Ah… hmm… Welcome on board, Ladies… all three of you and the gentleman.' He doffed his cap, smiled and read out the emergency instructions.

'He's turned on the engine. We're off!'

'Good. Do you remember the last time we came here? We had the school children to look after, Frankie.'

'No responsibilities this time. Calm. Peaceful.'

The engine throbbed low. Frankie became conscious of the lapping of the swell as one of the other boats docked as they headed out. Paula leaned back in her seat.

'Frankie, this is idyllic. How did you and Sr Sheila manage to get Paddy to agree to let me go on this river trip? He has not allowed me out of his care for weeks. Besides, I thought that Sr Sheila would not forgive us for suing the school when I broke my arm.'

'Sr Sheila worked her magic.' Frankie tapped her nose. 'Secrets.' She doesn't bear grudges. Besides, the school insurance is there for incidents like that. She was only too happy to arrange this adventure. She loves you, Paula. We all do.'

'This is wonderful. Look, there's Windsor Castle. Those majestic grey stone turrets are towering over steely Lady Thames.'

'You're a poet, Paula. Are you warm enough?'

'Oh yes. I'm wearing lots of layers. Paddy insisted that I wrap myself in this gorgeous woollen cardigan that he bought as a surprise last time he returned from the famous Galway Woollen Mills.'

'You're camouflaged in beguiling shades of brown. Those colours certainly suit you. You know me: Dressed in shades of green. I'm wearing layers too. T-shirt and two cardigans. Should be warm enough.'

'Isn't it fun, two girls together. I do miss all the fun we had at school.'

'Aren't those snow white swans graceful as they glide in pairs on the ebb created by the boats? Married for life, aren't they? Like Paddy and you.'

'Paddy's a lonely soul. Has no one but me.'

'Look, the mallards and moorhens are squabbling over the titbits. That old man has tossed them some bread.'

Paula rested her arm on the side of the boat. 'The stillness. It's only interrupted by a twitter, a warble and an occasional squawk. This is wonderfully peaceful.'

'When I see an upturned ducks I'm reminded of that old rhyme;

They both recited *Ducks Ditty, 'All along...'*

'I'm looking along the river bank for Ratty, Mole and Toad. I love 'Wind in the Willows'. The children always love hearing their adventures.'

As they approached the weir the engine revved. The boat began to turn round. They had reached Old Windsor Lock.

'I could ride on this boat forever, Frankie. Just switch time off and sail on and on and out into the big hungry sea.'

Frankie moved closer and stretched her warm shawl over both of them. She linked her arms in Paula's and felt her bones.

'Paula? Are you eating?'

'No, Frankie. Paddy tried to tempt me with very weak chicken soup. I couldn't swallow it.'

'Are you limited to the Fortifies Foods?'

'They're not too bad. Come in many flavours. I listen to Paddy when he quizzes Mr Laurd, my oncologist, about my food. I know my time is limited.'

'Are you frightened?'

'I am. Death comes to us all, doesn't it? I'm well cared for. Paddy does he's best. I think he is more frightened than I am.'

'You're very brave, Paula.'

'Not really, Frankie. You and I are never alone. I miss my friends.'

'I wondered about that. When I phone you, Paddy says that you are too weak to have visitors. He's told Sr Sheila not to come.'

'I know. I've heard him. That makes me angry. I know he loves me but I am not his possession. I must be my own person, Frankie. I should not be so ungrateful. Forgive me.'

'I would not want to feel that I was owned by anyone. It's not sinful to feel angry. Even Jesus was angry. Remember the time he threw the sellers out of the Temple because they were selling all sorts of things there? He upturned the tables with all their goods and sent them flying.'

'Sometimes I scowl or pull a face at Paddy. I immediately regret doing it. Paddy puts his arm around me and smothers me with kisses. He says, 'There, there. You have every right to be angry. I wish we could swop places. Why have you to suffer so much?'

'Oh, Paula… Paddy doesn't understand that you do not want to be smothered. He is doing his best to satisfy your every wish. He never had this experience before. He adores you. He can't bear to lose you.'

'We're nearly back. There's another man waiting to dock our boat.'

'Do you fancy a drink? There's a lovely little tea house near where we alight. Sr Sheila thought that we might like to wait for her there until she returns to drive us back home.'

'Good, Frankie. I want to enjoy every second of the magic of this precious time together.'

Frankie was aware that this visit might be the last time they would be together. She felt tears beginning to flow down her cheeks. She helped Paula step off the boat and put her arm through hers as they walked up a slope to the little café.

As they sat down in a quiet corner of the café, Frankie noticed that Paula's eyes were moistened. She fidgeted. She held her head in her hands resting on the table. She signalled to the waitress to leave them alone.

'I wish I could wave a wand and make you better, Paula.'

'I wish! I know the cancer has spread to my other lung. I don't want to know any details. That's Paddy's department. He's driving me crazy with information. Books and phone calls and enquiries and discussions with specialists.'

'He only wants to help you… to save you.'

'Frankie, I have had enough. It's *my* body. I want you to know I'm going into hospital for some probing on Monday. I'll be in for a week.'

'Is it St Richard's Hospital?'

'Yes. I'm going privately. I'd love you to visit me. Can you do that?'

'Of course. You're my dear friend. I promise to do exactly as you wish.'

'No questions. I'm driven mad with facts and all the watching of my every move. I can't blink or blow my nose or even twitch, Paddy's looking at me, analysing, comparing, enquiring… O God! I could scream. Give me space. Is this love? Oh, I'm sorry. Don't get me wrong. I couldn't do without Paddy. He takes such good care of me. Money is no object. He buys me very expensive jewellery. Look at this sapphire ring. But love can be all-consuming-over-bearing-suffocation.' She was breathless, agitated.

Paula's mobile phone rang.

'Here we go again! Paddy has a snack waiting for us. I said we'll be back by three.'

When Sr Sheila pulled up outside the café, they both greeted her.

'You look as though you enjoyed yourselves. Was the boat trip good?'

'I'm so grateful, Sr Sheila. It was simply wonderful. Can't thank you enough.'

'I'm so glad. Make yourself comfortable here in the front, Paula. Are you okay in the back, Frankie?'

'Yes Sister. Thank you for this perfect gift. We enjoyed such a very meaningful time together.'

They chatted about school as Sr Sheila drove them back to Paddy and Paula's home.

'Now Paula, I want to assure you that our community prays for you and Paddy too. Every day both in the bidding prayers in the Divine Office and at Mass, we ask God to grant you strength and peace.'

As Sr Sheila waved goodbye, Paddy rushed out to support Paula as she walked into their home. He accompanied her to a comfortable arm chair. 'Did you have a lovely trip? I missed you. Shall I help you take off that cardigan, love? I hope you were you warm enough? I've have the heating turned up a little.'

'Thank you, Paddy. I'm fine. We had a lovely river trip. I expect you went to Mass.'

'I had them all praying for you, Paula. Fr Dan mentioned you at the bidding prayers. He belongs to the Opus Dei group. He gave a fine sermon.'

'Is Fr Dan visiting, Paddy?'

'Yes, Frankie. He's covering for the parish priest while he is on holiday. Thank you for looking after my Paula.'

'My pleasure. The river was very smooth. Not a ripple. Very quiet except for the moor hens.'

'Do you know about the Opus Dei movement, Frankie? Fr Dan reminded us that his brother was a member of the Catholic Catenian Association.'

Frankie didn't want to be reminded of the Opus Dei take-over of the First Communion. She also realised that Paula most likely had not told Paddy how authoritarian they had been in their church. Frankie nodded. Paddy continued:

'Kieran would like me to join the Catenians but as a mere carpenter I'm not eligible. It's for professional men'

Paddy expected her to reply. She didn't.

'Paula, I know what you need. What can I offer you, Frankie? You said last time that you like ginger. How about a tiny drop of this ginger wine?'

The coffee table was strewn with tempting pastries. Frankie tried to show her appreciation by tasting most of them. 'Paddy, you've been to your favourite bakery! I'll have the vanilla slice, please.'

Paula was struggling to keep awake.

'Thank you very much for this lovely spread, Paddy and Paula. You need to rest, Paula. I'll go home now.'

'Let me give you a doggie bag, Frankie.'

'Thank you, Paddy. I'll be praying for you tomorrow, Paula.'

'Paddy will text you when I am ready for you to visit the hospital, Frankie. Is that alright?'

It was the third time that week that Frankie visited Paula in hospital. As she entered her room, she noticed how frail she looked.

'Hello Paula! Another new nightdress. Flowery-lemon. Don't you look pretty!'

'So good to see you, Frankie.'

Frankie watched her try to smile. She hugged Paula. Her body felt like a bag of bones.

Paula put her hand to her mouth. She pointed to a bowl. She heaved. She grasped her inhaler.

'Here. I'll help you.' Frankie helped her put the inhaler to her mouth. She wheezed. She gasped for breath. Frankie was about to pat her back. Paula began to gasp again. Frankie pressed the bell to get help.

Paula sighed and was sick into the bowl. Frankie helped her to wipe spittle from her mouth.

'So sorry, Frankie. I'm fine now.'

The nurse arrived. 'You've managed to be sick. Let's put you on the chair. I'll call Nurse Sadie.'

'Can I help you, nurse?'

'That's kind of you, Frankie.'

Frankie helped the nurse to slide Paula into her chair.

'That's better. I'll attach the breathing apparatus. That'll help you to breathe more comfortably.'

When the nurse left, Paula removed the breathing apparatus covering her mouth.

'Sor… sorry I can't…'

'Keep the apparatus on, Paula. I'll do the talking today. Don't want you to get breathless.'

Paula smiled. She lent over to reach a walking stick next to her bed and waved it menacingly.

'What a great collection of cards. I've brought a Mass card from Sr Sheila. Shall I open it for you?'

Paula pulled her mask away. 'Please.'

Frankie handed the card to Paula.

'Lovely. Beautiful red roses. All the nuns have signed it. A novena of Masses, too.'

Frankie noticed that Paula's eyes were struggling to keep open. The nurse popped her head around the door.

'She needs to sleep.'

'I'd better go now, nurse.'

Frankie was about to say goodbye to Paula. She saw tears roll down her pale cheeks.

Frankie stooped and gently cuddled and kissed her.

Paula clutched Frankie's hand. She mouthed, 'Love you.'

'Love you too, Paula. I will never forget you.'

Frankie walked out slowly, backwards, keeping her eyes on Paula struggling to smile and trying to keep her eyes open. She wondered if this would be the last time that she would see Paula alive. She went into the Ladies Toilets, tears rolling down her face. She walked outside into the grounds and shouted, 'God, why are you letting this cancer kill my friend? We call you Father… father's love their children. Jesus changed water into wine at Cana… do something now. At least take away the suffering. Please God, I beg you.'

WHEN FRANKIE ARRIVED in school after the summer holidays, Richard was standing at the entrance. He looked tanned and rested. He beamed a smile to Frankie.

'I've missed you, Frankie.'

'I missed you, too. How was Florence? '

'Sr Sheila told me that you have been so good to poor Paula.'

'Yes, I've tried to visit her as often as I could. She's very frail. How's your aunt?'

'She's doing well. She has the aches and pains that go with old age. But Paula. Poor Paula. Sr Sheila told me that she hasn't long to live. She's not that old.'

'It's heartbreaking, Richard. Cancer is such an unforgiving, relentless disease. Paula doesn't deserve this illness.'

'No one deserves this illness. It's so wicked...Frankie, don't cry. Come here. He reached out his arms towards her. Tonight, I'll drive you home.'

Frankie joined the staff going out to the playground to collect her new class of thirty-four seven year olds.

Linda, who taught in the classroom next to Frankie, leaned over to her. She whispered, 'Little angels! New uniforms. Smiling and ready to imbibe all you're ready to impart!'

'Angels? Look along my boys' line, Linda. Darling Rodney is kicking every stone in sight!'

'What a rascal!'

Richard overheard. He tapped Frankie on the shoulder. 'You'll have him eating out of your hand in no time.'

'Let you know by the end of the week. Need to up-date you on Paula.'

At break, when most of the staff were settled with their coffee, Sr Sheila clapped her hands to gain their attention.

'Many of you have been enquiring about dear Paula. As Frankie has been visiting her in St Richard's Hospital, I have asked her to update us on her condition.'

Frankie stood. 'Paula was very frail when I visited her on Saturday. They've kept her in hospital. The cancer has moved to her other lung. The chemotherapy seems to be very strong. She gave up wearing her wig and headscarf. She wants you to know that she loves you all.... The last time I was with her she was not able to speak...' Frankie felt her voice faltering.

'Please don't go on if...'

'Thank you, Sr Sheila. I'm alright now. Paddy phoned on Sunday. Her prognosis... I really don't. I wonder how long...' Tears welled in her eyes. She reached for a tissue.

'Thank you very much, Frankie. We'll continue to pray for dear Paula and for Paddy too.'

'Have you got a Mass card, Sister?'

'Good, Linda. We could send some flowers, too. Maybe you could do that?'

* * *

YVONNE, her landlady, tapped at her bedroom door.

'It's Paddy... your friend's husband. On the phone for you, Frankie.'

Frankie surmised the worst. She struggled to pull on her dressing gown and opened the door. She handed her the phone. Yvonne warned, 'He sounds sad. It's only just gone seven.'

'Bad news, Frankie. She struggled. She was peaceful at the end. Oh, Frankie! What am I going to do?'

'She's no longer in pain, Paddy. You did your best. What time did she die?'

'Midnight. I've lain beside her since. I know she's gone but I...'

'Paddy, you're not on your own? I will support you... as you supported Paula.'

'Marie Cure. The nurses have been taking care. I needed to talk to you. No use coming now. Everything is happening.'

'Paddy... I don't know what to say. Thank you for telling me. I'll tell Sr Sheila. It's so sad. I'll pray. We'll talk. I will see you soon.'

When Frankie replaced the receiver down and turned round, Yvonne handed her a cup.

'Drink this strong coffee. I'm so sorry, Frankie.'

'My best friend is dead. I can't cry. I…'

'You're in shock. Is there anyone you can talk to? Drink this. Then phone those you need to tell.'

'You're very kind, Yvonne. Thank you.'

The Sisters will be at prayer. I'll phone them first. I wonder if Richard is up yet?

When Frankie phoned the convent, Sr Sheila told her that Paddy had already informed them of Paula's death. The Sisters asked the priest to offer Mass for the repose of her soul.

'Richard, have I woken you? I'm sorry…'

'She's gone. Paula's dead. I've just heard the news. I'll come over, Frankie. I've been up a while. Twenty minutes, I'll be with you. Poor Paula.'

'You're an angel, Richard. It will be good to be together.'

Frankie thought, *Richard's not been in my little bed-sit. I'll get dressed quickly. I don't even possess two cups. Have I got enough milk? I'll ask Yvonne. She'll have some milk. Thank God for convent training... my room is reasonably tidy.*

'Thank you, Yvonne. I'll replace the milk later. Oh that's the door bell. Must be Richard.'

'I'm going down. Shall I open it for you?'

'Thanks Yvonne.'

'Come! Welcome into my little room. I only have the one chair.'

'Oh Frankie… I came to see you. Don't worry. Okay if I sit on your bed? Or shall I sit on the floor?'

'Make yourself comfortable. Would you like a cup of coffee?'

'I wondered if you would like to go to Mass first. We'd be in time for the nine o'clock Mass at the Sacred Heart Church, Frankie. What do you think, Frankie?'

'You're right. That would be best.'

'We can pray for Paula. Not that I think she needs prayers. She suffered so much. Paddy will need help. You told me that her adopted parents are dead. She has no family. Is that right?'

'Correct. She had no living family. Paddy's family are in Ireland.'

Frankie put on her coat.

Together they left the house wordless. Frankie and Richard sat together during Mass. The priest asked the congregation to pray for Paula RIP, Paddy and family:

'Let us ask God, Our Heavenly Father to comfort Mr Patrick Foley, on the death of his dear wife, Paula, who passed away early this morning. May she and the souls of our dearly departed rest in peace.'

Frankie felt tears flowing down her cheeks. Richard handed her some tissues. He put his hand on her shoulder. He whispered, 'So sad. Good to cry. She's no longer struggling.'

Richard took Frankie's hand as they walked from the church. 'You need a good strong coffee now, Frankie. You probably could do with something to eat. Shall we go to Eve's Café at the end of this road?'

'Thanks, Richard. I feel so many emotions. I'm sad and angry and...'

'Angry?'

'Yes. Very angry. Angry with God and Paddy. With God... why does he make good people die? I know we all die but why good, gentle Paula. She was so good to people... why?'

Richard stretched his hand to rest on Frankie's.

'A just anger, Frankie. I don't know why Paula got cancer. It seems unfair that people like Paula are singled out... I can't pretend that I understand God's ways. I don't suppose any of us do.'

'I know... sometimes I think it was Paddy's fault.'

'Paddy's fault? He couldn't give her cancer! What do you mean?'

'I know it sounds ridiculous, Richard, but maybe... could it be? Did Paddy suffocate Paula by loving her too much?'

'Frankie, that needs explaining... Love suffocating? How can that be?'

'I saw how possessive Paddy could be, Richard. Perhaps he didn't realise what he was doing but he controlled everything she did... even her friends. Often when she was with me shopping he would appear or phone to ask when she was coming home.'

'He loved her. He wanted the best for her. He gave her expensive jewellery.'

'Richard, on one or two occasions Paula told me that Paddy was too possessive. She said… Paddy loves me too much.'

'Oh, I see what you mean. I agree. If you love someone, you want them to be their person. I believe that each person is unique and special and individual. I'm safe with you, Frankie!'

A week later Richard slipped into Frankie's classroom, 'When is Paula's funeral? Has Paddy been in touch?'

'Sr Sheila called me into her office today. She said that the staff had been enquiring about Paula's funeral. She told me that Paddy had told her that he had arranged for Paula to be buried in Ireland.'

'She's English. Has she ever been to Ireland?'

'I don't think so. Paddy's Irish, of course. He's from Kerry.'

'Sr Sheila wanted to make sure that she had understood Paddy's intentions. She asked me if I would phone him from her office.'

'You did?'

'Yes. Very strange. Not only will the funeral take place in Kerry but only his immediate family are invited to attend. When I asked for the date, he replied that it was not necessary for me to know.'

'Unbelievable! You're not invited to your friend's funeral. That is strange.'

'Now do you understand what I said about Paddy being too possessive? Even in death he wants to have her for himself.'

'I really don't understand that mentality, Frankie.'

'I don't either, Richard, but I've done a lot of thinking. I've concluded that Paddy thinks that he is doing the right thing. He's heart broken. Ireland is the country that he loves. He intends retiring to Ireland. He wants the love of his life to be with him there.'

43

PONDERING

'Come in, Richard. I'm glad you phoned. I don't know what is happening to me.'

'Have you been cooped up in your bedroom since I dropped you off on Friday? What did you do yesterday? I invited you to meet me in town. You didn't answer.'

'I feel listless... I... didn't want to see anyone.'

'Frankie. Move over. I'll sit beside you. You can't sit here alone. Paula's death was expected. There was nothing more we could do. Not to be invited to her funeral...'

'I'm still trying to understand Paddy.'

'This is a beautiful picture of dear Paula that you have on the table.'

'A beautiful person.'

'I've been lighting that candle and sitting in front of her photo. I've been asking her to make sense of it all. It was past midnight last night, when the nightlight had burnt out.'

'You talk to Paula?'

'I do. I asked why Paddy won't invite me to her funeral.'

'You really needed to be able to attend Paula's funeral. To bid her 'goodbye.'

'There was something frightening about the kind of love that Paddy had for Paula.

Paddy's love was suffocating. He acted as though he owned Paula. Dominating.'

'From what you've told me it seems it was, Frankie. She was so ill that she became totally dependent of him. She needed him. What would she have done without him?'

'Paddy did dedicate every minute of his day to Paula. He could have been praised for being selfless. Did he make her dependent on him? Perhaps I am mistaken. Am I too judgemental? I have been pondering, thinking and analysing Paddy's love for Paula. Forget what I said. I'm thinking too much.'

'No, Frankie. It is important to discuss this. Can our love be selfless? I want to talk about this.'

'I don't know about you, Richard, but when I was in the convent I felt I was owned by the Superiors, the Church. I don't want that to happen again. I want to use my free will to choose how I want to live. That's why I left.'

'So true, Frankie. You couldn't have expressed it better. I don't want to be owned either.'

'Love means that we respect ourselves, our independence and our right to choose and want the same for other people.'

'Especially for the person with whom we want to live.'

'Especially for the person whom we have chosen to spend the rest of our life with.'

'Richard, I want to tell you… I'm in love with you.'

'I don't doubt that, Frankie. You know I love you, too.'

Frankie snuggled into Richard's arms as they moved closer on the edge of her bed.

'Please don't cry, Frankie. It makes me sad to see you sad.'

'You're an angel, Richard. Paddy's kind of love for Paula has made me realise that love manifests itself in different ways.'

'Had Paula many other friends?'

'Only those whom she met at church or school. She made friends easily. Paddy only seemed to have his brother and his family.'

'He must be suffering now. You said he was a religious man. The thought of being reunited with his love in heaven must give him some consolation.'

'Happiness for ever. Loving each other for all eternity. His Faith will help him.'

'The knowledge too that Paula is free from pain and suffering. She's united with her maker.'

'Heaven must be a very large place. Your mother and my father and my friend, Margaret, and now, Paula.'

'What do atheists do?'

'Death is the end of everything for them.'

'We each have our own set of beliefs. Where we were born and how we were educated influences what we believe. You must be wondering about me, Frankie. I've never invited you to my home. I was planning to invite you but I had to spend the holidays with my aunt.'

'No... well...'

'You ought to know more about my background.'

'You don't know much about my family either, Richard. Perhaps you will not want to love me when you have learnt about my lowly background.'

'That is certainly not true. It's so good to discuss these things, Frankie. Look what you have gleaned from Paddy's love for Paula. Be honest with me. I want to know all about your family.'

'I think that Paddy suffocated Paula. In the end she couldn't breathe. He took control of her life. She became so weak and worried that the cancer took over and spread. It leaked into every pore. She became helpless. He held her too tightly. He loved her to death. She died of lung cancer. She was unable to breathe. We don't know what causes cancer. Am I wrong in thinking that his suffocating love killed her? '

'You think that he was a control freak. Misconstrued love. It reminds me of the warning given in that hymn about a butterfly. If you catch hold of a lovely butterfly and grasp it too tightly, you will kill it. If you really love those beautifully coloured, fragile and delicate insects, let them fly freely.'

'Precisely. Paula was one of those beautiful butterflies.'

'When I'm struggling to understand, I find that reading poetry helps me.'

'Do you?'

'Do you know Oscar Wilde's 'Ballad of Reading Gaol? I love the rhythm.'

'Of course I do.'

'I've always loved that ballad. Years ago, when I travelled over to Ireland to take part in an Oscar Wilde Appreciation Course, I listened to this ballad being read. You could have heard a pin drop in the room. After pondering on the love that Paddy had for Paula, I have written my own version of that poem.'

'Is that it propped by the photo?'

'Yes.'

'Read it to me, Frankie.'

'It's long. I'll read part of it. You can read the rest if you wish. You know it begins, *Each man kills the thing he loves...* I have tried to pen my version like this:

Paula was the love that Paddy adored
By all let this be heard,
She was his precious treasure
With each blink, twitch or sigh
His princess gave him pleasure.

Her lungs felt the strain.
Cancer ravages quietly.
Lungs, sternum, bones
From head, down spine it travelled
Wracking, wrecking cancer.

Who knows when Paula looked
With such a wistful eye
Upon that little tent of blue
Which prisoners call the sky?

Her life was put to the test
Every organ, every cell
Paddy struggled to control:
Doctors, nurses, stop that pain
Torturing precious treasure!

Was it then that Paula looked
With such a wistful eye
Upon that little tent of blue
Which prisoners call the sky?

'Frankie, that is excellent. What a talented girl you are. You really summed up Paddy.'

'I've done so much thinking, Richard. It's the result of all the analysing and examining that we were trained to do in the convent. It's been so exhausting. Maybe Paula understands?'

'It's about time I told you about my family background.'

'Wait until you hear mine!'

'Tomorrow when we drive home. Shall we stop somewhere? Have a chat. That café near Putney Bridge. They'll probably have a fire. Christmas decorations.'

'Thank you, Richard. What a treat.'

44

LOOKING FORWARD

As Frankie was about to leave for school, she noticed an envelope had been pushed under her bedroom door.

An Irish stamp. Who's this from? Her address had been typed.

When Frankie slit open the envelope, she found a Christmas card with a black and white sketch of Mary and the child Jesus. Inside was written:

May the blessings of the Christ Child and His Holy Mother, Mary be yours this Christmas and always.

Fr Sean

After all these months, he remembered me with a card. Why would he do that? Was he playing with my emotions, stupid man... or did he really fancy me? He scribbled his name under the printed message. 'Fr' Why Father? So formal. Is this what priests do?

She thought about the night in the restaurant. His familiarity. She put the card back into the envelope. I know better now, she thought.

When Frankie rested the bags she had carried to school on the staffroom table, Sr Sheila clapped her hands.

'Frankie. So many bags! You're laden. How did you manage to carry them? What have you got in there? Did you carry all these on the train?'

'Treats for my classes' Christmas party, Sister. I got the bus to the station this morning. It's not too far from there. I bought these at Sainsbury's.'

'I'm walking towards your classroom. Let me carry one of the bags.'

'Thank you, Sister.'

'Here we are, Frankie. I'll open the door for you. Shall I put them near your desk? You look so happy.'

'Thank you, Sister. I am happy. Richard has been so understanding. We have grown closer. He's as puzzled as I am about Paula's funeral.'

'Good. Richard is very kind. It was he who suggested that the school has a memorial Mass for Paula in our Parish Church.'

'Staff, children, we all need to say goodbye to our lovely Paula RIP.'

'No doubt you'll miss her this Christmas.'

'I will. I want to throw myself into the celebrations. I want this to be a good Christmas. I bet children like little Barry or big, bold Iffey will probably have a bleak Christmas.'

'Ta tu fluairseach, Frankie!'

'Thank you, Sister. I had forgotten that lovely expressive word. 'Generous to a fault'. Am I right?'

'Yes. Literal translation. I suspect that your friendship with Richard has brought you great happiness. That's a lovely velvet skirt you're wearing.'

'I'm glad you like it.' Frankie twirled around. 'I bought the black shirt in Oxfam. I found this red top in Debenhams. Richard and I have planned to enjoy a drink to celebrate the beginning of the Christmas holidays on the way home tonight.'

'I'm delighted for you both, Frankie. It can't have been easy for each of you when you left religious life.'

'I enjoyed community life. When I left the convent I felt quite lonely. I think Richard did too.'

'You have this in common. You'll be able to understand each other. I wish you both happiness.'

'You're very understanding. Please remember us in your prayers.'

After school Frankie entered the busy pub with Richard. He steered her towards seating near the log fire.

'How about this sofa, Frankie. Just room for the two of us.'

'Perfect!'

'Drink up, Frankie. That hot punch will warm you. We can relax now. Christmas holidays have begun.'

'Did you enjoy the Infants' Nativity play?'

'Loved it! You always help the children to understand the Christmas Story, Frankie.'

'It was fun, Richard.'

'The way Mary dangled Baby Jesus made me wonder if she has ever been cuddled. And Joseph… he was a howl a minute… fancy him going off to get the innkeeper… when he… Oh, I can't stop laughing… when he was so busy waving to his mum that he missed his cue to come on. That was so funny, wasn't it, Frankie?'

'Barry has such a poor background. You know about that. He's a bit like me. Perhaps not as bad but…'

'Frankie, I don't care about your background. Besides, you've told me about your mother. You said that you have a brother and a sister. We were both locked up! Spent time inside. Okay, it was a nunnery and a monastery. We have that in common.'

'You look hilarious waving your arms about! That silly grin too!'

'It's the punch.'

'I have hardly any contact with my mother now. My sister looks after her. She drinks a lot. I can't cope with that. I carry a photo of her in my bag. Let me show you. It's all creased now. She gave it to me when I entered the convent. It's the two of us.'

'Let me see.'

'Oh! You look angelic. Lovely lady.'

'Skinny… Mam used to say that I was lanky. I hated my freckles. No, don't look. I keep them covered.'

'Had your father the same hair colouring?'

'The photos that my mother has of him are in black and white. We weren't permitted to keep photos in the convent. Sadly I don't have any of him.'

'Do you worry about your mother?'

'Yes. Sometimes I feel guilty that I don't spend time with her but I can't live the way she does. My life is so different. I'm confident that my sister, Mary, takes good care of her. She takes her out to restaurants. She makes sure that she takes her medication. They seem to be happy together. After I left the convent, I tried to visit and keep in touch. We had so little in common.'

'I promised that I would tell you about my background. I want to tell you everything properly, Frankie. Shall we go out for a meal tomorrow? Would you like that?'

'You yawned after I did! It's catching. So tired. Yes, let's meet tomorrow for a meal.'

45

RICHARD'S SURPRISE

The house felt eerily empty when Frankie woke on the 22nd December.

She glanced at the clock. *Nine o'clock already. I didn't hear Evelyn bang the front door after she collected the milk. She's must have gone to spend Christmas with her son and daughter-in-law.*

Richard! Richard is coming to take me to lunch. I must get ready. I'll make the bed. Empty my bag and put school things away. I'll hang some of the Christmas cards that the children gave me around the window.

I wonder if Richard lives on his own. He never said. I'll wrap my framed miniature of Dante, as a present. I know he will like it. Richard loves Florence. He's sure to know this famous painting of Dante meeting Beatrice on Santa Trinita Bridge.

Frankie slipped out of her nightdress and into the shower. She decided to wear a fine pale pink woollen dress that Sr Sheila had given her from the clothes donated to the convent.

Frankie glanced at the clock. Midday. She had tidied her room and was about to string up the Christmas cards.

The door bell. That can't be Richard? We didn't agree on a time. I hoped he would phone to arrange a time. I'll look out of the side window on the landing to check that it's him.

Oh dear God. It's Richard! I haven't wrapped his gift.

Frankie ran downstairs to open the front door.

'Happy Christmas, Frankie!'

'And to you too, Richard.' He reached out his arms to hug her.

Frankie couldn't resist. She buried herself in Richard's bright red woolly scarf. She delighted in being smothered in kisses and hugs.

He held her at arms length. 'Richard, you look so debonair in your leather jacket. Is it new?'

'Thank you! Yes. An early Christmas present to myself. I bought you a surprise. I hope you like poinsettias.'

'I adore poinsettias. How beautiful they are. We always placed them in front of the crib when I was in the convent.'

'We did too.'

'Oh Richard, isn't Christmas wonderful. Come up to my little room. Chair or bed? I have so little to offer you. I have a small present for you too. I hope you like it.'

Frankie watched Richard's eyes widen as he held the picture depicting Dante and Beatrice. He reached out and pulled her to him. He embraced her.

'I love this scene. How did you know, Frankie? What a thoughtful gift. I will put it on my desk at home. Tender love on the ancient Ponte Vecchio… so touching. Thank you.'

'I'm so glad you like it. I bought it at the art and craft exhibition in the church hall.'

'I love it. Every Florentine walks that bridge.'

'Would you like a cup of coffee and a mince pie?'

'Sounds good to me…… !'

Frankie noticed that his eyes were dancing as he looked round the room.

'Lunch is almost ready at my house. Will you join me… us?'

'*Us*, Richard?'

Richard's beating his chest and shaking his head.

'Mea culpa! Among the many things I haven't told you about myself. I live with my father.'

Frankie felt a flush of relief.

'Your father? I'd love to join you both.'

'Good. Your carriage awaits!'

She felt Richard's hand around her shoulder as he helped her to put on her long, mauve knitted coat. He held her hand on the way to the stairs. They walked together down the polished staircase. Frankie opened the door.

'Wow! Lovely car, Richard. Is this an early Christmas present too?'

'No, no it's not mine. It's my father's. Comfortable as well. Here, let me open your door.'

Richard turned on the ignition. They glided off in the Wimbledon direction. He proceeded into a more secluded, residential area. He drew up outside wrought-iron gates. Pushing the button on the dashboard, he opened the gates.

'Do you live here? Is that your home?'

At the further end of the drive Frankie caught a glimpse of a red brink Tudor-style house.

'I'm fortunate. I live in a house that belongs to my parents. It is very lovely.'

'Very grand... you never said... You teach in a poor area...'

He parked in front of a big oak door. 'Such a magnificent home. You are lucky, Richard.'

Frankie wondered if a butler was about to rush out to open the car door.

'Allow me to do the honour, Frankie.'

'Richard, this is wonderful.'

'My father worked hard. We have lived here all my life. I think you will like my father. Come, let's ring the door bell.'

Frankie marvelled as Richard escorted her to a big oak door. She heard the door bell clanging. Richard opened the door. He called out, 'Papà, come! Meet our guest. Papà, this is Frankie, my friend from school.'

'Benvenuta. Buon Natale! Welcome. Welcome.'

Frankie watched a tall, stately man appear from the side of a beautifully carved carpeted staircase. He hurried towards her with open arms. He kissed her on both cheeks. His dappled beard tickled her face.

'What a pleasure to meet you, Signor Canto.'

As he stood back, Frankie admired his maroon velvet jacket. He might be in his late sixties, she thought.

'Grazie. Buon Natale! Piacere. Mi chiama, Frankie.'

'Mi chiamo, Giovanni.'

Frankie loved the friendly way he tilted his head to one side and wiggled his finger towards her.

'Ah no! Ricardo told me that you are Irish. You are from that great land of saints and scholars. Davvero? How is it that you speak Italian?'

'That's a long story. I will tell you, Signor.'

'We have plenty of time.'

Frankie felt Richard gently placing his arm behind her back. He pointed to an open door at the other side of the stairs. 'Enrico will be waiting for us.'

Enrico? Who is he?

Frankie and Richard walked behind Papà Giovanni along one of the quadratic corridors flanking a piazza with a fountain and trailing vines.

It's all too much to absorb. What would Cousin Joan think of the hanging tapestries depicting the Il Duomo against the Florence skyline?

She heard another voice.

'I am pleased to offer you an 'appy Christmas. Buon appetito.'

'Frankie, this is Enrico.'

Frankie shook his outstretched hand and smiled.

'Pleased to meet you, Enrico.'

'Come, Francesca.'

Enrico pulled out a heavy leather-bound chair. Frankie seated herself on one side of a table covered with a cream table cloth. Richard was seated opposite her. His father sat at the top.

'Benvenuto, Cara Francesca.'

'Mi scusi, please, am I allowed to ask you, Francesca, how you know some Italian?'

'Si, certo. I was a nun in an Italian order.'

'Did I hear correctly? You are a nun? Una Suora? Religiosa?'

'Si Papà. Frankie was a nun but she is not one anymore. Papà, I think that as she is our guest, you should tell her a little about yourself first.'

'Certo! First we pray. Then while we eat, I'll explain.'

While they ate their first course of salmon mousse, Richard's father described how he came to Reading in the fifties to lecture on Italian literature at Oxford University. 'There is a photo of Papà in his academic gown on the mantle piece.' Richard placed the photo at the end of the table.

'Ah! Bellissima, Laura. My darling moglie… wife. I met Laura at Oxford. She is one of the Levy family. An only child. She had spent many years in Florence.'

'Is she Italian?'

'No. No, she was English. She died many years ago. She converted to Catholicism.'

'I'm sorry. I…'

'Unfortunately, she was unaware that she had a rare blood disease that resulted in her death while giving birth to Richard.'

'Oh! What a tragedy.'

'It was in February. Each year after commemorating her death in Wimbledon where she was buried, I go back to my family, where she spent so many happy years in Florence.'

'That's where you spent the summer holidays, Richard.'

'Went to help my aunt. Thank goodness, her wrist has mended well.'

'They have adopted you there, Richard, have they not?'

'Yes, even though there are not many of the actual family still alive, the next generation always make me feel so welcome.'

After the Tiramisu, cheese, more wine, coffee was served. Frankie was invited to lounge on a massive leather armchair in front of a roaring fire.

'That was a delicious meal. Grazie per tutti!'

'I'm delighted to meet you at last, Francesca.'

'I can't believe I'm here, Signor Giovanni. I feel overwhelmed. I am very grateful that you have invited me. Richard and I teach in a poor area. I was so pleased to remain in that job when I left the convent. It was hard to adjust after spending half my life in a religious environment.'

'That must have been difficult for you. You entered the convent when you were young?'

'Sixteen. I was just sixteen when I left home. Been out nearly eight years.'

'Frankie, my father and I are very pleased to have you here.'

'Si! Here you can spend time together. Enjoy each others company.'

'Papà, will you be alright if we go for a walk? Perhaps you are tired?'

'Good. You two walk. I'll have a nap.'

As they went out through the French windows Richard whispered, 'I've been longing for you to come to my home, Frankie.'

'Richard, I wonder why you bother to teach in our little school? Sorry… I'm mesmerised with the magic of your wonderful home.'

'I love our school and all the children. Wouldn't change it for the world.'

'Nor would I. That was such a delicious meal, Richard. I feel so satisfied.'

'Okay. At end of the lane next to our house there is a lovely pond. Why don't we go there? A brisk walk will do us good.'

'Good. I'm glad I'm wearing my boots. Shall we march?'

'Arm and arm we march together!'

'Did you come down to this pond as a child, Richard?'

'Yes. My father used to make sure that I had crumbs to feed the ducks. This place holds many fond memories for me. When we go back I want to show you another very special place in our garden, Frankie.'

'Oh! About turn then, before the afternoon draws in.' Frankie held his arm tightly.

She felt so comfortable walking arm in arm. They pushed open the back gate of the garden.

'Follow me. I'll lead you to the garden seat that my father had commissioned in memory of my mother. See over there.'

'Oh Richard, how beautiful! Is it marble?'

'Only the best. Carrara marble. Italian of course. Pure white.'

'I love the way it curves slightly inwards and the little marble table in front… and the angel wings over the backrest. Such a serene face.'

'Under the angel can you see the plaque?'

'Oh yes. In gold lettering: Laura Canto… she was only 28. Oh Richard, what a beautiful memorial to your dear mother.'

'My parents really loved each other, Frankie. My father has tended the plants round this shrine to my mother all my life.'

'The garden is lovely even in winter.'

'Yes. I helped to plant the winter Jasmine and the Alpine Edelweiss. In spring the vibrant Aquilegia adds so many colours. We'd tend the garden and then Dad used to show me photos of my mother.'

'I feel so privileged to be taken to this special place, Richard. Thank you.'

'I wanted to bring you here, Frankie. There is a rug in the bag on the seat. If I spread it out, shall we sit here for a while? You're not too cold?'

'No, that would be lovely, Richard. I doubt your mother needs prayers but maybe you might want to say a prayer to… for her?'

Richard sat next to Frankie. His arms encircled her. She enjoyed the aroma of his aftershave.

'I'm feeling safe in your arms, Richard.'

'Frankie, I want to tell you a little about myself.'

'You're an only child?'

'Yes. My father made sure that I was well educated. He encouraged me to follow all sorts of academic pursuits including teaching, even lecturing. He even insisted that I learn how to play the piano. Then as you know, like you, I gave up everything up to follow God's call. I entered the Carmelite Order.'

'Why did you leave?'

'My biggest weakness is that I can't seem to stick at things. My poor father despairs of my indecisiveness. God alone knows how patient he has tried to be with me.'

'Oh Richard, don't be too hard on yourself.'

'No. I want you to know what I'm really like.'

'You dedicated your life to Christ. We both did. You have also spent some years teaching needy children at our school. It hasn't been exactly easy for you.'

'You mean Anna?'

'Anna drove me to cruelty. Anna was never a girlfriend. She was forced on me by the church with Opus Dei. You've borne the brunt of that, Frankie. I often wonder what came over me. I'm ashamed of the anger that I felt. Never again. I'm determined that I will not get into that mood again. I've made my mind up now, once and for always.'

'You must have had other girl friends?'

'No, Frankie. Have you fallen in love with anyone else?'

'I thought I had. I often mention her. Margaret.'

'Another women?'

'It was a deep friendship. We wanted to share ideas... be together. But of course the nuns were afraid of us developing particular friendships. It was the same with the brothers, wasn't it?'

'Yes. Men and women living so close together. They had to safeguard relationships.'

'Once I left, I wanted to find someone to love. I love children. I have been puzzled about love... I used to feel guilty about enjoying pleasure...'

'That's what we have in common, Frankie. We were constantly reminded that we had to be pure in thought, word and deed. I used to confess indulging myself when I listened to Elvis Presley. I was on the verge of suffering from scrupulosity.'

'Me too. Constantly examining my conscience. Analysis. Sin loomed large.'

'Maybe we were both too conscientious. I know priests who are happy in their vocations. Nuns too. Let's put all the soul-searching behind us. Start afresh.'

'I'm glad you've brought me to this special place. We can talk freely here.'

'I want my mother to watch over us today, Frankie.'

'Shall we pray for, or better still, pray to her?'

Richard's bending... falling to his knees. Kneeling.

He's pleading eyes are sparkling... there are tears... he's smiling

He's kissing my hands.

'Frankie, I love you. I want to spend my life with you. Will you marry me?'

'Oh... oh Richard... I'd love too... Yes! I will. I will, Richard...'

'Oh darling, I can't tell you how happy you've made me. I love you, Frankie... I want us to be together forever...'

'Richard, of course I will marry you.'

He's holding a ring out to me... sparkling... gold.

Frankie hold out her left hand. He gently eased a diamond-studded ring on her finger.

'Forever and ever. Promise me.'

'Forever and ever, Richard.' *I cross my heart. My body quivers. He's moved up beside me and enfolded me in his arms.*

'This is the happiest day of my life. I have loved you for years. I didn't think you loved me.'

'I do love you, Richard.'

He is hugging and kissing me from the crown of my head, my shoulders, my waist. He is holding me in such a tight embrace. I'm abandoning myself to him. I've close my eyes. I've never sensed such happiness... such closeness before. Am I dreaming... I can feel the ring. This must be real love.

Richard must have felt her twiddling the ring. He asked, 'I hope you like the ring, Frankie. It was my mother's. My father wanted you to have it.'

'So your father knows that you have proposed to me?'

'Yes. We planned this special day, Frankie. We hoped that you were at home today.'

'I'm so happy. This ring is beautiful. Gold! One, two, three diamonds.'

'It's special. My mother must be looking down on us today.'

'I love it but it's your love that I treasure. Even if you put a... I don't know... a brass ring on my finger...'

'You're so good, Frankie. That's what I love about you. You're a straight-forward girl. Not scared to speak your mind.'

Richard kissed Frankie as he drew her to him.

'Richard, I love you. I am so happy. I could dance around this beautiful garden. Just think maybe your mother is smiling at us, too.'

They rubbed noses. He held her at arm's length. He drew her closer. He put his arm round her waist and tilted my head. He kissed her tenderly on the cheek.

His kiss on my lips lingered. We gradually unfolded. He held me at arms length. My body quivered. Weak yet strong. Deliriously happy.

'I want to stay here forever.'

'I'll race you to the path.'

'I'll win!'

'What a view up here, Frankie! That's Crystal Palace over there, where the light are flashing. Come closer. Let me wrap this scarf around you. I don't want you to be blown away with the wind!'

Frankie snuggled into his strong arms. She felt his lips press on her lips. His face looked so gentle, so kind. She had found love.

46

SO THAT'S LOVE

Did we really walk back to his house? I was floating on air. Richard was smiling, his arm on my shoulder.

Richard's father knew of his intention to propose. He was at the door to greet them.

Richard declared, 'Congratulations are in order, Papà!'

'Congratulations! Bene… bene! Finalmente, Ricardo caro. My dear Laura will be so happy, bless her soul. Allora vino! Una celebrazione!'

Richard pointed to the chocolates and bouquet of flowers on the dining room table. 'Welcome to our family, Francesca.' Papà Giovanni kissed and embraced Frankie. 'Soon you will be my daughter-in-law. Daughter…'

Frankie felt Richard's arms encircle her. His father poured the wine. He offered them the chocolates. 'Oh, you have made an old man very happy.'

'Andiamo. Let's sit. I have plans.'

'Dreams of being a grandfather, Papà?'

Frankie noticed that Richard's father didn't answer. He clasped his hands and looked towards the photo of his wife, Laura. The clocked ticked. Eventually he asked.

'How would you like to celebrate your engagement in Firenze... Florence?'

'Florence. That beautiful Italian city. I have seen so many picture of it. How romantic.

That would be wonderful, Signor.'

'Giovanni... you can call me Giovanni. I have tickets for your flight.'

Richard clapped, 'Bravo, Papà! Our flight is for Christmas Eve. The day after tomorrow. I hope that is alright for you, Frankie.'

'Christmas in Florence. How wonderful! Mille Grazie, Papà Giovanni!'

'Bene. If you will excuse me, I have a headache.'

'A headache, Papà? You look pale. Maybe you should rest while I drive Frankie home.'

RICHARD DROVE Frankie back to her flat in a daze of excitement talking, smiling. Tears of happiness ran down her face.

'I want to keep hugging you, Frankie.'

'And me, you. I love you, Richard.' They tiptoed up the stairs to her bedroom. 'This has been the most wonderful day of my life, Richard. I feel that I am dreaming. I won't be able to sleep tonight.'

Frankie hugged him. He kissed her.

'You make me very happy, Frankie. Papà is happy too.'

'He is very proud of you, Richard. Maybe, he dreams of us giving him a grandchild... you love children... you do... ?'

'Of course I do. We've dedicated our lives to children. I can't wait until we have a child of our own.'

'Oh Richard, when you eased the ring onto to my finger, a surge of love welled up inside of me. I felt so warm, so loved, so happy. I wished... I long for us to share our love... to have a child of our own. We have so much to talk about.'

'That's why I agreed to go away together. To be alone. I'm shy... In company I still find it hard to be demonstrative.'

'In spite of being half-Italian... ? They're so loving... so uninhibited.'

'It's that blo... blessed religious training... it knocks all spontaneity... all natural reactions...'

'Bloody! Go on say *Bloody*!'

Richard stamped his foot and clenched his fists. 'Bloody! Bloody sin! There... it makes me angry... I don't want to be angry. I'm sorry, Frankie.'

'Richard, let's forget the past. Let's live for our happiness. We are so lucky to have found each other.'

Frankie noticed that Richard's face became contorted. He looked like this when Anna was around. We have so much to be happy about.

'I don't know what came over me. We won't worry. When we are in Florence, we'll just love each other every minute. You're so right. Italians are demonstrative. My father has arranged everything. We'll have the upstairs rooms of my aunts' home to ourselves. There are two bedrooms next to each other. They're good Catholics, you know! We'll have a wonderful Christmas together.'

'This beautiful ring... It's a perfect fit... How did you manage that? Is my finger the same size as your mother's was? Your father adored your mother.'

Richard, restored to his gentle self, grinned... his eyes twinkled

'Am I right in thinking that the day you sent little Steve into my classroom to measure fingers...'

'You've found me out...' Richard waved his hands above his head...' How else was I to be sure. Strange thing is that it was the exact same size as my mother's. It didn't need altering. Isn't that significant?'

'A heart-shaped cluster of diamonds set in a gold mounting. How beautiful.'

'It's a slim band. The diamonds are not big. I thought you wouldn't want any thing too pretentious. I wanted you to have my mother's engagement ring. That their great love for each other would become our great love.'

'You know me well. Nothing big and flashy. This is perfect. I feel privileged to wear your mother's ring. I'll put it safely under my pillow.'

Richard combed his hand through Frankie's hair. 'Frankie, our flight is on Christmas Eve. I'll have to drag myself away now. Let me kiss you goodnight.' They stood and held hands. He kissed her again. 'Try to sleep. We have only one day left before we fly out. Don't worry about anything. We have everything arranged.'

Frankie waved as Richard crept down the stairs. They blew kisses until he closed the door behind him. Frankie went to the window and waved until his car disappeared into the night.

I can't go to bed. I don't want this day to end. I want to sing and dance. Do as I please. My diamond ring reflects the light. I'm not tired. If I close my eyes this balloon will burst. No I must hold tightly to its strings. Keep tugging until I am back in Richard's arms again. Can all this be happening to me?

'Hello mirror!' *All my time in the convent we didn't have mirrors. I'm not used to looking in a mirror. But tonight I need to check that it's really me. I can't believe all this is happening either! My DVD is playing Elton John, Step into Christmas. I seem to have boundless energy as I dance round my room in my nightie watching my precious ring sparkle. I'm in love! Richard has asked me to marry him. Now I know how love feels. I am ecstatically happy!*

47

THE DREAM

It's nearly three am. I can't sleep. Where's my ring? Under my pillow... it's mine... Richard put it on my finger. I know he loves me... I can't go back to sleep. I'll make a cup of cocoa.

Tomorrow evening, Richard and I will fly from Gatwick to Pisa Airport, then on to Firenze. I'll begin to pack. No need to worry about waking others. The landlady's family are at their son's house for Christmas. I've never been to Florence. I expect Richard's relatives will probably have a big villa. They seem to be rich. How lucky I am to be invited. Richard will be with me. I'll sleep in a room next to his. A dream come true. What will his aunts think of me? I must look my best.

Frankie pulled her suitcase from the cupboard.

Richard said that we will return in time for school. Frankie surveyed her wardrobe. I haven't many clothes. I'll take them all. Thank goodness Sr Sheila gave me a lovely, long blue woollen dress and black, fitted trousers. I'm glad that I bought black, leather knee-high boots at the sales before Christmas. I will take my bank card in case I need to buy anything else in the airport. I will look for gifts to take to Richard's aunts in the airport. Richard will know what they like.

Frankie looked around her little room with its bookcase in the corner. Floral curtains covered the window. The very thought of being with Richard gave her goose bumps.

Frankie wondered if Richard and she would embrace on Ponte Vecchio; the very bridge where Dante met Beatrice all those years ago. *Together we will marvel at the statue of Michelangelo's David. We will have time to plan our lives... our first home...our child.*

The phone's ringing. It's six o'clock. I'm nearly ready. I'd better run downstairs. Just as well the family have gone away.

It was Richard. 'Frankie... I hope you managed to sleep.'

'I was too excited. Couldn't sleep.'

'Can I come over to see you... now?'

'Of course... you sound... are you alright, Richard? Has something happened? Is your father alright?'

'I'll come straight away. I need to tell... talk... I'll come...'

'Come.'

Richard's voice was shaky. *What could have happened? Maybe he's caught the 'flu. I need to get dressed.*

When the door bell rang, Frankie rushed downstairs to open the door. Richard's eyes were red. He looked flushed. His hands were gripped together. He fell into Frankie's open arms. She held his hand as they climbed the stairs.

'Whatever is the matter, my darling? Are you ill? Have you hurt yourself?'

'No... I...'

'Let me take your coat. I'll sit next to you on the bed. Take your time. What's the matter? Tell me what happened, my love. Nothing can be that bad.'

Richard took a folder from the inside pocket of his coat. He put it on the bed next to him.

'I hope you'll understand, Frankie. I can't believe... you won't believe.'

'My darling.' She put her arms round him. 'What's happened to upset you so much?'

'Last night I was angry... disappointed... so many emotions...'

'Why? What made you angry? Did I upset you?'

'Was it something I said? Did? It was me, wasn't it?'

He pulled his handkerchief from his pocket. He blew his nose. He lifted his head to look into her eyes. He looked ill-at ease. He stretched both hands out towards her. She held his hands and pulled him nearer.

'I… I can't speak. It's so awful. No, it's not you, Frankie. It's me.'

'Tell me what happened, Richard?'

'I was so happy when I arrived home. My father had drinks ready. We relaxed in armchairs in front of a blazing fire. He congratulated me on our engagement, again.'

'So what happened. Tell me.'

'My father asked me if we had made any plans. If, eventually, I wanted him to help us move into a home of our own.'

'Obviously he's thinking of his future. You both live in a big house.'

'Agreed. It's sensible to plan ahead. Then I mentioned having a grandchild. I thought he'd love to have a child in the family.'

'I thought he would, too. Most parents want their lineage to continue.'

'He seemed to become agitated. I watched him scratch his head. Rub his hands up and down the front of his legs. He looked over to the photo of my mother. Gazed into the distance.'

Richard dropped his hands back to his lap.

Frankie rubbed her eyes.

'Papà… my father asked if you… if you were still… could you still have children. I'm sorry to be blunt, Frankie.'

'I'm not forty yet. Of course I want a child. He must have worked out my age when I told him I was sixteen when I entered the convent and I spent half my life… why is that important?'

'That was it. 'I'm forty-three. He didn't know how young…'

'What significance has that…'

'He said he had something very serious to tell me. This is why I had to come to talk to you, Frankie. I wanted to come to you last night. I couldn't sleep. He persuaded me to wait.'

'Oh.'

'There is a problem. I am angry that my father didn't tell me years ago. It's about my mother.'

'You said she died in childbirth. Poor woman.'

'My father always told me that she had a rare blood disease.'

'That's what he said the other night. Did something else cause her death?'

'Frankie, what he said was true. She died of hypertrophic cardiomyopathy. It is an inherited disease of the heart muscle, where the myocardium becomes thickened, making

the heart muscle stiff. It's not uncommon for this to be the cause of women's death during childbirth.'

'Your dear mother died a long time ago. Richard. There's been a lot of medical progress since then.'

'It was what my father revealed next that concerned me most.'

'He told me that her mother, my grandmother, had Huntington's Disease. That is what caused her death.'

'But the cause of your mother's death was a blood disease.'

'My father talked about inherited genetic diseases that are related to cardiomyopathy. He mentioned mutations... here he gave me a paper to read. I talked about genetic conditions inherited... all kind of ailments and conditions even Huntingdon's disease.'

'You said that your grandmother suffered Huntington's disease... but your mother died of a blood disease. Is there a connection? '

'My father's reasoning is that my mother could have been a carrier of Huntington's disease. It usually manifests itself when a person is aged between thirty and fifty. My mother died when she was only twenty-eight. It is an inherited disease. I might be a carrier... a fifty percent chance.'

'A fifty percent chance that you have not inherited... what did you say it was? Huntington's disease... what is this disease?'

'I'd never heard of it. When I asked Papà for an explanation, he looked as though he was about to faint. His soot-black eyes seemed to sink deep into his emaciated skull. I watched him heaving himself out of his armchair. He held onto another chair as he padded across the floor. He pulled a file out of his cabinet. He handed a faded sheet of A4 sized paper from an old brown leather folder.'

'Your poor father.'

'Frankie, I do feel sorry for my father. It must have been hard for him to lose his wife. To bring me up on his own. But he should have told me the truth.'

'I don't understand, Richard. I can see you're angry… and sad.'

Richard took a sheet of paper from the folder that he had brought with him. He handed it to Frankie. He rolled his lips. 'Rather than me struggling to explain, you will understand better if you read the bits I have unlined in this paper.'

It looked technical so Frankie did as instructed and read:

Huntington's disease is an inherited brain disorder that results in loss of physical control and mental capacity. Symptoms typically appear between the ages of 30 and 50… HD is characterised by progressive physical, cognitive and psychological deterioration…

Frankie looked at Richard. He was sitting upright, gazing into the distance.

She tried to continue reading. Neither of them said anything. The fridge switched on and off. The room door shook a little with the wind. Frankie shivered but not because she was cold.

'Richard! Richard! Come back to me.'

Richard seemed to have gone into a trance.

He shook himself. He stared past Frankie. He relaxed his shoulders. He screwed-up his face. He cleared his throat.

'Father said that he had not told me about the possibility of my inheriting this disease because he thought that I did not intend to father a child.'

Richard looked as though he was about to crumple like screwed-up paper. He twisted his handkerchief. He coughed.

'In addition to me becoming an invalid, I could pass this disorder to children we might have. I can't do that. I will remain celibate.'

Frankie cleared her throat.

'Was your father worried about your health?'

'Yes!' Richard stamped his foot. 'He was worried but he did nothing about it! That's why I shouted at him.' Richard stamped his foot again. 'He never told me. All these years!'

'He loves you, Richard. Did he say why he didn't tell you?'

'He said he watched me as I grew up to see if I displayed any of the listed symptoms. When I entered the Carmelite Order, he was able to assure the priests that it seemed that I was fine. I passed their medical. The Order was aware. I was under thirty. He had done his duty in informing them. He said that he told the Carmelites that he would provide for me should anything happen.'

Frankie felt herself shaking. Her mind was racing.

What are the consequences if Richard has inherited this disease? The details I've read said that symptoms appear between the ages of 30 and 50. What symptoms? It mentioned physical, cognitive and psychological deterioration. This disease is passed on... yesterday we were blissfully happy. Frankie said, 'You don't have any of the symptoms. You are forty-three.

Minutes passed in silence.

Frankie saw Richard rubbing his hands up and down his face. It looked as though he was mouthing words. They were inaudible.

'Coffee? I'll make coffee. The kettle boiled earlier.'

Richard nodded and rocked to and fro, rubbing his hands together.

Frankie watched Richard out of the corner of her eye.

Is Richard exhibiting some of these symptoms? she wondered.

They sipped coffee. Frankie tried to understand what she had read. Was anger a sign? Was that why he treated her badly when Anna was at school? Surely not. He said it was the Opus Dei.

'I don't know how much you know about this disease, Frankie, I know nothing about it. I researched it on my computer. It's a progressive brain disorder. If I have inherited it, I will be a hopeless husband.'

'*If*, Richard. How do you know? What are the symptoms?'

'You won't want to know. Horrible things happen. Brain changes that cause abnormal involuntary movements, depression, mood swings, anger… the list is long. It's better we call off the engagement, Frankie. I can't ask anyone to put up with… I might become a total invalid… dependent on you.'

'You don't know if you have inherited this awful disease, Richard. You don't know all that there is to know about it.'

'Frankie darling, why do you think my father nearly fainted when I spoke about us having children? This is an inherited disease. Should I discover that I have it, I would be an unbearable burden. Just imagine the consequences if I passed it onto a child. I love you too much to expect you to take this risk.'

'You're breaking my heart…'

Frankie held her head in her hands. She rested her hands on her knees. She struggled to comprehend the consequences of what Richard was explaining.

Richard drew Frankie to him. He fondled her hair.

'This is what I didn't want to do. This is my dilemma. I had to tell you the truth. I wanted you to know as soon as I knew. I'm sorry, Frankie. It's better that I walk out of your life now. Christmas is the worst time to do this but…'

Richard kissed Frankie. He stood to go.

'No Richard! I'm not leaving you. You need to find out if you have this disease. You don't know.'

'What? What if I have inherited it? The closer we become, the greater the heart-break. Why don't you use these tickets and fly to Florence with… You must have a friend. I'm sure you have a friend you could take? I'll drive you to the airport.'

'Go to Florence without you, Richard! No Richard. Never. My heart will be broken worrying over you. We will spend Christmas together. Together we will find out. I'm not leaving you on your own… your father… you're angry with him. Poor man. He must be heart-broken too. He wants to be a grandfather.'

'You're too kind, Frankie. I can't expect you to…'

'Kind? My heart is broken. I want to be with you. I need to be with you. Will you come to Florence with me? What will happen after, who knows? We can't find out the medical answer on Christmas Eve. All the offices will be closed.'

'Are you sure, Frankie?'

'I am certain.' Frankie smiled. 'Besides I've always wanted to go to Florence!'

Richard laughed. They hugged. Richard traced his finger down her nose. 'You make me happy. My father will be surprised that we're still going. I'd better get ready.'

'Go! I've just enough time to finish packing.'

When Frankie had waved Richard off, she collapsed onto her bedroom floor with her back to the door. *Why does life have to be so difficult? One moment, flying high... now this disaster. I wish I had a mother to whom I could talk.*

She prayed, 'Paula please intercede with God for us.'

Are we being punished for leaving religious life and falling in love? she wondered.

Something clicked deep inside. Frankie suddenly jumped up. She punched the air. She stamped the floor. 'No! I'm determined to make the best of life!'

48

DAZED

The phone rang. 'Just checking that you haven't changed your mind, Frankie? I wouldn't blame you if you have.'

'Certainly not! My case is by the door. I want to be with you, Richard. I love you, Richard, no matter what happens.'

'You sure?'

'Perfectly sure! What did your father say?'

'He's singing your praises.'

'Will he be alone over Christmas?'

'No, no. Couldn't leave him alone. He has invited Enrico and his wife.'

'Good.'

'Thank you. Thank you, Frankie. The taxi will be with you in fifteen minutes. I don't know what I threw into my case.'

Richard held Frankie's hand as they travelled to the airport. Not a word was said. Frankie looked at her beautiful ring. *I'm with Richard. That is all that matters today.*

Seated on the plane, Frankie squeezed Richard's hand. 'It's Christmas Eve. We're going to enjoy ourselves Richard. Try not to worry.'

'Thank you, Frankie. You're an angel. I'll do my best over Christmas. I promise.'

IT WAS dark when their taxi reached Florence. The car turned into the drive of Richard's aunts' house.

'It's a big house, Richard. Look! The lights on those trees! Someone's looking from the window.'

'That'll be Aunt Margherita.'

'The door's being opened.'

Aunt Margherita hugged Richard. She turned to Frankie and kissed her on both cheeks.

'Benvenuta! You are welcome, Francesca.'

'Grazie!'

'Come. My name is Margherita. My sister's is Rosina. We both speak a little English. It's very late. You're tired? We've been waiting for you. Rosina has prepared something to eat.'

'Giovanni sends tanti auguri.' Richard kissed and embraced his aunt.

'I'll phone Papà to let him know you've arrived safely.'

'It was a long journey. A bowl of pasta with tomato, sprinkled with cheese and some salad. Is that alright for you, Frankie? Richard loves pasta.'

'Thank you. I love pasta, too.'

When Frankie met Margherita she thought that she resembled her brother, Giovanni. Fathomless brown eyes. Tanned skin. Tall, upright, a good head of curly hair. Wearing a pale pink silk blouse and long woollen skirt, she reminded Frankie of the elegantly dressed mother of the Foundress of the Italian order of nuns she entered. The distinctive Florentine manner in which she enunciated every word reminded Frankie of Richard's mannerisms.

'Eat first. Your rooms are ready. We'll take you and your luggage in the lift. Fa bene?'

'Grazie! I'll carry them up.'

'Meet my sister, Rosina, Frankie.'

Shorter, rotund, with the collar of the cotton dark blue blouse peeping from under a long apron, she wiped her hands before hugging Frankie.

'We've prepared in the kitchen, Frankie. Here's a chair for you.'

She gestured. Frankie and Richard sat.

'Homely. Thank you.'

'Shall I serve you, Frankie?'

'Thank you, Signora. You broke your wrist? It's healed well?'

'Ricardo told you. Yes. See.' She pulled up her sleeve. 'Thank you for asking. Call me, Rosina, Frankie. We've eaten.'

She pulled over two stools. 'We'll join you for a glass of wine.'

'I feel privileged being invited into the heart of your home.'

'We're delighted to welcome you. Christmas is a time to be together. We'll get to know each other tomorrow. Sleep first. I must phone Giovanni to let him know you have arrived safely.'

Richard said, 'I phoned him to let him know we've arrived here. Enrico's wife, Clarissa, has most likely arrived to join him for Christmas.'

Frankie wondered if Richard's father had spoken to his sisters since he had told Richard about the cause of his wife's death.

Richard carried the cases to their rooms. He peeped into Frankie's'. 'Should you need anything, Frankie, just ask.'

'I'm sure I have everything. What more could I want. This bed looks very comfortable.'

Frankie patted the bed. Looked round pointing, nodding, marvelling at everything.

'It's such a lovely room. Vaulted ceiling. Terracotta-tiled floor. Autumn-coloured rugs, parquet wooden floor.'

'I'm glad you like it. I like to think that my aunts have good taste. Let me give you a kiss.'

As they embraced, Frankie patted Richard's back. 'Try not to worry. I love you dearly, darling. You're probably fine. We'll fight this together.'

Frankie placed her engagement ring safely between two firm pillows. Emotionally exhausted, she slept on and off until she heard a door, close-by, being closed. She remembered that Richard's room was next to hers.

Sounds like footsteps. Richard must be up. Quiet steps on the stairs.

Daylight streamed through the shutter that she had left half-open. She gradually opened her eyes. She heard what sounded like a card being pushed under her door.

It's Christmas day! I wonder if Richard slept. That was probably him tiptoeing down stairs. I'd better see what's written on the card.

BUON NATALE! Happy Christmas, carissima, Frankie!

Didn't want to disturb you.

I've just gone for a short walk. Back soon.

Everything for breakfast is in the kitchen next to our rooms.

My aunts have gone to early Mass in the Duomo.

I'm going at midday. It's very near.

Want to come with me?

Our Christmas meal is at three o'clock

Amore! Richard xxx

FRANKIE WORRIED. *Richard is restless. I hope he managed to sleep. I must be there for him. I'll have a shower. I'll wear my pink woollen dress. He might be waiting for me to have breakfast together.*

FRANKIE PEEPED INTO THE KITCHENETTE. Richard sprang from his seat. They embraced. A deep long hug. 'Happy Christmas, Frankie! I hope I didn't wake you. I had to get out… walk… walking helps. You look lovely. Pink suits you. That pearl necklace is beautiful… you're beautiful.'

'You're pretty handsome yourself.'

'There's worry in those eyes. We need to find out… we will. Can you hold out until tomorrow?'

'I can't switch off… I'll try.'

'It's so hard. Let's try. Your woolly jumper... it's knitted. Shades of brown to match those deep-brown eyes of yours...'

'Knitted by aunt, Rosina. It was on my bed last night. Each Christmas she presents me with a lovely woollen jumper.'

'The wool looks fine... light... let me feel it.'

'Only the best for their nephew! Alpaca wool.'

'Sit here, Frankie. Would you like cereals?'

'Have you eaten, Richard? You need to eat.'

'I will. I've waited for you. I had a few grapes. My aunts haven't returned from Mass. It's only ten. Did you adjust your watch to continental time?'

'I did. Thank you for the note... and the Christmas wishes. That looks like muesli. A bowl of that and a cup of coffee will perfect for me, Richard.'

Richard placed a bowl in front of Frankie. He began to shake some muesli into it. 'Tell me when to stop. I'll have some too. Was the bed comfortable?'

'Very comfortable... fell asleep puzzling how... Richard... Did you sleep at all?'

'Eventually, Frankie. I'm so worried.'

'You must be, Richard. It's the not knowing. We need to find out. Hospitals, clinics... How do ...?'

'I found a few sites on my laptop. That's what I was doing last night... searching.'

Frankie grasped Richard's hand and squeezed it. 'Remember you're not alone, Richard. I'm by your side... I will be there forever. You can never escape from my love.'

'Are you sure, Frankie? I'm damaged goods.'

'Richard. You're probably perfectly healthy. You're bound to be worried. I would be. For your own sake, can you try to enjoy Christmas day?' Frankie stood. She held Richard's hands between hers. 'We'll pray at Mass.'

'I'll try my best, Frankie. Promise.'

'Do you think your father told your aunts that you know?'

'I wish I knew. No doubt they've known for years. I've been

thinking about that. I've been watching for hints. I thought Rosina might have said something when I was alone. She's very sensitive. So far though...'

'She might be waiting for you to tell her. They most likely don't know if you're going to be affected either. '

'Frankie, after Mass, would you like me to take you to the Ponte Vech...'

'The Ponte Vecchio... I'd love that...'

The cathedral bells were tolling. The air was crisp. Children were calling out to each other. They walked towards the Duomo. It was half past eleven.

'*Tu scendi dalle stelle*...' Frankie joined Richard singing this carol as they neared the cathedral of Florence.... *Oh bambino mio Divino...*'

'You know it too?'

'We sang it every Christmas. Remember I belonged to an Italian Order. I love this lullaby carol.'

'Look at the crowds, Frankie. I hope we can find a pew.'

As they edged their way past those praying at the huge crib they managed to find space in a side aisle.

Frankie whispered to Richard, 'What a magnificent cathedral! Marble floors. The cupola... Every alcove is strewn with such a variety of beautiful white flowers. Look at the high altar. Tall candles flickering... the excited sounds of people gathering for Mass.'

'It will be a Latin Sung Mass. Traditional. Gregorian chant. Evokes so many memories. You must have sung that too, Frankie. I love it.'

'Where are the children, Richard?'

'They will have gone to the earlier Mass.'

An older couple waved to Richard. He crossed the aisle to greet them and a few others.

Frankie noticed that everyone was dressed smartly. Men and women were wearing tailored coats. Even the nuns wore habits that seemed to be made from fine serge material. She wondered if her wine-coloured woollen coat was smart enough. Richard's lightweight black tailored coat looked as though it might be cashmere.

Seated to one side of the altar, the choir stood. The orchestra started. The choir began to sing *Alleluia*. Altar boys slowly processed up the main aisle, in front of the cardinal, to the high altar. When the incense in the thurible was blessed, an aromatic fragrance pervaded the cathedral. The introit was intoned. Mass had begun.

Frankie was glad that she and Richard joined in singing the Latin responses. She sensed the power of Richard's devotion. Supporting himself on the bench in front, he stood upright. He sang with vigour. His feet tapped in time. Was he listening intently to the scripture readings or pondering on his health? He seemed to want to hear every word of the homily. It was as though he was transfixed. She reached out to hold his hand. He smiled so broadly that her heart swelled with love.

Frankie reflected, *I love the Mass too. The incense, bells, prayers, the Latin, are familiar. For part of my life, that was very meaningful. I wonder how Richard looks back on his training to be a priest. Does he miss the rituals? Is he praying? Is he angry with God? He must be very worried about the Huntington's disease.*

She bowed her head, *Dear Jesus, am I being selfish? I love Richard with all my heart. I'm frightened. Please grant that he has not inherited this awful disease. If he has, that it can be cured. I wish I knew more. We want to be married. I would like... I've always wished to have a baby. Richard wants to be a father. Please Jesus, help us. Help Richard. We need your help now.*

The choir and congregation sang *Adeste Fideles* as the Cardinal and altar servers processed towards the main door at the end of Mass. Frankie sat again. Friends came to Richard. He introduced them to Frankie. They reached over to kiss and hug her. 'Buon Natale' their greeting.

'It's a quarter to two already, Frankie. We've enough time to walk to the Ponte Vecchio.'

'Let's go! I've always longed to stand on that bridge.'

'I hope you won't be disappointed, Frankie. You know that it's had shops built on it. It's changed since Dante's day. It's no longer exactly like it was in the beautiful painting you kindly gave me.'

'Oh! But it is the same bridge...'

They walked hand in hand across the city. The streets were almost deserted. A few footsteps echoed in side streets. An old man was singing a carol. Frankie surmised that most people must have gone home for their Christmas meal. She knew that they usually had their Christmas dinner on Christmas Eve.

'When we reached the middle of the bridge, we can look down on the mighty River Arno.' 'I could imagine what it was like before shops were built on it.'

Frankie and Richard stood next to each other on the Ponte Vecchio gazing on the winter sun shimmering on the Arno.

Frankie put her arm over Richard's shoulder. 'Richard, on this bridge I pledge my love to you. Dante pledged his love for Beatrice here. I promised you, Richard, that I will stay by your side whatever you discover about this Huntington's disease.'

Frankie felt Richard's body tremble. They held each other closely. His tears trickled down her cheeks too. 'My darling, I am so lucky to have you...'

In silence, arm in arm they slowly made their way back to the house. As they were about to ring the door bell, Richard's aunts opened the door. Their arms embraced both Richard and Frankie.

'Povero Ricardo... Giovanni phoned. You know... we wondered...'

'Oh! What are we to do? We're just engaged...'

The aunts drew them closer. They kissed each of them.

'Speriamo... we hope there is nothing to worry about. We find out. Hospitals... tests...'

'Papà will phone...... Oh... the phone. You answer, Riccardo.'

Aunt Rosina held out her hand to Frankie. 'We'll wait for Richard.'

She led Frankie into their ornate front room. Side by side they sank into dark brown leather chairs. Rosina slid a cushion behind Frankie's head.

'You... you, Francesca. We hope he will not have this disease. So far no signs.'

'Rosina, I want you to know that I have promised to stay by Richard's side whatever the medical prognosis is. Be his wife. I will help him.'

'Bene.' Rosina squeezed Frankie's hand and smiled. 'Pregiamo. Christmas day. Gesu Bambino. Ask Jesus. Ecco! They're coming.'

Marguerite's arm was on Richard's shoulder as they entered the room. Richard face was puckered. His eyes moist. He had a soggy tissue in his hand. Margherita was biting her teeth. Her eyes looked as though she was struggling to keep them fully open.

Frankie rushed to embrace Richard. The aunts encircled them. Silently they remained enfolding each other.

'We'll help each other. Now we need nourishment. Let's try to eat. Shall we?'

'Si Margherita… Papà made me promise to enjoy… to eat. We can do nothing today. Tomorrow we…'

'Bravo, Ricardo! You know we love you. Together united as a family we can fight any battle. Today we'll enjoy Christmas. Let's go into the dining room.'

Frankie felt the warmth and care of Richard's aunts. She was relieved that they could speak openly of what they were facing.

'You two have been mother to me all these years,' said Richard.

'I treasure such fond memories of your mother, Ricardo. We often looked through the photo albums that we used to show you when you lived here with us. Such a beautiful lady. Beautiful in every way. We'll show you, Francesca.'

'Aunt Margherita, how could I doubt your love for me. Mamma was indeed very beautiful. I'm certainly not going to spoil you're… our Christmas. Come on. Let's celebrate!'

'Giovanni and Laura loved each other very much. He adored her. She worshipped him. It was a wonderful marriage. They had so many dreams. They were looking forward so much to having a son, the fruit of their love.'

'So sad, Margherita. If only she had lived.'

Rosina led the way. The dining room table was covered with a green and red table-cloth. Richard lit three red candles. Places were laid with silver cutlery and matching linen napkins. Wine was poured into crystal glasses.

They raised their glasses. 'I hope you are hungry. Margherita and I have prepared a feast. We decided to have our dinner today.'

'We walked to the Ponte Vecchio after Mass. We should be hungry. I can smell it already. You're wonderful cooks.'

'This will be a traditional Italian Christmas meal, Frankie. No turkey. Instead, ravioli, lamb, and we have a delicious desert called Zuppa Inglese… English soup. But it's not soup. It consists of layers of cake brushed with a rum and jam mixture, sweetened whipped cream and fruit.'

'I feel so fortunate. Thank you very much.'

'Richard told me that your mother lives in London, Frankie. I hope you gave her our phone number.'

'Thank you, Rosina. My mother will be spending Christmas with my sister and her family.'

Frankie thought that if her mother knew she was in Florence she might want to be there too. Besides, she considered that she seemed to be content in her sister's company. She hadn't told her about her engagement. She had been swept off her feet so suddenly. She wondered why she had not felt she needed to turn to her mother immediately. She surmised that most young girls would.

Garnished olives and various cheeses were followed by spinach-filled ravioli.

Frankie became aware that when her mother was mentioned Richard, gazed at his ravioli. She caught Rosina's eye.

'Richard's Mamma and Papà enjoyed Christmas here too. You dear mother must be looking down from heaven at us enjoying our dinner.'

'She loved Italian cuisine. Dad said she appreciated your cooking so much, Rosina.'

'Giovanni said that Enrico has promised to bring his wife to your house, Richard. No doubt they're enjoying the taste of Italy too.'

Richard smiled. He nodded. Aware of the silences, Frankie thought that she should try to help the conversation, 'I remember one Christmas in the convent when we had prayed before starting our meal. One of the nuns announced, 'While we're tucking into this delicious meal, remember the many starving people in this world.'

'Did she succeed in making you feel guilty, Frankie?'

'I confess that images of starving African children did come into my mind. But another nun called out, 'Enjoy your meal today. Our Sisters are in Cape Town helping these very people.'

Frankie noticed that Richard seemed to be finding it difficult to swallow. She wondered if he tried to eat too big a portion of lamb. Maybe he hadn't cut it into edible portions. Maybe he was preoccupied.

'Were the meals good in the convent, Frankie?'

'Most of the time. Some of the sisters didn't like cooking. At Christmas we all helped.'

The aunts continued to enquire about Frankie's life in the convent. Frankie was aware that they were watching Richard. He did not contribute to the conversation even when they enquired about that morning's celebration of Mass.

When Rosina brought the Zuppa Englese to the table, Richard put one hand over his chest and waved the other about. 'Grazie per tutti... lovely meal. I hope you won't mind but I need some fresh air. Such a rich meal. Will you excuse me? I'll take a short walk.' Richard stood.

'Wait, Richard! Don't go alone... I'll..'

'I'm sorry, Rosina... I can't seem to concentrate on anything. I don't want to spoil everyone's Christmas...'

'Mea culpa! It's my fault. Margherita was right. You need to find out...'

'I need to go back to London. I want to go to a hospital.'

'I'll come with you... if you want...'

'Oh Frankie, would you think me awful if I book a flight? Difficult on Christmas Day.'

'Do that straight away, Richard. You must be so frightened. Of course I don't mind.'

'Thank you. I'm sorry.'

Margherita turned to Frankie.

'Thank goodness, you understand, Frankie. There'll be no flights today. Maybe a walk would help him. He knows that he can drive our car. I'll suggest that the two of you drive outside the city. Take a walk in the Tuscan hills. Breathe fresh air. Is that alright, Frankie?'

'Good idea. He's frustrated.'

'Fisole. We're not far from Fisole. Did Ricardo tell you that this home is named 'Angelico', in remembrance of Fra Angelico?'

'I love his art. Are we near Fisole?'

'Si. Our home is situated on the route to Fisole.'

Margherita joined her hands as if to pray. She looked straight at Frankie. She seemed inspired. Those fathomless, dark brown eyes are unmistakably a distinctive Canto family trait.

'Angels to look after him. Calming and reassuring. I'll suggest you visit Fisole.'

Richard returned to the room. 'Thank you. Each of you. I managed to book our flight. No flights today. Tomorrow at noon.

'Why don't your drive to Fisole, Ricardo? You could walk up the hills. Angels will protect you.'

'You'll love Fisole. It is beautiful. Its history goes back into the mists of time. We believe in angels. Nurses, doctors... they're my angels now. Wait until you see Fra Angelica's angels, Frankie. You'll love them. Fisole is only about eleven kilometres away. Takes no more than 30 minutes.'

'That sounds like a perfect place to visit. Thank you.'

Frankie felt relieved. She realised that Richard needed to de-stress.

En route Richard pointed out places of interest. 'That's the Piazza della Liberta to our right. Lovely arch. Did you know that Florence was once the capital of Italy?'

'You seem a little better, Richard?'

'I hope you don't mind. I've brought my laptop with me, Frankie. I found a good site on Huntington's Disease. Would you mind looking at it with me?'

'That's good. We can search to see where to go for help in London too.'

'Exactly. Will do. I am anxious to research as much information as I can.'

'Of course.'

'We can do both. We will research and also enjoy his art.'

'The hills are so steep. My feet keep sliding. Oh! Could we stop here, Richard? The view is spectacular. We have climbed up so high... Terracotta-coloured Florence down below. I can see the Duomo... the villas in the hillside... wonderful!'

'The best view is along the climb to the monastery of San Francesco at the crest of the higher hill on which Fisole sits. But let's park here in the Piazza Mino near the cathedral of Fiesole.'

'I don't need my coat. My woolly cardigan will keep me warm. Fresh air, beautiful scenery, not many people. So much to enjoy.'

'The antique markets are not open today. They are usually crowded. Fortunately the Museo Bandini is open. Shall we visit there first?'

'That would be lovely, Richard. I'm longing to see Fra Angelico's altarpieces, especially the Virgin and Child enthroned with the saints and angels.'

'There are so many artists' works to admire here. Florentine paintings from the 12th-14th century. I love Fra Angelico's *The Virgin of the Annunciation*. Gabriel dressed in pink and gold with multi-coloured wings stooping down with his gaze fixed on Mary. Mary looks so sweet and innocent and taken aback by Gabriel's arrival. Her innocence and virginity and her acceptance, humility, and submission.'

'What a tender description you paint Richard. I don't know much about this fourteenth century monk. I really wanted to see the originals because I remember these were the angels that one of our nuns painted in the convent where I was an aspirant.'

Frankie watched Richard. He looked disinterested. He seemed to be gazing past the art work.

'I feel a little dizzy, Richard' She lied. 'Would you mind if we went outside?'

'Fresh air. Let's. A walk would do us both good, Frankie.'

'You probably want to make our way to Fiesole's Etruscan-Roman Archeological area which is across the street from the museum? Or we could head up the hill from the square to reach the monastery of San Francesco located at the very crest of the hill.'

'There is so much to see in this historic city, Richard. The cobbled path up to San Francesco seems very steep. Maybe, it would be good just to sit and admire the beauty of this place.'

'I agree, Frankie. We'll come back again. Today let's sit on the steps in the archeological area for a while. I have a flask of coffee and my laptop in my rucksack.'

'Coffee would be good.'

As they walked down hill Frankie tried to distract Richard from his anxiety. 'What's so important about this archeological area?'

'Oh Frankie! There's so much to tell. While the Etruscan settlement likely dates back to the 9th-8th century BC, the first record of it in history is when it was conquered by the Romans in the 2nd century BC.'

'This must have been a prime hilltop location for the Romans. It would have been easy to see any enemies approaching from up here.'

'The sun is still shining in the amphitheatre, Frankie. Shall we sit on the step for a while?'

'Perfect. You'll probably have to sit on the top step in order to get a signal.'

We sipped coffee. Richard switched on his laptop.

Huntington's disease symptoms:

Huntington's disease usually causes a wide spectrum of signs and symptoms...

As Frankie read this, she grasped Richard's arm. 'That's... I didn't realise... You...'

Richard placed his hand over Frankie's. 'I wanted to let you read this, Frankie. I guessed that you didn't really know the symptoms.'

Frankie rested her head in her hands. 'I... I thought... is there a list of symptoms? You don't know if you have this illness...'

'I'll scroll down.'

Frankie scanned: Involuntary jerking... something about balance and swallowing... anger!

As Frankie read the symptoms, she recalled the time Richard changed into an angry person. She had blamed it on Anna and the Opus Dei. Today he seemed to have to hold onto the church bench to keep his balance. And the swallowing... she remembered him struggling with the lamb during the Christmas dinner.

Frankie felt Richard watching her reaction. He squeezed her arm. 'Some of those symptoms, Frankie... I think I have them.'

'Nonsense. You are reading too much into this. None of us is perfect. I'm knocked-kneed. I have a bunion. One of the nuns accused me of bullying. I...'

'This is more serious. I want you to be aware of the consequences of this disease, Frankie. If I am diagnosed with Huntington's disease, I will eventually require help with everything... all activities... constant care. I'll be prone to infections. Sexual activities have a consequence. This disease is past on. My mother died in child-birth. I could be drawn to suicide. I could be dead within ten years.'

'Stop! Stop, Richard. You have not been tested. You don't know.'

'Maybe, I don't but I want you to know the worst scenario. I don't want you to tie your life to a man who might never be able to give you a child...'

'We could always adopt a child.'

Frankie felt herself begin to shake. Richard slipped his hand around behind her shoulders. 'Let's switch off the computer. Come on. See if we can see the River Arno from the hill top. Give me your hand..'

Frankie and Richard supported each other as they silently climbed up the hill.

'What a mighty river, Frankie.'

'Where does it rise?'

'The Arno River is 240 km long, rising in the Northern Apennines, Tuscany, central Italy.'

'Does it flow out to the sea?'

'It flows south to Arezzo where it turns northwest. Then it proceeds west, through Florence and Pisa and eventually empties itself into the Ligurian Sea.'

'Clever Richard! You sound like a guide, spouting all this information.'

'I'm your guide, darling.'

'Great! Didn't the Arno flood once?'

'It did. The 1966 flood of the Arno in Florence killed 101 people and damaged or destroyed millions of masterpieces of art and rare books. It is considered the worst flood in the city's history since 1557. With the combined effort of Italian citizens and foreign donors and committees, or *angeli del fango* - Mud Angels - many of these fine works have been restored.'

'Angels! Angels again. Let's ask our Guardian Angels to protect us, Richard. The Arno looks calm now. Maybe our angels will help us to keep calm while we wait for the medical report.'

'You're so positive, Frankie.'

'On the Ponte Vecchio, I pledged my love to you, Richard. Here surrounded by angels, I want you to know that whatever happens I will be with you. Together we will be as strong as the rock we are sitting on... as strong as the mighty Tuscan Hills, part of the Apennines the backbone of Italy. We will be strong.'

Richard enfolded Frankie. His tears splashed her face. 'I couldn't ask for any greater love.'

49

DREAM ON

That evening Richard and Frankie clung to each other on the way up the stairs at his aunts' home. They found a bottle of red wine on a table on the landing.

'Oh, Richard! There's a note, too.'

'Ah! Sleep well! Amore.'

'Your aunts are so kind.'

'I'd love to sleep with you tonight, Frankie.'

'Me too. I... You know your aunts best.'

'We need the Almighty on our side, Frankie. Let's wait un...'

'Until we're married, Richard?'

'Even if I discover... !'

'No matter what you discover. I've done a lot of thinking and praying. Let's open the bottle of wine. Let's celebrate our love.'

They sat next to each other on cushions on the landing. When their glasses were full.

'Were you frightened of falling in love, Frankie? I know I was.'

'I was and I wasn't, Richard. I became infatuated with Sean, the priest I followed to Ireland on an art course. Then I even went out to dance with a bunch of youngsters one night, Richard. That was a disaster.'

'Did you love Sean?'

'I was in such a muddle in relating to Sean. I was attracted by his Irishness… the fact that he was a priest and unattainable… does that make sense?'

'But did you love him?'

'He was very persuasive. He played with my feelings. I became angry with him. He justified his approach to me by telling me that he was showing me that I was capable of falling in love.'

'That seems cruel… taking advantage of your vulnerability. So that's counselling!'

'I'm sure not all counselling. Maybe priests who become counsellors can be more easily tempted. Did you fall in love with anyone else, Richard?'

'I suppose living with my father kept me from experimenting. He always questioned any relationship. In the light of what I have discovered now, I suppose he was worried.'

'Since I left the convent I have watched and reflected on other people's relationships. I know Paula and Paddy had a possessive relationship.'

'What do you mean, Frankie?'

'Paula used to say that she could do and go whatever she liked. When we were out together, Paddy would make contact and she would respond. He seemed to act as if he owned her. It was as if he wanted to be her only friend. He tried to tie her to him. I'd hated that. It would like being back in the convent again.'

'Frankie, if I have Huntington's disease and we're married, you will be tied to a dependent invalid!'

'Firstly, you do not know if you have this illness. If you do, I want you to know that I fully realise that I might have to care for you every day…'

'You do? You would?'

'Yes, Richard. Hopefully I have learnt more about life and love. That's what I want to tell you. I know now that life is messy. Life is not perfect. Never will be.'

'You want a child. You said you love children. I love children too.'

'I know. We could adopt. Think of all the children who have no one to love them. Wouldn't you love to have a dear little boy or girl call you Dad?'

Frankie and Richard leant nearer to each other. She felt his warmth. They kissed.

'I can't believe you would sacrifice your...'

'I love you, Richard. I don't love anyone else. Perhaps you will change your mind when you meet my mother... and the rest of my family. And more personally... there is my bunion, my bandy left knee. I think I snore. I could go on...'

'What have I let myself in for?' He laughed. 'You really are a mess!'

They clinked glasses. Kissed again. Richard accompanied Frankie to her room.

THE SONOROUS SOUNDING of the Duomo Campanili awoke Frankie the following morning.

Wheelchairs and weddings... I seem to have had so many dreams lately. The wine. I must have slept soundly.

She rubbed her eyes and peeped into daylight. *We've talked it all out... cleared the air. I'm glad. Poor Richard. God give me strength to support Richard whatever... I hope he is in a good frame of mind. We fly home today. Packing...*

Frankie showered, dressed and was about to pack when she heard Richard's bedroom door being closed. Frankie opened hers. She heard the aunts talking. She took the presents that she had brought for them and went down stairs.

'Buongiorno, Francesca! The bells woke you. Come and join us. We're just going to have breakfast.'

'Thank you! It's so cosy in this kitchen. Comfortable chairs and a proper wooden kitchen table. I see you've been knitting Rosina. Richard loves his jumper. It's so lovely and warm in here.'

'Rosina always heats the bread. Sit here. Richard has gone for a walk. He'll be back.'

'Thank you, Margherita. I wanted to give you the Christmas

presents that I brought for each of you. You have been so welcoming. I know that it is customary in Italy to exchange presents on the Epiphany. But we will be back in England by then.'

'Befania. Yes, on the sixth January, the feast of the Epiphany. National customs! For us today is the feast of St Stephen. I believe you call it Boxing Day?'

'It's St Stephen's day for me too. I'm Irish. It was a custom in some parts of Ireland for people to dress up on this day. They would dance and sing this song. Would you like to hear my poem?

'The Wran, the wran, the king of all birds,
At Stephen's Day was caught in the furze.
Although he was little his family was great
So rise up land lady, and give us a trate.
Up with the kettle and down with the pan
And give us a penny to bury the wran.'

'Oh! Difficult to understand!'

'I know. Open your presents. They are so little in exchange for all your wonderful hospitality.'

Frankie kissed the two aunts and gave each their wrapped silk scarves. Margherita carried them to their front room.

'Mille Grazie, Francesca. I'll put them under our Christmas tree.'

'Francesca, we are worried that Richard may have inherited Huntington disease.'

'Margherita, I want you and Rosina to know that I have promised Richard that no matter what he discovers about Huntington Disease, I will stay with him. This ring…'

Frankie held her hand out to show the aunts. 'This ring ties us together. We're engaged.'

'Beautiful ring.' They bent their heads to look. 'Laura's engagement ring. You are very kind, Frankie. We promise to support you both. We always will. You will always be welcome here.'

They hugged. They ate salami with their bread and drank coffee.

'I saw your case outside your room, Frankie. I ordered a taxi for ten. I always find goodbyes difficult. It's particularly hard…'

'I'm ready, Richard.'

'We know Ricardo.'

'Our flight is not until midday. Good to be early. Once we've booked in our luggage, you need to eat. I don't think you've had anything.'

'Good. I'll queue for a roll. You'll have coffee? Maybe a roll too?'

'A latte and a biscuit. Any biscuit.'

'Frankie, while I queue would you mind reading the information that I have put on my computer desktop? I want you know what you're promising.'

Frankie glanced through the Huntington's disease association fact sheet. She noticed that there were 'Genetic tests.'

She listened to a video on an NHS site. She learnt about the various therapies. It was stated very clearly that there was no cure for Huntington's disease. She scanned through information: cells in brain dying, irregular movements, depression, twitching, stress, clumsiness, speech therapy, swallowing and memory loss. Mention was made of laboratory test.

'You look as I feel, Frankie.'

'I'm fine, Richard. Really I am. I think that wine helped me to sleep soundly. I was trying to remembering my dreams.' Frankie lied.

'Frankie, I'm frightened. You must be too. I'll make an appointment with my GP as soon we land at Gatwick. My father tried earlier. They gave him an emergency number.'

'I'll come with you… that's if… maybe your father.'

'Honestly Frankie,… I'

'You gave me this beautiful ring, Richard. I promised that I will be at your side, come what may. We'll board that plane and fly off together and be together always. I intend keeping this promise. I love you, Richard.'

'I love you too, Frankie! I'm a lucky man.'

50

EXPECTATION

Richard's mobile rang. He recognised the number. His Dad's.

'I'll be at Gatwick to meet you. Please forgive me, Richard.'

'That was my Dad. He's going to meet us.'

'Good. He's kind…'

'No Frankie! He's not. He should have told me…'

'You look angry. Maybe he hoped…'

'I should have known.'

'Don't take it out on your Dad. He has supported you… Given you money…'

'No, it isn't about money… It's about honesty.'

'Sorry, Frankie. It's not your fault.'

We found our seat. Nobody took the remaining seat in the row. Richard's eyes closed. He relaxed, asleep. Frankie wondered how the day would end. Frankie hoped he would not argue with his father.

As they landed Frankie put her hand on Richard. He woke with a start.

'Frankie, I'm sorry. I must have dozed off. I'll get our bags down. Dad will be waiting for us. He's always punctual.'

They collected their cases from the carousal and pushed the trolley towards the Nothing to Declare exit. As they came through Richard's father was waving a woolly hat that matched his Aran polo-necked jumper.

'Benvenuti! Welcome!' He opened his arms to embrace Richard.

'No Papà. Take your hands off my shoulder.'

'Povero Ricardo! Figlio mio!...' His face fell.

'Come, we'll have a drink. Francesca, you'd appreciate a drink?'

'Yes. Thank you, Giovanni.'

'I know just the place.' Giovanni linked arms with Frankie. He kissed her. Richard noticed that she smiled at his father.

Giovanni led the way to *Prêt A Manger.* Richard pushed the trolley with the cases.

'This looks like a quiet corner. What do you think? Okay?'

Richard nodded.

'Would you like white wine?'

'I'll get the drinks. Three Sauvignon Blanc? Is that okay? Richard and you want to talk.'

'You can't do that. Let me...'

'Oh yes I can. Remember, I'm a liberated woman.' She winked at him. 'You've done so much for me. It won't take me long.'

'Thank you, Frankie.'

As soon as Frankie began to walk to the cabinet to select the wine she heard Richard's voice addressing his father begin to address his father. Perche? Importante... tanti anni... They were both gesticulating. Their voices grew louder.

It's better that they talk it out. Difficult for both of them. She paid the cashier and made her way past tables of holiday-makers and their luggage.

Richard wasn't speaking. They both stood to help her take the glasses and bottles off the tray.

'Grazie, Francesca. I am sorry. It is my fault. I should have told Richard that he might have inherited Huntington's disease.'

'You could have told me when I was old enough to understand.... when I was ten...'

Frankie intervened, 'Papà... no one is to blame. Life throws up these problems. I want you to know that no matter what happens, Richard and I are going to support each other. We love each other. Disease will not keep us apart.'

Frankie saw Giovanni's eyes moisten as he peered over his praying hands propped up on the table. 'My dear Francesca. You forgive me? All the worry I have caused you.'

"There is nothing to forgive.'

'Frankie, Papà... my father has booked me an appointment at the hospital. Nine-thirty tomorrow to see a specialist.'

'Look!' Giovanni pulled the appointment card from his pocket.

'The hospital was so attentive when I explained the problem. Gave me the first available time. Richard has an appointment with a consultant.' Frankie read the name.

Richard rolled one lip over another. He put his hand over his chest. He nodded towards his father.

'Richard, aren't you pleased to know that you will be seen quickly?'

'I am. Thank you, Papà. You are so forgiving when I am angry with you.'

'I want to come with you.'

'You really want to come, Frankie.'

'Of course, I want to come with you. We're in this together.'

'I want to come too. I'll drive you to the hospital. We'll pick you up, Frankie. We'll need to leave about eight o'clock.'

RICHARD DROVE BACK from the airport. He concentrated on the heavy traffic. Frankie turned from the front seat to tell Giovanni how much she enjoyed Christmas with his two sisters.

When they arrived at her flat Richard carried her case upstairs.

'You seem calmer now, Richard?'

Richard drew her to him. 'Forgive me, Frankie. Papà... I ..he tries...'

'It's not easy for either of you.'

Richard kissed her. 'You're a rock of strength, Frankie.'

WHEN FRANKIE UNPACKED HER BAGS, she opened the aunts' presents. *What dear women they are. So caring. So contented. And Richard. What an emotional merry-go-round he was on.*

She sat in front of her photo of Paula, lit a candle and began to talk to her.

'Paula, my darling friend. Pray for me. You know that I am engaged to Richard. He might have a life-threatening disease. I am gradually learning more about Richard. He's a wonderful man. I love him deeply. Have I rushed into this commitment? Paula, I really love Richard. I loved him before I knew about his family. When I left the convent I watched my Aunt Joan almost trap her husband into marrying her. You said Paddy's love for you was too possessive, Paula. Forgive me if I was mistaken. Am I being the possessive one? I wanted so much to be loved by someone. I didn't want to spend my live alone. I found Richard. He found me. You warned me about becoming attracted to Sean. I thought I would be safe with a man who was a priest. It seems he had no intention of leaving the priesthood and marrying me. Maybe I was conscious of that I was choosing someone whom I knew was unobtainable? Was I so crazy to find someone, that I imagined that he loved me? Am I reckless to love Richard who may be terminally ill?

'We all want our lives to be perfect. I wanted to be loved... to have a child. If Richard is diagnosed with Huntington's disease, life will be full of difficulties for both of us. If his disease progressed rapidly, we will not be able to adopt a child. While I was a nun I aimed to be as perfect as I could. When the cause of Margaret's death was not made known, I learnt that even nuns can withhold the truth.

'I realise now that life is a struggle. Nothing is perfect. Every fibre of my being is telling me that I love Richard. He loves me. He has told me many times. I am determined to walk with him for the rest of my life. Paula, I feel you near me.'

The candle flickered.

'You are near, dear Paula. Talking to you has convinced that as the Great St Teresa said, 'All will be well...'

Richard sat in the back seat of the car with Frankie while Giovanni concentrated on the traffic. Frankie put her hand over Richard's. He hugged her. She tried to distract him by telling him how delighted she was when she opened the present from his aunts.

'They are so kind. Beautiful silk scarf with scenes of Florence. The Duomo. Such happy memories. What a lovely family you have.'

'Happy memories? If only...'

'Be positive, Richard. You'll see... all will work out. We will be happy. All will be well.'

Giovanni parked. They slipped out of the car. Giovanni put five one pound coins in the meter. 'Good for four hours,' he said with a chuckle. Richard and Frankie held hands. Read the directions to the hospital entrance. Giovanni followed them. Once they had checked-in, they sat in silence. There were only two other couples there. Giovanni leaned over to Richard. 'You want me to go in with you?'

'Yes, Papà. Need you to explain.'

'Mr Richard Canto.' The nurse called out.

Richard placed his hand on Frankie's. Giovanni followed him into the consultant's room.

Frankie squeezed her praying hands. *Heavenly Father, please grant that dear Richard has not inherited this awful disease.*

Frankie picked up a magazine. She flicked through a few pages before she realised that it was full of ideas for wedding. This prompted her to think about her wedding to Richard.

Nothing too elaborate. Simple but classic white dress. Where? When? Our parish church?

She was smiling when Richard and Giovanni were ushered out of the consultant's room. She searched their faces. They weren't smiling but looked less tense. They sat either side of Frankie.

Giovanni called out, 'We've made progress, Frankie. This consultant has given me an appointment to see a neurologist who specialises in Huntington's disease Richard was given an appointment to attend the clinic where tests would be carried out.' Richard showed Frankie the card.

'I go for blood tests tomorrow.'

'Good. Not long to wait. Must keep strong and healthy, Richard.'

'Good food. You didn't eat much this morning, Richard. Look for the restaurant there. Shall we have something to eat?'

While Giovanni queued for coffee and muffins Richard and Frankie found a seat overlooking the Thames.

'Richard, have you thought of a date for our wedding? While you were with the consultant I flicked through a magazine…'

'We haven't told the staff we're engaged. When we return to…'

'We've got an Inset Day on Monday. Better tell Sr Sheila first.'

'She'll be so happy, Richard. Shall we go to the convent this afternoon?'

'This afternoon? Yes, Frankie. Let's'.

'I'll phone her now. See when it's convenient for her.'

While they drank their coffee, Frankie told Giovanni that they had arranged to visit Sr Sheila at four o'clock.

'Bene! Have you fixed a date for the wedding?'

'Soon. We'll look at the calendar this afternoon. Easter is early this year.'

'So much to fix. The church. The wedding. The invitations. From your family. My family. Our home. Our favourite things. The rest of our lives together!'

'Happiness. That smile. The twinkle in your eyes. You bring me so much happiness, Frankie. We're both so excited. Maybe we'll have to go a little slower… but I love it all.'

Frankie noticed Richard waiting in his car in the staff car park when she turned the corner into school on the Inset Day. He jumped out to hug her. When he opened the staffroom door, the clapping began. Frankie bit her lip. The 'Congratulations' banner was facing them on the opposite wall. There were plates of iced buns on a lace table cloth. Sr Sheila clasped her hands. 'May God bless you both. We're all delighted at your wonderful news.' She held out a card. Congratulations on your engagement.

'Let me see the ring.'

'Sit at the top of the table.'

'You both look so happy.'

Frankie felt herself blushing. When she looked at Richard, she saw that he was beaming smiling at everyone.

'Waiting for results is the worst time, Frankie. Three weeks have passed now since I went for blood tests. Each day I hope a letter will be waiting for me when I return home after school.'

'No news is good news, Richard.' When they tested Paula to see if she had cancer, they called her into hospital straight away.'

Later that evening Richard phoned Frankie. 'The letter has arrived.'

'What does it say?'

'Asked me to attend the hospital on Monday. I will receive the results of the tests, Frankie.'

'Great news, Richard! Be strong. Remember that we belong to each other.'

'Suppose I've inherited this awful disease?'

'Suppose you haven't? Remember, a fifty percent chance. If you have... you won't be alone. We'll get through this together, Richard.'

'Oh Frankie, I hope I'm okay.'

'Half-term holiday on Monday. I'll be going with you.'

At 9 a.m. Frankie heard a tap on the door. 'Frankie, Dad's driving. Are you ready?'

'Have faith! Our prayers will be answered. Fr John announced your intentions at Mass yesterday Richard.'

'I hope God is of the same opinion as we are, Francesca.'

The waiting room was crowded. Looking round a sea of faces of differing nationalities, Giovanni pointed to two places. He seated himself across from them between two older men. Richard handed his appointment card to the nurse. She noticed his name on the screen above the checking-in desk. The appointments were on time.

'Mr Canto. Room 3.'

Richard and his father stood at the same time. Richard led the way. Once Richard and Giovanni stood to enter the room, she rested her praying hands on her hips supporting her face and prayed:

'God, Our Father, help us to accept whatever answer that the specialist tells them. Grant us the strength we need. Amen.'

Frankie looked at her watch. Five minutes. Ten minutes. She heard chairs being pushed back. She heard Giovanni saying 'Thank you for your time.' When the door opened, she scrutinised their faces. They looked calm. Richard almost ran over to her. He pulled her off the seat and hugged her.

He whispered in her ear, 'I'm clear. I am not a carrier of Huntington's Disease. My blood tests proved that conclusively.'

Giovanni beckoned them into the corridor. Once they went through the door, he embraced them both in a huge hug. 'What a relief! Oh Ricardo we need not worry any more. Francesca, your patience has been rewarded.'

Frankie and Richard clasped each other's arms as they skipped along the corridor.

Frankie smiled as they listened to Giovanni repeating, 'Grazie Dio! Grazie Laura! I'm so happy!'

Richard turned to his father and kissed him. 'Papà, you deserve to be happy. Forgive me for judging you. You lost the love of your life. I must have been a constant reminder of my dear mother. You must have been torn asunder inside.'

'Cara Ricardo, you were deprived of the love of your mother. I tried to do my best. Now I am a very happy man. Hopefully, I'll be a very happy grandfather.'

'Come Papà, let's go home and plan our future.'

Richard hugged them both.

'We're a family! Our love for each other is as strong as... as... as the Tuscan Hills.'

ACKNOWLEDGMENTS

Barbara Large, MBE, has been my tutor over the past four years. I owe a great deal to her. Barbara Large was the Founder-Director of the Winchester Writers' Conference for 33 years. She is director of CreativeWordsMatter and a member of The Society of Authors and The National Association of Writers in Education.

Bead Roberts, writer, tutor, broadcaster and lecturer encouraged me to write in my own voice and conversational style. I am indebted to her for giving me the title of my autobiography 'Dropping The Habit'.

My parents Frank and Patricia Dante (nee Colivet) and my brothers Tim and Des RIP

My sisters Pat Stay and Ber Collins

Jenny Hattersley tutor, preacher, lecturer, friend and much more.

Barney Cantillion for the checking my use of the Italian language. I take full responsibility for my mistakes, though.

St John Bosco founder of the Salesian Order St Mary Mazzarello Co-Founder of which I was a member for thirty-three years.

My nephew Mark Stay for formatting both books and imparting his vast knowledge of publishing matters.

Ray Lane who has always been on hand for technical support.

ABOUT THE AUTHOR

Marion Dante B.Ed.

Marion Dante hails from Limerick and has lived in England since 1955. When her family arrived in Shepherds Bush, London, there were signs on some door saying 'No Blacks. No Dogs. No Irish.'

Aged fourteen she began training to be a nun in the Salesian convent in Chertsey Surrey. After her aspirantade and noviciate, Marion made her vows of poverty, chastity and obedience in Friar Park Henley-on Thames in 1965. (These premises were later purchased by George Harrison.) She finished her three year teacher training course at Digby Stuart College in 1970. Having taught in Chertsey, Henley on Thames, Battersea, Rotherhithe, Glasgow and Farnborough she gained her degree in education (Bachelor of Education) London University in 1979 and continued to teach when she left the Salesian Order.

Many changes brought about in the Catholic Church as a result of the second Vatican Council resulted in Marion pondering on her future role in the convent and the realisation that she did not have to be a nun in order to live a fulfilling life. Mother Provincial of the Salesian Sisters strove to help her to prepare for life outside the convent. Initially, Marion was sent to Ireland to study theology and related religious studies. She graduated from Maynooth University, Kildare 1987. The following year she completed a Secretarial and Business, Pitmans word-processing and typing Course at Language, Secretarial and Business Centre, Balfe Street, off Grafton Street, Dublin 1988.

On returning to England at some financial cost to the Salesian Sisters, Marion benefitted from further support, counselling and various therapies in a Heronbrook House in the Midlands. While there she became convinced that she could no longer remain in the convent and eventually wrote to the Pope to be dispensed from her vows in 1991.

Anxious to equip herself for her future life, while still teaching, Marion gained further qualification from several courses: Two years at Tavistock Clinic to meriting Counselling Aspects in Education certificates. City and Guilds Further Adult Education run by University of Surrey in Family, Language and Literacy. TESOL qualification enabling her to teach English to speakers of other languages. Information Technology at Brooklands College Surrey.

While teaching in St Patrick's School, Farnborough, Hampshire, Marion was diagnosed with breast cancer in 1995. She eventually retired but continued to teach privately. Soon after becoming a member of Camberley Writers' she began to pen her autobiography. Encouraged and supported by Charlotte McDowell, who had been her radiographer and became co-founder of The Fountain Centre in St Luke's Cancer Centre in the Royal Surrey County Hospital, Guildford, she enlisted and continues to be a volunteer helping to raise funds for this therapeutic centre. To this end she was sponsored when she climbed Machu Picchu and on three occasions endeavoured to trek the last hundred kilometres of the Camino Compostela in northern Spain.

Marion Dante's autobiography 'Dropping The Habit' was well received in Ireland, England, USA and was translated into Polish. She is invited to give talks to many different groups:

Women's Institute, The Townswomen's Guild, Probus, Rotary, Inner Wheel, Tangent and various retirement groups.

Marion was on RTE television and radio as part of the publicity at the launch of her autobiography.

She has featured in BBC Programmes such as Heart and Soul BBC World Service, Radio Four Saturday Live and this February 2017 to speak on BBC Radio Surrey taking part in the BBC Listening Project. (Stored in the British Library).

She is a member of The Three Counties Cancer Support Group, The Kindred Spirits Choir, Camberley and Farnborough U3A in which she takes part in Italian, yoga, walking and ukulele groups. Marion also attends aqua aerobics and is a Member of National Women's Register discussion, dining and reading group.

66798374R00201

Made in the USA
Middletown, DE
15 March 2018